"What's tomorrow night?"

The fat man leaned back in his chair. This time it didn't creak or pop like before. Somewhere in his brain, that seemed wrong to Jack. "I don't know what, I swear!" Ramin squealed. "I am not a terrorist."

"You only handle their money," the FBI agent snapped. He leaned down, gripping Ramin's shirt in two club-like fists.

"But not their information!" He clasped his sweaty, bejeweled hands over Burchanel's. "I only know that Yasin will be leaving the next day, so it must be tomorrow night! He would not stay longer."

"What's the target?" Burchanel demanded.

"Hold on . . ." Jack started to say.

Ramin squeaked again. "I don't know! I only know that with Yasin you must think in threes! I heard talk of three points of attack, three opportunities—three, three, three all the time!"

"This is bull," Burchanel said. He braced with his legs and heaved the fat man up and out of his seat.

Jack heard another pop. "Down!" he yelled.

The chair blew up, vanishing in a spray of light and heat, wood and metal. Jack hit the floor while a thousand angry bees tore at his clothes, some at his skin, trying to pull him in pieces away from the center of the blast.

24 DECLASSIFIED Books
From HarperEntertainment

TRINITY
COLLATERAL DAMAGE
STORM FORCE
CHAOS THEORY
VANISHING POINT
CAT'S CLAW
TROJAN HORSE
VETO POWER
OPERATION HELL GATE

7⁰⁰

DECLASSIFIED

TRINITY

JOHN WHITMAN

Based on the hit FOX series created by Joel Surnow & Robert Cochran

HarperEntertainment
An Imprint of HarperCollinsPublishers

This is a work of fiction. Names, characters, places, and incidents are products of the author's imagination or are used fictitiously and are not to be construed as real. Any resemblance to actual events, locales, organizations, or persons, living or dead, is entirely coincidental.

HARPERENTERTAINMENT
An Imprint of HarperCollins*Publishers*
10 East 53rd Street
New York, New York 10022-5299

Copyright © 2008 by Twentieth Century Fox Film Corporation. All rights reserved. No part of this book may be used or reproduced in any manner whatsoever without written permission, except in the case of brief quotations embodied in critical articles and reviews. For information address HarperEntertainment, an Imprint of Harper-Collins Publishers.

ISBN 978-0-06-143119-7

HarperCollins®, 📖 ®, and HarperEntertainment™ are registered trademarks of HarperCollins Publishers.

First HarperEntertainment paperback printing: May 2008

Printed in the United States of America

Visit HarperEntertainment on the World Wide Web at
www.harpercollins.com

10 9 8 7 6 5 4 3 2 1

After the 1993 World Trade Center attack, a division of the Central Intelligence Agency established a domestic unit tasked with protecting America from the threat of terrorism. Headquartered in Washington, D.C., the Counter Terrorist Unit established field offices in several American cities. From its inception, CTU faced hostility and skepticism from other Federal law enforcement agencies. Despite bureaucratic resistance, within a few years CTU had become a major force in the war against terror. After the events of 9/11, a number of early CTU missions were declassified. The following is one of them.

DECLASSIFIED

TRINITY

PROLOGUE

One month ago

It used to be easier, Claire told herself as she pushed the refreshment cart down the narrow aisle. The plane hit a pocket of turbulence and bucked like a horse. She didn't like horses. She liked planes, or at least she had for the first thirty years of her career. In her twenties, it had been fun to be a stewardess (she was old enough to have been called that once upon a time). Her thirties had been good, too, even her forties. But now, in her fifties, the rides had grown too hard on her feet, and the aisles had shrunk too narrow for her hips. The men didn't look at her anymore, either. They had stayed the same age, but she'd grown older. They liked her still—thirty years of dealing with grumpy travelers packed in like LEGOs had taught her how to survive on charm—but these days they smiled at her the way her grandson's friends smiled at her, and where was the fun in that?

"Something to drink?" she said, snapping down

the brake and smiling at the boy in 29A. The young man wore an REI jacket and a leather thong choker with a wooden Inuit-carved pendant dangling from it. Claire had seen the boy a hundred times. Not the same boy, of course, but annual versions of him, flying back home from Alaska after a season aboard a fishing boat. Sometimes they were rich people's sons "toughing it out" for the experience. Sometimes they came from the underside of middle class, really needing the money. They all came back looking the same. She liked to guess as much as she could about them. Thirty years of practice had made her pretty good at it. 29A took a Coke. She poured the fizzy soda into the plastic cup and handed it over.

29B and 29C were together, a couple in their late twenties, no wedding rings, coming back from a trip up to the Alaskan wilderness. She was a redhead with a bright smile. Schoolteacher, Claire thought. He had a smile, too, but he was thinner, like a sword. She wondered if he was an athlete. The way he said, "Thanks" reminded Claire of Chicago.

On the other side of the aisle, a young man sat alone in 29D. He had short black hair and a clean-shaven face. He smiled at her warmly and said, "Tomato juice" in answer to her question. He spoke with a bit of a lilt in his voice that didn't sound Hispanic, though he looked it. She poured tomato juice into a plastic cup. "Is L.A. home?" she asked pleasantly.

"For a while," the young man replied.

"Everyone says that at first." Claire laughed. She handed him the tomato juice.

Claire never heard him reply because the plane exploded.

1 2 3 4 5 6 7 8 9
10 11 12 13 14 15 16 17
18 19 20 21 22 23 24

6:00 P.M. PST
Panorama City, California

"I promise you, there will be no need for anything rough."

Jack Bauer believed him and lowered his SigSauer. He motioned for Ed Burchanel to do the same. The FBI agent hesitated, not as sure as Jack. Finally, he lowered his Glock .40 but did not holster it.

The fat man on the wrong end of Burchanel's gun chuckled nervously. "Your Agent Bauer knows when he's won. I am not the type to give you trouble."

Burchanel's expression hadn't changed since the moment they'd kicked in the door. "You gave us trouble back in '93."

Jack knew Burchanel was barking more than he

planned to bite. Burchanel wasn't even aware of the entire package. All he knew was that the fat man, Ramin, had been connected to terrorist activities. But Jack was CIA, and by law the CIA was not allowed to operate domestically. Burchanel's presence made it legal.

"Not me, not me," Ramin insisted. He lowered himself heavily into the armchair of his own living room, like a guest not sure the chair was permitted to him. There was already a deep indentation where he usually settled his wide ass. The chair creaked heavily and made a sound like one of the springs popping. He kept his hands on the armrests in plain view. He wore thick gold rings on most of his thick fingers. His nails appeared unnaturally neat and shiny. His mustached face smiled at them, a smile that was neither arrogant nor deceptive. It was the anxious smile of a man who had no desire except to please whoever might do him the most damage, and right now that honor belonged to Jack Bauer of the CIA and Ed Burchanel of the FBI. Ramin smiled again. "I wasn't involved directly at all in the truck bombing."

Jack motioned for Burchanel to stay with Ramin while he cleared the rest of the house. It was a small bungalow in Panorama City, in the dirty heart of the San Fernando Valley north of Los Angeles. Master bedroom, extra bedroom, bathroom, kitchen. He was done quickly and returned, nodding to Burchanel. Jack sat on the sofa that put his back to a wall and gave him full view of the front door and the hallway. Burchanel's position blocked the door itself, although with Ramin's size there was no way he could outrun them, even if he were the type.

The search had taken a few seconds, but Jack spoke as if no time had passed. "Not directly, but you used to go by the name of Mezriani, and you were friends with Sheik Omar Abdel-Rahman."

"Sheik Omar was the man behind the '93 bombing," Burchanel added. "You moved money around for him."

Ramin sighed at Burchanel, then appealed to Jack. "Agent Bauer, look at me. I am an aging fat man of moderate resources. I am neither a patriot nor a zealot. I have one goal in life, and that is to make myself as comfortable as possible. I do not find interrogation or imprisonment comfortable, so I will tell you everything, everything I can."

"Start by taking us through '93," Jack said. "Tell us what you know."

Ramin obeyed. He talked freely, but ultimately he told Jack nothing the CIA agent didn't already know. Seven years ago, Sheik Omar Abdel-Rahman, "the Blind Sheik," had inspired several members of a Jersey City mosque to park a truck bomb in the parking structure of the World Trade Center. Most of those responsible had been caught, including the Sheik himself. One terrorist, Abdul Rahman Yasin, had been taken into custody and then mistakenly released. He'd slipped away to somewhere in the Middle East, probably Iraq. With most of the main culprits in jail, the media considered the case closed, but the World Trade Center bombing had been a wake-up call to a few entities inside the U.S. government, and they had started watching more carefully. Ramin hadn't been missed in the first rounds of investigation. He'd been brought into custody and interrogated—something, he repeatedly told Jack, that he did not find comfortable at all—but his only real connection to the World Trade Center bombing was an association with some of the Blind Sheik's zealous friends, and a knack for investing their money profitably. The FBI and Federal prosecutors had chosen not to pursue a case against him. Since 1993, Ramin had been interviewed several times by the Feds, and each time he insisted that 1993 had scared him into a much more cautious and upstanding circle of friends.

Jack had come to Ramin from the other end of operations. Jack was currently "on loan" to the CIA, although he couldn't explain even to his wife what "on loan" meant. In the early days, in the military and with LAPD, it had been easy. You were assigned to a unit and you worked in that unit. You reported to a commanding officer, and that was that. But over the years Jack had risen (or fallen? he wasn't sure which) into a murkier stratum of operations. It was as though the closer he got to the source of decision making, the more complex the network became. Communication channels crisscrossed. Organizational charts looked like Escher drawings. It was, to coin a phrase one of Jack's CIA colleagues had used, the "fog of deniability."

But one thing did remain clear, even in that fog: the bad guys. They were out there, and if Jack couldn't pierce the heart of his own government's workings, he sure as hell could pierce the heart of the other guy's. So when the chance to be seconded to the CIA had come up, he'd taken it in a heartbeat. CIA meant overseas work, and that's where the enemy lived. Ironically, Jack's most recent task with the CIA had led him right back home.

"Farouk tells me you have been in bed with Al-Gama'a al-Islamiyya," Jack said. Ramin winced at the term *in bed* and wiggled his bejeweled fingers.

"Farouk likes to sound more important than he is," the fat man said. "Ask anyone in Cairo."

"I did and you're right," Jack said. "If I believed everything Farouk said, Burchanel here would be asking the questions, not me." Burchanel smiled unpleasantly. "But I do believe that you've gotten cozy with some unsavory types again, Ramin. And I also believe that somewhere in all of Farouk's stories about terrorist attacks on U.S. soil, there's a little bit of truth. You're not the type to blow yourself up for the sake of Allah, and you're not the type to go to jail for someone else's sake. So tell me everything you know about Abdul Rahman Yasin trying to get back into this country."

Ramin sighed. "If you know about Yasin, then you must know about tomorrow night."

Jack reacted, startled, despite his training. Burchanel, too. "What's tomorrow night?"

Ramin looked equally surprised. "I thought you knew. I don't know what it is, but I know that it is tomorrow."

Burchanel stood up and snarled. "Tell us what it is."

The fat man leaned back in his chair. This time it didn't creak or pop as before. Somewhere in his brain, that seemed wrong to Jack. "I don't know what, I swear!" Ramin squealed. "I am not a terrorist."

"You only handle their money," the FBI agent snapped. He leaned down, gripping Ramin's shirt in two clublike fists.

"But not their information!" Ramin clasped his sweaty, bejeweled hands over Burchanel's. "I only know that Yasin will be leaving the next day, so it must be tomorrow night! He would not stay longer."

"What's the target!" Burchanel demanded.

"Hold on . . ." Jack started to say.

Ramin squeaked again. "I don't know! I only know that with Yasin you must think in threes! I heard talk of three points of attack, three opportunities, three, three, three all the time!"

"This is bullshit," Burchanel said. He braced with his legs and heaved the fat man up and out of his seat.

Jack heard another pop. "Down!" he yelled.

The chair blew up, vanishing in a spray of light and heat, wood and metal. Jack hit the floor while a thousand angry bees tore at his clothes, some at his skin, trying to pull him in pieces away from the center of the blast.

6:14 P.M. PST
Westwood, California

"Dare," Kim Bauer chose.

Her best friend, Janet York, grinned mischievously. "Kiss Dean. French!" Everyone oohed and giggled.

There were six of them, three girls and three boys, sitting in the den of Lindsay Needham's house. The housekeeper was supposed to be watching them while Lindsay's mother was at a meeting, but housekeepers were easily gotten rid of, and the six thirteen-year-olds had gotten down to a very intense game of Truth or Dare.

Kim Bauer looked at Luke, hoping she wasn't blushing too badly. She was just glad Janet hadn't chosen Aaron. Aaron was cute, but he was brother material. Luke was a hunk. He was most of the reason Kim had been willing to play Truth or Dare in the first place. Kim had kissed boys before—she was thirteen, after all!—but she'd never French kissed. She didn't think Luke had, either. Their lips locked; something warm and wiggly, strange and uncomfortable, happened; and then it was over except for a lot of squealing and giggling.

"Okay, okay, my turn!" Kim said. Her heart was racing, but she felt no need to remain the center of all that attention. "Aaron!" she declared to a boy across the circle from her. "Truth or dare!"

Aaron had just recovered from laughing and applauding. "Truth," he chose.

Kim knew that Aaron and Janet had been going steady, and that they'd been caught behind the gym once. Janet denied anything was happening, but Kim wasn't so sure. "Has anyone ever touched you?" she asked.

Aaron's laughter thinned. "Touched me? Well, sure . . ."

"Uh-uh." Kim grinned. She glanced wickedly at Janet. "I mean, *touched* you. Down there."

"Kim!" Janet shrieked. The others shrieked, too. All except for Aaron. Kim had expected him to blush, but instead he'd gone ghostly white.

"Well, spill!" Dean demanded, oblivious.

"Spill!" repeated the others.

Aaron was not playing along. He fidgeted, the color gone from his face, his lip trembling. He looked at Kim with wet eyes, then looked down. All the laughter died.

"Aaron?" Kim asked quietly.

The boy got to his feet and hurried from the room.

6:19 P.M. PST
Panorama City

Jack stumbled out of a cloud of dark smoke and into a sea of red and blue flashing lights set against black and white. He was vaguely aware of the police cars and uniformed officers. He knew someone was trying to talk to him, but the words came through as a muffled buzz, distorted by the ringing in his ears.

Booby trap, he said. Or at least that's what he meant to say. He couldn't hear his own words. *Bomb in the chair. Pressure release, like a land mine. The fat man sat down and that triggered it. They're ahead of us.*

The uniformed officers asked him a few more questions, but he couldn't hear them yet. *They're ahead of us*, he kept thinking and saying. *They're ahead of us*. The uniforms didn't know what that meant, so they left him sitting on the curb and went back inside to search.

Jack breathed in the cleaner air and worked his jaw as though that would open up channels and let the ringing sound leave his head. The muffled voices became a little more distinct as he watched figures in firemen's jackets carry two people out of the house on stretchers—the fat man covered by a sheet, and Burchanel. Jack couldn't see much of the FBI agent with the emergency personnel around him, but what little he saw looked bad.

They're ahead of us, Jack told himself. *They knew we'd talk to Ramin and they tried to put him out of service. They're ahead of us*. It occurred to him that he kept repeating that same phrase. It was not a good sign.

Someone knelt behind him, tearing the back of his shirt open. The someone—a paramedic—daubed his back with soft, wet gauze. The wetness felt cool at first, then it stung. Jack gritted his teeth but said nothing. This was easier to deal with than the ringing in his head. He could focus on pain. Sounds came into his head now as separate and distinct stimuli. Soon enough he was able to focus on two people standing in front of him. One was a paramedic—maybe the same one who had treated his back. The other was a tall man with steel-blue eyes. It occurred to Jack that he knew that man.

". . . got to be a concussion," the paramedic was saying. "And his back is torn up a little from chair fragments, but there's nothing serious. Not like the other guys. I can't believe he survived it, that close."

"That's Jack," said Christopher Henderson. Henderson stooped in front of Jack to look him in the eye. "You okay, buddy?"

Jack was. Henderson's voice came from farther away than it should have, but otherwise, Jack's head was clearing. "I'm pissed," he said. "How are they?"

Henderson shook his head. "The fat guy's dead. Your FBI man would be, too, but the fat guy shielded a lot of the blast. Still, they're taking him to ICU."

Jack nodded. Every passing moment brought him a little more clarity. Still, he'd had concussions before, and he knew that clarity came in layers—at each stage you felt fine, until the next layer came and you realized how groggy you'd still been a moment before.

"Was the fat guy Ramin Ahmadi?" Henderson asked.

Jack nodded again, and this time he smiled wryly. "This unit of yours is coming along, eh?"

Henderson managed to nod proudly and dismissively at the same time, the way a man takes a compliment on a golf swing he knows is good. "We're on the distribution list, now. I still think you should come over. Speaking of which . . ." He spun on his heels and sat down on the curb next to Jack. "What's a CIA agent doing operating domestically?"

Jack rubbed his eyes and pointed down the road, where an ambulance had just taken Ed Burchanel. "I was just along for the ride. It was Ed's investigation."

Henderson snorted. "If you joined the Counter Terrorist Unit, you wouldn't have to tell tall tales."

"Like I told Richard Walsh, you guys seem set up to deal with things on this side of the ocean. The real action is overseas."

Henderson looked over his shoulder at the smoldering house. "Is that so?"

It occurred to Jack that the evidence was against him.

"Well, at least let me give you a ride," Henderson said.

Jack shook his head. "Can't. I've got to clean this mess up," he said, referring to the informational debris, not the damage to the house.

"No, you don't," Henderson said. "It's our mess now. CTU's mess, I mean."

Jack bristled, but then put his hackles down. He could see it. CIA recruits the FBI to pursue a domestic investigation. The shit hits the fan, and CTU, eager to make its bones, steps in as the new agency in charge of a terrorist case.

"It's my case," Jack said. "I want in."

Henderson winked. "Like I said, let me give you a ride."

Kim found Aaron sitting on the curb outside the Needham house. She knew boys didn't like to be caught crying, so she pretended not to notice as he wiped his eyes. When he was done, she sat down next to him.

"I didn't mean to freak you out," she said. "I mean, it was just a game—"

"It's cool, it's cool," he said, still sniffling. "You didn't freak me out. I kinda did that myself."

"It wasn't . . . it wasn't because you and Janet—"

"No!"

"—because I was just joking—"

"No, it's not." His breath caught in his throat, making her stop, too. "It's not Janet or anything. It's . . ."

He adjusted himself in a way Kim couldn't really explain. It wasn't like he fidgeted or anything. But she could tell that some machinery in his body or his head, a cog or a wheel she couldn't see, had shifted, like when you clicked a button on a computer and could sort of sense it gearing up to perform its appointed task.

"I've never told anyone before."

She didn't say, *You can tell me.* Thirteen though she was, she was old enough to understand that prompts of that kind were reserved for gossip and rumors in the girls' room and e-mail. This was more important. She didn't have to tell Aaron he could trust her. He would know, or he wouldn't.

"It's weird no matter what, but it's especially weird because it's, it's the priest at my church." She nodded, still not sure what he meant or what "it" was, just knowing that somehow all the air had been sucked away from both of them. "He's been one of the priests there for my whole life, and when he asked me, I didn't know what to say. I mean, I didn't know how to say no or whatever."

"No to what?"

Aaron shivered. "He . . . did that. What you asked about inside. He did it a lot."

6:31 P.M. PST
Los Angeles, California

Michael dialed the number and waited. The phone rang three times before it was picked up. No one spoke on the other end. "Hello?" Michael said in mock confusion. "Hello? Is Michael there?" When no one spoke, he hung up.

His cell phone rang a moment later. "Is this Michael?" said a voice on the far end.

"Speaking," Michael replied.

"This is Gabriel." Gabriel, of course, was not his real name, but that hardly mattered. "What happened?"

"Ramin is dead."

"What a tragedy. Before the authorities got to him, no doubt?"

"Well, no. During."

The voice on the far end hissed, somehow sucking all the warmth out of Michael. "Did he pass on any information? Anything that could cause a problem?"

"I don't see how," Michael said. "He knew almost nothing. If he told them everything, it would be no more than they might have guessed on their own."

"Probably you are right," Gabriel said. "We should meet. We need to move forward. Write down this address."

Michael wrote.

6:35 P.M. PST
CTU Headquarters, Los Angeles

The Los Angeles headquarters of the Counter Terrorist Unit looked like a technological garden run amok. Phone lines and optical cables sprouted out of the ground. More cables draped themselves vinelike from the ceiling. A few desks sat, steady and alone, as certain and determined as rocks in a Zen garden.

There was a picnic going on in this garden—about a half-dozen staffers were camped out on the floor, sitting around a blanket of paper napkins, sharing cheddar cheese and Wheat Thins and sucking bottles of Sam Adams beer.

"This looks cozy," Jack said as he and Henderson entered the room. "You guys make a great first impression."

A muscle in Henderson's jaw pulsed.

"Hey, sir, did you hear the good news!" one of the picnickers said. She stood up and walked toward Henderson with an unopened bottle in her hand. "We made our first bust!"

Henderson did not lighten up. "And it's big enough so that you're already drinking on the job?"

The young woman, in her late twenties, glanced at Jack and realized that she didn't know him. She hesitated, then clearly decided that there was no backtracking. "Well, just to baptize the place, you know? None of us are on call anyway."

Jack didn't think she was an operator. None of them looked like operators to him. Even the most by-the-book operator toeing the line for a superior had a certain don't-fuck-with-me quality about him, and would lean on you the way your dog leaned its weight against you, just to test you, even though it knew you were the alpha. None of these people had it.

"Tell me about the bust," Henderson said.

The woman glanced at Jack. "He's all right," Henderson said, waving away any concern about classification. "Bauer, this is Jamey Farrell, one of our analysts. Jamey, Jack Bauer, CIA."

She nodded, then said excitedly, "We're pulling together field reports for the formal summary, but basically we nailed those three guys from the Hollywood mosque."

"What three guys?" Jack asked.

Jamey said three names he didn't recognize. "They were leads we were working out of here," Jamey said, taking obvious pride in the half-assembled office. Or, rather, taking pride in her accomplishments despite her surroundings. "We caught them using Internet café computers and Skype technology to contact members of al-Gama'a al-Islamiyya . . . um, you know what—"

"I know who they are," Jack said.

"Right. We couldn't get anything definitive, and the

conversations we recorded weren't incriminating. It took us a while to convince the judge to let us go in."

Henderson grunted. "Damned warrants. It's a pain in the ass to get them. It oughta be easier."

Jamey continued undeterred. "Finally, we got evidence that one of these three had tried to call the Blind Sheik's number, and the judge decided we had probable cause."

"Are they booked?" Henderson asked.

"Will be. We found plastic explosives in their house."

"Who is this?"

The voice that spoke was thin and tight as a wire. All three of them turned to see a narrow-faced man with a balding head staring at them. He wasn't particularly small, but, oddly, Jack got the impression that he thought of himself as small. His shoulders seemed to cave in, but his chest puffed out, as though he was at once collapsing under, and resisting, his own self-image.

"Jack Bauer, CIA," Henderson said quickly. "Jack, this is Ryan Chappelle, Division Director of CTU."

Jack reached out to shake Chappelle's hand, but Chappelle only looked at it and raised an eyebrow. Jack realized what he was waiting for, withdrew the hand, and produced his identification. Chappelle read it like he was studying a driver's test, then nodded. "Welcome," he said finally. "Excuse me a moment." Chappelle turned to berate the carpet picnickers.

Jack took that opportunity to turn to Henderson. "I thought George Mason was Division Director," he whispered.

Henderson shook his head. "Mason is District Director."

Jack rolled his eyes. Henderson shrugged. "We're new. We're a little confused about titles, but it all works out."

"Yeah, I can see that."

Under Chappelle's scolding, the picnickers had vanished as if they'd never been. The room successfully cleared of any joy, Chappelle returned to Henderson and Bauer. "Bauer, Richard Walsh tells me you're considering coming on board with us."

Jack bit his lip to avoid scowling. "It's a discussion we've had, but I'm not sure I'm right for it. I'm pretty happy over at the CIA. But I am interested in what you're going to do with Ramin Ahmadi. I thought I—I mean, the CIA—had turned this over to the FBI."

"It should have come to us," Chappelle sniffed. "That sort of case is our jurisdiction now."

"I didn't know."

"Now you do."

Jack smiled thinly. He was reminded suddenly of a story of Abraham Lincoln, who was overheard talking about another guest at a reception. "I don't much like that man," Lincoln was heard to say. "I'll have to get to know him better." Jack suspected that such efforts would not pay off with Ryan Chappelle.

"I'd like to continue with the case," Jack said. "It started with some of the work we did in Cairo."

Chappelle tipped his chin. "My people will tell you it started with our work in Los Angeles, but whatever. You're welcome to read the reports. But I can't have CIA working a domestic case for obvious reasons."

"The FBI didn't have a problem."

Chappelle's laugh was derisive. "Oh, well, if the

FBI didn't have a problem!" He shook his head. "Aren't they the ones who let Abdul Raman Yasin walk out the front door?"

Jack decided he'd had enough. "It's easy to pick on the other guys when you don't have any track record at all."

"We're one for one," Chappelle replied.

"Impressive," Jack sneered. "Three wannabe terrorists talking on the Internet. You saved the planet."

"Jack," Henderson soothed. "There's coffee down that hall. Why don't you get some."

Jack glared at Chappelle a moment longer, then turned away. Chappelle watched him go. "That's the guy you want to bring in here?"

"Richard Walsh says he's the best," Henderson said. "We need him."

"I need him like a hole in the head," Chappelle replied.

. . . .

THE FOLLOWING TAKES PLACE
BETWEEN THE HOURS OF
7 P.M. AND 8 P.M.
PACIFIC STANDARD TIME

. . . .

7:00 P.M. PST
CTU Headquarters, Los Angeles

Jack found the break room. There was a woman pouring herself a mug of coffee. She was thin, with sharp features and a wry look, but somehow it all came together in a nice-looking package.

"It's barely worth drinking," she said, stepping out of his way and leaning against a counter, sipping.

"That's okay. I just had a conversation barely worth having. The coffee will go great." He found a mug in the cabinet and poured it full.

"Nina Myers," she said.

He lifted his cup at her. "Jack Bauer. You're part of all this?"

She nodded. "Yep. Are you the new kid?"

Jack shook his head. "You guys are the new kids. And the teacher's pets. You just pulled jurisdiction and took over my case."

"Yep, there's a new sheriff in town," she said with mock pride. "Sorry you get stripped of the ball." Her eyes lingered on Jack over the rim of her coffee mug. "Was it something to do with these three guys we've got in storage?"

"Maybe," Jack said. "I was working a case that may lead to a terrorist attack in L.A. You guys seem to have found three Muslims with plastic explosives. I'm sure they're connected."

"You want to ask my three young Turks?"

"Your three—?"

"I collared them. I'm going down to interrogate them in a few." She let her eyes rest on him again. "Come on, watch the tape with me first."

She led him down the hall to a room that wanted to be a technical bay, but wasn't yet. There was a large console, but only one screen, surrounded by empty cubbyholes with a few wires poking out like snakes. A computer had been set up. Nina woke it up and clicked a few times. The large inset monitor came to life. Jack began to watch the shaky, high-definition video footage of the backs of Federal agents wearing blue Windbreakers with "ATF" and "FBI" written across the back in yellow block letters. Jack watched with interest, but most of it was routine footage recording the interior of a house in the mid-Wilshire area. The house was totally unremarkable until the police videographer arrived at the detached garage at the back of the property. The garage was lit by only a single bare bulb sticking out of a cobwebbed socket high up on the wall. A very old, rickety, homemade workstation had been built along one wall. But next to it stood a brand-new white cabinet, the kind that could be purchased at a big box store and assembled at home. An agent opened the cabinet to reveal a crate, which two agents pulled out and placed on the floor. It was long and low—the voice narrating the description said it was four feet long by three wide by three feet high. The agents popped the lid off the top and removed it to reveal the contents.

The plastic explosives had been molded into gray-blue bricks, stacked five high and six across in the case. There were two gaps in the top layer.

"What do you think?" Nina asked. Jack had the impression she'd been watching him the whole time.

"I think there are more than two bricks missing," Jack said. "Freeze it."

She didn't jump to it, so he reached for the mouse and stopped the video, running it back to a closer shot of the crate. He pointed. "There's room for another layer. There's discoloration—"

"Along the edge. I think so, too." She waved her coffee mug at the screen. "Our boys denied it, of course. They say that's all there is."

"Oh, we should definitely ask them again," Jack said. "You have them here?"

Nina shook her head. "We're not set up for it yet. They're over at the county jail. Want to go for a visit?"

Jack smiled.

Diana Christie sat in her X-Terra, her fingers gripping the steering wheel. "I won't take no for an answer," she said out loud. "They are going to listen this time."

She jerked on the door handle and pushed the door open. A moment later she marched determinedly toward the doors. The glass was dark, and she saw the reflection of a thin woman with dirty-blond hair, in a blue pantsuit, moving double-time. As she reached the glass doors, her image morphed into that of a tall blond man. He was on the far side of the door and he pushed it open, exiting just in front of a thin, short-haired woman with a determined look on her face. He held the door open long enough for Diana to pass through. She smiled and nodded her thanks, then she was inside.

The offices had improved since her last visit. The phones worked now. There was some furniture. There was still no receptionist or security, so she walked into the main room and looked around until she spotted the ferret-faced man in charge.

"Director Chappelle," she said firmly. "Diana Christie, National Transportation Safety Board."

Chappelle looked away from his conversation with a square-jawed man. "National Transpo— oh, right, Agent Christie. Was that today?"

She nodded and held up a manila folder. Chappelle shrugged and led her into the conference room. There was a table in it surrounded by chairs. The chairs themselves were covered in plastic. Chappelle tore the plastic off two of them and offered one to Diana. "Okay, Ms. Christie, I assume this is still about the Alaska flight?"

She opened the folder and spread out several reports and diagrams. "Yes. I'm still convinced it was bombed."

Chappelle pointed at one of the reports in Diana's folder. "The official FAA reports decided that it was a malfunction in the fuel tank. Some kind of faulty wiring. You were on the team that wrote the report."

"I didn't write it," she reminded him. "I didn't agree with it. The fuel tank explosion was secondary. The first blast was in the cabin. The rest of my team thought the tank blew first, and sent a fire line up into the cabin. One of the oxygen tanks then blew up. I think it went the opposite way. I think something inside the cabin blew up, igniting the tank, and sending a line down to the fuel supply."

She handed a sheaf of papers to Chappelle, who tried to make sense of them. There were several columns of numbers—something·about pounds of pressure per square centimeter, and comparisons of the expanding volume of several gases based on several temperatures. There was also a diagram of the Boeing 737 that had flown from Alaska on its way to Los Angeles, but had burst into flames over the Pacific.

"Isn't this the same data as before?" Chappelle queried impatiently.

"No, no it's not. Look at the schematic of the wiring system. It's—"

"To be honest, it's outside my field of expertise. I don't know enough about avionics and airplane design to know—"

"I do. I do, and I'm telling you that plane was brought down by an explosion inside the cabin, and that means someone set off a bomb."

"And the rest of the Federal Aviation Administration disagrees with you—"

"I'm with the NTSB, Director Chappelle. We have autonomy."

"And the NTSB isn't backing you," he pointed out. "You're off the reservation on this one. We're the Counter Terrorist Unit, Ms. Christie. We're professionals. We don't act on the impulse of one maverick agent."

7:17 P.M. PST
Pacific Coast Highway, North of Los Angeles

Sheik Abdul al-Hassan stood at the wide restaurant window, watching the waves curl and crash on the shore. Light from the restaurant cast a huge rhomboid of light out onto the ocean. Beyond its borders, all was pitch-black.

"Beautiful," said the man next to him.

Abdul glanced over at Father Collins. He hadn't realized the priest was standing there. That was how much of an impression Collins made.

"I was just thinking," Abdul said, more to himself than to the priest, "that this frame of light is a metaphor for our work."

"How do you mean?"

"The tide keeps rolling, never changing, like generations and generations of people. We are the light, casting ourselves out over them, trying to illuminate."

Father Collins smiled. He had a round, almost obese face under a shock of red hair that stood out starkly from his black shirt. "I have to say I always took you for kind of a cynic. I didn't know you were a poet."

Abdul shrugged. "I meant to be cynical. The light only reaches a tiny patch of the ocean. And the water never changes anyway."

Father Collins frowned at this. Abdul was afraid he would say something, but instead the priest lifted his frown up to a weak smile and turned away. Abdul watched him waddle gingerly through the crowd of clerics, protecting his left arm, which was in a sling.

"There goes the face of the interfaith Unity Conference," said a new arrival. Rabbi Dan Bender moved his considerable girth into the spot vacated by Father Collins. Bender was a big man, certainly overweight, and yet somehow able to move with a nimbleness that eluded thinner men. Abdul knew him to have run marathons.

"You are speaking metaphorically," said Abdul, who was no Father Collins. "He is a gentle, harmless man without teeth. Without toughness. I suppose that is a good summation of the conference as a whole."

Bender dabbed a kerchief on his cheek and neck, then dabbed around the rim of the yarmulke that somehow managed to keep its place on his bald head. "The conference will never have muscle as long as Collins is running it. I don't care that it has the backing of the Pope. It is a local event, and that means Cardinal Mulrooney is in charge. He is no great fan of his Pope's policy."

Abdul raised an eyebrow. "You sound like you disapprove of Mulrooney. But isn't he more like you and me?"

Bender looked offended. "You don't believe that, Sheik. You and I are realists. We know that the problems that divide us aren't just about making religions coexist. But we can respect one another. Mulrooney is cut from a different cloth. Pardon the pun."

Abdul said wryly, "Well, I'm in a whimsical mood now, so I guess I'll suggest that maybe it is the Pope's way that is the best. In the face of our cynicism and Mulrooney's isolationism, maybe hope and prayer are the best third option."

Bender shook his head. "What's the old Arab saying? Trust God, but tether your camel."

A dark cloud settled over Abdul's face. His cheeks seemed to sink under the line of his black beard.

"I said something?" Bender said, noting the change.

"No. No, it's just . . . the last person to use that expression with me was my brother."

"Oh, I didn't know you had—"

"A twin, actually," Abdul said. "He used that same phrase with me the last time I saw him."

"I get the feeling you two are not close."

"He's a fundamentalist," Abdul said.

Bender looked around the restaurant at the collection of clerics from so many faiths. "A fundamentalist? What would he think of this, then? What would he call it?"

Abdul considered. "An opportunity for martyrdom."

7:24 P.M. PST
L.A. County "Twin Towers" Detention Center

A phone call and the words *Federal anti-terrorist unit* had oiled the machinery of the jail system, and Jack and Nina were inside in no time. Sheriff's deputies brought the three suspects to three separate holding cells at the bottom level of the Twin Towers on Bauchet Street.

It also helped that Jack knew the watch commander, Mark Brodell, from his days with the LAPD.

"Hey, Mark," he said, shaking the man's hand as he entered the detention center. "Thanks for letting us in."

Brodell rolled his eyes at Jack and Nina. "Are you kidding? You're the Feds now, aren't you? We roll out the red carpet for the Federal government."

"That's not what it was like in my day," Jack replied.

Brodell winked. "Still isn't. But your partner's cute." Nina did not return his smile with anything like a thank-you.

"We lined 'em up for you. Three holding cells right this way."

Take away the existence of the plastic explosives, and the three suspects were completely unremarkable. They were Abu Mousa, a marketing coordinator at an advertising agency on Wilshire Boulevard; Omar Abu Risha, a small-time electronics wholesaler; and Sabah Fakhri, a clerk at Nordstrom's. None had a criminal record in the United States. Mousa and Fakhri had been born in this country. Risha was a naturalized citizen, but had no flags or warnings in his file.

"It was grunt work, really," Nina had explained on the way over. "We did what the FBI had done back in '93 to get the Blind Sheik. We just looked at the names at the center of the web and started following strands outward. It was really supposed to be a practice run to test our procedures. We didn't expect to find anything."

"But you found—?"

"Abu Mousa's brother was a member at the New Jersey mosque. He changed his name and someone missed it. Mousa wasn't a recorded member, but he had lived with his brother in Jersey. We found him here in Los Angeles and knocked on his door. Lo and behold, he and his housemates are sitting on a crate full of plastic explosives."

Jack nodded. "You mind if I—?"

"Go ahead and take the lead," Nina allowed. "But just this once."

Jack opened the door to the holding room. *Holding room* was a much more politically correct term than *interrogation room*, although the latter was more appropriate. The room was barely ten feet by ten feet, with a metal table and an uncomfortable chair for the subject to sit in. A single light hung down from the ceiling. The bulb wasn't bare, but it might as well have been from the light greenish pall it cast over the room.

Abu Mousa sat in the chair, his wrists shackled together and attached to a chain that had been bolted into the floor. He looked short sitting in the chair, and although his face was young, his hair was already thinning. He wore a frail mustache and a short beard. His eyes were brown and muddy, staring out over huge black bags that, by the looks of them, were permanent.

Jack walked over to the chair on the far side of the metal table and sat down, staring at the prisoner. Nina stayed behind Mousa, not moving, but she was adept at emitting malice. Jack stared at Mousa for a while, silent, until the prisoner began to fidget.

"I would like to see my lawyer," Mousa said finally.

"I haven't even asked you anything," Jack said. He continued to study the prisoner as though he were a zoo exhibit. Mousa caught on to his game and tried to return his gaze. It worked for a while, but Jack was patient, and it was easier to feel that you had the upper hand when you weren't shackled to the floor. Finally, Mousa gave in. "Come on, man, what is it you want?"

Jack said, "We want to know what you were planning on doing with that plastic explosive. And we want to know who has the rest of it."

Mousa clenched his shackled fists. "Man, I told you guys already, I wasn't going to do anything with it. Guy I know asked me to hold on to the crate for him. He said it was modeling clay, but expensive so I shouldn't mess with it. I didn't even open the thing, so I don't know if any of it is missing."

"Who gave it to you?"

"A friend."

Jack lunged across the table and grabbed Mousa by the front of his prison jumpsuit.

7:35 P.M. PST
L.A. County "Twin Towers" Detention Center

Mark Brodell watched the man in the suit approach, walking like he had a flagpole up his ass, flag and all. When Brodell said the word *Fed*, this was who he had in mind.

The man gave Brodell's hand a perfunctory shake and showed his identification. It read: "Ryan Chappelle, Division Director, Counter Terrorist Unit." "Is there a Jack Bauer here interrogating one of our prisoners?"

7:36 P.M. PST
Holding Cell, L.A. County "Twin Towers" Detention Center

Jack had pulled Mousa up across the table. Because the shackles held his arms back, Mousa was bent over the table with his arms pinned painfully beneath him.

"You don't have any friends," Jack was saying. "All you have are the names you're going to give me and the names I'm going to beat out of you. Understood?"

Mousa looked genuinely terrified, which was very informative. It told Jack that Mousa wasn't a professional, and that he had no real training. To Jack's way of thinking, that ruled out Syrian or Iranian intelligence, and probably Hezbollah as well. No trained intelligence officer would be afraid of a beating—not because he could take the punishment, but because a beating rarely gathered any significant information. The real tools of interrogation were sleep deprivation, drugs, and psychological duress. Only an amateur afraid for his own skin balked at physical punishment.

"Please," Mousa whimpered. "My arms . . ."

"Stop complaining, they're still attached," Jack said.

"What the hell is this!"

Ryan Chappelle walked into the room, flanked by a couple of suits Jack didn't know.

"Get your hands off that man. Now!" Chappelle barked.

Despite the order, Jack didn't let go immediately. He kept his eyes on Mousa and thought he saw, as Chappelle shouted again, the faintest hint of a smile on the man's face. Maybe he was wrong about Mousa's training.

"Let him go!" Chappelle practically shrieked.

Jack released Mousa. The man slumped forward over the table edge with a yelp, then slid backward to the floor. He winced as he stood up and took his seat in the chair again. His wrists around the manacles were red and raw. The fact created in Jack no sense of pity.

"What the hell do you think you're doing!" Chappelle was in his face. "This isn't even your case. That is not your prisoner. And you are not allowed to use force in interrogations."

Jack weathered Chappelle's shrill storm with antipathy. When the Director paused for breath, Jack said calmly, "Someone is going to blow up something with a bunch of plastic explosives tomorrow night. We need to find out who they are and what they are planning, and we need to find out now."

Chappelle flapped his hands in the air. "Not this way!"

Jack's tone was like ice. "Then what way? Show me." He looked at Mousa. "Should we just ask you where Abdul Rahman Yasin is hiding?"

He had asked facetiously, but he kept his eyes on Mousa, searching for any signs of recognition. He was disappointed. If Mousa knew the name of the World Trade Center bomber, he hid the fact like an expert.

". . . drummed out of the CIA when the Director of Operations hears about this," Chappelle was saying.

"Sir," Jack said, bringing his attention back to Chappelle. "It probably isn't good to be arguing in front of the prisoner."

Chappelle's neck turned purple, but he realized that Jack was right. He spun around and stormed out, gesturing for Bauer to follow. Jack did, casting a wry look at Nina Myers, who seemed to be enjoying herself.

Outside, in the hallway, Chappelle fumed. "You had no right to be here. You are not part of this unit, you are not authorized to perform operations on U.S. soil. You are not even on this case!"

Jack had no idea how much authority Chappelle really had. Even if he was the big dick in this Counter Terrorist Unit, the political influence of these agencies waxed and waned with their budgets and their successes. Unless CTU had some heavy hitters backing it in Congress, it was doubtful Chappelle could pull many strings. Domestic terrorism just wasn't that big an issue, even after '93.

"Take it up with the Director." Jack shrugged.

"I'll do better than that," Chappelle said. "You, Brodell!"

Several sheriff's deputies, including watch commander Brodell, had gathered around to watch the pissing contest. Chappelle had spotted the watch commander and called him out. "I want you to arrest this man. Jail him here, and call the Central Intelligence Agency."

Brodell's brow furrowed deeply. "Arrest him? Him? For what?"

Chappelle waved dismissively. "Excessive force. Assault. Violation of the Executive Order 12036 banning domestic surveillance. Trespassing, for all I care. Just lock him up and let the CIA come find him."

The watch commander looked perplexed, but then said, "Uh, no, sir."

Chappelle's neck reddened again. "What!"

"Well, sir, we didn't see any harm being done. We can't arrest him for nothing."

"Arrest him because I'm telling you to. I have the authority to do it."

Brodell nodded and scratched his head like a lazy farmer. "Well, sir, that may be true. If you could just get on the phone to my supervisor, and have him contact the sheriff, then I'll know for sure."

If Chappelle had been red-faced before, now he looked purple. But he wasn't a stupid man. He knew when he'd been defeated. "Stay away from our prisoners," he warned.

1 2 **3** 4 5 6 7 8 9
10 11 12 13 14 15 16 17
18 19 20 21 22 23 24

• •

THE FOLLOWING TAKES PLACE
BETWEEN THE HOURS OF
8 P.M. AND 9 P.M.
PACIFIC STANDARD TIME

• •

8:00 P.M. PST
CTU Headquarters, Los Angeles

Christopher Henderson was scratching out work assignments on a pad of paper because his computer wasn't booting up. Someday soon they'd have an entire tech department of their own, he told himself, but right now he'd settle for a guy from the Geek Squad.

He needed more staff. There was funding for it—in fact, he had to talk to Chappelle about spending more money, or someone in Washington would cut their budget for next year. But CTU was still having trouble recruiting, especially in field operations. Most of the top-quality operators saw the domestic agenda as the boondocks of counterterrorism work. Yes, the World Trade Center bombing had served notice that the bad guys could and would try attacks on U.S. soil, but the truck bomb hadn't brought the building down, and memories faded.

That's why Henderson wanted Bauer so badly. Jack had military experience, law enforcement experience, and hands-on intelligence work. Hell, the man had even studied literature at UCLA. He was a complete package. CTU could really use a man like Bauer.

"Jack Bauer will never work for CTU!" Ryan Chappelle howled. He'd managed to maintain his level of rancor all the way from the Twin Towers.

Henderson nearly jumped. "What? Why?"

Chappelle described the events at the holding cell. "He's a loose cannon. Insubordinate. Dangerous to the completion of any case, unless we want to give the terrorists a get-out-of-jail-free card for civil rights violations!" He glared at Henderson as though the entire affair had been his fault.

Henderson rubbed a hand on his head. If Jack did come on board, he told himself, this would not be the last of such conversations. He sighed. "He's a doer, sir. He gets the job done. If we're facing the kind of people you and I both think we are, that's going to be important."

Chappelle shook his head furiously. "There is no way that man is working for CTU. Ever."

8:08 P.M. PST
West Los Angeles, California

"Hey," Jack said, putting a hand on Teri's shoulder and kissing her neck from behind.

Teri Bauer leaned back into the kiss, mewed with pleasure, then said, "Who is this?"

Jack laughed. "I'm the blond one." He walked around her and the café table, and sat down in the lounge chair across from her. Knowing his habits, she had chosen the chair with its back to the room.

Teri put down her book and sipped her latte. "You want one?"

He shook his head. "No, I'm already pretty wired. I need to unwind so I can get some sleep."

"Rough day?" she asked, reaching across and putting her hand over his. Her hands looked small compared to his; she had always liked how strong his were.

He nodded, but didn't say more, and she didn't ask. She understood that his work with the CIA was often sensitive, and she had long ago decided not to ask too many questions. But there was one area that was open for discussion.

"That man, Christopher Henderson, called again today. Did you speak with him?"

Jack laughed. "Yes. And I got to see the CTU offices. Our garage looks more organized."

"Oh," she said.

He leaned forward and connected his free hand to hers. "You want me to take this."

She shrugged in a what-do-you-want-me-to-say? manner. "It might keep you in Los Angeles more often. That would be good. You'd still be doing work you like. And with Kim going into high school, it'll be good for you to be around as often as you can."

Jack nodded. "Where is she?"

"Home. Asleep, I think."

"I still can't get used to the fact that she's old enough to be left home alone."

"Still young enough to want her daddy around."

"I've thought of that. I'm not married to the CIA—" They both balked at the expression. He regretted using it, but said nothing and moved on. "I like it, but I could leave if the right thing came along. But I'm just not sure what CTU is all about, what their mission is. I'm not even sure they know yet."

"You like Christopher Henderson."

"Who's not really in charge. Some guy named Chappelle is. I met him today. He's a tool." Jack laughed. "I think if I work for that guy I'll end up shooting him in the head."

Jack's cell phone buzzed, and a number he hadn't seen in years flashed on the screen. "Bauer," he said.

"Jack, it's Harry Driscoll, Robbery-Homicide—"

"Hey, Harry, long time." He mouthed an apology to Teri, who shrugged. "How's business?"

On the other end of the line, Harry Driscoll chuckled. "Never slow, always plenty of customers. Listen, word gets around, and I know that you've got some interest in the Sweetzer Avenue thing."

Jack hadn't heard the term before, but he recognized Sweetzer Avenue as the street where the three suspected terrorists shared a house. "If you mean the Three Stooges and their box of goodies, yeah, I'm interested."

"Well, we've got a kind of lead on it. Thought you might be interested in tagging along."

Jack paused. "So now LAPD is involved? What's Robbery-Homicide got to do with it."

"Long story. Well, actually a pretty short story. It's a turf war. Some new Federal unit is trying to throw its weight around. We think they've got their head up their ass, we want to get involved, especially when houses blow up in our backyard."

"Yeah, houses with me in them," Jack said. "Tell me where to go." He snatched Teri's napkin and a pen and scribbled down some directions. "On my way.

"I've got to go, honey," he said, standing and kissing her. "I shouldn't be too late. We can talk more about whether I should work for CTU."

His back was already to her when she said softly, "Seems like you already are."

8:14 P.M. PST
Brentwood, California

Aaron Biehn kept tugging at the collar of his shirt. It was his favorite T-shirt, bright yellow with squiggly monsters drawn on it and the name of the band Lido Beach. It was his favorite, but it felt too small on him now. He was choking.

You have to tell someone, Kim Bauer had said. *Tell your dad. He's a police officer. He can do something.*

What if no one believes me? What if I can't prove it, or what if I have to tell . . . to describe what he did?

Aaron shuddered again thinking about that. He wanted to forget that it had ever happened, but it was there, the guilt in his mind, the horrible feeling in his body, every time he thought about the Mass or said his Hail Marys or went to confession, which his mother insisted they do each week.

He knew he couldn't tell his mother. She wouldn't believe him. She was a devout Catholic and very active at St. Monica's. "The priests are the apple of God's eye," she always said, copying the phrase from her mother, Aaron's grandmother, who lived in Dublin. And if she did believe him, she'd be crushed.

But Dad was different. He was a Catholic, too, but more because his parents had been and it pleased his wife. He was sure his father would believe him, but he was afraid he would be ashamed. Don Biehn was big on self-reliance. He had always made Aaron deal with elementary school bullies on his own, rather than telling his teachers.

But Aaron had to do something. The thing of it . . . he wasn't sure what to call it; was it guilt, or a vile memory, or terror? Whatever it was, it lived in him like a snake wriggling inside his body. Its head lived in his chest, gnawing at the bottom of his heart. Its tail resided at the very bottom of his spine and wriggled there, sending shivers up his back and making his lower half feel somehow cold and wet.

Aaron tugged at his shirt again and walked into the den where his father was watching *Survivor*. Aaron sat down next to him on the couch. His father, tall and lanky like Aaron was clearly going to be, punched him in the shoulder absentmindedly and kept watching.

"Dad . . ." Aaron began.

"Yep," his father said, eyes still on the television. There was a good-looking girl in a bikini walking along the beach.

"I . . . I need to talk to you about something." He paused. His dad nodded. "It's . . . about church."

"You gotta go, pal," Don Biehn said. "I'm sorry

about that. You and I will both hear an earful from Mom if you—"

"Not about that. Dad, it's about Father Frank. It's about the priests."

Don Biehn glanced sidelong at his son. "They're not perfect, Aaron, no matter what they think. Don't ever let them fool you. Forgive the expression, but don't take everything they say or do as the gospel truth."

Aaron blushed. "Um, yeah. Okay. Thanks, Dad." He turned away.

8:23 P.M. PST
St. Monica's Cathedral, Downtown Los Angeles

His Holiness Pope John Paul II, the Vicar of Rome, washed his hands after using the bathroom in the cloister of St. Monica's Cathedral. Such acts had humbled him during the course of his many years as leader of the Catholic Church. Each year on Holy Thursday, he washed the feet of the poor, and that was supposed to remind him that Christ himself had practiced such humility. But, though he never would have admitted it aloud, the practice had taken on too much of the feeling of ceremony, of show. He did not feel humble on Holy Thursday, he felt like an actor.

But these human acts, these needs of the body that had not ended when he was made Pope, and indeed became more difficult as time passed, constantly reminded him of his frailty. There was a Zen saying he had always liked: "Before enlightenment, chop wood, carry water. After enlightenment, chop wood, carry water." He liked that.

There were those among his cardinals who would

have frowned at his use of the Zen maxim, but he was a pluralist, this Pope. Through all the years of his religious life, from altar boy to Pontiff, he had never forgotten the original meaning of that word *catholic*—of or concerning all humankind. All humankind, he thought, and he believed. His belief in the one true church was deep, of course, but he refused to turn his heart or his intellect away from the rest of the world. He had studied deeply of Islam and Judaism, but also of Buddhism, Hinduism, and other, less popular beliefs. Though he dwelt within the profound understanding that a man's soul could be saved only through Christ, only through the church, he refused to exclude those who failed to accept this fact.

The Pope walked gingerly out into the small hallway and thence to the sitting room, each step a quick but careful feat of engineering for his ancient body. His once-straight spine had long ago curled like the pages of a well-read paperback. His knees hurt. His hands were gnarled as the bark of pines back in his childhood home of Krakow.

It is only the body, he said to himself in several of the languages he spoke. *It is only the body.*

Cardinal Mulrooney was waiting for him in the sitting room. As the Pope entered, Mulrooney stood. The Cardinal towered over the shrunken Pope.

"Your Holiness," Mulrooney drawled.

"Your Eminence," the Pope said in his distinctly accented English. "Was the reception well attended?"

"A full house, Holy Father," Mulrooney said. He placed strong emphasis on the titles, like a man uncomfortable with them, grasping them firmly to maintain control. "The papers will carry a good story about the event."

The Pope tottered over to a chair and sat down, and Mulrooney swept toward a seat opposite. "That is quite an achievement," the Holy Father said, his tiny eyes glittering, "despite your disapproval. And your attempts to undermine the Unity Conference."

The tiniest quiver ran along Mulrooney's thin lips. He cursed himself inwardly. This was the Holy Father's latest weapon, and he should have been better prepared. John Paul gave the appearance of a doddering old fool. He often used this facade to lay traps for those he mistrusted.

"You are mistaken, Holy Father," Mulrooney said at last. "I am as much a supporter of your peace efforts as any—"

"I am old, Your Eminence," the Pope said impatiently. "I don't have time for games. Nor do I have the interest I once had." His face had collapsed in on itself, a caved-in melon. But his eyes gleamed out of the wreckage like two bright wet seeds. "You disdain my efforts. You disdain me."

Mulrooney smoothed the hem of his black shirt. "Your Holiness, it was you who chose to hold the Unity Conference here, in my diocese. You insisted."

"The United States is the logical place to begin," John Paul said wearily. "And either New York or Los Angeles was the logical city." The Pope sighed. "War is coming, Your Eminence. War of a kind we have not seen before. Someone must defuse it, and I intend to put the full power of the church behind the efforts of peace."

Mulrooney felt the Pope's words resound in his chest. Even in his failing years, John Paul was a powerful orator. A man did not become Pope without mastering the tools that bent others to his will. "But some of those you want to make friends with are the enemies of the church. I don't know how we can make peace with enemies."

"There is no point in making peace with friends, Your Eminence."

Mulrooney scratched his nose to hide his sneer. There was no use debating with this old man. The truth was, as unsupportive as the Holy Father thought he was, Mulrooney's true animosity went much, much further.

John Paul seemed to read his thoughts. "I wonder, Your Eminence, if this is the extent of your rebelliousness, or if we are only scratching the surface?"

Something clutched at Mulrooney's stomach. He ignored it. "Your Holiness?"

John Paul's eyes bored into him. "There are rumors."

Mulrooney brushed them aside. "You know better than any of us that the church is a political animal. There are always rumors." When John Paul continued to stare, Mulrooney added, "I swear, Your Holiness, that I am loyal to the church, and to its Pope."

John Paul nodded. "That will be all. For now."

8:37 P.M. PST
Brentwood

Aaron Biehn sat in the tub of warm water. The snake slithered inside his body. He could feel it in his heart, wriggling through his guts, its tail dampening and violating the base of his spine. He shuddered.

He had hoped that telling his father would give him some relief. He wanted to be held, to be told it wasn't his fault. He wanted something . . . something he hadn't gotten, because he couldn't bring himself to say it. He wanted a hug that would squeeze the snake out of him.

But then his father would tell people. And he, Aaron, would have to talk about it to strangers. And friends. And confront Father Frank. And others. He would be asked what had been done to him. He would have to use words he did not want to use. Say things he did not want to say. He would be asked if he had wanted it. Someone would say that he had wanted it. He shivered.

The snake squirmed joyfully, horribly, inside him. The snake would love the attention. Feed on his despair. Like a snake eating a cat that ate the rat, it would swallow his humiliation whole and digest it slowly, growing fatter as it did, so that even when the public humiliation passed, the snake would still be there, consuming him from inside.

He could not bear that. He had to get the snake out of his body now. He could not stand to be violated any longer. Aaron sat up in the tub and fumbled with his father's shaving kit.

8:41 P.M. PST
Parker Center, Los Angeles

"Remember to check for the Adam's apple," Jack Bauer said, leaning into Harry Driscoll's office.

Driscoll looked up from his desk, which was crammed face-to-face with another empty desk in the tiny office. He grinned. "Like I said, it wasn't the Adam's apple that bothered me, it was the rest of the equipment."

Jack laughed. It was an old joke, inspired by an old story from when Driscoll was a detective in Hollywood Division and Bauer was LAPD SWAT. The two men shook hands. Driscoll was shorter than Jack, but nearly twice as wide, a black fireplug with a cheesy mustache. He clasped Harry's outstretched hand.

"You been good?" Driscoll said, standing up.

"Not bad."

"How's the dark side treating you?" the detective asked as he reached for a jacket that covered his shoulder rig.

Jack shrugged. There was no point in hiding his CIA status from those who knew of it, but he still couldn't discuss much. "I'm still hoping to get promoted to Robbery-Homicide someday. How'd you know I was on this case?"

Driscoll laughed. "You were in a house that blew up, Jack. That doesn't happen every day, even in L.A. Word gets around, you know?"

8:45 P.M. PST
Brentwood

"Aaron? You okay in there?" Don banged on the door. "You've been in there awhile." He waited. He pounded again when no answer came back. "Aaron?"

"Is something wrong?" Carianne, his wife, asked, coming up behind him.

"Aaron!" Don yelled. "Answer me! I'm going to break down the door." That was the cop in him, and the father, talking at once.

His wife pointed upward. Resting atop the door frame was a little key, just a loop of wire with a straight tail. He nodded and pulled it down, then jiggled it into the bathroom doorknob. It popped open, and he shoved the door inward.

Carianne screamed. Don thought he screamed, too, but he was only aware of himself rushing forward, slamming his knees against the side of the bathtub and plunging his hands into the pink water and dragging Aaron out onto the floor.

8:47 P.M. PST
110 West

"It's a screwed-up case, really," Driscoll said. Jack hunkered down in the passenger seat of Driscoll's Acura as the detective drove up the 110 Freeway and hurtled toward the 101. "Carney's okay with you?"

"Fine," Jack said. "Go on."

"The case really started with LAPD. We got a whiff that these guys had something to do with illegal importing, so we were watching them. Then along comes this Federal group. Counter Terrorist Unit? Who the fuck are they?"

Jack laughed. "Doesn't matter."

"Maybe not to you, but they stole our case away. They were kind enough to keep us updated—"

"I've heard that before," Jack interjected.

"We were there when CTU collared them. You saw the box, right?"

"Yeah."

"Looked to me like some of that stuff was missing."

"I thought so, too. They're working on the three suspects."

Driscoll nodded as he exited the 101 and dropped

down to Sunset, heading for Carney's hot dogs. "I hear they're acting tough now. They'll break down."

"I'll be honest, Harry, I don't have the time. I had an informant who gave me the idea that something's happening tomorrow night."

Driscoll's mental wheels spun. "Informant . . . the guy who blew up?"

"Yes. I need leads. Did you guys have anything else?"

"We came in behind CTU and dusted for prints. There was lots of them and not much else. They had a cleaning lady, but she's fifty-eight and from El Salvador. The other was the mailman. We had his prints on file. He was arrested in Pakistan for some violent protests against the prime minister. Came here a few years ago, but hasn't caused a problem since. He's a person of interest, but we don't consider him a suspect at this time . . .'course, technically none of them are our suspects."

"None of them are my suspects, either. Mind if I question him anyway?"

"Right after a chili dog."

8:50 P.M. PST
Playa del Rey, California

Yasin sat in the lobby of the Windows Hotel in Playa del Rey. He rubbed a hand along his smooth jawline. It felt wrong to be clean-shaven. A true Muslim wore a beard, of course. But this couldn't be helped. He was known now in this country. It had been a risk just to return.

The man he'd been waiting for entered the front doors. Clean-shaven, including a shaven scalp, dressed in jeans, blue T-shirt, and court shoes, he looked like any one of the thousands of fit, middle-aged, multi-cultural Angelenos that formed the image of the city. As the other man approached, Yasin smiled to himself, satisfied in the knowledge that it was America's pluralism that would help defeat it. The United States had too many open doors, too many faces, too many acceptable modes of behavior, to keep them out. They could blend in so easily. Because Allah was great, Yasin probably could have stood in the middle of the lobby dressed as a Bedouin and no one would have given it a thought. The Americans were so arrogant, so ignorant, that they were not even aware of the masses who hated them halfway around the world.

The bald, fit man arrived at his seat. He said to Yasin, "Good to see you, Gabriel," using Yasin's code name.

"And you, Michael," he replied tersely. "You seem unhappy, Michael. Is something wrong."

A look of disdain crawled across Michael's face. "We're in this together, but I don't have to pretend to like you."

"It will be over soon. Tomorrow. Let's talk about the C–4. I assume that what the authorities found was the extra?" Yasin asked.

Michael nodded. "And the ones in custody don't know anything. That, plus the fact that the police are inept, means we're both safe."

Yasin was not comfortable with this. "Don't underestimate them."

Michael laughed. "The FBI let you walk out their front door."

"They were idiots then," Yasin agreed. "The events of 1993 took them by surprise. That was the idea, of course. But we can't let success cloud our judgment. Look how quickly they recovered. My blind friend is in jail. So are several of the others. I was caught, and it was only the will of"—he almost said Allah aloud—"it was only good luck that I was set free. If we make mistakes, they will take advantage of them." Yasin sat back for a minute, rubbing his bare chin again. Michael sensed a lecture. "My blind friend's mistake," Yasin began, "was that he put all his trust in hiding his trail. The trail cannot be entirely hidden. You cannot hide water from a Bedouin. They will find a trail. We should have left false leads. The word for it is subterfuge. You Americans call it a red herring, though I don't know where the expression comes from."

Michael raised an eyebrow. "You seem to have more than one."

Yasin grinned. "I have been lately interested in the number three."

8:57 P.M. PST
Brentwood

The sirens had stopped, but Carianne was still wailing. The paramedics had shoved Don out of the room as they tried desperately to resuscitate their son. Don and Carianne had clutched at each other for a few minutes. Don, horrified, in shock, could only wonder morbidly how the bathroom had looked so clean. All the blood had spilled into the big tub of water, clouding it pink.

Mandi had come from next door, responding to the commotion, and wrapped herself around Carianne's grief. Don had peeled himself away. It was the man in him, or the cop, he wasn't sure which, but he felt the need to act. And he had a horrible feeling that Aaron had been trying to tell him something earlier.

Don walked away from the urgent calls and commands passing back and forth between the paramedics, and away from the ululations of his wife and neighbor. He went into Aaron's room. There was a journal on Aaron's desk. Don Biehn the police officer picked up the journal and began to read.

A few pages later, it was Don Biehn the father who knew that he was going to kill someone.

1 2 3 **4** 5 6 7 8 9
10 11 12 13 14 15 16 17
18 19 20 21 22 23 24

• •

**THE FOLLOWING TAKES PLACE
BETWEEN THE HOURS OF
9 P.M. AND 10 P.M.
PACIFIC STANDARD TIME**

• •

*9:00 P.M. PST
Mid-Wilshire Area, Los Angeles*

Jack pulled up in front of the bungalow on Edinburgh Avenue just north of Melrose. Like all the houses on the street, this one was well-tended. The front yard was small, but the porch light revealed a well-cut lawn and a flower-lined walkway that serpentined through the grass up to the porch. The door itself was a massive slab of well-varnished oak. Jack rapped on it with his knuckles.

Lights were already on inside, shining through the curtained windows to the left of the door. Jack saw one of the curtains draw back for a moment, then fall into place. Beyond the thick door something rattled, then the door opened a bit, and a tall, thin man stared out at him uncertainly.

"Yes?"

Jack held up his identification. "Mr. Ghulam Meraj Khalid? My name is Jack Bauer. I'm with the State Department. Can I have a word with you?"

Khalid managed to look frightened, annoyed, and accommodating all at once. He stepped back and pulled the door open wide. "Um, State Department, of course, come in, come in."

Jack smiled and entered onto hardwood floors as well-maintained as the yard out front. There was not much in the way of furniture—a simple couch, a chair, a wooden dining table with a clean-lined credenza beside it. A flat-screen television hung on the wall across from the couch and the chair. It was on, broadcasting a rerun of *CSI*.

"Please, sit," Khalid said, indicating the couch. "Would you like something to drink?"

"No, thanks," Jack said, though he did sit down. He looked at Ghulam Meraj Khalid as the other man lowered himself into the chair. Khalid was lean, the kind of lean that was always genetic. His nose was hooked, and his hair was thinning. He reminded Jack vaguely of the Goon from an old *Popeye* cartoon. But he had a friendly smile and an animated expression.

"This is about Abu Mousa," Khalid said.

"What makes you say that?" Jack asked.

Khalid laughed. "I hope it's about that! What else have I done?"

"You tell me," Jack said casually.

Khalid laughed again, nervously. "Nothing. It's just you're the third or fourth police officer or whatever to talk to me about this. At least this time I get to answer questions here. Or . . . ?" Khalid looked toward the door as though other men might appear to escort him out.

"Here's fine," Jack said. His demeanor was casual, almost bored, but he was assessing the other man carefully. Khalid was appropriately nervous, but no more than one could expect from a man being questioned by the Federal government. "So first, your full name is Ghulam Meraj Khalid, yes?"

The man nodded. "You can call me Gary."

"And how are you involved with Abu Mousa?"

Gary said, "I'm not. Involved with him, I mean. I know all three of those guys a little, but only through my job."

"You work with them?" Jack asked.

Gary looked confused. "No. I'm a mailman. I mean, mail carrier, that's what they tell us to say these days. A U.S. postal worker. I figured you'd know that already."

Jack did. He'd read Khalid's file. But the simplest way to trip someone up was to play dumb and ask every question under the sun.

"They are on my route," Gary continued. "I pretty much know them as much as I know anyone on my route."

Jack smiled charmingly. "So we'll find your fingerprints in everyone's house?"

Khalid blushed. Jack wondered if he might find Khalid's prints in the homes of a housewife or two. "Well, I don't really know them that well. But they're Muslims, too, you know? I pray five times a day, and sometimes they invited me in to pray in their house. It's a little more convenient than the back of the truck."

"How often did you pray with them?"

Khalid shrugged. "I couldn't say. Once or twice a month, I guess. You know, if they're home, if they see me, if they invite me in, I say yes. It didn't happen all that much."

"But they were home sometimes during the day. What do they do for a living?"

Gary the mailman shrugged. "I don't know. I heard one of them, not Mousa, one of the other guys, talking about computers once, but mostly we just prayed, talked a little, then I went on my route."

"You knew Mousa the best," Jack said.

Gary tilted his chin. "I don't . . . I guess. Why?"

"You just said, 'not Mousa, one of the others.' You sound familiar with him."

Gary nodded. "I guess so. He was the most talkative. The friendliest."

"How long have you been a mailman?"

"Seven years. I've been in the U.S. for almost twelve," he added with a smile. "Like I said, I've had this conversation three or four times already. I figured that was your next question."

"You're like an expert," Jack agreed. "What are your politics?"

Gary looked confused. "My politics? I . . . hmm, what do you mean? Are you asking me how I vote? Does that matter here?"

Jack reassured him. "No, not really. I don't mean your politics here. I mean your politics back home. Pakistan."

Gary calmed noticeably. "Oh, that. Yeah, I left because of politics. Look, I don't know if this gets me into trouble or not, but I came here because I didn't like what was happening in Pakistan back then. Benazir Bhutto got elected. They made her Prime Minister! I didn't want to be in that country."

"Was it Bhutto herself? Or the fact that she was a woman? You don't like women?"

Gary grinned. He did have an infectious smile. "Oh, I like women well enough, you know? But there's a place for everything. I'm not sure a woman's place is in charge."

Jack laughed. "So you came here? Women here have more freedom than—"

Gary interrupted. "No, yeah, that's what they say here. I mean, that's part of the propaganda, right? But no one here's dumb enough to elect a woman."

Jack's mobile phone rang, and he saw Driscoll's number appear on the screen. "Sorry," he said, and answered.

"Bauer, it's Harry," Driscoll said. "This case is getting stranger all the time. I got a lead on the plastic explosives. Coming?"

"Yes," Jack said. He stood up and shook Gary Khalid's hand. "Thanks. We'll be in touch."

9:09 P.M. PST
Brentwood

The sirens had faded. Carianne had gone in the ambulance as it rushed Aaron to the hospital. They were going to try to save him. Don had said he would follow behind in the car. But first, he had a quick chore to do.

Don Biehn, police officer and caretaker of his household, owned several guns but kept them secured in a gun safe. Only he knew the combination. If he'd opened it, he would have found inside a Heckler & Koch .40 caliber semi-automatic, a Kimber Custom II .45 caliber, and a Smith & Wesson .38 caliber six-shot revolver. All of them were fine weapons that had seen a lot of use in his practice shooting.

But Don didn't go to that safe. Instead, he went to the garage and got his ladder. Dragging it over to the tall, do-it-yourself white cabinets he had built, he climbed the ladder so that he could reach the top of the shelves. There was dust everywhere, on and around old boxes they had never opened from their last move, laid thickly over two antique-looking blue lamps that Carianne insisted on keeping, and a box containing a fondue set they had received as a wedding gift nineteen years ago, but never opened.

Don pushed these useless artifacts aside until he found a small box with the words "Old Lecture Notes" scribbled in black marker. He pulled it out, sneezing at the dust, and rested it on the flat top of the ladder. The box top slid off easily enough. Don dug through the piles of bent and yellowed paper from his days at Cal State University Northridge. Beneath them lay a rolled-up piece of canvas—right where he'd stashed it seven or eight years earlier. Dan unrolled the canvas, and a Taurus 92F semi-automatic fell into his hand.

It had been his first year as a homicide detective. He and his partner had been working a bank robbery case involving a couple of career criminals. Don managed to arrest one of them in his home. He'd found several weapons, including the Taurus, and discovered that the Taurus was unregistered. Untraceable. Don had stashed it away, and no one had noticed. As a cop who had tracked suspects through their guns and watched prosecutors nail them with ballistics, Don figured that it might be useful to have a weapon that was completely unconnected to himself.

He had been right.

9:16 P.M. PST
Pacific Coast Highway

At quarter after nine on a weeknight, the Interstate 10 Freeway worked the way it had been designed to work: it got you from the middle of Los Angeles to the beach in just a few minutes. A tunnel marked the end of the I–10. When you emerged on the far side, the world opened up onto a gigantic postcard of Los Angeles: the beach, the ocean, and the Pacific Coast Highway.

Jack was moving up the coast highway—also easily navigated this time of night—with his speakerphone on as Driscoll recited the nature of the lead they were going to investigate.

". . . telling you, it's the weirdest lead I've ever followed. But it's very L.A."

"So tell me," Jack called out to the cell phone resting on the console of his SUV.

"You ever heard of Mark Gelson?"

Jack considered that. "I know Mark Gelson the actor. The *Future Fighter* guy."

"That's him. You don't see him much anymore, but he used to be on the A-list back in the eighties. Anyway, the story is that he got pulled over on the way home to Malibu for drunk driving. He was raving, talking about how he was going to set things straight, blow some people to pieces, just like in his movies."

"So what?" Jack said skeptically. "Some has-been actor gets sauced and—"

"He mentioned plastic explosives."

Jack nodded at the cell phone. "Ah."

"Yeah. It could be nothing."

"No, it's something," Jack said wryly. "It's an over-the-hill actor who misses being in the headlines, and we're helping him. He have a movie coming out?"

"Thought of that," Driscoll replied through the phone. "He's got zilch. A new version of the complete set of *Future Fighter* movies came out on DVD, but that was two years ago. I don't see this as a publicity stunt. If it's anything, it's just a drunk old guy trying to sound as tough as he used to look. But I'll catch hell if we don't check it out. You want to leave this one to me?"

Jack shrugged, mostly to himself. "I'm almost there anyway. See you in the driveway." He hung up.

Mark Gelson. Jack had been a fan of the *Future Fighter* movies when they came out. He was the target market, of course. The Future Fighter lived in a post-apocalyptic world. He was a hero, but an amoral one willing to do whatever it took to defeat evil. He was a maverick who literally lived outside the law. Jack recalled that Gelson had made the headlines a few times for erratic and scandalous behavior. Back then the media weren't quite as ruthless as they were these days, so the news didn't stay in the papers long, but Gelson had been in his share of barroom fights and nightclub scuffles. Most people figured he was just trying to live up to the heroic, tough-guy image he portrayed on screen.

Jack reached the exclusive beach colony of Malibu and drove down along Malibu Colony Road until he reached the address for Mark Gelson's beach house. Driscoll was waiting for him outside on the street, smoking a cigarette. Jack watched the cigarette tip glow momentarily brighter in the darkness beyond the light atop Gelson's gate and stared at Driscoll quizzically.

"Took it back up," the detective said unapologetically. "Otherwise I'd be perfect and no one could stand to be around me." He dropped the cigarette and crushed it with his heel.

Gelson's house was screened by a tall, ivy-grown wall with an iron gate. There was an intercom set next to the gate. Driscoll buzzed it and heard a female voice say in a Hispanic accent, "Yes, who is it?"

"Los Angeles Police Department, ma'am," Harry Driscoll said. "Mr. Gelson is expecting us."

The intercom buzzed irritably. The gate rattled and chugged, swinging back and away from them. Jack and Driscoll walked up the wide circular drive to a white, very modern house that looked like several large white cubes stacked irregularly together. Something about the way the giant cubes were stacked triggered a sense of recognition in Jack. It was nothing definitive, but he had the sense that the cubist architecture had meaning.

They could hear the ocean murmuring in the darkness beyond the house.

"Those residuals must be nice," Driscoll said enviously.

The door opened as they approached, and a sturdy Latina nodded at them. She motioned for them to enter and guided them toward the living room. The walls of the hallway were white, like the exterior of the house, and entirely bare except for a single, ornate crucifix fixed at eye level. The view was stark. The living room matched. It was huge, and the entire west wall was glass. Light from the room spilled out onto the sand and the waves beyond. There was a painting over the couch that appeared as white as the wall on which it hung. But as Jack studied it for a moment, he began to see faint discolorations that pulled his vision out of focus, or rather into a new focus in which he saw the faint image of a man's face painted white within white.

"That's a Stretch."

Jack turned, mildly surprised that he'd let someone enter a room without his knowledge. "Excuse me?"

"The painting. It's a Stretch. Ronnie Stretch, the artist. You know his work?"

"I didn't even know it was a painting at first," Jack admitted. "But it's interesting how things come into focus if you give them time."

He turned fully to face Mark Gelson. Somehow, Jack always expected actors to be taller than they really were. Gelson was about five feet, seven inches. He looked younger than his fifty-plus years, and still carried the square jaw and bright blue eyes Jack remembered from the movies, even though there was more salt than pepper in his hair. He was wearing blue jeans and an American Eagle T-shirt, the kind of clothes you might see on twenty-somethings at Chia Venice.

Gelson approached and shook Jack's hand firmly. "Detective Driscoll?"

Jack pointed over at Harry. "My name is Bauer. That's Driscoll."

"Detective Bauer, then," Gelson said before turning to Harry. "Can I get you guys something to drink?"

"No, but thanks for seeing us so late in the evening," the detective took over. "We have some questions about—"

"Last night." Gelson sat down. He shook his head gravely. "Look, I'm not sure why detectives are involved, but I don't make a habit of driving drunk. It was stupid. I know I'm going to take a hit in the papers tomorrow."

"It's not the drunk driving part we're here about, Mr. Gelson," Harry interrupted. "It's about what you said. You talked about—" Harry flipped a page in his notepad. "You said, 'I hope my guys blow your fat asses up with the rest of them.'"

Gelson blushed. "Doesn't sound like me, does it. Jesus, I hope not, anyway. I'm sorry, I was drunk . . ."

"And then you said, 'I'm so fucking glad I bought them the plastic explosives.'"

Mark Gelson froze like a DVD on pause. "What do you mean?

Harry Driscoll folded his notebook and said simply, "The question, Mr. Gelson, is what did you mean? When did you get the plastic explosives? Who are your friends?"

"I don't . . ." The actor's face had gone from red to white in a split second. "I'm not . . . Do you mean explosives?"

Abu Mousa had been a better actor. Driscoll's disdain showed clearly on his face as he said, "We can just as easily do this downtown. In fact, I'd rather do it down there. We've got video cameras, tape recorders, it's more convenient; isn't it, Jack?"

Bauer nodded.

"Yeah, so let's go down there—" He reached for Gelson's arm. The actor squirmed away and sank back into the couch.

"No, look, okay. Okay." Some of Gelson's good looks seemed to have faded away, the reverse action of the picture on the wall. "Look, can I tell you the truth?"

"That is the general idea," Jack said.

Gelson put his head in his hands. He didn't cry, but he was close to it. Jack was just about to step forward and shake him when the actor rubbed his face and looked up. "I've got some friends. They're guys I hang out with sometimes. It's stupid, maybe just something I do to relive the old days, you know? There was a time when I used this whole town like a cheap whore, and all anyone did was scream for more. I rode bikes with gangs, I did coke like it was vitamin C. I used to fire directors off the set. I—"

"The plastic explosives," Jack demanded.

Gelson jumped a little. "Okay. Um, I didn't really buy it. I just gave money. I was hanging out with some guys I knew from back then. They said they could buy some stuff to raise some real hell. I gave them the money."

"Who were these guys?" Jack asked. "Were any of them from another country?"

Gelson looked bewildered. "Another . . . ? No. They're from here. They're bikers."

"Where were they buying the plastic explosives from?"

"They didn't tell me. Look, I'm sorry. I didn't know they were serious. I don't want anyone getting

hurt. I swear. I just . . . I just wanted to raise a little
hell, you know?"

"Nice job," Jack grunted.

Gelson looked "Is this . . . will this get into the
papers?"

Driscoll rolled his eyes. "Why don't you just tell us
where to find your biker friends."

9:27 P.M. PST
St. Monica's Cathedral, Downtown Los Angeles

Cardinal Mulrooney swooped down the hallway
of St. Monica's cloister. The walls looked shabby
to him. The decor was old and worn; Mulrooney
could see ruts worn into the tiles before his feet. St.
Monica's was old and rickety. The Cardinal feared
the next earthquake.

He was embarrassed at the look of his cathedral in
the eyes of the Pope, and angry at himself for being
embarrassed. As if he should worry about the opinion of that sanctimonious old man. A person able to
hear Mulrooney's thoughts at that moment would be
surprised to learn that he did, indeed, believe in the
infallibility of the Pope. Just not this Pope.

9:28 P.M. PST
CTU Headquarters, Los Angeles

Christopher Henderson was finishing his review of
an early forensics report from the Panorama City
explosion. Someone had used plastic explosives to
rig a homemade land mine into Ramin's chair. The

fat man's enormous weight had activated it, and the minute he stood up, it had gone off. Ramin had been killed instantly, and Burchanel was in critical condition. CTU was coordinating with the CIA and foreign agencies—mostly the Israelis, who'd had plenty of experience with this sort of thing—to compare this bombing strategy to the methods of any known terrorists.

What bothered Henderson most was the wide-ranging nature of the operation. Bauer's investigation had started in Cairo. CTU's had started in West Los Angeles. Ramin's original connections were in New York, and if Abdul Rahman Yasin was involved, the most recent reports put him in Iraq. This suggested a fairly extensive network.

Henderson looked at the notes he'd put together from his brief conversation with Bauer. The only pertinent piece of information was the timing. Ramin seemed certain that whatever Yasin and his people were planning, they were going to do it tomorrow night. Ramin's murder lent credence to that belief. That gave CTU twenty-four hours, maybe less, to disrupt the plot.

Henderson's cell phone rang. "Henderson."

"Christopher, it's Jack Bauer."

"I was just thinking about you," Henderson said. "I know you're declining the offer, but I could really use help on this, Jack."

"I'm already helping," Bauer replied. "I've got a lead on the source of the plastic explosives." He explained his call from Driscoll and the interrogation of Mark Gelson. "You know how some of the explosive seemed to be missing? I'm thinking whoever sold it to the Sweetzer Avenue group also sold some to Gelson's people. If we find them, we may be able to track it back to the source."

"How do you know it's even the same batch of plastic explosives?" Henderson asked.

"I don't," Jack replied over the phone. "But how much plastic explosive is there floating around the city?"

"Jesus, I hope not much."

"Exactly. There's a chance that Abu Mousa and the other guys in custody don't know much. Maybe if I track the plastic explosive back to its source, I can get a stronger lead." Jack paused. "Christopher, you know the clock is ticking on this, right?"

"Yeah."

"So, listen, if I get my hands on someone who knows something, I'm going to ask them a few questions before I turn them over to Chappelle."

Henderson wasn't sure whether to wince or smile. "I didn't hear that."

"Good, just as long as you didn't hear it loud and clear. In the meantime, I was hoping your new CTU group could lend a hand on something. We have to assume that Ramin was right and the target is going to get hit tomorrow night. I'd like your CTU people to run an analysis of Yasin's profile, and the Blind Sheik's profile, and come up with a list of likely targets in Los Angeles. You can probably coordinate with LAPD. I would cross-reference with Beverly Hills PD, too, because a lot of dignitaries stay in Beverly Hills when they visit L.A. Also, there's a large Persian population there, and the target may be an Iranian immigrant trying to influence politics back home. You can probably coordinate that with the State Department. If you guys have any facial recognition equipment up and running, I'd download as much video from the Los Angeles airport as you can get and start running it. We may get lucky. Bauer out."

Henderson laughed helplessly to himself as Bauer hung up. He stood and went to his office door, looking out on the big empty space hanging with data lines, phone wires, and a few desks. It was approaching ten o'clock. Everyone had gone home for the evening, and Jack was asking for a multijursidictional, multiagency data search. "Yeah, right." Henderson sighed. "We'll get right on that."

9:33 P.M. PST
Downtown Los Angeles

For years the Cathedral of St. Monica, more often referred to simply as St. Monica's, stood like a proud matron brooding over the poverty and squalor around her. She'd been completed in 1876 at a time when downtown had been the beating heart of the city. That heart had grown frail and sickly over the decades. So, too, had Monica. The matron no longer stood quite so proudly, as though beaten down by more than a century of misery creeping toward her from nearby Skid Row. Earthquakes had played their part, too, especially the Northridge earthquake in 1994 that had torn holes throughout the city. Neglect also played a role. The diocese, led by Cardinal Mulrooney, had long ago wanted to tear the old girl down and replace her with a gleaming modern cathedral. Mulrooney's efforts had been stymied by preservationists who protested the destruction of one of the city's few remaining works of nineteenth-century architecture. Still, even in decline, St. Monica's was an admirable old lady compared to the soulless steel and glass spires around her. Her Italianate bell tower rose elegantly into the sky.

Don Biehn never could memorize the directions to St. Monica's. He just drove downtown and looked up for the bell tower, then followed it to the corner of Main and Second Street.

He parked his car at a parking meter on Second, a block away. During the day and on the weekend, street parking was impossible to find, but at night the city center was a ghost town and Biehn had no trouble. As he got out of the car, he touched the journal in his coat pocket to make sure it was still there. He did not check for the Taurus. He knew exactly where it was.

Biehn turned onto Main Street and walked past the front of the cathedral, then around the corner. He knew the rectory was behind the main chapel. He didn't know how many priests lived there, but he believed there were only one or two besides Father Frank. He didn't really care about them. They would either be in his way or not. If not, all the better for them.

He found a whitewashed wall and jumped it easily, landing in a flowering border on the inner side. Beyond it was a manicured grass lawn and a fountain, now silent for the evening. He listened for a minute, but heard no sound. To his right stood the cathedral proper; to his left, the rectory. He turned left and stalked up to the rectory door. It was unlocked. He opened it calmly and stepped inside as though he belonged there. This was, he knew from long experience, the very best way to walk into any building.

The rectory parlor was dark. There was an open door to a large room off to the right and a long hallway leading straight ahead. Stairs rose to his left. Biehn recalled that there had been a school on the site at one time. The thought of it made him shudder, and added to his anger like gasoline tossed onto a fire.

Biehn climbed the stairs and found himself looking down another long hallway. Several of the doors were open and led into bare rooms. Two or three were closed. Biehn took a deep breath to calm his pounding heart. He knocked on the first door.

No answer.

He moved down and knocked on the second closed door. It opened, and a startled man appeared. He was wearing a T-shirt and sweatpants, holding a book the title of which Biehn could not see.

"Yes, who—?" the man said gently. "You know, the rectory is off-limits."

Biehn nodded apologetically. "I'm sorry. I'm looking for Father Frank. He's expecting me."

The man looked down the hall at the last closed door. "Are you sure he didn't say to meet him in the chapel? This is the priests' private residence."

The detective stepped back as though shocked. "Oh, I'm sorry. I'm really sorry," he feigned. "I just thought it would be here. I'll go back and wait there."

The priest nodded, said good evening, and closed his door. Biehn walked back toward the stairs for a few steps in case the priest was listening. After a few minutes, he padded quietly back up the hall toward the door the priest had glanced at. He knocked very gently.

No answer.

He knocked a little louder. The door opened, and Father Frank appeared. Biehn didn't know him well, but he'd picked his son up from church functions often enough to recognize the priest.

Father Frank looked as puzzled as the other priest had. "Yes, what is it?" he asked.

Biehn punched him in the throat.

9:37 P.M. PST
Rectory of St. Monica's Cathedral,
Downtown Los Angeles

Father Frank didn't know what had happened. One minute he was staring at a stranger on the rectory floor; the next he had smashed into the back wall of his cell, having tripped backward over his narrow bed. His throat throbbed, and he was coughing and gagging uncontrollably. Something hit him in the nose, and his eyes began to water.

By the time he had blinked his vision clear, he was lying facedown on the floor. A hand was in his hair, pushing his face into the tile floor, and there was a heavy, sharp pressure on his back. He didn't know where his own hands were.

"Listen," said a voice that might have belonged to the devil himself. "Listen and don't make a sound. You are not to make a single sound or I'll kill you. Painfully. Nod if you understand."

To nod, Frank had to drag his face up and down on the tiles, but he did it.

"I'm going to sit you up. You are going to keep your mouth shut or I'll ram your own dick down your throat. Nod again."

Frank did so. He was utterly terrified.

Strong hands grabbed his shoulders and pulled him up to a sitting position, his back resting against his bed. He realized that his hands were fettered behind his back with something metal. Handcuffs.

The man who had done this to him crouched in front of him, sitting on Frank's straightened legs. He studied Frank for a minute calmly. It was almost as though he was giving Frank a moment to calm down himself.

The terror didn't go away. He knew, in the way of all predators, when a bigger and stronger predator had caught him in its grip. But his fear slid into the background for a moment as other survival instincts kicked in: cunning, acquiescence, obedience. Anything that might remove him from the grip of this obviously ruthless man.

As his higher functions took over from his reptile brain, Frank realized that he recognized this man. He wasn't sure from where, but he'd seen the face before. He was a parishioner. A parent. A father.

And the minute he realized that his captor was a father, Father Frank's terror rushed back to the forefront of his brain, and all the pleasures he had enjoyed, all the moments of thrilling power and sexual release and sweet, sweet fulfillment of desire—all of them seemed ephemeral compared to the cost that was surely about to be rendered.

The intruder read his face and nodded as though Frank had said something. "I'm Aaron Biehn's father."

And there it was, like a shirt ripped off his body, revealing the ugly, naked body beneath; like a story told so often it seems true suddenly revealed to be a lie by the simplest honest statement. Like an object of beauty suddenly, obviously discovered to be a cheap and ugly bauble.

The truth of himself flowed into Frank's veins like a poison finding its home.

Then the man, the father of Aaron Biehn, was standing on his ankle. The pain turned him back to the world outside.

"Aaron tried to kill himself tonight," the father said.

Frank started to speak, but remembered his vow.

"Do it quietly," the father said. He could read Frank's thoughts through his body language.

Frank spoke. "Tried to kill himself?"

"Don't you dare ask why," Don Biehn hissed. "You know why. Because of what you did to him. Because you . . . violated him." He slapped Frank. Hard. For no purpose other than because the rage in him needed some expression more than words.

9:39 P.M. PST
Rectory of St. Monica's Cathedral,
Downtown Los Angeles

Don watched the priest's eyes roll back in his head. If he were an iota less enraged, he'd have enjoyed it. But he was too far gone, too bound inside his anger, to feel anything. However, he waited until the rapist's head cleared.

"He tried to tell me about it. I didn't know what he

was talking about. He gave up." Don spoke in simple declarative sentences. He did not feel able to do more. He felt focused. Lucid. His thoughts demanded declaratives the way a knife required a sharp edge.

"I read his journal afterward. It told me everything." He pressed his foot down on Frank's ankle again. The priest sobbed.

"Father Frank," Don said in a voice dripping with irony. "I am the father here, Frank." He crouched down and grabbed Frank's hair, forcing him to look directly into Don's eyes. They burned too brightly for Frank to bear them.

"You can't have any idea what that word really means," Don said, his voice half a whisper, half a sob. "Father. Father is a job, Frank. Father is a duty. Do you know what that duty is?"

"Please," Frank pleaded quietly.

"It was my job to protect that boy, Frank. To. Keep. Him. From. Harm." He jerked Frank's head up and down with each syllable. "But I didn't do that, did I? I guess I drove him right up to harm's front door. And you. You fucking raped him."

Frank felt hands clasp his throat. All his air went away as his windpipe closed. He struggled, but the man was straddling him, pinning him. Terrifying urgency built up in his chest; he needed to breathe, breathe, but he couldn't. He thrashed, but didn't really thrash because he couldn't. He was going to die.

Then the man let go of his throat and he could breathe again. He gasped, coughed, and sucked in oxygen. Again, Don waited until the priest could focus.

"That's what he said it was like," he explained.

"He said it was like suffocating. Like being choked. Strangled. Every time you—" He couldn't say it this time.

Frank was crying now. "I'm sor—"

Biehn slapped him again, hard enough to draw blood from his lip. "Don't apologize. There's no meaning in it. There's no value in it. There are two things you're going to do that have value, though."

Biehn reached into his pocket and pulled out a notepad and a pen. "You're going to give me the names of other children you've destroyed. And you're going to tell me what other monsters there are in this place so I can kill them, too."

Kill them, too. Frank noticed it. He didn't want to die. "I'll tell you. But you have to promise to let me go—"

Pain. Pain in his testicles. He tried to scream but Biehn was covering his mouth, muffling the sound of agony. Don had stabbed the pen into his groin as hard as he could.

"We aren't negotiating," Biehn said firmly. He pulled the pen out of the priest's groin and wiped it on the man's pant leg. He kept his hand firmly over the rapist's mouth until his sobs subsided. "So listen to me, you sick little piece of shit. You tell me who else did this to little children. That geek down the hall?"

Frank whimpered but shook his head.

"Then who?"

"I don't know!" Frank sobbed again. "It wasn't a club!"

Don raised the pen again.

Frank pressed himself back against the bed. "Collins!" he squealed. "Father Collins! I heard him . . ."

He hesitated, terrified of angering Biehn further. "He said something once to me. About Aaron. Kind of . . . of a joke."

Biehn's face softened into agony. "A joke. Is he here?"

"He doesn't live here, I swear." Frank gave him a mid-Wilshire address for Father Collins.

"Who else?"

"Dortmund. That's it. That's all I know about. And Mulrooney. I know he had heard about them from other parishes. That's all I know. You have to believe me."

Biehn heard the terrified sincerity in his voice. "I do," he said. He reached past Frank and grabbed the pillow off the bed. He stuffed the pillow over the priest's face, jammed the weapon into the pillow, and fired.

9:47 P.M. PST
El Segundo, California

Nina Myers shook hands with Millad Yasdani at his front door and said, "Thanks for your time, Mr. Yasdani. I'm sorry to bother you so late."

"I suppose," the man said wearily, "you have to do your job. I'm sure you can understand that it's hard not to take it personally."

Nina adopted a remorseful, world-weary pose that usually appeased the offended in these cases. "I guess so. But I hope you know that we don't mean anything personal by it."

"We're not all terrorists," Yasdani stated. He pointed back over his own shoulder at his comfortable, middle-class house in El Segundo, south of Los Angeles. His wife was still in the living room, thoughtfully sipping some of the tea she'd made for Nina. "Do we look like terrorists?"

What do terrorists look like? Nina wanted to snap back. But that was poor public relations.

Yasdani moved his head so that he caught her eye again. "You know that ninety-nine percent of the Muslim world is peaceful, don't you?"

"Mr. Yasdani, I am not out to stop Muslims. My job is to stop bad guys. The bad guys I'm trying to stop happen to be Muslim. That's the end of the story."

"But you come to my house at night," he pointed out, his voice straining just a little. "To interview me. Because I'm a Muslim."

"Because you attend the same mosque as some of the people we're looking for. You're not a suspect, I told you that already. You and . . ." She checked her notes again. "You and Abdul Ali. You're sure you don't know him?"

Yasdani shook his head. "It's a big mosque. And he sounds Arabic, maybe Iraqi. Most of my friends are Persian."

"Is it common for Persians and Arabs to attend the same mosque?" Nina asked. She had a degree in Middle East studies, so she already had a fairly clear idea of the answer, but Yasdani seemed to be a thoughtful man, and she was curious about his perspective.

Yasdani's nose twitched, a sign Nina had recognized during the interview as an indication of annoyance. "If his name is Ali, he is probably Shi'a, like me. So yes, we would go to the same mosque. But that doesn't mean we are best friends. You do understand that we are not all alike, don't you?"

"Yes, sir," Nina said amiably. "Thank you again."

Nina turned and walked back to her car, disappointed and frustrated. She'd known this would be a dead end. Millad Yasdani was exactly what he appeared to be: chief information officer for a small insurance company, who lived in El Segundo with his wife and three children, and happened to be a Muslim. The only reason he'd shown up on her radar at all was that he drove a long way to go to a mosque in Los Angeles. It was a pathetic lead, but with the Three Stooges in jail not talking, she was reduced to chasing pathetic leads until they'd stewed for a while.

Her other lead, Abdul Ali, was no better. No criminal record, no suspicious activities, no political affiliations. He was hardly even an active member of the mosque where the Three Stooges belonged. But he traveled a lot, and according to the State Department, he'd visited several Muslim countries in the past few years. Again, a pathetic lead.

Nina got into her car and pulled away from the curb, thinking about the weak trail she was following. Jack Bauer popped into her thoughts. She wasn't sure what to make of him, yet, but she always appreciated the direct approach, so she could only applaud what he'd tried with Abu Mousa. Unlike Chappelle, who missed the subtlety and simply assumed that Bauer was a mindless thug, Nina had understood Bauer's tactic immediately. Mousa had been comfortable. It seemed clear to her that everything they'd done to him had been worked into the equation. Bauer had tried to shake him up a little. She wasn't sure it had worked, but at least Jack had tried. On the way to Yasdani's house, Nina had made some calls and dug up a little more information on Jack Bauer. He was, indeed, an interesting one. She hoped he stayed around CTU. She knew some people who might be very interested in getting close to him.

9:53 P.M. PST
Lancaster, California

Jack turned the borrowed Ducati motorcycle into the Killabrew, a bar on Carter Street in Lancaster. He'd had to hustle to make it on time. He hoped the RHD detective they'd borrowed the bike from didn't mind the wear and tear he'd just put on the engine.

Mark Gelson had given them one name—a biker mechanic named Earl "Dog" Smithies. Dog was definitely the kind of character a wannabe like Gelson would hang around. That is, Dog's rap sheet full of misdemeanors, and his one four-year stint for mayhem was significant enough to impress Gelson but not hard-core enough to scare him away. The fact that Dog lived out in Lancaster added to his mystique. To a Malibu celebrity like Gelson, Lancaster—a former boondock turned suburban sprawl perched in the desert flatlands north of Los Angeles—was far enough away to seem dangerous and exotic, but still close enough for him to get home by bedtime.

Jack walked into the Killabrew just before ten o'clock, which was perfect. They'd managed to scare up Dog's parole officer, who told Driscoll that Dog usually shut his garage up and was in the bar by ten. Jack wanted to be there before him. Jack had already been wearing jeans, and his plain black work shoes passed for boots in the dim bar light. Driscoll had an old NASCAR T-shirt in his trunk. It was musty and wrinkled, which didn't please Jack but added to the effect. In moments he'd transformed himself from a CIA field agent to a scruffy barfly.

He sat at the bar and ordered a beer. There was some kind of electronic keno game at one end of the bar and a television at the other. The bartender was a thick, heavy woman with a wide face that accounted for every year of her life in blemishes and wrinkles. But she smiled jovially under thin wisps of blondish hair, and she handed Jack his Bass Ale with a friendly nod.

Dog Smithies showed up a minute later. He was big everywhere. Big hair tumbling down from under an oily Harley-Davidson baseball cap. Big beard exploding from the bottom and sides of his face. Big chest, big arms, and a very big gut spilling over the top of his jeans. Big voice, too.

"Aaaaaggh," he sighed loudly as he eased himself onto a bar stool. "Thanks, Gabs," he added as the bartender brought him a glass full of beer. He drank. "Shit, that's good." Dog behaved like a man in his own home. He eyed the two or three customers in the Killabrew, including Jack, before calling out, "Which one o' you guys rides the Ducati?"

Jack waited just long enough to seem surprised at the question, then said, "Who's asking?"

"Me. Didn't you just see my mouth movin'?" Dog rose without an invitation and moved down to the stool next to Jack, resettling himself noisily. "That's a nice bike," he said. "Who you gotta blow to get a bike like that?"

Jack thanked Driscoll silently. He'd have thought of some way to strike up a conversation with Dog, but the RHD detective had formed this plan the minute they'd learned Dog's occupation. One of his fellow detectives was an avid motorcycle rider, and Ducati was considered one of the best bike makers in the world.

"It's who you know, man," Jack answered. "You know the right people, they just give you stuff. Really, you take it from them. They just don't know it."

"You take that bike?"

"Why do you like the bike so much?"

"I work on 'em. Ducati makes a nice bike. I'm just makin' conversation is all. You don't like talkin'?"

"My experience, strangers who start talkin' aren't what they seem to be," Jack said. Perfect. The trick to any good setup was to make the mark think he was steering the conversation. As far as Dog was concerned, he had initiated this conversation and he was pursuing it. Jack was the reluctant follower.

"What, you got somethin' to hide?" Dog laughed. "You don't strike me as the kind to make trouble."

Jack nodded. "That's my point. Trouble is what I'm trying to avoid." Jack downed his beer and ordered another. "So if you're another one of them trying to set me up, forget it. I'm clean."

Dog blinked at this, the conversation having moved a little too fast for him. "One of them? Them who?"

Jack eyed him now, as though appraising the big, hairy man for the first time. "You're a cop."

Gabs the bartender shrieked with laughter as she dropped off his beer.

"Bullshit," Dog laughed. "Bullshit." He laughed

awhile longer, loud just like he talked. When he settled down a bit, he said, "So why are cops looking
for you? What'd you do?"

Jack smirked. When he spoke, his voice was con-
spiratorial. "Nothing. I was just interested in something and I made too much noise about it."

Dog grinned mischievously. "What was it?"

Jack hesitated, then shrugged. "You know that
bombing thing in Oklahoma City a few years back.
I was just curious how they blow things up. How to
make bombs and shit like that."

Dog's eyes lit up when Jack said *bomb*. "You shit-
ting me? Why you want to know about bombs?"

Jack laughed. "What the hell, you never wanted to
blow something up?"

"The thought has crossed my mind," Dog said,
raising his glass in a toast. He took a sip. "Listen,
you really want to know how to make a bomb, I can
show you the real shit."

"What do you mean?" Jack asked, lowering his
voice.

"Come on outside. My truck."

Jack followed the hairy giant out of the Killabrew.
There was a dirty white Dodge Ram 1500 parked
off to the side of the parking lot, a tarp thrown over
the bed. "I got cool shit back here," Dog said, his
voice growing more animated. "I think you're gonna
like it. Help me with that cover."

Jack put his hands on the heavy tarp to lift it, but
his fingers lost all strength as something cold and
heavy struck him on the back of the head.

• •

THE FOLLOWING TAKES PLACE
BETWEEN THE HOURS OF
10 P.M. AND 11 P.M.
PACIFIC STANDARD TIME

• •

10:00 P.M. PST
National Transportation Safety Board,
Los Angeles Field Office

Diana tried to blink the sleep from her eyes. She'd been up since last night, trying to find the clue that would help everyone else see what she, bleary-eyed though she was, saw so clearly. Alaska Airlines Flight 442 had been deliberately bombed.

Diana Christie was not prone to hysterics. One did not become an investigator for the NTSB without a large supply of objectivity, not to mention patience and meticulousness. NTSB investigators had access to the finest investigative forces in the world, but they often worked alone, working their way through tiny scraps of evidence, minuscule warps in the fabric of shattered aircraft, minute scars on the wheels of locomotives, and usually under the watchful eye of the media. The pressure was enormous, and only the coolest and calmest were chosen for the job.

Diana was one of them. She'd worked on the go team that investigated TWA 800. She'd headed the investigation of the American flight that went down over Chicago, and the Amtrak derailment in Denver. She was an expert.

Which made her current investigation all the more frustrating. She had no vested interest in this particular disaster, no emotional attachments. She certainly had no agenda beyond the truth, and no reason to bang her head against the brick wall of other people's incompetence . . . except that her job was to find the cause of a particular effect. That was her raison d'etre, and she took it seriously.

Diana was investigative by nature, but the mystery she currently attempted to pierce led her into unknown territory. She examined equipment and shards of blasted metal, not people. Her work led her to the conclusion that the blast had originated in seat 29D. The airline manifest told her that the seat had been occupied by one Ali Abdul. Now, Diana wasn't a police detective, but she could pick up the phone as easily as the next person, so she'd made telephone calls. The address Ali Abdul had listed was out of date. To make things more frustrating, it appeared that every Ali Abdul residing in the city of Los Angeles was alive, which was very inconvenient considering that her theory was Ali Abdul had blown himself up.

There was, undoubtedly, an answer to this mystery. However, to resolve it she needed someone with the right sort of investigative skills. She decided to try the jerks at CTU one more time.

Shoemacher was one of those streets you rarely see on television programs about Los Angeles: a beautiful, well-landscaped street lined with elegant mid-sized houses and set in the heart of the city. The television usually showed the nice houses only on the west side or in the suburbs, but the truth was a vibrant community existed south of Hollywood and east of downtown. There were vibrant communities in south central and east L.A., too, but the television rarely hinted of that.

Don Biehn knew all this. A cop of twenty-two years, of course he did. But he didn't know why he was thinking of it at that moment. Self-distraction, maybe. Compartmentalization of emotions. Sheer madness, for all he knew.

Whatever it was, it allowed him to get from St. Monica's to Shoemacher Avenue without eating his own gun. He parked his car at a metered spot near the corner of San Vicente and Olympic, then crossed Olympic and went up Shoemacher, a diagonal street cutting a swath through a mid-Wilshire neighborhood. It was a short walk from there down the darkened sidewalk to the pretty brick house occupied by a monster.

Aaron hadn't known his name. In his journal, he'd simply called him "the other father." Father Frank had brought him in for "special visits." Don now planned to pay a special visit of his own.

The first time down the street, he walked right by the house, taking in as much information as he could without pausing. Lights were on, and the flicker of colors against the thin rice-paper panel blocking the large front window told Don that the priest was watching television. He went halfway up the block, paused and looked around as though lost, then turned back. This time, he favored the shadows, and when he reached the brick house, he glanced around to see if anyone was looking, then turned in a quick and businesslike way up the side lawn to the gate. It was unlocked. He opened it slowly, keeping the creaking to a minimum, then closed it himself so the self-closing spring didn't slam it shut. He had to negotiate some trash and recycling bins, but in a moment he was around the side of the house and into the backyard. There was a set of French doors between the backyard and the kitchen. It was locked.

Undiscouraged, Don hurried back around to the front of the house. There were several cars parked on the street right in front of the priest's house. Don wasn't sure which of them was owned by Collins. It didn't really matter. Once again glancing around to see if any neighbors were out, and finding no one, the detective slapped first one and then the other car hard.

Car alarms wailed. One of them was the annoying kind that changed its pitch and tempo every few seconds, and both were loud. Don hurried back around the house to the French doors. Even from here, the alarms sounded shrill and loud on the quiet street. Inhaling deeply, Don wrapped his fist in his jacket and wound up to punch out one of the glass squares.

But before he could, something covered his mouth and nose. He inhaled sharp, eye-watering fumes, and everything went black.

10:14 P.M. PST
Desert Outside Lancaster

Jack's head shook clear when he hit the ground. He wasn't sure how long he'd been totally out. He'd been groggy for the last few minutes, lying in the back of Dog's truck with his hands and feet bound with what felt like duct tape and a tarp thrown over his head. He was going to have a massive headache and a good-sized lump on his head, assuming he survived this.

Jack was vaguely aware that the truck had pulled off the road somewhere and was bumping along the pathless high desert. Eventually, the truck had stopped. The tarp disappeared, and Jack had felt himself lifted and then dropped. That's when the impact shook his head clear.

It was pitch-black. They were far from Lancaster's faint glow of lights, somewhere out in the desert off the Pearblossom Highway that ran south and east. There wasn't enough starlight or moonlight for Jack to make out Dog's face clearly, but he could see the hulking shape crouched down in front of him.

"So we don't misunderstand each other," Dog said out of the gloom, "you wouldn't be the first cop I killed."

Jack didn't say anything. Dog grunted and continued. "It was a good one, the bike thing. I do like Ducati. But I'm not dumb, just country dumb, and don't nobody start talkin' about blowing things up in a bar."

Jack allowed himself some silent absolution. He hadn't had much time to lay out and execute a longer, slower, less obvious sting. This was still a failure, but the risks had been unavoidable.

"I figure it's Farrigian sold me out," Dog said. He grabbed Jack by the throat. "Was it Farrigian? You tell me who it was and I'll end you quick."

Jack fought the natural panic of suffocation and stared into the shadows where Dog's eyes would be. He wasn't going to give this two-bit scum the satisfaction of seeing him struggle. After a second, the big man let go. Jack willed himself to breathe in slowly, easily. He didn't gasp.

"Tough sumbitch." Dog laughed.

"You should just let me go now," Jack said when his lungs stopped burning.

Dog laughed. "What, you think I'm a moron?"

Jack heard the faint *whup-whup* of the helicopter first. "Yes," he said, "I think you're a moron."

Spotlights ignited like a half-dozen suns leaping into the sky all around them. A voice blared over an unseen bullhorn. "This is the police! You are under arrest! This is the police!"

Dog whirled, blinded by the light and stunned by the noise. "Get down, get down, get down!" a voice shouted, and footsteps thudded toward them out of the darkness.

The hairy giant threw a hand up to shield his eyes from the blinding light as he reached under his shirt. His arm swung up, holding a huge revolver.

Jack never heard the shots, but he saw Dog's body shudder three times as three red flowers blossomed across his back. One of the sniper rounds hit the ground near Jack's leg with a soft puffing sound, like someone punching a pillow, and grains of dirt sprayed into Jack's face. Dog's body hit the ground before the SWAT team could reach him.

The next moment or two were controlled chaos as the SWAT team swarmed Jack to protect him and secured the area. Some of the spotlights were dimmed and cars were rolled up. The police helicopter continued to circle overhead for a few minutes, its powerful beam sliding around the scene. Finally someone spoke into a microphone, and the chopper dropped away loudly.

"You good?" Harry Driscoll said as Jack was freed and hauled to his feet.

"Yeah. I wish you hadn't shot him."

Driscoll nodded. "Me, too, but he was waving a gun at our badges."

Jack looked at Dog, still lying where he'd fallen. "I get it, I just wish I could ask another question or two. But I think I got what we needed. You know anything about a guy named Farrigian?"

Driscoll had driven Jack's car, and they walked to it now as the detective called in any information on that last name. By the time Jack was behind the wheel, he knew that Farrigian was an importer with a history of minor scrapes with customs. He'd also been brought up on charges of possession of illegal weapons, but the charge had been thrown out on a technicality. He was on a number of Federal, state, and local watch lists, but he was considered small-time.

Jack stuck his hand out the window. "Thanks, Harry. I owe you."

Driscoll shook his hand. "Bet your ass. And I'm collecting now. Keep me up on this. I want to stay in the loop."

"What, you don't have enough work?"

Driscoll checked his watch. "If you're right about your shit, then something's going down in less than a day. I don't want terrorist crap in my town. You keep me involved." He smacked the side of the car.

Jack pulled off the dirt field and onto the highway. Driscoll was a good man. If CTU could get him, or people like him, they'd be okay.

As he drove, Jack picked up his phone and called Christopher Henderson. "You're still there, right?" he asked when Henderson answered.

Henderson didn't sound happy. "What do you think? I've been on the phone with the State Department for the last forty minutes. Jesus, you think *we've* got bureaucracy!"

"I've got something," Jack said bluntly. "Not much, but I'm on the trail." He told Henderson about the meeting with Gelson and the encounter with Dog Smithies.

"I'm following this plastic explosives back to its source. I'm going to figure out who has the rest of it."

"Hold on, I'm going to conference in Chappelle." Jack waited on hold, then heard several beeps, then Henderson's voice again. "Jack, you there? Chappelle?"

"Present," Chappelle said unhappily. "You know what time it is, right?"

"Justice never sleeps," Henderson quipped. "Jack has an update."

For the second time, Bauer explained what he'd been up to for the last two hours. Chappelle was quiet, except for the occasional resentful grunt. When Jack was done, all his questions were cynical.

"You're assuming it's the same set of plastic explosives?"

"For now. I'll know for sure once I get to Farrigian."

"Your theory is that this Farrigian sold some of the plastic explosives to this biker and some to the terrorists. You think if we find the seller we'll be able to track it back to the terrorists?"

"Yes."

"But what if Abu Mousa, the guy we have in custody, was the buyer?"

Jack shook his head at the phone. "I don't see Mousa as the brains. They were storage and fall guys."

"Probably right," Chappelle agreed reluctantly. "But I still don't see the urgency. Even if Ramin was right about some plan for tomorrow, we've stopped it. We have the plastic explosives. If you're worried about some missing bricks, then you just answered your own question with this biker. He got the rest."

Jack shrugged. "You may be right," he conceded. "I just want to make sure."

There was silence, except for the faint white noise of the cellular transmissions. Jack knew that Chappelle was trying to decide whether to give his authorization for this. Of course, neither one of them was sure what the District Director could do to stop him. Chappelle could help him by endorsing him, but could not hurt him directly. If Jack, acting as a CIA operative, was going to get in trouble for operating domestically, he'd get called to the carpet by the CIA's Director of Operations, not by Chappelle.

In the end, Chappelle made the decision worthy of a government employee at any level. "I don't want to know about this," he said. "As far as I'm concerned, this is a CTU case and CTU personnel are working on it." He hung up.

Christopher Henderson said, "That's as close to approval as you're going to get."

"I wasn't looking for approval," Jack replied as he turned south on the 405 Freeway.

"Come into the office. We'll plan a move on Farrigian from here. It'll make Chappelle feel better."

"On my way."

10:31 P.M. PST
Baldwin Hills, California

There were oil wells in Los Angeles. You could see them when driving down La Cienega Boulevard toward the airport. Where the street passed between the shoulders of two hills, on the west side you could see the pumps, like metallic dinosaurs bobbing their heads up and down. Nearby was the growing suburb of Baldwin Hills, but the oil wells were surrounded by undeveloped land and the expanse of Baldwin Park. Plus the pumps themselves emitted a continuous dull groan.

So there was no one to hear Don Biehn scream.

His captor had rolled the tire of his car over Biehn's handcuffed hands, crushing them and pinning him face-up on the ground. Biehn's legs were strapped together with something he couldn't see, and tied off to the metal base of one of the great pumps, which nodded its giant hood over him as he stared up at the dark sky.

Biehn didn't know who had kidnapped him, or why. The man hadn't even asked him questions yet. Biehn had woken from his drug-induced stupor (chloroform?) to find his fingers already crushed under the car. He'd played possum for a few minutes while his captor stood a few feet away, whispering into a cell phone. Biehn heard very little of the conversation, but what he heard was startling. If he could survive this, he might be able to use that conversation to avoid prison or the gas chamber.

The captor, not quite visible in the gloom, had hung up his phone. He knelt down beside Biehn and slapped him to wake him. Then he cut Biehn's shirt away and carved a bloody line down his chest, causing Biehn to scream despite himself.

Now his captor came close. There was a dim light somewhere nearby on one of the pumps. In the very faint light, Biehn saw a gleaming bald head and a handsome, clean-shaven face staring down at him.

"That is to let you know I am serious," said his captor, holding up his knife. "Don't make me show you how truly, truly serious I am."

Biehn said nothing. What the hell was going on? Was this guy with the church?

The man held up Biehn's badge. "Were you there to arrest Father Collins?"

"Yes," Don lied.

The captor cut away a sickle-shaped piece of skin below Biehn's left nipple.

"No," he said calmly as Biehn sobbed. "Police officers do not sneak around the backs of houses to break and enter. They do not come alone, either. Don't lie to me again."

This time, Biehn had not screamed, but the cut hurt like hell. He blinked away tears of pain. "Who the fuck are you?" he demanded.

The man cut him again. Biehn thrashed in his confinement, feeling his fingers tear and nearly break under the weight of the car tire.

"I see that you want to ask questions, too," the man said. "Well, I'm not unreasonable. I will let you ask questions. But your questions will come at a cost. Every time you ask one, I will cut a piece from you. Now, do you want to ask something?"

"Do you work for the church?" Biehn asked.

"Yes," the man said. "You can call me Michael."

Biehn spat into his face.

The man cut a thin fillet, just below the epidermis on Biehn's left side. Biehn cried out and thrashed again. He felt two of his fingers dislocate. But he also felt them start to wiggle in the space he'd created.

"Now it's my turn," Michael said. "What did you want with Father Collins?"

"To kill him."

"Why?"

"Because he deserves to die."

That answer seemed to strike Michael as curious. He started again. "What do you know of the plan?"

"What plan?"

"That was a question," Michael said. He gouged a piece from Biehn's right side. Blood trickled from both sides of his body down into the mud. "What do you know of the plan?" Michael asked again.

Biehn didn't know how many more cuts he could

take. He was losing blood, and the pain was excruciating. "I don't know about any plan."

"I will make deeper cuts for lying."

"I really don't!" Biehn sobbed. "I have my reasons for killing that piece of shit!'

"What reasons are those?" Michael asked.

"Fuck you."

"Who are you working for?"

"Nobody!"

Another cut, not deep, but in the sensitive area of the armpit. Biehn thrashed again, felt another finger dislocate, and this time his arms came free. Michael looked genuinely startled when Biehn sat up. Gripping his two battered hands into a club, Biehn smashed Michael across the jaw, and the torturer crumpled sideways. Biehn snatched up the knife and cut the leather strap—a belt, it seemed to be—from around his ankles. Michael stirred, and Biehn turned to stab him. But his feet were cramped and asleep, and his hands were too battered to hold the knife well. Michael slapped the blade from his grip. Biehn clutched at Michael's shirt with his handcuffed hands and headbutted him in the face. His position was weak and the strike wasn't strong, but it was enough to stun Michael again. Biehn stood up, his legs feeling like dead wood beneath him. He wanted to stay and fight, but he was weak from pain and blood loss. He ran into the darkness.

• •

THE FOLLOWING TAKES PLACE
BETWEEN THE HOURS OF
11 P.M. AND 12 A.M.
PACIFIC STANDARD TIME

• •

11:00 P.M. PST
CTU Headquarters, Los Angeles

Jack walked into CTU's shell of a headquarters
looking like a dog's chew toy. His hair was tousled,
and his clothes and face were covered with dust.
His wrists were still sticky from the duct tape. But
his eyes were on fire, and he was all business as he
walked through the office toward the bare meeting
room. He passed a woman sitting impatiently in a
chair. He recognized her as the same thin, pretty
woman he'd passed earlier in the evening. She seemed
eager to talk with anyone who would pay attention
to her, but Jack hurried past her into the room where
Christopher Henderson waited. Nina Myers was
there, too. The analyst Jamey Farrell was also present, as were a few others Jack hadn't met.

"Everyone's up to speed?" Jack asked.

"You want to clean up first?" Henderson offered.

Jack waved him off. "Do we have a list of likely targets?"

Jamey Farrell spoke up, but she spoke to Henderson out of deference to his position. "Yeah, but it's so long it's not usable." She passed around packets of paper. "Sorry, our monitor isn't hooked up to the network yet. These will have to do. Look at the first six pages." They did, and saw a long list of Los Angeles landmarks. Jack frowned. With the exception of a few financial institutions, he could have found the same list in any Los Angeles guidebook.

"We have to narrow this down," he said.

Henderson observed, "Our working assumption is that the weapon is plastic explosives. If that's the case, they can't have much of it. Even if they have twice as much as we've already uncovered (and that's next to impossible), they still don't have huge amounts."

"Which means their target is specific," Jack added. "Something small."

Nina Myers made a skeptical noise in the back of her throat. "That doesn't fit their MO." She sat down, leaning back in one of the brand-new chairs. "I mean, our theory is that this is Yasin, right? One of the Blind Sheik's guys? Maybe even al-Qaeda. You all know al-Qaeda, right?"

Jack did. Al-Qaeda was an Arabic phrase that literally meant "the base." It was the catchphrase for a network of Islamic fundamentalists with very anti-Western, anti-American sentiments. The loose network had gotten its start during the Russian war in Afghanistan. In 1991, al-Qaeda turned its anger on the United States when that country dared to maintain its troops in Saudi Arabia, the land of the two mosques, Medina and Mecca. Al-Qaeda had bombed an embassy in Riyadh, Saudi Arabia, killing a number of Americans. One of the primary terrorists in the 1993 World Trade Center bomb attack was Ramzi Yousef, a known associate of al-Qaeda. Although the al-Qaeda name hadn't gotten much play in the media yet, operators in intelligence circles were already talking about them as the next big threat.

Nina continued. "They don't seem to pick small targets. They go after headlines. Embassies. The World Trade Center."

Jack studied the list while she spoke. "Always the big-ticket items?"

Nina considered. "The Blind Sheik was implicated in the death of Meir Kahane, the ultra-rightist Israeli rabbi. But if it's just an assassination, why use plastic explosives?"

Henderson added, "And if they want an explosion, they've already proven they can make homemade explosives."

Jack knew what they were thinking, what they were trying to tell him through the facts. This wasn't adding up. All of them were trained investigators, accustomed to uncovering facts that began to form a pattern. There didn't seem to be a pattern here.

"Here's what we know for certain," he said, returning to the beginning. He picked up the laser pointer, but the monitor was as dead now as it had been before.

"Sorry," Henderson apologized.

Jack snatched up a pen, flipped over one of the

packets Jamey had provided, and started scribbling a flowchart. "One: Israeli agents contacted the CIA a while ago with intelligence that some known terrorists were planning an attack in the United States. After tracking down leads in Cairo, I was given the name of Ramin, who I knew had been distantly associated with the Blind Sheik. When I tried to question him, someone blew him up. But he did say that Yasin, another WTC bomber, was involved, and that he was planning an event for tomorrow night.

"Two: you guys uncover some Muslims in Los Angeles who are hiding plastic explosives under their bed. Some if it is missing.

"Three: a washed-up actor apparently gave money to some low-level troublemakers to buy plastic explosives from an arms dealer who got his hands on some."

Nina Myers rubbed her temples. "There's enough here to tell us something is going on, but not enough to know what."

"No luck with the guys in custody?" Jack asked.

Nina scowled and said sarcastically, "They are holding up under our most ruthless interrogation methods. We're only serving them tea twice a day now. They still won't break." Jamey Farrell chuckled.

"If it is a smaller target," Jack mused, "what would it be? What people or events are happening tomorrow?"

Jamey ticked off a few things from memory. "The Pope is in town for the Unity Conference. The Vice President will be attending, but he's not scheduled until the day after tomorrow and isn't in town until the early morning of that day. The Governor of California will be in the city for a huge Democratic fundraiser, which is a likely political target. The space shuttle is scheduled to land tomorrow, although Edwards Air Force isn't the primary landing site, always the emergency one."

Henderson held up a hand to stop her. "Actually, it's not. I read there are issues with the landing strip at Kennedy Space Center. Edwards is the primary zone now. Has been for over a month."

They all paused. "The shuttle would be an interesting target," Jack said. "If it's Edwards, that adds new meaning to the fact that these bikers are somehow connected. Lancaster is a lot closer to Edwards than we are down here." He looked at Henderson. "Do you have someone you can put on that?"

Henderson opened his arms wide. "I've got a whole room full of people," he said humorlessly.

"Can you borrow—?" Jack started to say.

"Relax, Jack," Henderson drawled. "You're not the only resourceful one. There's someone I've been after to join up. Guy named Almeida. I'll see about him."

"Another recruit?" Jack laughed.

"You're not the only fish in the sea."

"Okay," Jack said. "So we'll pursue the space shuttle angle. I'm going to deal with this Farrigian issue. I guess that's it for now. Thank you all."

The group started to disband. Nina Myers hung back until only she and Jack remained in the room. "You look like hell," she said.

Jack looked up from the target list and grinned. "I don't look much better when I'm cleaned up. Although my wife does try."

She walked halfway to the door, then turned back toward him. "I like the way you take charge here.

You're going to help us get this unit into shape."

"I turned down the job. I'm just working my own case through here."

"Uh-huh," she said dismissively. "You're what this place needed. Oh, and by the way," she said with a Cheshire cat smile. "You didn't have to mention your wife. I saw the ring. I just don't see it as an issue."

Jack wasn't often surprised, but her boldness left him momentarily speechless. She laughed charmingly at it. "You just keep that thought in mind. Might be a reason for you to stick around CTU. Meanwhile, I've got to keep up this ridiculous search for Abdul Ali, a man who seems to have vanished."

"Excuse me."

That same woman was standing in the doorway. Her arms were crossed in front of her and her feet were planted, as though she was prepared to be defiant. But she wore a look of astonishment. Jack had the impression that he'd caught her halfway between two different attitudes.

"I'm . . . I'm sorry," the woman said. "Did you say you were looking for someone named Abdul Ali?"

Nina's own expression had turned instantly from flirtatious to judgmental. "You're the NTBS investigator, aren't you?" she asked coldly.

"Diana Christie," the woman affirmed. "It was Abdul Ali, right?"

Nina shook her head. "All respect, but this is a Federal case we're discussing. You shouldn't be eavesdropping—"

"I'm on a Federal case, too," Christie interjected. For all her frail prettiness, she clearly had a hard, determined core. "And if I hadn't just eavesdropped, you'd be out running your ass off for no reason. If I'm right, the guy you're looking for is dead."

11:12 P.M. PST
Shoemacher Avenue, Los Angeles

Father Sam Collins crouched down beside his back door, trying to sweep up the glass one-handed. He'd broken his left arm a few weeks ago in a car accident, and it was causing him a lot of trouble. The break had been bad, apparently, and they'd put a steel rod in his arm and popped his dislocated elbow back into place. He hadn't had his own doctor, and the archdiocese had recommended one to him. Collins wasn't sure the man was any good. His arm hurt a hell of a lot.

The pain in his arm wasn't the only thing making Collins grumpy. Someone had broken one of the glass squares in his beautiful French doors. At first he'd thought it was a robbery, but nothing had been taken. The door itself was still locked from the inside. Probably the gardener, Collins had thought with a sigh. It was probably time to get rid of his current guy. Melanie across the street had told him that you had to change gardeners every year or so because their work got sloppier. Collins didn't like to believe that—he liked to believe the best in everyone. But someone had broken his window, that was certain.

Collins swept the big shards of glass into a paper grocery bag. Then he got out a Dustbuster and used that to suck up the smaller bits. By the time he was done, his left arm ached. He wished he could take a Vicodin, but they left him groggy for hours, and tomorrow was an important day. Tomorrow he would sit at the right hand of the Holy Father at the Unity Conference. It was going to be a glorious day.

11:17 P.M. PST
CTU Headquarters, Los Angeles

"This might be a break for both of us," Diana summarized. "And it's such a simple, stupid thing."

"I've been looking for a dead man," Nina said. "Abdul Ali, Ali Abdul. Just a mix-up of names. But why doesn't anyone know he's dead?"

"Someone knows," Jack said. "Someone knows and doesn't want to make a lot of noise about it, especially if Federal investigators are already asking."

While Jack and Nina's tension increased, Diana Christie was obviously relieved. "So this is an answer. At least part of one. If Abdul Ali is a suspect in your case, if he's involved with this plastic explosive, then maybe he brought some on board. That's what caused the detonation."

Nina frowned. "Why would he want to blow up an Alaska Airlines flight? Could a bomb have gone off accidentally?"

Diana shook her head doubtfully. "If the plastic explosive was primed and ready with a detonator, if it was in a state where it might go off accidentally, it'd be hard to get it through security."

"Same question, then," Jack repeated. "Why blow up that flight? Was there anyone special on it?" He knew it was a callous question, but it was the kind of question that had to be asked if they were going to find the bombers.

But Diana put a stop to that line of thinking. "I researched everyone, trying to find a motive so I could convince the rest of NTSB that this was a bombing. There was no one on board that made any headlines or would be a target for any of the kinds of groups you guys are after."

"Maybe Ali was the target," Nina suggested. "Maybe he knew something and they wanted to shut him up. They blew up Ramin, didn't they?"

The NTSB investigator agreed. "Okay, but even so, he had to have been holding the bomb. That blast originated in his seat."

"A gift. A going-away present. Something," Jack said. "They offed him because he was a witness." He nodded approvingly at Diana. "So our first clue that something was going on came at us a month ago, and no one listened to you. Sorry about that."

A look of gratitude unfolded out of the exhaustion on Diana Christie's face. She might have cried if she weren't in the presence of the two anti-terrorist agents. "Thanks," was all she said.

"Okay, but now what?" Nina asked. "We're still working on lots of hypotheses here, but no concrete evidence and no target. An airplane blows up, either accidentally or on purpose, with a possible terrorist on board. I can already tell you Abdul Ali's record won't give us any real leads. He's a nobody as far as your people are concerned," she said, meaning Jack's CIA. "He's a cipher."

"Farrigian is still our best lead. I'm going to talk to him."

"He has something to do with the airline explosion?" Diana asked.

Jack shook his head. "Seller. He may be the source of the explosives, though."

"I want to go," the NTSB agent said firmly. "I want in on the investigation."

"This is undercover work," he replied, rejecting her.

"I don't care. I've been on this thing from the beginning. Before either of you. If this guys deals in explosives, I can help. I may hear or see something you don't."

Nina waited for Jack to say no again. To her surprise, he hesitated, then said, "No promises. I don't know what the play is yet. I'll let you know. If you want to wait around, that's your business. Now will you excuse us?"

Diana accepted this answer, and the dismissal, reluctantly, and left the room.

"What the hell?" Nina said when she was gone. "She doesn't even work for us!"

Jack laughed. "Neither do I."

11:28 P.M. PST
Rectory of St. Monica's Cathedral,
Downtown Los Angeles

If you asked Harry Driscoll, he'd already put in his time tonight. Interviewing Mark Gelson and throwing together the Dog Smithies sting with Jack Bauer were, in his opinion, enough for one night. He'd only returned to the Robbery-Homicide office to finish up his paperwork, and he absolutely planned on coming in late tomorrow. But while he was straightening up his desk (*straightening up* being a relative term among the detectives, whose desks ranged from untidy to ludicrous) when the 187 call came in from St. Monica's. He wasn't inclined to take it, but the city had apparently been lively that night, and there was no one else to respond.

So he found himself, just before eleven-thirty, walking into the rectory of St. Monica's Cathedral, tramping up the stairs and past the yellow police tape and down the hall. A uniformed officer Driscoll had never met gave him the facts: Father Frank Giggs, one of the priests at St. Monica's, in charge of the youth program. There was one possible witness, another priest who'd encountered a stranger in the hallway. A uniform was sitting with him in his room.

Driscoll nodded and walked into the crime scene. The victim's body was on the floor, his back propped up against the bed. A pillow, its center black with powder burns and shredding by a hole, had slid down onto his chest. The priest's face had turned to bloody pulp, already drying to gray crust. His hands were hidden behind.

"Shit," Harry said to no one in particular. "There was serious malice here. Forensics?"

The uniform muttered into his radio, then waited. "Two minutes out. Been busy tonight."

Harry nodded. He crouched down and examined the area, careful not to touch anything, not even the bedspread. He tried not to look at the ruined face, now that he was so close to it. The pillow had obviously been used to muffle the sound of a gunshot. Harry's eyes, long used to searching for details, slowly scanned down the victim's chest to his stom-

ach and waist. He missed the groin puncture at first.
Then he saw the blood smear on the priest's pajama
bottoms, and his eyes moved back up. Taking out his
own pen, he gently moved the bunched-up gusset of
the pajamas to reveal a hole in the cloth surrounded
by blood. Harry could just make out tiny streaks of
the blood that had undoubtedly drained downward
below the body.

"Jesus," Harry muttered. The man had been tortured. Who would torture a priest?

Harry put his pen back in his pocket. As he lifted
his eyes a bit, he saw something on the floor, half
hidden by the hanging bedspread. Out came the pen
again. Harry dragged it into the open with the pen
tip. It was a book of some kind—actually, a journal.
Harry again used the pen to flip it open. He read
only a few pages before he knew that his night was
far from over.

11:39 P.M.
Culver City, California

Abdul called himself a schoolboy because he couldn't
sleep. He wandered around his apartment in his
robe, sipping club soda and listening to a Julia Fordham CD. This was haram, of course. His secret sin.
Listening to music was not itself forbidden. Abdul
was not one of those extremist imams, like those
among the Taliban, who forbade music altogether.
Abdul, rather, sided with ibn Hazm, who had declared music to be halal. Music could inspire the soul
to submit more fully to the will of Allah; at least,

Abdul found this to be true. Of course, ibn Hazm had lived a millennium ago, and had not conceived of music like this, or a voice as seductive as that of Ms. Fordham. And therein lay the sin, for Abdul did not simply listen to music in general, he longed for the voice and image of that singer. He played her music as he lay down to sleep, and in his dreams the messengers of Allah spoke with her voice. That was haram.

Yet on this evening even the gentle measures of *Porcelain* drifting through his apartment could not lull Abdul to sleep. Tomorrow was the opening of the Unity Conference. Intellectually (and, truth be told, Abdul al-Hassan's intellect was formidable) he knew the conference was doomed to failure. Upon opening, the conference would flare like a television screen turned on: all light and noise, but no heat. Soon it would flicker and die. Abdul had said as much to his friend and opponent Rabbi Moskovitz, and both had felt pity for the Catholic Pope and his minions who struggled valiantly to assemble the Unity event. Yet, even as he laughed with Moskovitz, Abdul felt a romantic hope nestle itself in his heart. Wouldn't it be nice if it worked? Would it not be grand to find that rival forces, so far apart, could build bridges across the chasm that divided them.

"Maybe," he said aloud. He would not mind being wrong. To be called a cynic, a pessimist, a skeptic would be a small price to pay if the powerful religions of the world could come together and forge peace now, with the world teetering so close to the edge of chaos.

"Maybe," he said again.

His doorbell rang.

Abdul was so startled that he stood in the center of his living room, not sure he had heard correctly. Who would ring his bell at this hour?

But the bell rang again, sounding somehow more insistent now. Abdul hurried over to his stereo and stopped the CD. The bell rang a third time before he reached the door and he opened it, intending to declare the lateness of the hour in his sternest tone.

But when he looked into the face of his visitor, he was stunned into silence. It was not a stranger's face. It was his own face, but it was grinning happily, eagerly. There was wicked light in his reflection's eyes.

"Hello, brother," said his reflection, raising his right hand. Abdul just had time to see that his reflection's left arm was in a sling, before he stopped seeing altogether.

1 2 3 4 5 6 **7** 8 9
10 11 12 13 14 15 16 17
18 19 20 21 22 23 24

· ·

THE FOLLOWING TAKES PLACE
BETWEEN THE HOURS OF
12 A.M. AND 1 A.M.
PACIFIC STANDARD TIME

· ·

12:00 A.M. PST
St. Monica's Cathedral, Downtown Los Angeles

"Your Holiness."

The Pope lifted his head from his hands. "It's all right, Giancarlo. I am not sleeping."

Giancarlo Mettler stepped into the room, gliding across the carpet. Giancarlo was skinny and balding, with watery brown eyes and a weak chin, the very image of an anonymous mid-level Vatican functionary. Only that fluid, catlike glide revealed him as the highly trained Swiss Guard that he was. Among all the many, many layers of security that surrounded the Holy Father, Giancarlo was the last and greatest, save for God alone. Only divine grace lay closer to the Pope's skin than Giancarlo Mettler.

"There's been a disturbance in the rectory, Holy Father," the Swiss Guard said quietly. "Local law enforcement agents are investigating."

The Pope slowly climbed up from his kneeling position beside the bed. Giancarlo politely took his arm, politely ignoring the loud creaking of his knees. "Do we need to evacuate?" the Pope asked.

"Not yet, Holy Father," Giancarlo said. "But I wanted you prepared in case that becomes necessary."

"The disturbance?"

Giancarlo hesitated. "Sadly, a murder. A priest."

John Paul crossed himself. "You're sure there is no danger . . . ?"

"Not sure, Your Holiness. There was an eyewitness. We are certain the killer has come and gone. The grounds have been thoroughly searched. We believe it has nothing to do with your presence here."

A soft knock interrupted them. Giancarlo frowned irritably. "Cardinal Mulrooney, Your Holiness. Security will have let him through. He insists on seeing you. I have not said you are available. I can send him—"

The Pope patted Giancarlo on the shoulder. "I could not sleep anyway, Giancarlo. Let him in, please."

John Paul arranged himself on a stool at the foot of his bed as Giancarlo opened the door and stepped aside, becoming instantly invisible as Cardinal Mulrooney swept into the room. He knelt perfunctorily and stood quickly. "Your Holiness, you have been informed?"

The Pope nodded. "I understand there is no danger."

"Not of that kind," Mulrooney said. He glanced back at Giancarlo, aware of him despite the guard's ability to fade into the background. "May we speak privately?"

Ever alert, Giancarlo stepped forward, his face a question. John Paul nodded, and Giancarlo departed without a word.

Mulrooney said, "Your Holiness, the murder is terrible, but the danger is not to your body. I believe . . ." He hesitated, reluctant to speak of the topic, even in the most circumspect terms. "I believe this murder may have something to do with . . . the *issue*."

The Pope did not immediately take his meaning. "Issue?"

"Yes, Your Holiness," Mulrooney snapped, annoyed at the man's thickness. "The issue. The one that we had hoped would never become a problem. A very serious, very public problem."

John Paul was still for a moment, his mind scrolling through a list of possible problems, the vastness of which only he could know. Then he trembled ever so slightly as he summoned, from some locked place in his mind, one of the greatest of fears. "How could it possibly . . . oh." John Paul was much quicker than Mulrooney wished to admit. In a flash, he grasped the possibilities: discovery, a vengeance killing, the police, capture, a trial, exposure, a suspect on trial beyond the reach of the church, embarrassment beyond measure.

"Was this one of the priests that was relocated?" the Pope asked.

"Twice, Your Holiness," Mulrooney said. "And . . .

it seems the police discovered a book of some kind. Written by one of the children. The killer was the father."

12:11 A.M. PST
West Los Angeles

Big cities were sometimes the best places to hide. Andre Farrigian operated a small import/export business out of a nondescript warehouse on Pico Boulevard just a few blocks west of the 405 Freeway. His warehouse was a mile away from Sony Pictures, a few miles west of UCLA, and only a few blocks from a police station, but no one noticed him. Who cared about one more gray and blue building surrounded by a plastic-sheath and chain-link fence?

Farrigian's import business was legitimate, but it was a loser, and had operated in the red for all three years of its existence. Neither Andre nor his two brothers cared. The business offered plenty of cover for their more profitable hobby—small-scale arms dealing. They were small-scale because they were smart enough to realize that they weren't smart enough to get bigger. A bigger operation meant greater danger and more watchful eyes. A bigger operation required better contacts among various governments, and bolder action to secure both equipment and customers. The Farrigians were neither bold nor well-connected. Besides, they made a decent enough profit distributing small quantities of automatic weapons to local gangs, snatching up explosives for the mob, and sending the occasional ordnance overseas to a few Palestinian and Lebanese organizations they had come to know. Big business just sounded like big trouble, a thing that Andre had avoided with an almost religious devotion.

So when the man called saying he was named Stockton and using Dog Smithies's name as a reference and giving out Dog's cell phone number, Andre was only a little suspicious. He told the man he'd call back, then he dialed Dog's number, which he already knew, of course. No answer. This didn't surprise Andre since he knew the motorhead usually parked his carcass at the Killabrew around this time of night.

Farrigian called over to the bar.

"Killabrew," said a gruff, vaguely feminine voice.

"Hey, it's Andre Farrigian," he said, not remembering her name. "Dog there?"

The bartender lady snorted. "What's left of him. Drunk out of his gourd. Can't get him off the floor. Sure can't get him to the phone."

Farrigian frowned. He didn't know the bartender well, but Dog had told him that they moved in the same circles, so he thought the risk was minimal. "You ever hear Dog talk about a guy named Stockton?"

The bartender lady hesitated . . . but maybe it was the usual thief's hesitation before speaking on a telephone. The untrustworthy trusted no one. "Maybe," she said at last. "Kind of blondie. Raspy voice."

Farrigian nodded. "Thanks. Gaby," he added, remembering her name at last.

12:14 A.M. PST
Killabrew Bar, Lancaster

Gaby hung up the phone and turned to the Federal agent standing next to her. "Okay?"

"Good enough," the man said, already walking out.

"Just don't take my liquor license!" she yelled.

"We'll be in touch."

12:15 A.M. PST
Farrigian's Warehouse, West Los Angeles

The blond man and the skinny chick walked into his warehouse at about a quarter after midnight. Farrigian was sitting at the steel desk in his cramped, frosted-glass office in a corner of the warehouse. The desk was piled high with invoices, customs forms, shipping manifests, and other assorted documents. All of it was as real as it was neglected. Andre hated paperwork. He stood up and moved toward the door as they approached.

"Hey there," Andre said. His English was perfect and his slang very American, but he could still hear traces of that clipped Armenian accent he cursed his parents for. "No sense going in there," he said. "Not even room to fart."

"Glad you could see us," the blond man said, holding out his hand. "Stockton. This is Danni."

Farrigian smiled. Smiles seemed to relax people and cost nothing, so he doled them out freely. "How's Dog?"

"Drunk, last time I saw him," Stockton said.

"Most of the time." Farrigian laughed. "So, what can I do for you two?"

The blond one, Stockton, said, "I'm looking to buy something kind of like what you sold to Dog."

Andre kept the big, friendly grin on his face, which was easy. He was the jovial type. But he wasn't stupid. "Hmm, I guess I sold some stuff to Dog. I sell a lot of stuff, you can see. We talking about imports here? I got these great office decorations. It's like a crystal ball, but there's a Chinese scroll inside, all decorated."

The woman spoke up. She was hot by American standards, but Andre liked his woman with more hips and ass. "We're talking about something a little more interesting. Some people are throwing a party. We're looking for something that will make a big bang."

That was corny, Farrigian thought, but he was used to it. Truth was, he'd spoken more than a few corny lines in his time. No one wanted to come right out and ask for illegal weapons.

"Well, I don't usually deal in party favors," he said, trying to help her out. "You mean something like Chinese firecrackers?"

"Chinese or whatever," Stockton said. "Whatever you can get your hands on right away."

"Oh, a rush order," Farrigian said. "There's a delivery charge for that, okay?"

Stockton nodded irritably, but not because of the money. The man had no patience for the obvious. Rudeness never bothered Andre, as long as the customer paid. "We're looking for something in plastic," Stockton said purposefully. "Dog told me you found him some plastic, too."

Farrigian scratched his chin. This was getting a little

too close for comfort and moving a little too fast. "I am sure I can help you," he said. "But I'll have to call a distributor or two that I know. Give me a number and I'll call you back. An hour, no more," he said in response to Stockton's impending objection.

Stockton nodded and handed him a piece of paper with a phone number on it. They shook hands and Stockton and Diana walked out.

12:19 A.M. PST
West Los Angeles

Jack and Diana walked casually out of the warehouse and into the narrow parking lot on the inside of the fence. They hopped into Jack's SUV and drove slowly out of the gate, turned on a side street, then made another turn onto Pico.

"Do you think he'll call back?" Diana asked.

Jack nodded. "If he's suspicious, he'll make a few calls. We've covered everyone we can find connected to Dog Smithies, so any of those people will back up our story."

"How long can you keep those people under your thumb?"

"Not long. Rumors will start flying, but by tomorrow night it won't matter anyway. We don't know what kinds of sources Farrigian has. I doubt he's all that sophisticated, but if he is connected and has a way to check out the cell number, it'll come up as James Baker, giving Tom Stockton as an alias. That'll make us more believable.

"I'm not worried about him checking us out, though. I want to know who his people are." Jack tapped a phone number into his cell while keeping one eye on the road. Henderson answered immediately, sounding a little surly about working so late.

"Christopher, I want to get wiretaps on this Farrigian character. He's going to start making calls right away, and I want us to trace them."

There was a moment of faint white noise. "Jack, Chappelle has to authorize all wiretaps and surveillance."

"Well, let's get him to authorize it!" Jack urged.

Henderson made a noise. Something more than a grunt and less than an actual word. Whatever it was, its meaning was clearly miserable. Jack waited. There was some shuffling and several clicks, then Henderson came back on. "The District Director is on the line with us," Henderson said simply.

"What?" Chappelle snapped.

Jack told his story. To his credit, Chappelle listened without interrupting once. When Jack was done, Chappelle actually agreed. "Don't sound so damned surprised, Bauer. You play by the book and I'll back you one hundred percent. You're following a lead, you got a suspect's name, you investigated and got probable cause." Jack was indeed surprised by Chappelle's cooperation. "As far as I'm concerned, though, this is LAPD, CTU, and NTSB investigating, not the CIA. But I'll let your people sort this out when the time comes. I'm fine authorizing your wiretap. Just get the paperwork to me in the morning and we'll proceed."

Jack's heart sank. "In the morning? No, I need it right now. Not the paperwork right now, the wiretap. Right now!"

"Never happen," Chappelle said matter-of-factly.

"There's me, there's the judge, then the actual surveillance guys to do the wiring. We're looking at mid-morning, tomorrow evening at the latest."

Jack squeezed the phone till his knuckles turned white. "You don't seem to get the urgency."

"And you don't seem to get that the plot has been stopped!" Chappelle snapped back. The moment of cooperation vanished. "We need to make arrests, but we have some of the plotters and we have the plastic explosives! You even found the few bits left over. So get them, but get them by following procedure! Henderson, deal with this jack-off before I have to deal with you!" The phone clicked.

"That went well," Henderson quipped.

"I think he's warming up to me," Jack agreed. "Don't worry about it, Christopher, I'll take care of everything."

12:23 P.M. PST
Brentwood

Harry Driscoll was used to knocking on doors after midnight, but usually all the cops were on the outside when he knocked. This time the cop was on the other side.

Driscoll didn't know Don Biehn. He thought he'd met him once or twice, at the funeral of a slain police officer, maybe, or the retirement party for another. But he'd never worked with Biehn and couldn't have told anyone a thing about him . . . except that his son's diary had been found at the scene of a priest's murder, and that, according to that diary, the priest had molested Biehn's son repeatedly.

Driscoll held up his hand, balled into a fist, but hesitated. He stood there for more than a minute, reluctant. No good, no satisfaction, would come from knocking on that door. That door would open on nothing but horror and politics and most likely the destruction of a fellow badge. Harry wanted no part of it. The man, the father in him protested that justice—real justice by any definition he could muster—had been served the minute that child-violating son of a bitch had his face blown off. The man, the father in him told him to lower his hand and walk away. Leave the door unopened.

But the cop in him replied that there were rules and laws, and those laws allowed the just to live among the unjust with the belief that they were shielded from iniquity. But the only way for that shield to work was for men to pin it to their chests and walk around day and night, enforcing the laws it represented, opening the doors that did not want to open. All the doors.

Harry knocked.

To his surprise, the door opened almost immediately. The man standing before him looked like the victim of a car wreck. His face was battered and swollen. Three fingers on one hand were splinted together with tape, and the fingers of the other hand looked like a dog's chew toy.

"Detective Don Biehn?" Harry said.

Biehn nodded.

"You're under arrest for the murder of Father Frank Giggs."

Biehn didn't panic, nor did he look relieved at being caught. He nodded matter-of-factly and said, "I figured as much. Won't you come in?"

Driscoll was nonplussed. Procedure told him not

to, of course. Take control of the suspect; don't give him any control. But this battered man was no threat of any kind. Even so, Driscoll motioned to the two uniforms behind him, and all three walked into the house together.

Biehn walked them into the living room. He didn't seem to mind at all when the two uniforms took up positions at right angles to each other—positions that would allow them to draw and fire without risk of hitting each other. Only Driscoll sat down, in a seat opposite Biehn's.

"Is your wife home, Detective Biehn?" Driscoll asked.

Biehn shook his head. "Hospital. Our son is in critical condition."

"I'm sorry to hear—"

"He tried to kill himself a couple of hours ago. He was tormented by the idea that his priest had been sodomizing him for the last three years." Biehn delivered the message with a dryness more vicious than any venom. Driscoll steeled himself against sympathy.

"I'm sorry for your trouble," he said weakly. "But you're still under arrest. I need you to cooperate with us, Detective. You're in no condition to resist."

Biehn smiled. "I want to do more than cooperate. I want to make a deal."

12:33 P.M. PST
St. Monica's Cathedral, Downtown Los Angeles

Pope John Paul sat by himself in the first pew of the chapel of St. Monica's. The chapel would have been empty at that hour in any case, but at his request Giancarlo had positioned Swiss Guards at each entrance.

He had spent the last half hour here in private meditation. He could have remained alone with his thoughts in the rooms Mulrooney had provided him, but truth be told, John Paul did not feel the presence of God in private. He had wished all his life for God to speak to him as he had spoken to Abraham. Instead, the Lord spoke to him through inspiration that he felt here, in the great echoing cathedrals throughout the world.

For twenty minutes he had prayed for guidance in this most delicate matter, but for once the majesty of the cathedral failed him. God's word did not speak to him out of the echoing corners. He was truly alone with his thoughts.

Mulrooney appeared again, his face taut. As the Holy Father had ordered, Giancarlo allowed him through. Mulrooney hurried forward, discarding all pretense of humility. "Your Holiness, we must act," he declared.

John Paul looked at him with his pale blue eyes, his gaze far away. Mulrooney nearly grabbed the man and shook him. "There is no more time."

The Pope's eyes hardened and focused on the Cardinal. "I've been thinking of it, Your Eminence. You are right. We have to do something, if there is still time. I am not happy about it."

Mulrooney relaxed visibly. "It's for the sake of the church."

John Paul nodded. "We have a man who does this sort of thing. In the service of the church. I can have him here in ten hours—"

Mulrooney interrupted. "I have a man here."

Now the Pope's eyes turned hard as sapphires, gleaming suspiciously at Mulrooney. The Cardinal was reminded that they did not send up the white smoke for just an ordinary man. "Your Holiness," he said appeasingly, "you and I may not agree on some things, but on this we are in accord. These accusations must not become public. Certainly there must be no trial. I have a man who can handle the job."

John Paul did not trust Mulrooney, but he was right on this count. "Very well, Your Eminence. But I want Giancarlo to meet him."

Mulrooney stood immediately, executed the briefest of bows, and turned away.

12:40 A.M. PST
CTU Headquarters, Los Angeles

Jack was just walking through the now-familiar doors of CTU when his phone rang and flashed Driscoll's number. "Jack, where are you? I need you to meet with someone right away."

"I'm at CTU. Counter Terrorist Unit headquarters."

"Give me the address. You need to meet this guy."

12:41 A.M. PST
St. Monica's Cathedral, Downtown Los Angeles

Mulrooney brushed past the Swiss Guard and out into the hallway. He knew Giancarlo had fallen into step behind him, though he could barely hear the man's footsteps. It was a few minutes' walk across the cathedral grounds to his private quarters, where the man he had in mind waited.

"We are on," Mulrooney said as the man stood up. He indicated Giancarlo. "This is one of the Holy Father's security men. He wanted to meet you."

The man extended his hand. "You can call me Michael."

Mulrooney watched the two men shake hands. They were similar, he thought, though they looked nothing alike. Giancarlo was gangly with thinning hair and a sunken chin. Michael was bronze-colored, with a sleek bald head and a very fit appearance. Yet both of them emitted the same aura.

"Michael has worked for me before," Mulrooney said. Giancarlo nodded and smiled faintly, but didn't take his eyes off the man. "He has some expertise in work that has been useful in the past."

"I caught someone trying to break into the house of another priest," Michael explained. "I stopped him, but he got away. I am sure he has a list of priests he wants to murder."

"Did you know he was going after this other priest?" Giancarlo asked. "Do you already have the list?"

"No," Michael said, glancing at Mulrooney. "I was watching that priest for other reasons."

"Unrelated," Mulrooney said.

Giancarlo shrugged. "You're not from the U.S.," he said to Michael. "Your accent is very good, but there's a hint of something."

"Lebanese Christian," Michael said. "And I lived in Jerusalem for a while when I first started working with the church. But that was a long time ago. I've been here for a long time."

This answer seemed to satisfy Giancarlo. "Please keep me up to date on anything, even the smallest thing. His Holiness will want to know." Mulrooney promised, and the Swiss Guard took his leave.

"Will they check on you?" Mulrooney asked.

Michael stared at the spot where Giancarlo had stood as though he could still learn something from the invisible air, and said, "Yes. They will find a Michael Shalhoub who was born in Beirut as a Christian and moved to Jerusalem to join the Catholic Church."

"But that's not your real name," the Cardinal inquired.

Now Michael turned his bronze face toward the priest. "No. You don't want to know my real name, Your Eminence. All you need to know is that, for the moment, our goals are in alignment. I will stop this policeman's vendetta because it's a danger to my own plans, at least until tomorrow."

"How can I be sure you'll keep your promise after tomorrow?" Mulrooney fretted.

Michael looked at him disdainfully. "I am not interested in your filthy church secrets. Our deal is intact. Help us, and I will remain silent. Betray us, or get in our way, and the pittance this policeman knows will be a drop in the bucket compared to the flood of crimes that we expose."

Mulrooney stiffened slightly. "Like you said, our paths are in alignment."

· ·

THE FOLLOWING TAKES PLACE
BETWEEN THE HOURS OF
1 A.M. AND 2 A.M.
PACIFIC STANDARD TIME

· ·

1:00 A.M. PST
CTU Headquarters, Los Angeles

Jack watched Harry Driscoll escort another man through the main doors of CTU. The bags under Harry's eyes looked big enough to pack a lunch. Jack wondered how he looked himself. He wondered if there might be a moment or two to catch some sleep. But he stifled a yawn when he got a clear view of the man Driscoll escorted, walking with his hands cuffed behind his back and the detective's arm firmly planted on his. He looked like someone had beaten him with a stick. That wasn't Driscoll's style, so Jack assumed it had happened prior to his arrest.

"What's up, Harry?" Jack asked with more energy than he felt.

"Conference room?" Driscoll replied.

Jack led them to the empty room, and Driscoll sat his prisoner down. Jack closed the door. "What's the story?"

"Jack, this is Don Biehn. Detective Don Biehn, by the way. I'm arresting him for murder. But he says he's got—"

"There are terrorists in Los Angeles," the man, Biehn, reported.

"No shit," Jack said. "We already knew that. That's why we set up these great offices."

"I can tell you what one of them looks like," Biehn said. "I can tell you his real name, and his alias. I can also tell you part of what their plan is."

Jack's confusion and annoyance fused into a laser-like focus. "Okay, tell."

"Two things," Biehn said. "First, amnesty. I killed a monster tonight, there's plenty of evidence to convict me, but I want to go free. Second, you let me finish the job I started."

"Forget it," Driscoll said. "I told you in the car that was—"

"They're monsters!" Biehn snapped.

"Then put them behind bars with all the other monsters!" Driscoll shot back.

Biehn looked at Jack. "My son was being molested by priests at our church for years. I never knew it. I even made him go to Sunday school some days. He would cry about it. I figured he was being a baby. I made him go!" Biehn shuddered.

Jack felt sorry for the man, but he knew he couldn't help. Even he was willing to bend the rules only so far. "I'm not going to release a murderer. I'm sure as hell not going to let him loose to go kill more people."

"Abdul Rahman Yasin."

Jack felt the hair on the back of his neck rise. "What?"

"He's a terrorist, right? I can tell you when he arrived in the city. I can tell you a lot more, but let's start with that." Biehn sat back in his chair, smiling out of his haggard, exhausted face.

"How the hell do you know that?" Jack was stunned.

"I'll tell you that, too. After you let me go."

"Let's start with your proof," Jack said. "When did he arrive?"

Biehn had overheard a conversation between Michael and Yasin just before Michael had begun to torture him. He had heard quite a few interesting details. "I don't know what airline. But I know that he arrived at LAX four days ago, in the afternoon, I think. And that he's leaving tomorrow."

Jack really had no idea how this battered, broken cop with murderous intentions had gathered information on a terrorist suspect, but he knew he had to check it out. "Wait here," he said.

He walked out of the conference room and through the main room, toward Christopher Henderson's office. He entered without knocking to find Henderson sitting at his computer, though his eyes were closed. Jack rapped his knuckles on the desk.

"That's impressive," he said as Henderson started awake. "I haven't learned to see through my eyelids yet."

Henderson shuddered himself further awake. "Long friggin' day. What's up?"

"Is that Jamey Farrell around? I need someone to run down some intelligence."

"Try bay one. It's one of the data banks down the hall past the conference room. She has a cot in there."

"A cot?"

"She's dedicated."

Bauer hurried down the hall and into the same technical bay he'd visited with Nina Myers. There was indeed a cot there, and Jamey Farrell was asleep on it. She was a light sleeper and popped up as soon as Jack entered.

"What?" she demanded.

"I need some data analysis," Jack said. "Did Henderson give you any instructions earlier about downloading feed from LAX for facial recognition?"

Jamey yawned. "Yup. For the last week. That's a lot of data. If you don't narrow it down, it's gonna take—"

"Four days ago. Afternoon. Let's do 1200 to 2100."

Jamey hopped out of the cot, grumbling, and went over to the half-finished tech bay. "It's all here. Let me get to the right area." She fired up the monitor and punched in some time code. A series of squares appeared within the monitor like a checkerboard, each square representing a camera. In each square was a time code set at 12:00:00. "Starting facial recognition." Jamey punched in a few more commands, and the video started running at high speed, the travelers hurrying through the frame like Keystone cops. For a brief instant, each face flashed as the facial recognition software captured it. Jack and Jamey watched for a while as the time code ran forward from 12:00 to 13:00, then 13:22, and then suddenly pinged.

"Oh, shit," Jamey said. She clicked on the warning window that had appeared. A face in the security footage opened up in a new window, and the system summoned another face from its own data banks, an older picture. The older picture had a mustache whereas the security photo did not, and the hair was different, but the features were the same. Under the older photo appeared the name "Abdul Rahman Yasin" and in larger letters under both pictures appeared the word *MATCH*.

"Right," Jack said. "Now please get me a list of all flights landing at gates—"

"—coming out of that area and passing that security camera. You want about thirty minutes prior?"

"You're good," Jack said. "This CTU might be in good hands after all."

"Better damned believe it," she muttered as he walked out.

Jack hurried back to the conference room, but his phone rang on the way. He stopped in the hall when he saw the number flashing on his screen.

"Bauer," he said quickly. "Thanks for answering the page, Carlos."

"Sure," said a throaty, cigarette-induced voice on the line. "No reason I should be sleeping anyway. I mean, why should I still be sleeping when it's already . . . oh, damn, look at that, I should be sleeping!"

"Can't be helped," Jack replied. "I need help only the NSA can give me at the moment. I need a wiretap run immediately."

When Carlos was truly annoyed, as now, all the sarcasm left his voice. "Wiretap? Call the locals."

"I need speed," Jack explained briefly. "My window to gather information is hours, not days. I need it yesterday and I'll deal with the FISA court." The Federal Intelligence Services Act had been estab-

lished in the early seventies. It allowed intelligence agencies broader surveillance powers under the supervision of a secret court. One of its primary benefits was the ability to set wiretaps and other invasive forms of surveillance prior to getting a court order.

Jack practically heard the espionage man's shrug through the phone. "It's your head, Jack, not mine. Gimme the info. I'm on it."

Jack passed on Farrigian's information, then hung up and hurried into the conference room, where Biehn and Driscoll sat in silence. Jack threw a you're-not-going-to-believe-this look at Harry. "Abdul Rahman Yasin was identified passing through LAX four days ago, in the afternoon."

"Told you," Biehn said. "We have a deal?"

Driscoll said, "So what? So cooperate and you'll get a reduced sentence."

Jack said, "What you know has to be worthwhile, or I'll scrap any deal we make."

Driscoll turned on Jack as though he'd just suggested they mug a cripple. "Jack, you're not serious. No one's making a deal with him—"

"I might be," Jack replied firmly.

"He killed someone, Jack. Let the DA talk to him. He can cut a deal for a reduced charge, maybe even manslaughter, but—"

"I don't have time!" Jack snapped. He knew he didn't have to snap like that. He was getting tired, too. He steadied his voice. "I still don't know what the hell is going on, but I've got all kinds of circumstantial evidence that it's going down tomorrow. You're talking about booking him, interviewing him, getting the DA down to talk to him, paperwork, an attorney . . ." Jack was frustrating himself with the

list, so he stopped. "The last time Yasin was in this country, he tried to blow up the World Trade Center. Whatever he's doing tomorrow, we need to stop it."

Driscoll was still staring at Jack, aghast. It was as though he was staring at a stranger. "To stop it you're going to make a deal with a murderer."

Now it was Jack's turn to stare at Harry, but his look was pure disdain at his old friend's naïveté. "You mean am I willing to get information on a known terrorist by releasing a guy who killed a child molester? Yes."

It occurred to Driscoll that he had never really known Jack Bauer. Or perhaps the CIA had changed the former LAPD SWAT officer. Either way, it was clear that Jack Bauer was willing to leave closed the doors that Driscoll felt obligated to open, and was probably willing to open doors Harry wouldn't touch. "That's against the law," he said quietly.

Jack pretended he hadn't heard.

1:18 A.M. PST
CTU Headquarters, Los Angeles

Nina Myers had tried to go home and sleep. She had told herself there was nothing left to do that night; that Jack Bauer seemed to want to play with the little blond chippie from NTSB; that she would be a better investigator after a good night's sleep.

But that hadn't lasted much beyond midnight. As the clock swung around toward one A.M., she was out of bed and pacing her living room, trying to think of angles she hadn't covered. When the clock struck one she was in her car, and fifteen minutes

later she was walking into CTU. She saw the log and knew Bauer was there, but he looked busy and she was feeling competitive. He hadn't responded to the direct approach at all. Maybe he'd warm up to a girl who could keep pace with him.

Despite what she'd said earlier, she thought that the Ali Abdul/Abdul Ali mix-up might actually produce some new data. She hopped on to one of the office's working terminals—these were in short supply during the day, but this late at night, with most of the analysts gone, she had her pick of stations—and logged into the FAA's records. Through the FAA, she was able to look at Alaska Airlines' manifests. That's when she started to learn something about Abdul Ali. According to the airline, he'd been traveling in Pakistan under the mixed- up name. His flight back to the United States had been canceled. For some reason, he had been eager to get home, so he'd jumped airlines to get back to the United States—a flight up to Moscow and then another one to Juneau, then down to Los Angeles. It had been a crazy and uncomfortable jaunt, but it had gotten him into Los Angeles sooner than any other combination of flights.

"So the first thing I know about you, Mr. Abdul Ali, is that you really, really wanted to get home," she said to the humming computers.

She knew there was nothing to be learned by his contacts in Los Angeles. All had been dead ends. If he was part of some plot, he'd been chosen well. But Pakistan was a very interesting country for a cipher to visit. Nina switched from the FAA's logs to her list of intelligence reports—a collection of reports from the Department of Defense, State Department, CIA, and NSA. Someday, she hoped, someone would come along and gather all these reports into one official album. It was ridiculously inefficient to have to cull through so many different reports. She did searches on "Pakistan" and "terrorism," which did almost nothing to narrow the field. Limiting the reports to a window of one week prior to the Alaska flight—which would have been about five weeks prior—helped somewhat, and Nina began skimming the articles.

The list was still long, and Nina couldn't do much more than spot check the more likely sources. This was ten minutes of boring, frustrating work at that late hour, but it was the kind of work that got the job done. Nina had gotten into fieldwork for the excitement, and there was plenty of that, but every moment in the field was backed up by hours of research. She remembered something Victor had told her: *Before you pull the trigger, you must know where to aim the gun.*

She was just about to give up when a string of words caught her eye. It was a report on a meeting in Peshawar, in northern Pakistan, close to the tribal regions that bordered Afghanistan. That area was a hotbed of Islamic fundamentalism, and was an unusual place for an American to visit. The meeting itself was a bit dubious: it had been billed as a Sunni-Shiite détente, which was itself unusual. Not malignant, but unusual. And why would an American with no apparent ties to Islamic fundamentalism be in Peshawar, Pakistan, at the same time as an Islamic conference?

Whoever had done the reporting on the Peshawar conference had been thorough. The report included a complete list of registered attendees. Nina felt herself in the groove now, like a bloodhound latching on to the scent, nose to the ground. She knew his name would be there even before her eyes settled on "Abdul Ali."

Nina could have gotten an analyst to help her, even woken one up if need be, but her own computer skills were nothing to sneeze at. In seconds she had the computer running a match between her list of "persons of interest" in Los Angeles and the guest list from Peshawar. Aside from Abdul Ali, there was one match: Sheik Abdul al-Hassan.

Nina sat back and stared at the name as it burned a mark into her screen and into her brain. This was interesting. Al-Hassan was already on her list. She had questioned him briefly. If he was a terrorist, he was so deep under cover, even he had forgotten who he was. According to a very thorough background check, al-Hassan was an avid promoter of Islamic causes, but an equally avid promoter of peace. The Imam al-Hassan had proven himself to be an outspoken critic of Western intrusion into the Middle East . . . but an even more outspoken critic of Islamists who used violence to achieve their ends. According to the report, the conference had been a small part of a global religious peace effort. Even if Peshawar was an unusual place for the conference, the meeting's purpose fit with al-Hassan's file. From what Nina could tell, Ryan Chappelle was more likely to attack the United States than Sheik Abdul al-Hassan. And yet the Imam hadn't mentioned that trip during his interview. That bothered her. Bothered her enough, in fact, that she was going to go wake Mr. al-Hassan up.

1:31 A.M. PST
West Hollywood, California

Jack had no intention of letting Don Biehn kill anyone. He didn't care at all if Biehn never served a day in prison for killing a child molester, but Jack wasn't an accomplice to murder. But letting Biehn confront his son's molester in private, away from the public eye, was a small price to pay for information that might save hundreds of lives.

He was still thinking of Abdul Rahman Yasin as they turned off Sunset into a West Hollywood neighborhood. Yasin, the Blind Sheik, and others had tried to bring down the World Trade Center about seven years earlier. Their plan had been simple: they'd parked a vehicle filled with homemade explosives in the parking structure beneath Tower One. They had hoped to blast loose the support foundations on one side, causing that building to fall into its twin. They had also included cyanide gas, hoping the gas would expand through the ventilation system and cause additional deaths.

The explosion had injured more than one thousand people and killed six. But considering its potential, the plan had been a failure. Tower One's foundations stood, and the heat from the explosion had burned the cyanide away.

None of this made Jack feel any better. Yasin and whoever he was working with now had had years to learn from their mistakes. It was the grandeur of their schemes that worried him. Had the WTC bombing been even a moderate success, thousands of people would have died. If that was the scale on which they still operated, Jack had to find out what they were planning and stop it. And he had only a few hours left in which to do it. Until Carlos and the NSA plucked any information out of Farrigian's communications, Biehn was Jack's best lead. He had to follow it, and Harry Driscoll's righteous indignation be damned.

Father Dortmund's bungalow was a holdout against the redevelopment of West Hollywood, a one-story cottage holding its ground against the six- and eight-story condominium complexes on either side. It was not unkempt, but it was plain—a square lawn with no flower bed, a small white porch front, and white paint. The porch light was the kind of tolerable but unimaginative light sold at big box hardware stores across the country. Jack had the distinct impression that Father Dortmund wanted his residence to be livable without investing too much time or affection, as though he might need to move at any moment.

Jack parked a few houses down and used a second pair of handcuffs to hobble Biehn's feet. "I'm not in running condition," the detective protested.

"Now you're not," Jack agreed. "I'll be back in a minute."

Jack got out, moved toward Dortmund's house, and performed a quick reconnoiter. One car in the detached garage, which sounded right for a priest living alone. A light went on in back when Jack hopped the fence, but it was one of those motion-sensor lights so it meant nothing. Jack checked for the alarm certification that was required by the city for any residence that contained a burglar alarm, and found none. Just to be sure, he checked one or two windows, searching for telltale wires or tabs that indicated an alarm circuit. Nothing. Apparently Father Dortmund trusted his safety to God.

Jack hurried back to his car and uncuffed Biehn's legs. "I'll get us in," he said firmly. "I'll take control of the situation. You talk to him when I say so." He didn't ask if Biehn understood. If there was a problem, he would make Biehn understand.

Jack led Biehn over to the porch and left him there, then walked around to one of the side windows. The bungalow was decently maintained, but it was almost all original. The old-style casement window was easy to jimmy, and Jack slid it open in a few seconds. He hopped up and slid himself through the window into what appeared to be the living room. No alarm had sounded, and there was no noise inside the house. Jack stood and walked carefully and quietly to the door. He unbolted the door with only the faintest of clicks, and opened it. Biehn was standing there, his bruised face ghastly in the porch light. The man looked eager, perhaps manic, and it occurred to Jack that he might be collecting information from a madman. Still, Biehn had known the time and place of Yasin's arrival. There was bound to be more.

The two men, one cuffed and the other guiding him, entered the house, and Jack closed and relocked the door. Together they moved down the hallway and easily found the one bedroom. Jack's heart started to pound as a rush of adrenaline hit him. Now was the time for both speed and stealth. He moved forward quickly.

Dortmund was a light sleeper. He was sitting up, drowsy and startled, as Jack reached him and clamped a hand hard over the priest's mouth, shoving him back down into the pillow. He put a knee across the priest's sternum, robbing him of breath. Dortmund panicked, thrashing ineffectually under his blankets. Behind Jack, Biehn hopped onto the bed, straddling Dortmund's legs and pinning them down. Madman or not, he knew how to gain control of a suspect.

"Stop. Listen," Jack commanded.

Dortmund, realizing he was trapped, went limp.

"Good. Don't give me any trouble and you won't get hurt. Don't change positions. Don't move at all. Don't make a sound unless you're told to. When you speak, speak quietly. Understood?"

He could see Dortmund's eyes wide and gleaming in the dark bedroom and felt him nod his head. He released his grip over the priest's jaw and face, but kept his knee on the chest. Dortmund did not say a word.

Jack lifted his knee away and nodded at Biehn, who crawled awkwardly off the priest's lower half. He stepped back and allowed the detective to step forward. Dortmund was frantic to ask a question, but the authority in Jack's voice still held him in silence.

"You're Father Dortmund from St. Monica's," Biehn said menacingly.

"Y-yes," the man said. He was mid-sized, perhaps 160 pounds, Jack guessed, with close-cut brown hair. His face was slightly chubby. There was terror in his eyes.

"You know Aaron Biehn?" the detective asked. He fidgeted, shifting his weight from foot to foot. His hands twitched inside the cuffs, but Jack could see that they were still on.

Dortmund looked bewildered for a moment, then replied, "Y-yes, I know him. He's a good kid—"

"Shut the fuck up!" Biehn said, his voice quiet but as intense as a scream.

"Please, what did I—?"

"Don't ask what you did! Don't ask. You know. You tortured my son. You molested him!"

Had Jack been present for Frank Giggs's interrogation, he would have seen that Dortmund's reaction was entirely different. Giggs had been forced to confront his monstrous self for the first time, and in public, and it had sent a shudder through him. Dortmund's reaction was fearful, of course, but there was more disappointment and resignation than sudden self-loathing.

"I . . . don't know what you're talking about," the priest said. "I didn't do anything."

Biehn's hands twitched again, and Jack knew that he wanted to strike the priest. He was glad he'd kept the handcuffs on. "You violated my son. My son, you sick son of a bitch."

"Please," Dortmund said. "I don't know what you're talking about."

Jack needed this all to happen much faster. "We already have one confession," he said. "You might as well confess, too."

"Confess—?" Dortmund said. "Are you . . . are you the police? I want a lawyer."

"We are the people who decide what happens to you next," Jack threatened. "And that depends on what you say next. Did you sexually abuse Aaron Biehn?"

Despite the darkness, he could see Dortmund look from one of them to the other, trying to decide what to do. Jack suspected that the priest saw the madness in Biehn's eyes, and that it scared him, because he finally said in a tiny voice, "Yes."

Biehn said something that was lost behind a choked sob.

"Who else?" Jack demanded. "Who else did this? We know there were others. Tell me now, or I won't be able to control him." He pointed at Biehn.

"Giggs. Father Giggs," Dortmund replied. "And Mulrooney."

"The Cardinal?" Biehn said.

"Not . . . He didn't . . . didn't do it," Dortmund said. "But he knew why I moved to this diocese. He helped make the arrangements."

Why I moved to this diocese . . . Jack guessed what that meant. "Are you saying you did this in other places? Is that why you moved here?"

Dortmund nodded. "In my old parish. The church moved me after the parishioners complained. They moved me here. I was supposed to . . . was supposed to control myself."

Jack's phone vibrated in his pocket. He pulled it out and checked the number. Shit. This couldn't come at a worse moment. "Wait," he said. He stepped back so that he'd be out of earshot, but kept his eye on Biehn. The man was still twitching, still asking Dortmund a question, but Jack had to answer this.

"Carlos, go," he said quickly.

"Hey, man," the NSA operative said. "We got you something. Your boy works late, like me. He made a call a little while ago. Having a meeting at three A.M. at his place with someone. They were definitely talking about plastic explosives. He wants to get hold of more for a new client, he said."

That's it, Jack thought. *He's our man.* "Who'd he call?"

"That's a harder one, my friend," Carlos replied, a little dejected. "Someone with a little sophistication. It was a scrambled line, and sent our tracers all over the damned planet. Could have been right next door for all I know. But we're on it. He calls that number again, and we'll get 'em."

"Thanks, Carlos. This was helpful. I—"

What happened seemed to occur in slow motion. Jack saw Biehn's hands twitch again, but this time they twitched and came loose. The handcuff stayed on his good hand; the bandaged one came free. Jack was already in motion. He'd already taken one step by the time Biehn's good hand snatched up the loose ring off the handcuff, turning it into a weapon, and Dortmund's eyes were growing big as saucers. Jack was finishing his second step and taking his third when the detective punched downward, smashing the sharp edge of the handcuff into Dortmund's throat.

Life sped up again, and Jack was tackling Biehn across the bed. Biehn turned into a rag doll and Jack rolled him onto the floor, crashing against a dresser. He put Biehn on his face and dragged his hands behind him. He couldn't see the hands clearly in the darkness, but by the feel of it he could guess what had happened. Biehn's hand was more damaged than he realized. The fingers had dislocated. Biehn's twitching had been an effort to dislodge them further. He'd popped his own thumb out of its socket, letting him slip the cuff.

"Damn it!" he cursed. He cuffed Biehn again, this

time digging the cuff in so tight it drew blood. He couldn't leave the cuff like that forever or the man would lose his hand. But for the moment he was taking no chances. Jack pulled his second pair of cuffs out again and resecured Biehn's feet.

He jumped up and vaulted the bed to check on Dortmund. The priest was in the middle of convulsions, gagging and clutching at his throat. Jack reached for the small lamp on the nightstand and turned it on. He pulled Dortmund's hands away from his throat. A deep bruise was already forming there, and Jack knew what had happened. Biehn had crushed his throat with the blow. Dortmund was choking to death.

"Calm down. Calm down!" he said, slapping Dortmund. The man's thrashing was not helping. Shit, he had to do something. If he didn't, he was an accomplice to murder. Jack pulled open the top drawer of the nightstand. It was a gallimaufry. He dug through the odds and ends, shoe polish kits and old watches, until he found a Bic pen. Using his teeth, he tore the top off it and plucked out the ink tube in the middle, until all he had left was a hard plastic straw.

Dortmund was turning blue and clutching at his throat. Urgent, terrified, gurgling noises came out of him, and his eyes were shiny with tears and fear. "I'm trying to fucking help you!" Jack said, shoving him back down on the bed. He stuck the tube between his teeth and pulled a knife out of his pocket. It was a small folder. He snapped it open and held it over Dortmund. He made his voice calm. "Don't move. This is going to hurt. But it will help you breathe. Understand? Don't move."

Dortmund nodded but couldn't stop from twitching. Jack jumped on top of him, straddling him, his knees pinning the priest's arms to his sides. With his free hand, Jack grabbed Dortmund's forehead and pushed it hard into the pillow and mattress. Then, quick as he could, he touched the tip of the knife to the throat below the bruise. He made a quick incision. There was blood, but not much because Jack hadn't come close to the carotid arteries. Jack put down the knife and snatched the pen tube out of his mouth. Lining it up with the hole he'd just made, he pushed it, driving it steadily through the resistance he felt. A second later, a wet rasping sound emerged from the outer end of the tube. Dortmund's chest heaved and the wet sound was repeated. After a moment, the priest's natural color returned. He moved his mouth but could not speak.

"Don't try," Jack said. He touched his own throat. "Your throat was crushed. I gave you a kind of tracheotomy."

Dortmund's hands probed his throat.

"Don't touch. It's a pretty bullshit emergency rig. You need to get to a hospital."

The priest looked at Jack with something like tearful appreciation. Jack sneered at him. "Don't thank me. You're a piece of shit and you probably deserve to die. But I don't have time to deal with it right now."

1:49 P.M. PST
Culver City

The door opened on Nina's second loud knock. The man who answered was in his mid-forties, with a well-trimmed dark beard and soft black eyes behind a pair of wire-framed glasses perched crookedly on his nose. He was still arranging a robe about his body as he looked at her.

"Are you aware of the time?" he said indignantly. "What is this?"

"Mr. al-Hassan, Nina Myers again," she said. "I have more questions for you."

"I'm sorry, who are you? Why are you here so late?"

Nina was annoyed that he didn't remember her. She held out her Federal identification again. "Federal agent Nina Myers," she reminded him. "I questioned you once before."

"Oh!" he said, rubbing his eyes as though just coming awake. "Ms. Myers. I'm sorry, I was asleep. I . . . may I ask what is going on?"

"I'd like to come in."

"Of—of course."

He stepped aside, and she entered. "What happened to your arm?" she asked. His left arm was in a sling.

"I fell," he replied. "Off a curb on the street. I hit my arm on the curb and broke my arm, if you can believe it."

"I'm not sure what to believe, Mr. al-Hassan," she said bluntly. "Why didn't you tell me about the conference in Peshawar?"

Abdul al-Hassan looked genuinely shocked. "Peshawar? What conference?"

She put her hands on her hips, which brought her right hand that much closer to the gun at her hip. "The one you attended. A month or so ago."

"In Peshawar," al-Hassan said, as though piecing together clues. "The Muslim union!" he said at last, his eyes lighting up. Nina swore that he was legitimately pleased with himself for figuring it out. "The reconciliation conference in Peshawar. And I didn't tell you about it?"

"It's late to play games," she said impatiently. "Would you rather I take you into custody and we do this in a less comfortable situation?"

"No, no," al-Hassan said, recovering his composure. "I'm sorry, Ms . . . Myers. I had simply forgotten. I'd forgotten I hadn't told you about that conference."

Nina glared at him. "I specifically asked you if you'd had contact with any Islamic fundamentalists recently and you said no. I believe at that time you might have mentioned a trip to a hotbed of radical Muslim beliefs."

The imam shook his head gently. "Ms. Myers, the problem is just that our definitions of 'radical Muslim belief' are different. The conference was a debate between Sunni and Shiite clerics. An effort to unify the Muslim community. To me, that is hardly a 'radical' notion. It would not have occurred to me to connect that meeting with any discussion of terrorism."

"But Peshawar—

"Yes, I apologize," he said sincerely. "To you, northern Pakistan must seem like the end of the world."

"Don't patronize me," Nina snapped. Something about al-Hassan seemed different than her memory of him. If she recalled correctly, he had been superficially stern, but ultimately cooperative and concerned for justice. Now he seemed much more deferential on the surface, but harder underneath. "I understand the region pretty damned well. If I were going somewhere to meet with a terrorist organization, Peshawar would be ideal."

"And if I were going to confront a schism in my religion," al-Hassan retorted, "I would choose a place just like Peshawar, in Pakistan, which has seen much violence between Sunni and Shi'a since the 1980s." He shrugged at her. "Light does its best work in a dark room, Ms. Myers."

"I don't believe you," Nina said simply. "I don't believe you just forgot. I think you're hiding something from me. Tell me more about your brother." She was fishing now, but she wanted to keep him talking, and al-Hassan had proved in the past that he was more than willing to talk about his brother.

Al-Hassan's eyes flashed. "My brother. Someday, by the will of Allah, he will understand the truth. Until then, his actions are his own. I have not spoken with him in years."

"Do you think he is still involved with radical fundamentalists?" she asked.

"Most assuredly."

"And where is he?"

Al-Hassan shook his head. "I have no idea where my brother might be, nor do I care. If I had any such information, I promise I would tell you."

1:54 A.M. PST
Culver City

Marwan al-Hassan listened to the woman ask several more of her questions. He answered them in the voice he had known from childhood, the voice he hated so much. The voice of his ridiculous embarrassment of a brother, that poor excuse of a Muslim who tried so hard to make peace with the nonbelievers.

Despite his disdain, Marwan played his part well. He tucked his filial dislike into a secret place within him. There was plenty there to keep it company, not least of which was fury at being forced to answer questions from a woman. As far as he was concerned, she should be beaten. Instead, he stood there smiling innocently and answering her questions. Patience, he told himself. Patience. The time would come when Allah would give the faithful the opportunity to bring real Islam to this country.

"Are you aware that we could not locate your brother?" the Federal agent asked.

"Excuse me?" he said, genuinely startled. "I didn't know that."

"His last known location was Afghanistan, but he could be anywhere. What do you think the chances are of his coming here?"

"Here?" Marwan said, still using his brother's scholarly tones. "You would know that better than I, Ms. Myers. I don't know why he would want to come here. I can't imagine he would be allowed in. And surely you must have some sort of registration, or visa, or—"

"We do keep track," she said. "I was just wondering. Would he contact you if he came here?"

"His last words to me were filled with hatred and venom," Marwan said, which was very true. He remembered speaking them. "I doubt he would have anything new to say."

The Federal agent nodded. She spoke some more words—instructions on how to contact her, an urgent request to reach her if he heard anything out of the ordinary, and then she was gone.

As soon as the door was closed, Marwan al-Hassan

allowed the genial mask to slip from his face, revealing his utter and complete disdain. In his home, she would be beaten for impertinence, and for wearing such revealing clothing, and for so many other efforts to live and move beyond a woman's legitimate place.

Marwan looked at the clock. It was a matter of hours, now. Only hours left until martyrdom.

1 2 3 4 5 6 7 8 **9**
10 11 12 13 14 15 16 17
18 19 20 21 22 23 24

. . . .

**THE FOLLOWING TAKES PLACE
BETWEEN THE HOURS OF
2 A.M. AND 3 A.M.
PACIFIC STANDARD TIME**

. . . .

2:00 A.M. PST
Culver City

Nina Myers walked down the steps from al-Hassan's apartment with the nagging feeling of uncertainty, like the feeling of someone who's just walked away from a sale unsure if she'd been had. The only real purpose of her meeting had been to look him in the eye when she asked him about his trip to Pakistan. She had to admit to herself that he had looked genuinely startled. That genuine reaction, more than any words he might have spoken, suggested that he might be telling the truth.

What bothered her was his overall demeanor. She'd spoken with him only once, but she had a good memory for interviews, especially on an active case, and she was sure that al-Hassan had been much more abrupt, even abrasive, with her during their previous meeting. Frankly, she had appreciated his candor. Tonight he had seemed slicker, a little more polished. But she had little to go on—to get any information more thorough than her report on Peshawar would take days. Tracking down the elusive brother in Pakistan or the Middle East would be like looking for a needle in a stack of needles.

She shrugged. It was either that or go back to sleep. She headed for CTU.

2:03 A.M. PST
West Hollywood

Jack had called Christopher Henderson rather than the regular emergency services, laying a bet that CTU had set up some kind of exfil system or cleanup procedure. His gamble paid off. Ten minutes after his call, paramedics arrived, along with a dark-haired man in slacks and a dress shirt, but the sleepy look of someone who'd just dragged himself out of bed.

"Almeida," he said, shaking Jack's hand. "These are our people. We'll check him in and give a story. Is he going to give us any trouble?" He nodded at Dortmund, who was being stabilized by the paramedics.

"I don't think so," Jack said. "He's a pedophile and there is evidence on him. Tell him to agree with your story or you'll tell the real one."

Almeida nodded as though that sort of reply was commonplace. He indicated Biehn, still handcuffed on the floor. "We taking him, too?"

"I'm not sure yet." He studied Almeida's dark eyes. "You haven't even asked what's going on."

The other man shrugged. "My job's to solve the problem, not slow down the solution with questions. Although if you did ask me, I'd say this whole thing looks pretty f'd up."

Jack walked over and knelt beside Biehn. "What do you think of that?" he said sarcastically. "This guy thinks the situation here is fucked up, just because I let a suspected murderer visit a priest and then you tried to kill him. What do you think?"

Biehn, his words muffled by the carpet, replied, "I can give you another name in the plot."

Jack sighed. "In return for letting you try to kill someone else? I don't think so."

"I promise I won't try to kill him."

"Oh, well, if you promise! That's a whole different story," Jack said acidly.

"I just want to see Mulrooney's face. I want to know if he's guilty."

Jack grabbed Biehn by the shoulders and sat him up. He held Biehn's anguished, frantic eyes with his own. "Of course he's guilty. Everyone's guilty of something. He's guilty, but you're not going to kill him. Deal with that right now."

Almeida watched them. "You know, I am starting to get a little curious."

Biehn did not back away from Jack's stare. "You've got a daughter. I know her, she's friends with my son. What would you do if priests had been raping her for the last four years?"

Jack knew. He'd thought about it already, driving in the car with Biehn. He'd make them all disappear quietly and painfully, law be damned. The law was a fine instrument, a useful tool. But it occurred to him that it was a tool that was often too clumsy, like a shovel with too long a handle. There were times when you wanted to cut it short. *When did I start thinking that way?* he wondered.

To Biehn, he said, "Doesn't matter what I'd do. The only thing that matters is that I'm not going to let you do it."

"I can give you a name directly associated with the plot. I don't know if he's one of the terrorists or just a shill, but I know that he's a key component. And I can give you a description of the main guy."

"How do you know all this?" Jack demanded. "What's your source?"

Biehn said, "The guy in charge kidnapped me. He tortured me. I overhead a conversation and then I escaped."

Jack processed this. Biehn was not involved in the terrorist investigation. He was a detective from West Hollywood Division, not Robbery-Homicide. "Were you on a case?"

"I'll tell you that, too, if you let me look into Mulrooney's face."

Jack stood and helped Biehn to his feet. He turned to find Almeida practically in his face. The man was close enough to trigger Jack's fight response, but he held back. Almeida himself was like ice. "I should probably remind you that none of what you're doing is procedure. But I get the feeling you don't really give a shit."

Jack gave a curt nod. "You're a good judge of character."

While Almeida saw to the paramedics and Dortmund, Jack took a deep breath and gathered his arms around the situation. Biehn first, he thought. "Come on." He uncuffed the detective's feet and half-dragged him back out to the car. He put him in the front seat and recuffed his legs. "Are you going to—?" Biehn tried to ask, but Jack slammed the door.

He stood outside the car and dialed his cell phone. "Jack, what a surprise," said Christopher Henderson. "Does everyone at the CIA work this late, or do they regret hiring you, too?"

"You knew the job was dangerous when you took it," Jack quipped in reply. "Don't tell me you signed up for a nine-to-five job, anyway."

"Nine to nine, nine to nine-thirty, but this!"

"You want to gripe, go back to the military. Meantime, you're the one who wanted me on this thing, so here I am."

"Does that mean you're signing on?"

"It means I'm going to figure out why the hell Yasin slipped back into the country, and how a small-time dealer is getting ahold of high-end plastic explosives and passing it around like pot at a party."

"Does figuring that out include hauling a suspected murderer around the city?"

Jack chewed his lip. Driscoll. Of course Driscoll would have gone over his head. Why wouldn't he? "Yes," he said firmly. "I don't know how it happened, but this guy Biehn has information on Yasin. But in the meantime, I need another lead followed."

"Shoot," Henderson said wearily.

"The arms dealer is going to call me any minute. I'm not going to be able to meet with him. I need Diana Christie to go do it."

There was a long pause on the far end. "She's with NTSB, Jack. She's not undercover. She barely even knows fieldwork—"

"I know, but Farrigian met with the two of us. I can't go. If he makes the meet now, then there's no other choice."

"Let's just arrest him."

"For what?"

Henderson snorted. "Says the guy hauling around a murderer!"

"I'm serious, Christopher. Dog Smithies gave us Farrigian's name, but he hasn't sold us a damned thing and Smithies is dead. So we haul in a middleman who probably knows next to nothing about the actual plot, and put him in jail for two years for possession of illegal arms? Big deal. No, we are looking for the guys on either end of the deal, either the buyers or the sellers."

Henderson seemed to consider this for a moment. Jack watched the paramedics roll Father Dortmund out and load him up, then the ambulance drive off, black and silent. Almeida gave him a wave and hopped into an unmarked car.

"Okay," Henderson said at last. "I'll see if she's up for it. Shit, she's going to be all alone in there, Jack. We don't have any backup teams yet."

"She'll be okay," he said, willing it to be true. "Now, about Biehn—" He looked toward the car window, where Biehn was staring back at him. "I'm going to take him on one more little trip, then I'll bring him in. Can you run interference for me?"

"Do you mean can I keep that Driscoll guy away from Chappelle?"

"Something like that."

"Funny thing, I don't think Driscoll has the heart to go too much higher. He likes you. You guys have history, I take it?"

"When I was with SWAT I saved his ass during a raid that went sideways. I also saved his ass from a cross-dresser, but that's a different story."

"Chappelle's going to hear about it soon enough anyway. Other people know Driscoll brought his prisoner to us. Someone's going to be calling CTU to find out what's going on.

"Oh, and Jack. Your friend Driscoll didn't come to rat you out. He asked me for advice on how to stop you before you got into trouble. Thought you should know that before you see him in person."

"Much appreciated." Jack hung up. He pulled open the car door again, stared hard at Biehn, and lied, "I've got my bosses threatening to throw me into prison with you. But I won't have company long because they'll drag you off to the interrogation room."

"I'll go singing," Biehn said miserably. "After I let my son be molested by—"

"Save it!" Jack snapped. "Fucking crybaby. Your son got molested. Stop making this about you."

Biehn was dumbstruck by the sudden accusation.

"I've got a known terrorist in this city somewhere, a guy who tried to kill thousands of people a few years ago. I need to find him fast. So stop blubbering and help me. Give me one more piece to go on."

The detective hesitated, clearly reluctant to play the only cards he had left. "I'll tell you one more name. I have more. But I heard the name Abdul al-Hassan."

The name meant nothing to Jack, but he committed it to memory nonetheless. He wanted to be done with Detective Don Biehn, but something was nagging at him. Not a clue, exactly, but an absence of explanation. If Biehn had already started his vendetta (which Jack assumed was true), and that's when he was grabbed by Yasin, or whoever tortured him, was there some kind of connection? Why would Yasin bother with an LAPD detective? There was an enormous gap in the logical flow of events, and the only way to fill that gap was to follow Biehn down this dark hole into his own personal hell.

"Come on," he said at last. "We're going to see Mulrooney. "Then you're going to tell me everything you know, or I'll kill you myself."

2:15 A.M. PST
CTU Headquarters, Los Angeles

"You sure you're up for this?" Christopher Henderson asked again.

This time Diana Christie glared at him. "Yes. I met him before. He's not that hard to handle. I go in, I try to buy the plastic explosives. My goal is to figure out where he buys from or who else he sold to."

"Don't push it," Henderson cautioned. "It'll be enough for us to get the goods. We may be able to trace—"

"—them back to their point of origin. You said that, too," the NTSB agent interrupted. "Look, I'll admit. This is new for me. But I can always just play dumb. Jack's character was the boss." She twisted her finger in her hair and turned one knee in girlishly. "I'm just his girl Friday."

Henderson grinned. "Works for me. Good luck."

He watched her walk out the door, hoping to god that everything went well, and praying for the day CTU was fully staffed and able to send backup.

2:17 A.M. PST
Los Angeles

Michael was asleep when the phone rang. He had willed himself to bed. Years of experience had taught him that, although he needed very little sleep, his circadian rhythms demanded rest from around two o'clock to five o'clock in the morning. With those three hours of sleep he could operate at full capacity. If he remained awake during that block of time, he could sleep eight hours on any other cycle and feel exhausted.

"What," he said grumpily.

"This is Pembrook," said the voice of one of his men. "There's been more trouble. The police detective was taken by Federal agents, but he's disappeared since then. And another of our clerics, Father Dortmund, has just been hospitalized."

"Was he attacked?"

Pembrook replied, "According to our sources, it was an accident. A dresser fell on him while he was asleep. It nearly crushed his throat. A neighbor found him. But . . ."

"Finish."

"It's too much of a coincidence. Dortmund was one of the church's . . . relocations."

Michael considered this. Biehn had most certainly killed Father Giggs. He'd been taken into custody by the Federal government, but now suddenly another priest, whom Michael knew to have the same unsavory habits as Giggs, had been injured. "Get a man over to Dortmund. Find out what happened to him."

He hung up and then sat up in bed. He could feel the Federal government nipping at his heels. Federal agents had captured their extra plastic explosives—thank god he'd left it in the hands of those bumblers on Sweetzer Avenue for just such a reason. Federal agents had nearly gotten their hands on Ramin. Federal agents had spoken with al-Hassan, but the man seemed to have passed with flying colors. Federal agents were tracking the plastic explosives backward, talking to the middleman he had hoped would divert curious eyes. Well, he had shored up that breach as best he could. That was the key, and Michael hoped that Yasin was right about what tactics to use in that battle. According to Yasin, it was foolish to try to hide from Federal investigators. They were relentless, and they had the resources to break down any defenses, once they spotted their objective. They could not be blocked, only redirected. So Michael, following Yasin's advice, had prepared to redirect them. He would know within the hour.

Ironically, the government's actual terrorist investigation was leading them only in circles. But this rogue detective was ruining everything.

Damn that detective, Michael thought. *Damn his son. Damn those boy-fucking priests who can't keep their hands to themselves. And damn me for not killing Biehn when I had the chance.*

2:22 P.M. PST
St. Monica's Cathedral, Downtown Los Angeles

Jack had no way of knowing, but he parked in exactly the same spot that Don Biehn had used hours earlier. After freeing Biehn's feet, he pulled the man out of the car and escorted him down the street. Biehn was looking haggard, almost a walking corpse, except for his eyes, which were bright with an unhealthy glow.

"I meant it," Jack warned, speaking for the first time since they'd left Dortmund's. "You give me the slightest bit of trouble, and I'll shoot you. I'm already in enough trouble over this. Shooting you is not going to make it all that much worse."

"I'm thinking," Biehn said in a hollow voice, "that you and I aren't that much different. I'm throwing everything away for something really important to me. You look like you're willing to do the same. I'm doing it for Aaron. What's your story?"

Jack shrugged. "A terrorist kicked my dog when I was a kid."

"No, really. Why risk your career?"

"Because someone has to care more about saving the world than saving his job."

"Exactly!" Biehn laughed. "I knew it. You're the hero of the story."

"I guess that makes you the villain," Jack answered.

"Nope, but I bet you're about to meet him."

Jack didn't stand on ceremony. He led Biehn straight through the cathedral and into the grounds beyond. Biehn seemed to know his way around the place, and led Jack past the rectory to the small house standing alone at the far corner of the cathedral grounds. Lights were on in the house, and there was a man standing in front. He looked utterly dumbfounded by the appearance of the two men. "We need to see the Cardinal," Jack said simply. "It's urgent."

"I'll have to—"

But Jack hadn't stopped walking. He brushed right past the guard and pulled on the door of the house. It was unlocked and opened easily onto a small hallway. Jack, still holding tightly to Biehn's arm, walked down the hallway and turned left into the first lighted room, to find himself staring at an utterly average man. He had the look of a man of about sixty; his hair was medium brown and only slightly thin on top; he was of average height and medium build. Jack was immediately reminded of one of his daughter's old "Felt Friends," ambiguous human figures that could be dressed up in different costumes with different expressions. This man could have been dropped into the suit of a Washington politician, or a sales clerk at Nordstrom's, or an Iowa farmer's overalls, and he would have blended perfectly.

The nondescript man looked shocked, but said nothing to the newcomers. He looked past Jack, to the flustered guard who was coming up behind.

"I'm sorry, Your Eminence," the guard said. "He just walked right past. I didn't expect—"

"Apologize later," Jack interrupted. "You're Cardinal Mulrooney?"

The man, wearing black slacks and a white shirt, unbuttoned, nodded. "Tell me what this is about."

"It's about the perverts who abused my son!"

Biehn shouted. Jack should have known he'd find the
energy to work himself back into a frenzy. "The ones
you knew about!"

Mulrooney was extremely self-disciplined. For a
man interrupted at such a late hour, and so accused,
he remained impressively calm. Jack saw the Cardinal's eyes dart from Jack, to Biehn, to the placement
of his hands behind his back, noting everything. But
he said to both of them, "Are you the two who killed
Father Giggs?"

"No," Jack replied. "I'm—"

Jack felt the change in air pressure more than he
heard anything. The men who rushed in through
some unseen door were quiet as wraiths. Jack was
already dropping to a crouched position as the first
pffft! pffft! sounds of bullets leaving silencers spat
into the room. As the rounds thudded into the wall
behind him, Jack already had his own gun out and
put two rounds into the lead man. The report of his
SigSauer was loud and alarming in the otherwise
quiet room, and seemed to shock everyone into the
reality that there was a real gunfight going on. Mulrooney dove for the floor. Biehn dropped heavily to
the ground. The flustered guard flung himself backward, terrified of friendly fire.

The newcomers were all dressed in black, nonmili-
tary attire. As the first man dropped under Jack's
fire, the second stumbled over him. Jack fired again,
blasting the enclosed room with noise, but the third
attacker had rolled around the corner in the hallway.
Jack saw the muzzle of his gun stick itself blindly
around the corner. He rolled away, entering fully
into Mulrooney's living room.

Jack glanced at Biehn. He was lying facedown

on the floor over a widening pool of blood. "Stop!" Jack shouted. "I'm a Federal agent!" *Pfft-thunk! Pfft-thunk!* Silenced rounds sought him out, finding the floor and walls around him. "Federal—!" but he lost his voice as he rolled to the far corner to avoid a dangerous angle as one of the attackers moved down the hall, "slicing the pie" to cover more of the space with his muzzle.

Jack realized that these gun-happy security men were going to kill him first and ask questions later. He was sure Biehn was already dead. Jack fired several rounds into the hallway, then fired two more into a window behind him. He leaped up and hurled himself through the shattered glass. He hit the ground hard on the other side, making an awkwardly timed roll through some kind of wet ground cover. He couldn't be sure over the noise he was making, but he thought he heard more silenced rounds discharge behind him. As he stood and bolted for the cover of a nearby tree, he heard a definitive cough, a sound he recognized as the report of a weapon whose silencer has worn out its usefulness. They were still shooting at him. They weren't protecting the Cardinal. They were trying to kill him.

Jack's mind transitioned smoothly from the problem-solving, fact-finding mode of an investigator to the hunter-killer instincts that had served him well during his time in Delta Force. He swung around to the other side of the bole of the tree and leveled his weapon. The first man who tried to climb through the window after him fell back. Jack hesitated for only a moment to see if anyone was foolish enough to try that way again. No one appeared. Jack moved backward, dropped to one knee, then rose and retreated farther. He heard sounds in the darkness and knew that he was being hunted.

2:31 A.M. PST
St. Monica's Cathedral, Downtown Los Angeles

Michael checked to make sure Don Biehn was dead, then checked his fallen operative, also dead, before moving out onto the grounds where his team was hunting the Federal agent. They had only a few moments left—not to let him escape, but to kill him and claim that they did not know who he was. The opportunity had been ripe when the man first entered: an armed intruder, a man wanted for the murder of a priest. Michael had been hoping they would show. He'd put his least experienced man on the Cardinal's door and pulled back the additional security put in place after Giggs's murder. He had been hoping to lure Biehn in. The appearance of the Federal agent had been unwelcome but not unexpected.

"Station One, this is Station Four," someone whispered into his earpiece.

"Station One here. Go," Michael said softly into his collar mic.

"He's over the wall," his man said. "Station Five is down."

"Roger," Michael replied. "Maintain a perimeter. I'm going back to the residence."

Michael hurried back across the lawn. He had to admit he was enjoying himself. He liked this upfront tactical work much more than the idea of assassination, which he found necessary but repugnant. He jogged into the house, where two of his men stood, weapons drawn, with Mulrooney crouched down below them. It was hardly a fitting position for a Cardinal of the church, but it kept him safe. Michael motioned for them to be at ease, and they allowed Mulrooney to stand. "Check upstairs," he said to them, and the two men nodded and left the room.

Michael pulled a ring of keys from his belt and unwrapped a Velcro strip that kept them from jangling. He sorted through them until he found a handcuff key, then used that to free the hands of Biehn's corpse. Then he pulled a second handgun out of his ankle holster, wiped it down carefully, and then put it in the detective's cold hand for a moment, moving it around slightly. Then he tossed it forward where it clattered on the floor.

"Easier for us to explain if he came in with a drawn weapon," Michael said in answer to Mulrooney's bewildered look. He went on to describe to Mulrooney their version of events: how the insane-looking man had burst into the house brandishing the gun, with the other man right behind him, and how the security team had come in, shooting him down while his accomplice escaped.

"But . . . won't the other man tell a different story?"

Michael shrugged. 'Let the investigators sort it out. The more confusion, the better. Besides, this story will be hard to disprove, since this one already killed one priest. And the other man, whoever he is, was helping a suspected murderer. His position will not be very solid."

2:37 A.M. PST
Downtown Los Angeles

Jack stumbled back to his car, dirty, exhausted, and thoroughly pissed off. He wanted to go back into St. Monica's with a SWAT team at his back and burn the place down. That security team was a bunch of cowboys who needed to get their asses kicked. But it occurred to Jack that he could not call for backup. He had been the intruder, in the company of a man wanted for murder. He was beginning to realize how far behind the eight ball he'd put himself.

He jumped into his car and drove off, trying to figure out what to do next. His prisoner had been shot and, he was sure, killed. The Cardinal might or might not be able to identify Jack himself, but that hardly mattered. Everyone knew Jack and Biehn had been together. Besides, Jack's own sense of morality wouldn't allow him to just walk away from what happened. He had to tell someone.

Jack dialed a number in Langley, Virginia. Someone picked up on the first ring. "Bauer," he said simply. "Sixteen-twenty-two. Out in the open."

He heard several clicks as his call was routed through scrambled lines to a caseworker. He'd had to use this line only once before, and that had been in Ankara. He wasn't sure what would happen when he called from Los Angeles.

"Bauer," said an unfamiliar voice. "You were in L.A. Is this now a domestic issue?"

"As domestic as it gets," Jack said, turning onto the 110 Freeway North. As quickly as he could, Jack relayed the pertinent information. The person on the other end didn't complain or quote the rule book.

That wasn't his job. His only job was extraction, as neatly and cleanly as possible. Not because Jack was important, but because the secrecy and reputation of the Agency were.

"Stand by." There was a click followed by an emotionless hum that lasted from the Sixth Street on-ramp to the 101 Freeway. The voice came back on. "Stand by. We're gathering information. It sounds like your problem is being solved for you." This time the dull hum lasted from the 101/110 juncture all the way to Gower. Finally the caseworker returned. "Problem solved."

"How—"

"The church is reporting that a madman, probably the same one who killed a priest earlier, broke into the Cardinal's residence, but was killed by security. They are reporting that a second assailant escaped, but there is no description."

"I'm working with an agency here, Counter Terrorist Unit," Jack said. "They know I had Biehn in custody."

Another pause. "We'll make a call on that. Go to ground and let us take care of that. It's going to be messy, but we'll try to make it a quiet mess. There will be follow-up." *Click.*

There will be follow-up. That meant trouble, though Jack couldn't blame them. Although the Agency went to great lengths to protect itself, that didn't mean its agents got a free pass every time they colored outside the lines.

After a few more minutes of driving, Jack heard his phone ring and he saw Christopher Henderson's number, but when he answered, it wasn't Henderson's voice.

"You are in so fucking deep!" Ryan Chappelle

shrieked into the phone. "Do you know the phone call I just got!" Jack held the phone away from his ear until Chappelle had exhausted his rant. In the silence after the mini-storm, he wasn't sure if he was supposed to reply or not, until Chappelle said, "What do you have to say for yourself?"

"I assume that you've heard about St. Monica's?" he asked.

"Everybody's heard about it!" Chappelle snapped. "And I've got string pullers at Langley calling in chits, telling me to go easy on you. You know I don't work for them. I don't have to do any goddamned favors."

"Listen, there is something odd," Jack said. He told the story of his visit, and how he'd tried to identify himself as a Federal agent. "Those guys were determined to kill us no matter who we were."

He could practically hear the veins in Chappelle's forehead popping through the telephone. "That's not my case. Maybe that detective was on to something and they wanted him quiet. We don't investigate murders here, we stop terrorists."

"That's what I'm trying to do," Jack said. "Biehn had information—"

"And instead of extracting it, you chauffeured him around town. And got him killed."

"No one except us knows it was me. There's containment here," Jack said, trying to control his own temper. He didn't mind getting chewed out once in a while, but this pencil neck who wasn't even his commanding officer was starting to get under his skin. "I did what I thought necessary to get the information I needed as soon as possible. There have been no major consequences—"

"No major—!" Chappelle sputtered. "A priest in the hospital and three dead men!"

"A pedophile and two trigger-happy security men who were trying to kill me," Jack retorted. "Biehn, they murdered."

"Get into this office now. I'm going to decide whether you need to be put into custody or not. If you don't show up here in the next fifteen minutes, I'm putting out a warrant for your arrest."

2:44 A.M. PST
Parker Center, Los Angeles

Harry Driscoll could not work, but he could not go home, either. After leaving CTU, he had returned to his desk at Robbery-Homicide. But the work he had to do was unpleasant: to write a report on his transfer of Don Biehn's custody to Jack Bauer of the CIA, and to accuse Bauer of endangering the case and, further, currently unaccused citizens, in pursuit of an unrelated investigation.

The office lights at Parker Center were all dark. Only the fluorescent lights in the hallway were awake, casting their pale greenish glow down on the beige, speckled tiles on the floor. When it was quiet like this, you could hear the fluorescent tubes buzzing like bees in a glowing hive. The sound made Driscoll feel even more alone.

He had heard about Biehn's death a few minutes before. By morning, he'd have his captain breathing down his neck for an explanation. He'd be under water and he would have no choice but to describe

how he'd turned custody over to Bauer. What would
Bauer say? What was Jack possibly thinking?

As if to answer his question, Jack Bauer called him.

"Jack," Harry said sadly.

"You heard?"

"Yeah, one of the responding uniforms called me.
It's a mess over at St. Monica's."

Jack defended himself with an explanation of
how gun-happy the security men were. *No wonder*,
Driscoll thought, *with a murderer on the premises*.

"But something was wrong with the Cardinal.
And the security team. They were way more interested in killing us than protecting their man."

'So?"

"So they succeeded in doing one thing. I never
learned the connection between Biehn's vendetta
and the terrorists."

"Was there one?"

"You heard him talk about Yasin, the terrorist. And
someone did all that to him. I need you to help me."

Without hesitation, Harry said, "I'm not helping you, Jack, except to talk you into settling down
before there's any more trouble."

"Can you look into Cardinal Mulrooney for me?"
Jack asked as though Harry hadn't spoken. "I want
to know his background, who works for him. Any
skeletons in his closet."

"He's a Cardinal in the Catholic Church," Driscoll
said, as though that concluded the matter.

The tone in his voice alerted Jack. "Harry . . . I
never knew you were Catholic."

"Why would you?" the detective asked. "I don't
need to wear a sign on my back."

"No, I guess it's not my business," Jack replied simply. He wondered if Driscoll's faith had affected his view of Biehn. No wonder, at least, that it had been hard for Harry to turn the man over to Jack. "You're still the only guy I can turn to right now. This group I'm working with, it's a new unit, and they are stretched thin. I don't know what the CIA will have on Mulrooney. I need someone local. I just want to know the Cardinal's background."

Driscoll pinched the bridge of his nose with his fingers. Damn it. All he'd wanted to do was stay involved in the potential terrorist case the Feds had taken away from his unit. How had that morphed into this debacle?

"If I help you, then you need to help me," the detective said at last. "I'm just shy of twenty years on, Jack. This thing could kill my career when my captain hears about it in the morning. Shit, forget the Captain, I'll probably hear from the Chief himself, and you know I don't want to get the call."

"What do you want me to do?" Jack offered sincerely.

"I want off the hook on this. I want it clear that I turned custody of Biehn over to you at your insistence, and you made all the decisions from there."

Jack smiled unhappily. He remembered what he'd said to Biehn: *Someone has to care more about saving the world than saving his job.* "Don't worry, Harry. All the heat is headed at me anyway, I guarantee it."

"Okay. I'll do it."

"Thanks. Listen, if you need help, there's someone I want you to call. Name's Maddie Marianno."

He recited an unusually long number. "Give her my name."

"Okay," Harry said. "I'll see what I can dig up."

2:47 A.M. PST
St. Monica's Cathedral, Downtown Los Angeles

The regular police were still milling about the crime scene, and Michael could only give thanks that the Unity Conference would be held elsewhere. He was sure they would cancel the event rather than let civilians trample over any potential evidence. He had already given an immediate interview, and had been told to wait around until more detectives arrived so that he could answer the same questions again. At the moment, though, he was alone, and decided to make a call.

Abdul Rahman Yasin, still using the name Gabriel, answered after two rings. He listened quietly while Michael updated him. "It would all be easier," Michael said, not for the first time, "if I just did the job myself, quickly. I could probably do it right now."

And, not for the first time, Yasin replied, "But that is just murder. Assassination, nothing more. The tool we are using is terrorism. It must be a spectacle. It must be public."

Michael had known the answer before he heard it. He shrugged off the rejection. He had worked for enough men to be accustomed to following orders. Yasin was the man in charge at the moment, and Michael would do as he was told.

"But," Yasin said cautiously, "there is no danger of canceling the conference?"

"There is talk of it," Michael replied, "but I know this Pope, and he will push forward if he can. He doesn't get sidetracked easily."

"Good," Yasin said. "And how are our deliverymen? All in good condition?"

"Yes," Michael replied.

"Then all this trouble will come to nothing. Well done, Michael. We are going to have a very interesting day."

2:50 A.M. PST
CTU Headquarters, Los Angeles

Jack walked into CTU's headquarters, which seemed almost morguelike at this late hour. Overhead lights had been turned off, except in the conference room, whose doorway appeared like some extra-dimensional portal in the darkness. Jack walked toward it but was met halfway by Ryan Chappelle, wearing khaki pants, a sweatshirt, and a more than usually pinched look.

"You are fucked," Chappelle said to him.

"Right," Jack replied, following him into the conference room. Christopher Henderson was there, as was Diana Christie. Her left arm was heavily bandaged from her wrist all the way to her shoulder.

"What happened to you?" he asked.

"Later," Chappelle snapped dismissively. "Tell him the important part."

Diana looked chagrined. She was clearly embarrassed to relay her information—not embarrassed for herself, but for Jack. "I think . . ." she started, then winced a bit as she moved her injured arm. "I think you're headed in the wrong direction, Jack. Based on my meeting with Farrigian."

Jack felt a cold weight settle into his stomach. "What do you mean? Did he get you more plastic explosives? Can we trace his other customers?"

"Yes," Diana said. "But it's not Islamic terrorists."

"Or the Catholic church, which you just terrorized," Chappelle pointed out. Henderson dipped his head.

The weight in Jack's stomach grew heavier. "Tell me what's going on."

Diana Christie began, and no one interrupted her. "I met with Farrigian. He didn't suspect anything about me. You saw how he was before. We checked out, as far as he was concerned. He told me who the buyers were—they were more people like that Smithies character. Some biker gang coming down from the San Joaquin Valley. He gave me names. As far as I can tell, he has no connection to the plastic explosives found on Sweetzer Avenue."

Jack tried to process that, but couldn't. "That's ridiculous. Two different groups, both suddenly appearing on the scene with plastic explosives? It's pretty unlikely." That was obvious to him, and he hoped it was obvious to them, too. Henderson met his gaze just long enough to shrug, but he remained silent. "What's the point here?"

"The point," Chappelle said condescendingly, "is that you're on a wild-goose chase. You and the detective you helped get killed."

"Not possible," Jack argued. He listed the evidence for them: the assassination of the informant

Ramin; Biehn's knowledge that Yasin was back in Los Angeles, which had been confirmed by security cameras; the three Islamists in possession of plastic explosives. "You're going to put all that aside based on comments from a small-time arms dealer?"

"*Your* small-time arms dealer," Chappelle pointed out. "The one you dug up. If he confirmed your theories, you'd be calling him a vital source of information. Instead"—he pointed at Diana—"the evidence points elsewhere, so suddenly we should ignore him?"

"Just don't ignore all the rest of it."

"We're not, Jack." Christopher Henderson played good cop, speaking in slow, measured tones. "We've already got the three men with the plastic explosives. We think that did a lot more to mess up their plans than you realize. Maybe Yasin got here just in time to find out we'd fucked up his plans. But we'll get him, if he's still in town."

"And Biehn . . . ?" Jack challenged.

"Had his own agenda," Chappelle said, "which you fell for hook, line, and sinker."

It was possible. Jack hated to admit it, but it was possible. There was one gaping hole, of course—how did Biehn know about Yasin? That was an enormous question mark squatting on any other theory. But put it aside for a moment, and what they were proposing made sense. In that moment, Jack tried to step back and away from his ego. Ego was the enemy of a good investigator, he had decided long ago. Men fell in love with their own theories, and once enamored, held on to them like prize possessions. The very best investigators pursued their theories with determination but not tunnel vision. Jack hadn't been at this long enough to know if he was one of the very best, but he refused to stumble over his own ego.

Yasin certainly was up to something. But maybe CTU had shattered that plan. Maybe Jack, who had thought himself to be the man exposing the plot no one else had foreseen, was instead just a latecomer to a party that was already over.

"Jack, we'll get him," Henderson said, continuing to act the friend. "But according to Diana, that's not where the urgency lies."

Jack looked at the injured woman. She nodded. "Farrigian says the buyers were friends of Dog Smithies, who I guess you dealt with. They bought more plastic explosives than what was found on Sweetzer. A lot more. The buyer was a man named Dean."

"Jamey Farrell ran down his information," Henderson went on. "Dean runs a biker gang that is an offshoot of the Hell's Angels. They want the Angels to go back to the old days. Back when they'd take over towns and make themselves the law. One of their gang was arrested last night in Fresno. He said that Dean was on his way down to L.A. He said they were going to 'Blow some shit up.' He said everyone would wake up tomorrow morning to a big surprise."

Chappelle checked his watch. "Which gives us only a few hours to find them and stop them. And, much as I hate myself for saying this, Agent Bauer, you are going to help."

· ·

THE FOLLOWING TAKES PLACE
BETWEEN THE HOURS OF
3 A.M. AND 4 A.M.
PACIFIC STANDARD TIME

· ·

3:00 A.M. PST
Santa Clarita, California

His real name was Dean Schrock, but he'd just been Dean for so long that even he had mostly forgotten the last name. He was old enough to feel a long day's ride in his ass and lower back, but he was still young enough to bully the one-percenters who were part of his gang, and hell of bad enough to terrify the crap out of any cagers he saw on the streets.

Dean was part of a dying breed, and he knew it. Hell, he took pride in it. He'd been a kid during the heyday of Altamont, so he hadn't been busting heads back then, but he was old enough to remember when whole towns would head for the hills when the Hell's Angels rode down Main Street. These days most people calling themselves Hell's Angels were wannabes or squiddies who'd just as soon ride a rice burner as a Harley and pretend to be badass. Sure, there were still a few throwbacks; Dean had heard about a Hell's Angels club in New York City, and another up in Canada (friggin' Canada, of all places!) that were hard-core and full of one-percenters, but they were few and far between.

Dean pushed an empty beer bottle off his belly and sat up. They were in a house on the outskirts of Santa Clarita, in the upland valleys north of Los Angeles. He'd forgotten—or, more to the point, he never really cared—whose house it was. Four or five of his boys were sprawled out on couches or chairs or on the floor. A couple of women were there, too— nothing to look at, or he'd have taken them into one of the bedrooms and had them himself. A few more of his boys were crashed in the bedrooms or the hallways, sleeping off the ride down from Bakersfield and the six-packs they'd swallowed since then.

All Dean's boys were one-percenters—that is, part of the "one percent" of bikers that were outlaws, rather than the ninety-nine percent that the Hell's Angels claimed were law-abiding citizens—and in just a few hours they were going to prove that even if only one percent of the biker population were outlaws, it was one hell of a one percent.

Bleary-eyed, he checked his watch. Little bit of time left. That puke Dog Smithies was supposed to show up before sunrise. Dean was looking forward to meeting him face to face, see what that bullshitter was really like. But right now he could close his eyes a little bit and dream of the big explosion.

3:06 A.M. PST
Parker Center, Los Angeles

As far as LAPD was concerned, Cardinal Mulrooney
was a candidate for beatification. They maintained a
small dossier on him, but the contents might as well
have been provided by the Catholic Church's public
relations department. The report discussed Mulrooney's upbringing in a poor Irish neighborhood of
Chicago, his travel to Los Angeles as a teenager in
the fifties, where he slept on the floor of the Catholic
mission and then volunteered for their soup kitchen.
Soon after, he had promised himself he would
become ordained, and Allen James Mulrooney had
been a servant of the Catholic Church ever since.
There was, to Harry's utter relief, not even a whisper
in the dossier of child abuse or hushed-up scandals.

Harry would like to have stopped there. The Mulrooney file was flimsy, but it was official, and Harry
could rightly have told Jack that was far as he could
or would go. He sat in his office for a few moments,
fingering the number Jack had given him. Finally, he
punched in the long string of numbers. It didn't seem
like a phone number at all, but a few moments later,
his phone was ringing.

"Marianno," said a female voice on the other
end.

"Maddie Marianno, this is Detective Harry
Driscoll, LAPD," he said. "Jack Bauer asked me to
contact you. You have a moment?"

"Driscoll," she repeated, and he was sure she was
committing it to memory. "What kind of trouble has
Bauer gotten you into?"

"Ha!" Harry said. "You definitely know Jack. Listen, I'm sorry for calling you so early, but I need a little information if you can give it."

"It's not that early," Marianno said. "Fire away."

"Jack asked me to find out anything I could dig up on Cardinal Allen J. Mulrooney. He's the—"

"Cardinal of the Archdiocese of Los Angeles, sure," the woman replied. "Interesting guy. You know he's a schismatic, right?"

"A what?"

"Schismatic. This isn't even classified, really, so I have no trouble telling you this. You ever heard of Vatican II?"

"Is the Pope Catholic?" Harry replied. Vatican II, officially known as the Second Ecumenical Council of the Vatican, was a series of meetings held between 1962 and 1965 that made significant changes to the views and practices of the Catholic Church.

"Right. Some of the decisions made at Vatican II made a certain segment of the church unhappy. Some splinter groups were created within the church. Some are still inside the church, still follow the Pope, etcetera, but think the church has lost its way a little bit. Some are more extreme. They think there hasn't been a legitimate Pope since 1962. They believe there's been a schism. Schismatics."

"And Mulrooney is one of those?"

"Not publicly," Marianno replied. "I don't even think the Vatican has solid proof, or they'd out him. But, yes, he is. Mulrooney was groomed by very orthodox priests and didn't take kindly to the changes being made back then."

This was news to Harry. Although he was far, far

from the inner circles of the Catholic Church in Los Angeles, he'd been a congregant inside the archdiocese for most of his life. One heard rumors. But he'd never heard a whisper of this.

"Anything else? Anything about . . . about child abuse?" he asked.

"Ah," the woman said solemnly. "Child abuse and Mulrooney? No. Nothing directly related to him. But the child abuse issue is a hydra waiting to raise its head. When it does, the church is going to have serious problems."

No kidding, Harry thought. Aloud, he said, "Thanks for your time. Again, sorry to call so early."

Maddie Marianno laughed. "That's twice you've said that. It's not so early here. I'm having lunch."

"Oh," Harry said, surprised. "Where exactly are you?"

Marianno laughed again, louder this time. "Didn't Jack even tell you who you were calling? I'm in Italy, Harry. You've called the CIA's Section Chief in Rome."

3:12 A.M. PST
405 Freeway

For the second time in one night, Jack was riding up the 405 Freeway on a motorcycle. This time it was on Dog Smithies's impounded Harley-Davidson. There was no traffic at this hour, even on the northbound 405, and Jack literally flew out of the city and into the foothills.

The Hell's Angel in custody had given the police several pertinent pieces of information. First, Dean and his bikers expected to meet up with Smithies. Second, they'd never met him before, although they'd talked to him on the phone a lot. Third, Smithies was supposed to bring them more plastic explosives.

All this was now pretty goddamned far removed from CIA business, but Jack wasn't sure he had a choice. He'd gotten himself involved in this business, and like it or not, Chappelle did have a pretty big book to throw at him. The least Jack could do was try to clean up his own mess.

The plan wasn't very complicated: impersonate Smithies, find out what this Dean character was planning, and either call in the cavalry right away, or head him off and arrest him at the scene.

Alone on the bike, Jack had time to think about what he was getting into. Messes came with every job. Even on SWAT, which was as straightforward as it gets, he'd seen issues with other officers: questionable shootings, civilian complaints even when the shootings were righteous, guys jockeying for position to help boost their careers. Delta had been the same; even though every man in his unit had his back during an operation, when they were inside the wire, all of them had their own agendas and personal missions. The CIA was . . . well, hell, he wasn't sure what the CIA was. He just knew that they were the guys looking into the shadows. Jack liked that, but he had to admit that half of any day spent at the CIA was devoted to managing the politics of the place. This new agency, Counter Terrorist Unit, was certainly full of all the same bullshit. But Jack had to admit that they were seeing a lot of action. Maybe there was good work to be done on the domestic front. For all his smooth salesmanship, Christopher Henderson was right: his CIA status hurt more than it helped right now. If the borders were porous enough to let Yasin back into the country so easily, who knew what other scorpions had crept inside the wire?

It would make Teri happy, too, he knew. So far, his CIA work had sent him overseas only on short-term assignments. But he knew that any day he might be permanently assigned to a foreign desk anywhere from Djibouti to Jakarta, and then where would they be? Teri didn't want to move. Kim would have a meltdown. And Jack . . . Jack wasn't sure what he wanted.

Inside the helmet, sealed off from the landscape hurtling past him at eighty miles per hour, Jack said the words aloud. "I don't know what I want."

And if you don't know what you want, how will you ever get it?

"But Jesus," Jack said into the helmet. "Can I really work for a prick like that?"

There's a Chappelle everywhere. Besides, you wouldn't be working for him. You'd work for Henderson. Or for yourself.

This internal dialogue continued for another mile or two, but in the end, a more practical side of Jack Bauer won out, the part of him that simply could not abide indecisiveness. "Screw it," he said aloud. "Let's just take out some bad guys."

Ryan Chappelle sat alone in a darkened corner of the headquarters, away from the halogen lights in the conference room and the gentler yellow lights leaking out of Henderson's office. Chappelle put his feet up and rubbed his temples.

It's not always going to be like this, he almost said aloud. *I do my job right, this will all get better. More efficient. It'll be staffed properly.*

Chappelle knew some of his staff didn't like him. But he also knew that they liked their budgets, their computers, their access to classified materials. Their salaries. And those things weren't created ex nihilo. Someone went out and got those items, fought for them, justified them after the money had been spent. That someone was Ryan Chappelle.

The PDA in Chappelle's pocket buzzed, alerting him to something on his calendar. Chappelle shook his head and rubbed his cheeks, trying to shake off the sleep. He stood up and walked quietly to the conference room, activated the monitor, and signed in to the scrambled video conference. He had insisted the monitor and Internet connection be prepared for just this moment.

An efficient-looking middle-aged woman leaned into the screen frame. "Director Chappelle? Stand by for Mr. Harding."

Chappelle did not disguise his displeasure as Peter Harding sat down in the chair at the other end of the link. Harding had the kind of bright red, almost orange hair and freckles that looked cute on a ten-year-old-boy but unfortunate on a fifty-year-old man with jowls.

"Chappelle, how are you?" Harding said.

"Confused," Ryan said tersely. "I understood this meeting was with the President."

"Change of plans. Now you've got the Deputy to the National Security Advisor."

Ryan snorted. "So I see. Look, I need to know if the National Security Council is taking CTU seriously. I understood that the Division Directors were reporting directly to the President."

Harding scratched his remaining shock of red hair. "That may change. We're still sussing it out."

Idiots, Chappelle thought. *This is why mavericks like this Bauer character need me. Someone has to deal with this crap.* "While you're sussing, we are actually chasing terrorists out here. I've got people putting their lives on the line right now, and I'm giving my own people hell for not following protocol. How am I supposed to tell them that the people above us don't even know what the protocol is?"

Harding bristled visibly. "Don't talk to me like that, Chappelle. This is a new—"

Chappelle interrupted. "It took seven years to get a unit like CTU up and running. You think the terrorists have been sitting on their asses since then? Hell, one of our guys just got confirmation that Abdul Rahman Yasin came back into the country!" Harding's eyes opened as wide as saucers. "That's right. One of the terrorists from back in '93." Chappelle didn't bother to mention that the "guy" he was referring to was a cowboy from the CIA. His fledgling unit could use all the credit it could get. "If you want us to keep trying to stop terrorists on a shoestring budget and no real access to the big decisions, fine. But you get what you pay for."

He stood up and walked away from the screen, leaving Harding tripping over himself to respond.

Chappelle's fingers shook from the sudden adrenaline dump. He wasn't out there dodging bullets or facing down international terrorists. But there were many kinds of unsung heroism, and some of the most important battles were fought in little beige rooms by men like Ryan Chappelle.

3:31 A.M. PST
Parker Center, Los Angeles

Driscoll had tried three times to call Jack Bauer, but the calls went directly to voice mail. Though he was a detective with over ten years, Harry had no idea what to do with the information he'd received. Mulrooney's political affiliations within the Catholic Church had nothing to do with the current case, as far as he could tell. And the CIA (Jesus, had he really just called a CIA operative in Rome?) had no information on Mulrooney's involvement in any child abuse scandals.

There was a part of Harry Driscoll that wanted to be done. No one could say he hadn't played his role, put his career on the line, risked his neck. He should go home and sleep for a few hours.

But he couldn't. Maybe it was the Catholic in him. He was guilted into staying on the case. *It's your own fault*, some little voice was telling him. *You wanted to be a part of the big terrorist case. You wanted to turn Biehn over to the Feds. You got him killed as much as Bauer did.*

Oddly, it wasn't the terrorist angle that was haunting Harry as the clock leaned toward four o'clock. It was Biehn, especially his face as he described the horror of his son being abused. While Biehn was alive, his righteous indignation had struck Harry as melodramatic. Now that he was gone, the silence was far more offensive than his antics. No one now was speaking for that kid who got abused.

"Damn," Harry said to the empty building. "Hell and damn."

He stood up and grabbed his jacket.

3:38 A.M. PST
Santa Clarita

The 405 Freeway had merged onto Interstate 5, and Jack was now heading through the city of Santa Clarita. He left the 5 and turned onto one of the many roads that led into the hills. A hundred years ago the roads and homes built up here would have seemed like a world away from the city of Los Angeles. But the suburbs had crept steadily northward into the mountain valleys, and the dirt roads had been paved over. Jack followed one of these roads away from the residential streetlights and out into the hills, where a lonely one-story ranch house squatted at the top of a small rise. A garden of motorbikes seemed to have sprouted in the dry ground around the house. A porch light was on, and another light somewhere in the back of the house, but all was still.

The Harley made enough noise to wake the dead, so Jack didn't even try stealth. He roared up the S-shaped road to the top of the rise and then idled the engine as he rolled to a stop a few yards from the front door. He climbed off the bike and slid the helmet off his now-sweaty head. He pulled the package out of a pack strapped to the seat and climbed the steps.

He reached the top step to find a shotgun in his face.

3:45 A.M. PST
Brentwood

Amy Weiss dreamed that church bells were ringing, which was odd because she was in a grocery store, not a church. The church bells became cash registers that wouldn't stop ringing up her yogurt, and then telephones ringing at the cashier's stand, and then she was awake and it was just her telephone ringing shrilly at a ridiculous hour of the morning.

"Uh-huh," she groaned, having fumbled for the phone.

"Amy, it's Josh Segal." She struggled to remember who that was. She dredged up a recollection that Josh Segal was the assistant metro editor, and often got stuck on the night desk. "I need you up and at 'em."

"My dad said 'up and at 'em,' every morning for twelve years," Amy said. "Don't use that phrase, please."

"Either way, you need to get up. You're slated to have that interview with the Pope this morning, aren't you?"

"Interview. Yes. In, oh, five hours or so. Trust me, it doesn't take that long to do this hair." She yawned again, wanting to be sleepy, but sleep was fading away. Her reporter's instincts were tuned in to the excitement in Segal's voice.

"Drag it out of bed, Weiss," the assistant editor said. "There's been some serious stuff you need to be up on when you meet with him." Amy listened as the editor described, in as much detail as the police would allow, the violence that had taken place at St. Monica's.

"Jesus, and they're still holding the conference to-morrow, uh, today?" she said, now fully awake and pulling clothes out of her drawer.

"That's what they're telling us. The police haven't given any motive for the murder of this Father Giggs. They're not releasing the name of the intruder killed later that evening. We've been on the phone with a public relations person for the archdiocese, but we're getting a hundred variations of 'no comment.'"

"You think the Pope's going to tell me anything more than what you're getting from the archdiocese? I'm just doing a puff piece on the conference."

"You just graduated to the crime beat. I figure our article on the attacks will be a hell of a lot more in-teresting with a quote from the Pope in it. So get up and—"

"—at 'em. Bite me," Amy said genially, and hung up.

3:52 A.M. PST
Santa Clarita

Jack had spent several minutes facedown in the dirt beside the porch with the shotgun pressed against the back of his neck. He had thought about taking the gun away from the bearded, beer-gutted biker, but this was no time to make trouble. He tolerated the biker's boot in the small of his back while someone went in to clear things with Dean. Finally, he was let up. Jack looked at the biker, who was grinning out of the hole in his bushy brown-white beard, still lazily holding the shotgun in Jack's general direction.

"You want to point that thing somewhere else," Jack said, "before it accidentally gets shoved up your ass."

"Ha!" the biker said. "You give that a try someday. Come on."

He led Jack into the house. It stank of beer and farts and mildew that had been around much longer than the bikers. The living room was gloomy, lit by only a seventies-era table lamp and a small fluorescent in the kitchen. There were two couches and a tattered easy chair, the latter occupied by a big man with the kind of huge, uncut arms that indicated genetic size. The man, probably in his late forties or early fifties, still had a barrel chest pushing his T-shirt to the limit. CTU had been able to dig up only one mug shot, but that had been enough. Jack recognized Dean Schrock.

"I heard you was a fat guy," Dean said.

Jack shrugged. "Had to lose my gut. My cousin had a heart attack. My age, too."

"So, what," said the biker with the shotgun, "you eat bean sprouts and salads? Shit, we really doin' business with this dipshit?"

"I'm the dipshit with the shit you need," Jack said. "Besides, looks like every pound I lost was your gain, so shut the fuck up."

The biker gave Jack a fuck-off look, but Dean laughed. "Anyway, I made calls when I got here. I knew who to expect."

Jack shrugged, but inwardly, he knew what Dean meant. The bartender at the Killabrew had been Smithies's middleman, so having her under the Federal thumb had made impersonating Dog easy, despite the difference in their appearance.

"You heard from Peek?" Dean asked.

"Peek," Jack knew, was the nickname of the biker the Fresno police had picked up. From what he had confessed, his job had been to ride in early and meet with Farrigian.

"Nah," Jack said. "He told me to meet up here."

Dean and the fat biker exchanged glances, and Jack knew that Peek's absence had put them on edge. "You bring what I need?" Dean asked.

Jack hefted the sack. "You wanted one more brick, I brought it."

"What the fuck?" said a female voice out of the shadows.

Jack didn't know who she was or what she meant,

so he tossed the brick to Dean. A couple of the bikers flinched as the dormant explosive arced across the room, but Dean caught it casually and hefted it.

"What the fuck?" said the woman again, staggering into the lamplight. She was blond, in her late thirties, but with the used look of a much older woman. She blinked at Jack. "You're not Dog!"

1 2 3 4 5 6 7 8 9
10 **11** 12 13 14 15 16 17
18 19 20 21 22 23 24

• •

**THE FOLLOWING TAKES PLACE
BETWEEN THE HOURS OF
4 A.M. AND 5 A.M.
PACIFIC STANDARD TIME**

• •

*4:00 A.M. PST
Santa Clarita*

"Who the fuck are you?" Jack said lazily.

"Deb!" she said indignantly. "I lived down 'round here back in '94. Or maybe '95. Something like that." She blinked several times, and spoke in the overly enunciated speech of someone who is trying not to sound drunk. "I met him coupla times."

"You mean you screwed him a couple times!" The fat biker laughed. So did everyone else, including Deb, who was clearly no delicate flower.

"You know Deb?" Dean asked. He was laughing, too, but Jack could feel the energy between them change. A wall had gone up between them.

Jack looked at her and shrugged. "I don't know.

It's like four o'clock in the morning. At this point I'm too shit-faced to know what they look like. And if I wasn't shit-faced, I sure as hell wouldn't choose this one."

This elicited a roar of laughter from everyone except Deb, who was insistent. "No, no, I'm serious, Dean. I'm sure I met that fat slob before. This ain't him."

There were two directions: forward or backward. Jack wasn't usually one for retreating. He strode forward and plopped himself down on the couch at a ninety-degree angle to Dean, and put his booted feet up on the old scratched coffee table. "Look, I got you the first batch of stuff. Then I hear from Peek that you want more. I brought it. You gonna let this split tail give me a bunch of crap?"

Dean was shrewd. He played the controversy very casually, but Jack, just as shrewd, knew that the biker leader was on his guard. "Nah, she can't even remember what she looks like half the time," he said. "Besides, you said you talked to Peek, right?"

Jack leaned back as though he didn't care much as he corrected: "I didn't talk to him. He left a message at the Killabrew." That was how Dog did most of his business. And CTU had checked Smithies's personal phone records. No calls that day or night from anyone that might have been connected to Peek the biker.

Before Dean could respond, Jack found Deb in his face, her skin leathered yellow, undoubtedly from years of smoking. "You're way too good-looking. If I'd screwed you, I'd remember it."

"If I did you, I'd do my best to forget it," Jack answered. He put his hand on her face and shoved her backward. She fell sprawling on her backside, shrieked, and scrambled to her feet, coming at Jack like a harpy. Before Jack had moved, Dean was on her, catching her wrists in his big hands and shoving her aside.

"Give it a rest, Deb," he said. "Hell, I did you last year and you hardly remember it." To Jack, he said, "Thanks for bringing up the extra stuff. You want to help us use it?"

Jack nodded. "Yeah."

4:09 A.M. PST
Shoemacher Avenue, Los Angeles

Another door that Harry Driscoll did not want to open. This one, on Shoemacher Avenue, belonged to Father Sam Collins. But just as he had before, Harry knocked.

The door opened after a minute, and Father Collins, his eyes swollen from restless sleep, greeted him.

"Father Collins, Detective Driscoll. I hope I gave you enough time to—"

"Come in, come in, Detective," Collins said with as much congeniality as four o'clock would allow. "Yes, thanks for calling ahead. I put on some coffee if you want it."

Harry followed Collins's words and gestures into the small, well-kept house. There was an intricately carved crucifix hanging in a place of prominence in the entryway, but otherwise the house gave no indication of belonging to a man of the cloth.

"What happened to your arm?" Harry asked immediately.

Collins touched his right hand gingerly to his left arm, which was bound up in a sling. "Oh, it's been such a pain. Literally!" He laughed. "I was in an accident a while ago. My arm was really badly broken and I had to have surgery. I'm not sure how it's gone, though. I have a checkup scheduled for next week, but it's been hurting a lot."

"What kind of accident?" Harry probed.

"Car accident. Coffee?" Harry accepted, and Collins poured two cups in the open kitchen, then brought them into the living room. "I barely remember it. I didn't even wake up until after the surgery. I saw the X-rays, though. I have this huge plate in my arm."

Harry nodded absently. "I'm sorry to have bothered you so early."

Collins waved him off. Now that he was more awake, his face opened into a smile that Harry guessed was almost permanent. "It's a wasted night anyway. My arm's keeping me up, and I have a big conference today, and last night someone broke one of my back windows."

Biehn, Harry thought. Biehn had said he was trying to break in when someone kidnapped him.

4:12 A.M. PST
Shoemacher Avenue, Los Angeles

Collins had always been the weak point. The complication. Michael had known it from the beginning. But Yasin had insisted. He had wanted there to be three deliverymen—three, as an ironic joke for Yasin's own amusement—and Yasin had wanted at least one of them to be ignorant of the package he was carrying. At first, Michael had argued against this last idea, and won. But after that idiot Ali had gotten himself blown up on an airplane, they had to replace him with someone, and Yasin had insisted on returning to his original idea of the unwitting messenger. They had gone to immense amounts of trouble to make that happen, and now, of course, that one unnecessary twist was about to become the snag that might unravel the whole plan.

Michael was parked outside Collins's house again, just as he had been before, when Detective Biehn arrived. That last encounter had been sheer luck; this was foresight. Michael had bugged Collins's phone weeks ago, so that he could monitor any calls the priest made to any doctors he might know. That surveillance had paid off when another detective had called, waking Collins and asking him if he could stop by for a few questions. Michael had driven like a bat out of hell through the foggy Los Angeles morning to arrive just behind the detective.

Yasin could go to hell, as far as Michael was concerned. The power Yasin had over them depended entirely on the keeping of a secret, and that secret was unraveling as steadily as their plan. Michael was going to have to eliminate Collins for everyone's sake, and Yasin could go cry to Allah for all he cared.

4:14 A.M. PST
Shoemacher Avenue, Los Angeles

"Father Collins," Harry said, after spending several minutes asking simple questions designed to relax a suspect. "How well did you know Father Giggs?"

Collins sighed. "We were both priests at St. Monica's, so I knew him pretty well, of course."

"Were you both part of the youth program?"

Collins shifted ever so slightly. "Me? No, not officially. I helped out when I could. The program was popular, and Father Frank was sometimes overwhelmed."

"Did you molest the children like he did?"

Silence engulfed the room like a tangible thing, a thick blanket of tension tangling them both. "Ex-excuse me?" Collins said at last. He drank his coffee with a trembling hand.

"I said," Harry repeated, staring directly into the priest's eyes, "did you molest the children just like Father Frank did?"

Father Collins's face flushed, then went very, very pale. His eyes could find no place to rest. They flitted like nervous birds from Driscoll to the coffee table, to the window, until finally they fell, exhausted, toward his cup. "I . . . no . . . Oh, Mary, mother of . . ." Something struck him and he looked up finally, his eyes filling with a fearful realization. "Oh my Lord. Is that why Giggs was killed?"

"Answer the question," Harry demanded. His voice did not contain Biehn's righteous indignation. It couldn't, because he could not wrap his brain around the crime he was investigating. He recoiled from it. But his sense of justice would not let it be.

"I didn't!" Collins said quietly but urgently. "I mean, I haven't. Not in years." He shuddered. "It was such a sin. I should never have; it was Frank; almost always Frank."

The cup fell from Collins's hand, staining the couch and the rug with coffee. Collins put his head in his good hand and let out one long, strangled sob, his body convulsing.

4:17 A.M. PST
Santa Clarita

One wouldn't know it from looking at Dean Schrock, but he had a long memory. It stretched farther back than Altamont, farther back than the heyday of the Hell's Angels. It stretched back to the days when his father lost his farmland in the Owens Valley, way north of Los Angeles. The Owens Valley farmers wanted nothing from Los Angeles. Most of them had never even been there. But Los Angeles wanted something from Owens Valley.

Water.

Eighty years earlier, Los Angeles had all but won the California Water Wars and stolen the water from the Owens River, draining the Owens Lake dry and turning a fertile inland valley into a desert. Farms were ravaged. Spirits crushed. Families torn apart.

The farmers, poor in political power but rich in defiance, had fought back as best they could. Owens Valley in the 1920s witnessed numerous acts of sabotage against the aqueducts built to drain their water for Los Angeles taps. In the late fifties and early sixties, Dean had grown up on the desiccated remains

of the family farm, listening to his dad tell stories of
his grandfather using a pick to punch holes in the
pipes when he couldn't get his hands on dynamite.

That was when his father wasn't drunk and miserable, just miserable. Later, when the father drank too
much to tolerate, and Dean got too old to take it, he
beat up his old man and headed north on a stolen
motorbike.

The beating he gave his father never satisfied him.
It made him sorry for the old man. Dean always
thought that, if he ever decided to raise some real
hell, he'd do it to Los Angeles. And he'd do it for
Owens Valley.

Which was why Jack found himself riding Smithies's impounded Harley, hurtling toward Castaic
Lake with Dean's Hell's Angels all around him.
Castaic was a man-made lake, a reservoir that served
as the end point of the California Aqueduct. Basically, it was an enormous storage tank for most of
the water Los Angelenos drank.

And Dean was going to blow it up.

"Not just Castaic Dam," Dean told him when they
pulled over to get gas for some of the bikes. "Most
of that water comes from Northern California.
Stolen, too, I guess. No, my personal target is the
pumping station at Sylmar. That's where the Owens
water comes from. But hell, these days the water that
ruined Owens is barely a drop down in the city. So
I want to hurt them more. I figure I'll blow up both.
That's why I needed the extra shit." He hefted the
bag Jack had brought to him.

They kicked their bikes into gear and rode north on
the steadily rising Interstate 5 for a few miles before
arriving at Castaic Lake. Jack had never visited the

area, so he could do nothing but follow as Dean took an off-ramp that curved away heading toward a vast dark area to the east of the interstate. The road led to small collection of buildings.

There was a gate, and floodlights, but the bikers didn't seem bothered by them at all. One of the gang hopped off his bike and lifted a pair of bolt cutters off the back, walked boldly up to the gate, and snapped off the thick chain locking the gate closed. The sign on the gate read CASTAIC DAM—STATE WATER PRO- GRAM RESERVOIR—ACCESS RESTRICTED. The biker pushed open the gate and Dean's gang rolled in.

Jack felt a fist close hard around his heart as he realized just how easily terrorists could wreak havoc on vital locations inside the United States.

4:32 A.M. PST
Shoemacher Avenue, Los Angeles

It might have been the longest fifteen minutes of Harry Driscoll's life. It was certainly the most hor- rific. For that time period, he had become Father Col- lins's confessor, listening as the priest unburdened himself of many, many years of sins. And those sins were many: lust, gluttony, avarice, selfishness. But all his sins, in whatever form, were always, always visited upon children.

What horrified Driscoll most was the tender terms in which Collins spoke of the kids he had abused and sodomized. They were his lambs, his own flock, his tender charges. When Driscoll mentioned Aaron Biehn's name, Collins's face softened and his eyes drifted off nostalgically.

Harry resisted the urge to slap him.

"Oh God," Collins cried softly as he finished describing his many acts, and those of Father Giggs. "God, forgive me for what I've done. I've been terrible."

Harry stood up. His voice was hoarse. He'd spent a twenty-year career digging at the underbelly of the city, rooting out the bad things that grew there. He decided he'd never seen a more horrible or pathetic creature than this. "I don't know if God forgives people like you," he rasped. "I sure as hell don't. And I hope the judge doesn't, either. Get up."

Collins seemed to know he was beaten. He stood meekly. Harry grabbed the priest's good arm firmly and walked him out the door into the chilly morning air.

"Am I being arrested?" Collins said, as naïve as ever. Harry wondered if he was mentally deficient. "I . . . I have a presentation to give for the Pope."

"You're going to miss it," the detective replied. He opened the car door and guided Driscoll into the backseat. Harry couldn't handcuff the wrist on the priest's bad arm, so he hooked one ring around Collins's good right wrist and the other to his left ankle.

He closed the door and hurried around to driver's side, jumped in, and drove off toward Parker Center.

He was too disturbed by the images in his head to see the car ease away from the curb behind him.

4:51 A.M. PST
Castaic Dam

At least there was a night watchman, Jack thought ironically. Of course, he hadn't done much except sputter and wheeze as Dean strode up to him, beat him senseless, and then tossed him into a storage shed.

Beyond the buildings they could see the enormous bulk of Castaic Dam, not much more than a giant earthworks thrown across a ravine. Below it, a shallow gorge ran down toward Santa Clarita and, below that, to the main suburbs of Los Angeles.

"That's a whole lotta water behind there," said one of the bikers. "That flood the city?"

"Nah," said another. This was the tubby biker who'd put Jack down in the dirt earlier. "Too far to travel. It'll get Santa Clarita real wet, prob'ly, and mess up a lot of shit in the San Fernando Valley."

Dean nodded. "Yeah. I'm not trying to flood the city. I'm just taking away its water."

Jack understood enough about Los Angeles history to know what that dam meant. Los Angeles was built mostly on desert, and relied on the massive California Aqueduct to bring in most of its drinking water from the north. Castaic was the storage tank for all that water. Wreck Castaic, and millions of acre-feet of water just drained into the dust.

"Let's go," Dean said.

It was the tubby biker, whose name was Barny, who seemed to know what he was doing. He directed several of the bikers as they broke out packets of plastic explosives—some of which, Jack guessed, were the plastic explosives Farrigian had sold to them instead of the Islamists—and began telling them how to lay it along strategic points of the dam. The dam itself was nothing like Jack expected. He'd visited large dams before, and they usually looked like giant medieval castles. Castaic, however, was little more than a dirt dike reinforced with rocks and other debris to prevent erosion. It was, however, tall at over four hundred feet, and there was a huge amount of water behind it.

"You gonna help, or what?" Barny challenged. Jack realized that he had hesitated while the others were hiking out along the foot of the dam.

"Yeah," Jack replied. "I plan on helping a lot."

· ·

THE FOLLOWING TAKES PLACE
BETWEEN THE HOURS OF
5 A.M. AND 6 A.M.
PACIFIC STANDARD TIME

· ·

5:00 A.M. PST
CTU Headquarters, Los Angeles

"You could go home, you know," Christopher Henderson said.

"And miss all this action?" Nina Myers said, waving her arm across the empty conference room and the darkened main office beyond. "Actually, I don't feel right going to bed when there's someone out there undercover."

"Jack'll be all right," Henderson replied.

"He will?" Nina replied. "You know Chappelle screwed him over." She looked around, not sure if the Division Director was still lurking around the office. "He's out there with no backup, and if he goes under, Chappelle is going to chalk it up to the CIA instead of us."

Henderson had to agree, but he also knew that Jack hadn't been presented with much of a choice. "We have the same SWAT unit on call as we did before. It worked out when Jack was with Smithies."

Nina threw him a disapproving look. "Smithies was alone. This time it's a bunch of bikers. The response team isn't trailing them; they're a couple miles away. It's bullshit and you know it."

"Jack can take care of himself." Henderson shrugged, and the two sat in silence for a moment. Nina sipped her coffee before changing subjects. "What do you think of that NTSB woman?"

Henderson grinned. "You jealous that you're not the only queen bee at the moment? Get used to it when this place is really staffed."

Nina gave him a one-fingered wave. "She bugged me earlier. Her thing about Farrigian. I didn't like it."

"What?" Henderson was only half listening. It had been a long time since he'd pulled an all-nighter, and he was barely surviving this one. Thank god for coffee.

"Well, Jack was right. What are the odds of different agencies stumbling over two different groups with two different supplies of plastic explosives."

"Not all that likely, but we're brand-new here. Who knows what we're going to uncover."

Nina held up her hand to stop him. "That's right, we're brand-new. And we sent a brand-new investigator who doesn't do undercover. With no backup. Do we even have audio? Of course not. But we accepted her version of a story told by an arms dealer."

"And it's working out," Henderson said. "Jack's on to something."

Nina felt like she'd bumped her head against a wall. She paused a moment, then said. "What's the best kind of lie?"

"I don't follow."

"The best kind of lie isn't one that stops your investigation. It's the kind that sends it somewhere else. Somewhere that looks like a payoff."

"You think Farrigian lied," Henderson concluded. "Even though we got information that's leading us right to a terrorist plot we're about to stop?"

"I think I'm tired but I can't sleep," Nina said, downing her coffee. "And I don't like being the one sitting around. I'm going to go see what's up with this Farrigian."

5:06 A.M. PST
Castaic Dam

Jack followed Barny's directions, slid down a dirt slope next to the maintenance sheds, and started to walk along the base of the dam with the rest of Dean's gang. There was nothing high-end or technical about this area: it was a dry gulch. If there was a spillway somewhere, Jack couldn't see it. Maybe there was no need in thirsty Los Angeles.

Jack also wasn't sure how much damage the plastic explosives would do against that formidable earthworks dam. But as the group walked along the dam base, Barny was being very precise about where he wanted the charges placed. Jack drifted toward the back of the group, then reached behind his back to pull out the Sig that no one had bothered to take from him.

As his hand closed on the weapon, he felt tempered steel push against his temple.

"How fucking stupid do you think I am?" Dean's voice growled.

Jack's answer was a quick grab at the weapon, redirecting it, and a kick to Dean's groin. The biker grunted but didn't go down, while Jack felt a half-dozen hands and arms wrap him up and tackle him to the ground. He bit someone hard and managed to headbutt another biker, but there were too many of them, and they had him pinned a moment later.

Dean stood over him, his face mostly hidden by the predawn gloom but his bulk unmistakable. "You little shit," he said. "You think I wouldn't recognize a cop trying to get close to me? I thought you guys gave that shit up years ago."

Jack would have shrugged if he could have moved any part of his body under the pile of limbs. "Well, you can't have gotten any smarter."

Dean laughed. "We'll see. Stand him up."

They dragged Jack to his feet. He relaxed, hoping the two or three bikers that continued to hold him would loosen up, but they remained on guard. "We'll let our friend here plant the explosives for us. No sense in risking all our necks. Rig him up."

It was fast thinking, what they did to Jack—so fast that Jack couldn't help but wonder how Dean got the idea for it. Barny, who clearly had some knowledge of explosives, rigged a brick of plastic explosives to Jack's back where it was hard to reach, and added a detonator. Then he held up a cell phone, punching in a phone number. "I press send and you go boom," the fat man said. "You get it?"

Jack nodded.

"We'll be standing right over here. You make a run for it, and you die. I see you reach back there, you die. I'm going to mark the exact spots where I want you to put them."

Barny walked away along the base of the wall. Jack could feel Dean grinning at him, and he could feel the weight of the plastic explosives strapped to his back.

5:18 A.M. PST
Mid-Wilshire Area, Los Angeles

Traffic had started early, and like an early snow it had caught everyone by surprise. Almost a half hour after leaving Shoemacher Avenue, Harry Driscoll was still stuck on Wilshire Boulevard, where the irresistible force of L.A. traffic had met up with the immovable object of a CalTrans repair project. Checking the traffic news, Harry learned that Cal-Trans in its infinite wisdom had decided to effect repairs on Wilshire, Olympic, and Pico all on the same morning, clogging the three major surface arteries running east to west in the city.

"Your tax dollars at work," he muttered.

Collins had been quiet since they'd driven away from his home, but whether it was from fear or relief that his monstrous nature had finally been exposed, Harry couldn't tell.

"I'm getting off this street," Harry said, not really talking to Collins.

He jerked the wheel left and honked, inching his way through three rows of traffic heading in the other

direction, waving politely at the drivers who blared
their horns and flipped him off. Right of way in Los
Angeles was never given, only taken; that was Harry's
motto.

He found himself on Rossmoor, a residential
street in the Hancock Park neighborhood. A few
other cars had peeled off the main drag as well, but
after a block Driscoll was alone. He pulled up to a
stop sign at the next intersection and reached toward
his glove compartment to get his maps when he felt
something jolt his car hard, banging his head into
the dashboard.

Rear-ended. "Son of a bitch!" he grunted, pushing his hand on his head to squeeze away the pain.
'Worst goddamned day of my life. You stay here," he
snapped at Collins.

Harry got out of the car with a scowl on his face
and turned to look at the black Chrysler 300C that
had bumped into the back of his car. His scowl turned
to surprise and then fear as he saw the Chrysler's
door open and a small barrel jut out, aimed right
at him. Harry was ducking and spinning before he
heard the first sharp, angry cracks of gunfire.

5:27 A.M. PST
Farrigian's Warehouse, West Los Angeles

Nina reached the gate of Farrigian's Warehouse and
tested it; finding it unlocked, she slipped inside. She
had no plan, and no cover story, but she wasn't expecting much trouble from tepid criminals like the
Farrigian brothers. As she had told Henderson, she

hated just sitting around, but she wasn't expecting to glean much information from this field trip.

Which was why she was stunned by what she saw in the parking lot.

It was Diana Christie's car. She was sure of it. Christie had parked in one of CTU's brand-new authorized-visitors-only spots for several hours. What the hell was she doing back here?

5:28 A.M. PST
Mid-Wilshire Area, Los Angeles

Michael kept up a steady barrage of gunfire, his silenced .40 caliber semi-automatic puncturing the Acura the detective had been driving. The detective had managed to scramble around to the far side of the car for cover, and he wasn't sure if he had been hit or not. Michael had started to advance, but the man squeezed off a few rounds that kept Michael down.

Still, he couldn't wait much longer. Seconds were ticking by, and when enough of those seconds had passed the police would come, and he couldn't allow that for many, many reasons. "Go," he ordered the man in the passenger seat. It was Pembrook, the best of his small security detail. Pembrook bolted toward the Acura, even as the detective fired again. Pembrook flinched and dropped to one knee, but kept firing. Silenced rounds shattered the glass.

No! Michael thought. *We need Collins.*

Pembrook stood and fired. Michael saw the rounds shatter the window, saw Collins shudder and go limp. "Stop!" he yelled.

Pembrook halted at his shout, confused. "Get the body!" Michael yelled. "Get the body!" Pembrook started forward again, but now sirens wailed in the distance. The detective's gunfire had awakened the residents. "Forget it!" Michael yelled, causing Pembrook to stutter once again. Seeing Michael dive back into the car, Pembrook scrambled back to the Chrysler.

5:31 A.M. PST
Farrigian's Warehouse, West Los Angeles

Nina tested the doors of the warehouse but found them locked. She started to walk the wall, looking for a window or other entry, but as she neared the corner, she heard the door open behind her. She pressed herself against the wall and listened.

". . . you have to get it out. I did what you asked," said Diana Christie. She sounded near to panic.

"It's not me, I told you," said a voice Nina assumed belonged to Farrigian. "I've got nothing to do with that."

A car roared by, drowning out part of Christie's response. ". . . one I know," she was saying. "Please."

"You did what they asked. Go home. I'm sure they'll be in touch."

Nina heard the door close and footsteps walk away. A moment later a car door opened and closed, and Diana Christie drove away.

"What the hell is that all about?" Nina said quietly. "And who is she working for?"

5:45 A.M. PST
Castaic Dam

The sun was rising as Jack finished planting the armed C–4 along the base of the dam as Barny had directed. He resented every moment of it as much as he resented the weight of the plastic explosives strapped to his back. After placing the last brick and activating the detonator, he turned back toward the dirty slope where Dean waited.

The hike back took a few minutes, made longer by the smarmy grin on Dean's face as Jack trudged back up the slope.

"Well, I gotta say that made this more fun than I expected." The biker laughed. "I had time, I'd try to figure out who you are and how you got on to me, but I figure I'll find out soon enough. When you disappear, more cops are bound to sniff around."

"They're around now," Jack bluffed. "Wait a few minutes."

"Nah." Dean brushed off the attempt. "They'd have come down on us the minute we strapped a bomb on your back. You're alone. Why, I got no idea. But I'll take it."

"Can I blow him up now?" Barny asked.

Dean shook his head. "Go down and make sure he did it right. I don't trust him."

Barny nodded and trotted down the slope, followed by one of the other bikers. Jack glared at Dean's grinning face. "It was too easy," Dean noted.

Barny came back after a few minutes, puffing and sweating. "He tried to fuck us. He disabled the receivers on all the detonators. I fixed it, but I had to use the delayed fuse. The bombs will detonate about five minutes after we send the signal."

Dean nodded. "Dump him in the reservoir."

1 2 3 4 5 6 7 8 9
10 11 12 **13** 14 15 16 17
18 19 20 21 22 23 24

• •

THE FOLLOWING TAKES PLACE
BETWEEN THE HOURS OF
6 A.M. AND 7 A.M.
PACIFIC STANDARD TIME

• •

6:00 A.M. PST
St. Monica's Cathedral, Downtown Los Angeles

Pope John Paul woke suddenly, but gently, as he
always did. He liked to think it was the peace of
God, though in his heart he could not be sure. It
had been his career-long secret weapon, this ability to wake up gently, but immediately, with a mind
focused on the affairs of the day. That morning, he
woke up with the Unity Conference, and all it represented, clearly in mind. He understood, as so few
seemed to, what was at stake. East and West were
headed for a reckoning of tragic proportions. Someone needed to blunt the impact of the collision, bring
the two sides together with a handshake rather than
a clenched fist.

6:01 A.M. PST
Castaic Dam

Jack punched the closest biker in the face. The man staggered back, and Jack kicked him hard in the chest, sending him sprawling down the slope.

"Blow him—oh," Dean said, the grin falling off his face.

Jack had known it from the minute they allowed him to walk back up the slope. They couldn't detonate the bomb on his back when he was standing right among them. But they would scatter, and they were already trying. He had to get to Barny and his cell phone. Jack lunged at the fat biker, tripping him. But huge, viselike hands grabbed him, dragging him backward. Jack didn't resist. Instead he spun and traveled with the pull, tucking his chin and ramming his forehead into Dean's chest. He followed it with a knee that connected with Dean's groin. The big man doubled over like he was hugging Jack. Jack grabbed his hair at the temple and twisted it, peeling Dean's head away, and headbutted him again, this time in the face. He felt teeth give way.

But he couldn't stay with Dean. Barny had the phone that would trigger the bomb on his back. He spun and jumped down the slope. Barny, fat and slow, was just getting to his feet. He was holding a cell phone in his hand, his fingers fumbling at it, when Jack reached him and leaped, landing with both feet hard on Barny's back like a surfer atop his board. Barny grunted and his arms sprawled out, but he managed to keep his grip on the phone. Jack hopped from Barny's back and landed hard with one foot on the biker's right wrist. Barny howled but managed to press his thick thumb on the send button just before Jack crouched down and tore the mobile phone out of his clutched hand.

6:04 A.M. PST
Los Angeles

Harry Driscoll had been sitting on the curb on Rossmoor Avenue for nearly twenty minutes. He was in a daze. Twenty-plus years on the force, and this was only the second time he'd been in a firefight. The first time, Jack Bauer had saved his ass. This time, Harry had the funny feeling that Bauer was somehow the cause of it.

Though he was built like a fireplug and tough as iron, Harry hadn't joined the force out of machismo. He was no cowboy and had never wanted to be. He believed in justice, and wanted to keep his streets safe. He had been very satisfied with the role of a beat cop, and then been elated to move up into the ranks of detective, where he could pursue the criminals he knew were out there. His promotion to Robbery-Homicide, the elite unit in LAPD, had been one of the most gratifying moments of his life. He preferred rooting out the bad guys through solid detective work, and though he wasn't afraid to face danger, he'd never lusted for the thrill of bullets whizzing around him.

During the last twenty minutes there had been squad cars, ambulances, and other detectives. He had answered their questions the way dazed witnesses and victims often answered his: distantly, hollowly, as though the incident had happened to someone else.

But one thing kept going through Driscoll's mind, even while he finished answering their questions, even while the forensics guys worked on the cars and examined Father Collins's corpse. Why had one of the gunmen shouted, *Get the body! Get the body!*

6:05 A.M. PST
Castaic Dam

Jack stomped on Barny's head. He looked back up the slope, but none of the other bikers was in sight. His fingers tore at the backpack that had been strapped so tightly to his chest. They'd lashed the two shoulder straps together across his chest—a simple bind that wasn't meant to stop him indefinitely, just make it hard enough to undo without them seeing his struggles. He bent down and fished through the pockets of the now-motionless biker until he found a small folding knife. Flipping it open, he cut through the bindings and slipped the backpack off, hurling it from him and dropping flat, using Barny as cover.

But the bomb he'd been wearing didn't go off. The digital timer hadn't even started counting down.

Instead of relief, Jack felt a sickening pit open in his stomach. Jumping to his feet, he ran down the slope to the base of the dam and checked the first brick of plastic explosives. The digital timer on its face was counting down, the tenth-of-a-second digit flashing so fast it looked like a flickering 8.

Barny hadn't triggered the bomb on his back. He'd set off the explosives on the dam. Jack had less than five minutes to stop it.

"You can't call it off," Yasin told Michael over a mobile connection. "They will not find out in time. There are too many fail-safes and backups in this operation."

Yasin could afford to be calm. Michael could not, but he forced himself to sound relaxed anyway out of a sense of professional competitiveness. "None of the backups will work if the event itself is canceled. You can only push me so far."

"I know," Yasin agreed. "That is the reality of all blackmail. You know the power I have over you. You, not I, will decide whether it's worth it or not to follow my orders. But remember, I lose nothing by exposing the ones you try so hard to protect. I will do it willingly. And if you quit, you will lose them, and also the chance to kill a common enemy. The choice is yours."

Yasin dropped off. Michael was walking along Olympic Boulevard toward a bus stop. He had ditched the car and stripped off his black shirt, and wore only a fitted athletic T-shirt and his dark pants. He and Pembrook had separated.

Michael thought, just for a moment, about bolting. He had an escape plan, of course—a false identity, an open ticket to Venezuela, a small house there. Not really a life, but a place to bivouac. This carefully laid plan was fraying at the seams.

But his faith was too strong. Professional though he was, Michael was also a devout Catholic. A *true* Catholic. And though he despised Yasin for other reasons, the man was right in saying that they shared a common enemy. Michael had committed himself to destroying that enemy, and he would do so at any cost.

6:10 A.M. PST
Castaic Dam

Jack couldn't just pull the detonators. The triggers were not elaborate, but Barny had been clever enough to give each one a contact trigger—if the detonators were simply pulled out, a small wire still buried in the plastic explosives would trigger the brick. Pulling out the wire while the detonator was in place would have the same effect.

Disarming the detonator itself proved to be simple enough. Either Barny's knowledge did not extend to fail-safes and redundancies, or he hadn't had time to incorporate them. Jack's explosives training was not extensive, but he'd learned to both arm and disarm basic explosives while in Delta. That knowledge came in handy now as he careful removed the blast cap from each detonator. The process wasn't complicated, but he had to move slowly to prevent having the two brass connections touch. He finished the first one and saw that the digital counter had run down to 3:57.

And he had six more to go.

6:11 A.M. PST
Castaic Dam

Dean stumbled backward among the control rooms
west of the dam, still spitting out bits of his own
teeth and blood. One of his gang—Doogan, he
thought, but his head was reeling, too—was running
next to him, but the others were scattered. They'd
seen Barny go for the trigger that would blow that
Federal motherfucker to little pieces.

Dean was almost to his bike, and his head was
clearing, when he realized that he hadn't heard an
explosion of any kind. "Doog," he said through
swollen, bloody lips, "Less get back there."

6:12 A.M. PST
Castaic Dam

Jack wasn't going to make it. He'd disarmed all but
two, and the last timer had read 1:30.

Jack sprinted toward the second to last bomb,
took a deep, steadying breath, and disconnected its
blast cap. Without a current and a small charge to
set it off, the plastic explosive was now just so much
molding clay.

Forty-five seconds left. Jack sprinted toward the
last bomb, wondering if he might make it . . . but
even as he reached it, he knew the answer, and he
kept on running, reaching the far end of the dam
and driving himself up that slope until he reached
the height of the dam more than four hundred feet
above the gulch, and threw himself to the ground.

Behind and below him, hell erupted. A sound that

reminded him oddly of a lion's roar rent the air, and in an instant dirt was raining down on him, and dust filled the sky. The blast was powerful enough to make the solid earth beneath him tremble. With clods of earth still raining down, Jack leaped to his feet and ran back to the edge of the slope. A huge chunk of the dam was gone, as though scooped away by a giant hand. Water spurted through weak points in the wall in a half-dozen places. None of the newly made springs was very large, but erosion would loosen the dam further. Someone else would have to take care of that.

Jack hurried along the top of the dam, running gingerly over the weakened portion, then leaning into a full sprint as he headed back toward the maintenance sheds. His usual speed was not there because he was still carrying a stack of explosive bricks, but he was fast enough to reach the far side just as Dean's Angels came stumbling down the slope to his left. Jack dropped to one knee, letting them descend and pass, then he ran among the sheds. One of the bikers must have spotted him because he heard a howl from behind, but he didn't stop. He ran through the sheds and back to the bikes. He paused for only a second, to hang his backpack off the backseat of Dean's bike. Then ran to his own bike and, as fast as he could, lashed the stack of plastic explosives onto the seat behind him. Then he hopped on the Harley and started it up.

A bullet whined a few feet over his head. He spun the bike around, sending a spray of dirt and gravel behind him. He couldn't hear any more reports over the sound of his engine, but he thought he heard the hiss of more rounds falling and passing to the left and right. He felt a faint thud in his lower back and knew that a bullet had found its way into the stack of plastic explosives. The bricks had dispersed the bullet's force, so it hadn't penetrated his skin.

Jack raced down the access lane and onto the main road, knowing that they would give chase. He hurtled down the road for almost a mile before he found a good blind turn in the road, traveled past it, then turned and stopped in the middle of the road. He took Barny's cell phone out of his pocket. He flipped it open and pressed the menu buttons until a list of recent calls appeared. Two numbers appeared, one after the other, over and over again, and Jack knew that they were dry runs for the receivers attached to the detonators.

Just then, Dean and his bikers came roaring around the corner, not a hundred yards away. They saw Jack, and Dean's eyes lit up brighter than the early morning sun. Jack highlighted one of the two numbers and pressed send.

Nothing happened. Dean was now fifty yards away.

Jack scrolled down to the other number, held up the phone as though it were a talisman, and pressed send again.

It took a microsecond for the signal to flash from the phone to the nearest cell site to the receiver. When that fraction of a second ticked away, Dean and his bikers vanished inside a ball of fire.

6:30 A.M. PST
St. Monica's Cathedral, Downtown Los Angeles

". . . after last night's disturbances, Your Holiness,"
said Cardinal Walesa, "I don't see how we can possibly continue."

Walesa was speaking in Polish, and John Paul answered him in kind. "All the more reason, Your Eminence, all the more reason." In truth, John Paul was
somewhat rattled by the violence that had rocked the
cathedral all evening, but he refused to let it show.

He was sitting in the front room of his bedcham-
ber, surrounded by his closest advisors. Cardinal
Mulrooney was also there. It was Mulrooney who
spoke next.

"Your Holiness," he said in delicate English, "I
can only guess what His Eminence has said, but I
suspect he's urging you to postpone the Unity Conference. I am afraid I must agree."

"Postpone, yes!" Walesa said, seizing on the word.
"Postpone but not cancel. That is the word for it."

Cardinal Rausch from Germany, an old and dear
friend from John Paul's days as a cardinal, put his
own hand over the Pope's. "It might be best, Your
Holiness. No one would question the reason. The
media would be sympathetic."

John Paul looked for help from an unlikely
source—Father Martino, his press secretary. As
a calculating politician, John Paul had made use
of Martino many times, but he did not have much
affection for the man. Now, however, he thought
Martino might come in useful once again. "Father
Martino, what are your thoughts?"

Martino, perennially out of favor, was surprised to be consulted. He looked wide-eyed from cardinal to cardinal before stammering, "Well, Your—Your Holiness, on the one hand, His Eminence Cardinal Rausch is correct. The media would write a sympathetic story—"

"There!" Rausch said, patting John Paul's wrist. "You see?"

"—but, on the other hand," Martino continued, "on the other hand, the Holy Father has made a great effort, in many public statements, to define the importance of this first Unity Conference. If . . . if he were to stay, despite recent events, the media would talk about it for days. It would be a media coup."

The small congregation of cardinals murmured disapprovingly, and a few scoffed openly. Rausch turned pink. "These aren't 'recent events.' We're talking about murder! Right here!"

"But the conference will not be here," John Paul said firmly. "And murders take place every day, all around the world, in the name of religion. We must not be deterred."

He dismissed them with a nod. Only when they were gone did Giancarlo materialize out of the shadows. "Your thoughts, Giancarlo?"

The capable protector deliberated a moment. "My thoughts are always for your safety, Holy Father. My advice is obvious."

"And yet we cannot always do God's work and be safe."

Giancarlo shrugged. "The cardinals agree with me."

John Paul waved his words away. "Rausch is too

good a friend. His fear is for the flesh, when his mind should be on the church's mission. Mulrooney never supported the conference. Wait for me a moment, Giancarlo."

The Pope was too old to kneel comfortably, so in private he would pray in a comfortable chair. He did so now. His eyes closed gently, but the lids and lashes flickered ever so slightly like the tiny flashes of electricity pulsing in a radio. The security man was sure that the Holy Father was receiving some signal from heaven. Giancarlo had watched this many times. In these moments, the old Pope seemed both intimately vulnerable and utterly intangible, a holy relic that could not be harmed. Giancarlo, however, knew that was not true.

The old man sat there for more than a moment. Several minutes passed, but Giancarlo did not move. Though he felt like a traitor, he prayed that the Pope would open his eyes and decide to postpone the Unity Conference. Neither he nor the police could find any connection between the violence at St. Monica's and the Pope himself, but the murder was far too close to home for his own comfort. The prudent thing was to return immediately to the Vatican, where all the power of the church was assembled to protect the Holy Father.

Five minutes passed, then ten. Giancarlo stood, motionless. In his early years, in moments like these, he had said Ave Marias. Lately, though, he had taken to repeating to himself the poem "On His Blindness" by John Milton (even if Milton was a Protestant). It ended with the line, "They also serve who only stand and wait."

Finally, the Pope's eyes opened slowly and peacefully. He looked at Giancarlo with his keen eyes. "I will go forward, Giancarlo. If some violence should occur, will you be there for me?"

Giancarlo's expression, like his faith, never wavered.

7:00 A.M. PST
Los Angeles Department of Coroner
Forensic Sciences Lab

Harry had been down Mission Road, where the
coroner's office was located, many times during his
career. But there was something creepy about this
trip, because he didn't usually follow right behind the
bodies. He felt like a scavenger circling a carcass.

But he couldn't help it. As if being shot at wasn't
enough motivation, Harry was obsessed with the
driver's last words: *Get the body!*

What kind of assassins shot you up and then
wanted to keep the remains? What was it about the
body? Something telltale about the rounds? No,
there were plenty of rounds in and around Harry's

car, which now looked like Swiss cheese. To make sure he was dead? Probably not. *Get the body* already assumed Collins was dead.

It had to be evidence. The killers assumed that Collins was in possession of something incriminating and they wanted it. If that was true, then this case was turning into something much larger than a widespread child abuse ring. Whoever was involved was willing to kill to keep their secrets.

Harry's driver—a uniform who'd offered to give him a lift, thinking he was heading toward Parker Center—pulled into 1104 North Mission and stared white-faced at the building that housed the city's dead.

"You think they order lunch in?" the uniform said. "Who'd deliver?"

"They get plenty of deliveries," Harry said as he got out.

He showed his badge to the clerk at the front desk and waited until a coroner's assistant came out. In a city the size of Los Angeles, the coroner's office was open twenty-four hours a day, but even they had their off-peak hours. The man who appeared was young, with big curly hair that had been fashionable when Harry was this kid's age. The coroner looked sleepy, and was obviously just finishing the night shift.

"You're the detective?" he asked lazily.

"Driscoll," Harry said, flashing his badge. "I'm on the case with a body being delivered right now."

"Jason Keane," said the other. "Can we help with something? I mean, besides the obvious."

"I just want to have that body examined as soon as possible. Like, immediately," Harry underscored, a little dubious of the mop-headed kid's attention span. "Can you start now?"

Keane shook his head. "I'm not the guy. Just the assistant. The coroner left early because it was slow."

"And the morning guy—"

"Called in late," Keane said. "'S why I'm stuck here at almost quarter after."

Driscoll frowned. "Sounds like government work to me. Who's his supervisor?"

7:13 A.M. PST
Culver City

Marwan al-Hassan had finished the morning salaat and was sipping tea in his brother's breakfast nook. His left arm hurt, but he didn't care. The day he had committed himself to was now at hand, by the will of Allah. Not only would the pain in his arm vanish, but he would be gathered into paradise. And he would strike a blow against the infidels. Such a blow! Perhaps not the greatest blow, but a decisive one, like the stab of a dagger that leaves no great hole, but penetrates deep.

Yasin had explained to him the importance of the blow, especially to deal it here, on American soil. The fear it would cause, the chasms it would create between their enemies, would be significant. Marwan would be a hero, and his name would be praised.

Marwan decided to make another cup of tea.

7:16 A.M. PST
CTU Headquarters, Los Angeles

Jack hadn't felt this tired in a long time. There was a part of him that wanted to be pissed off at Christopher Henderson, or Ryan Chappelle, or both, for not providing him the backup he needed up at Castaic. Where had the surveillance been? Where was the cavalry?

These were legitimate questions, but Jack knew the answers would not satisfy him. CTU was an infant, disorganized, with unclear lines of communication. When Jack had gone after Dog Smithies, it had been with the help of Harry Driscoll and the LAPD. The Dean thing had been done strictly through CTU, and CTU definitely did not have its act together yet.

But Jack was too tired to chew anyone out, so when he staggered in the door and saw Christopher Henderson, he just shook his head reproachfully and took a seat in the conference room. He didn't know if there was going to be a debrief and he didn't care. He hadn't slept in a while, and since yesterday evening he had nearly been blown up twice and shot at twice. The phrase "third time's a charm" drifted through his mind in a very unsettling way.

There was some activity around Jack while he sat. Someone put a bagel and some coffee in front of him. Jamey Farrell had taken charge of the stack of C–4 and was examining it. Christopher Henderson was on the phone with the Santa Clarita police and the L.A. Sheriff, talking through the firefight and explosion that had left more than a half-dozen people dead near Castaic Dam.

Jack had lost his cell phone, so he dialed home

from one of CTU's landlines. Teri answered on the first ring.

"Jack?" she asked worriedly.

"Hi, it's me," he said.

"Were you home at all last night?" Teri said. "Or did you leave early?"

"Not home. I'm sorry," he said. Hearing Teri's voice was like a tonic that relaxed his muscles. But the effect was not beneficent. As he relaxed, his guard dropped, and the fatigue seemed to sink into the marrow of his bones. "You wouldn't believe the night I've had. It was like being in Delta again."

"I thought that kind of night ended with Delta," she replied. The reproach in her voice made Jack wince. "Is it over now?"

In his mind's eye, Jack saw Dean engulfed in a fireball. "Should be."

"Do you want to come home and have breakfast?"

Food, Jack thought. *Food sounds good. How long's it been since I've eaten anything?* "I'll be right there."

7:29 A.M. PST
Los Angeles Department of Coroner
Forensic Sciences Lab

Driscoll listened to the woman on the phone talking. ". . . I'm not annoyed at the early hour, Detective Driscoll. I'm annoyed that you won't listen to the facts."

"I've listened to your facts, ma'am," Driscoll argued into the receiver. "You won't listen to mine."

"You don't have any," the woman said gently.

Driscoll had to admit that he was most annoyed at her calm and rationality. She—her name was Patricia Siegman—was clearly accustomed to dealing with anxious investigators eager to receive data on their cases. She was currently handling Harry with an aplomb he would have admired, if only she were using it on someone else.

"You have a witness who was shot. I understand that, but something like sixty percent of the criminal forensics we conduct are shootings. We have a backlog, and I have two coroners out."

"But this is important—"

"—and I'll get to it today, Detective. I'll get to it by noon. I can't do any better than that."

Driscoll checked his watch. She was doing him a favor, he knew. A five-hour turnaround was ridiculously efficient. But somehow it wasn't enough for him. *Get the body!* The phrase haunted him, and maybe it was just his time around Jack Bauer, but he had a gut feeling that the explanation for that phrase was urgent.

7:33 A.M. PST
CTU Headquarters, Los Angeles

Jamey Farrell hadn't performed integral calculus since college, but she found herself dusting off her equations as she measured the bricks of C-4 that Jack Bauer had brought in. As soon as she'd measured the bricks, she took their average and scribbled it on a sheet of scratch paper.

Then she went down to the closet that currently

passed as CTU's evidence locker. The crate they'd
confiscated from Sweetzer Avenue was easy to
find—it was just about the only item in the closet.
Huffing and griping to herself, Jamey loaded it onto a
small mover's cart and pushed it back up to the computer bay she'd commandeered as a work space. The
crate still contained the C–4 they'd found. Looking
at the real deal, Jamey was struck by how obvious it
was that some of the plastic explosive had been missing. In real life the box looked much emptier than it
had on video. Just eyeballing the crate told her that
one could fit much more C–4 inside.

She frowned but continued working. Her next job
would be to measure the volume of the C–4 Bauer
had brought in, and then estimate how much (if any)
was missing. She had a sinking feeling that no one
was going to like the answer she came up with.

7:46 A.M. PST
Bauer Residence

Jack pulled into his own driveway and parked his
car. He flipped down the vanity mirror and took a
good look at himself. He'd splashed water on his
face at CTU, but he still looked dirty, sweaty, and
bruised. There were circles under his eyes the size of
gym bags.

I should have taken more time, he thought.
*Cleaned up more. Borrowed a shirt. This will be a
conversation.*

Jack didn't relish the idea of keeping secrets from
Teri. Given free rein, he'd have explained to her
every cut and bruise. But much of the information

about his job was classified, and though he told her everything he could, the result still left holes, and those holes became gaps in their relationship. Better to come home clean and happy, and avoid the need for stories altogether.

He walked in the door and entered a world entirely disconnected from the last few hours. In this world, bacon sizzled on a frying pan, channel four was broadcasting local news and traffic alerts, and Teri Bauer was trying to get Kim out of the bathroom.

"It's not that bad, Kimmy. Just come on!" She smiled at Jack as she saw him, then rolled her eyes, pointed to her chin, and mouthed the word *pimple*.

"It's huge!" Kim Bauer wailed from behind the bathroom door. "It's a volcano."

"It's stress," Teri said. "Last night was tough on everyone because of Aaron. Let me put some cover-up on it."

There was a pause, followed by a soft click as Kim unlocked the bathroom door. Teri threw her arms around Jack, kissed him, and said, "Eggs on the table. Teen crisis in the bathroom." She paused. "Did you know about Aaron Biehn?"

Jack nodded. "I heard."

"I want to know about it. After she's gone." Teri vanished behind the door.

Jack went into the kitchen and sat down at the small table there. The scrambled eggs were a little cold, but he didn't care. He felt as though he hadn't been home in weeks. While he ate, he listened to the news, simply because it sounded so wonderfully mundane: traffic on the I–10, a fight between the mayor and the city council. These were the crises most people faced. And they seemed to Jack as trivial as a pimple on the chin. But he wouldn't have it any other way.

He finished the eggs and decided that he would take a nap for a few minutes.

. . . .

THE FOLLOWING TAKES PLACE
BETWEEN THE HOURS OF
8 A.M. AND 9 A.M.
PACIFIC STANDARD TIME

. . . .

8:00. A.M. PST
Bauer Residence

Jack stretched out on the couch in his living room
and pushed the cushion under his head. And then his
cell phone rang.

"Bauer," he said unhappily.

"This is Jamey Farrell over at CTU."

"If this is about paperwork or reports, I'll come
in and answer questions in a couple of hours," he
grumbled, his eyes still closed.

"Nothing like that," she replied. "It's about the
plastic explosive you brought in."

"Uh-huh."

"Do we care if some is still missing?"

Jack opened his eyes. "What makes you think it's
missing?"

"I just analyzed the crate, and the volume of each brick of C–4. Even accounting for the bricks you dealt with, I think there still could have been several bricks left, maybe up to ten pounds of it."

Now Jack sat up, rubbing his eyes and trying to shake the sleep off his brain. "But you don't know that, right? That crate must have been a lot more full with the stuff I brought in."

"Oh, yeah," Jamey said. "But you know how a room looks bigger sometimes after you put furniture in it? Same with this box. I put the C–4 back in it, and no matter how I stuffed it, there are obvious spaces left. I did the math, too. Maybe ten pounds."

Jack didn't want to hear it. "The stuff Smithies had? The stuff that blew up Ramin?"

"Factored in."

"That is not what I want to hear," Jack admitted.

"Don't shoot the messenger. What do you want to do about it?"

Jack laughed. "Who says it's my decision?"

"I didn't ask anyone," Jamey said. "You just seemed like the guy who wants to know."

"Yeah," Jack agreed. "All right. I'm coming in."

8:05 A.M. PST
Crescent Heights Avenue, Los Angeles

Rabbi Dan Bender rarely used e-mail. He didn't trust it. Words sent electronically were as permanent as if they'd been etched in stone. He would certainly send nothing confidential over the Internet, and Rabbi Bender was in possession of many, many secrets.

He had written the first draft of the letter to his

brother on stationery, but in the end he decided against it. He needed to be sure his brother received this message, and the post between Los Angeles and Jerusalem had never been one hundred percent reliable. But, as he had already told himself, e-mail was like graven stone. His brother would see it eventually.

This is what he typed into his computer:

Dear Sam,

I hope Miriam is feeling better. You're both in my thoughts and I pray for her remission.

In the meantime, I want to send you a note of apology, and possibly a goodbye. I can't tell you why I am apologizing. You may or may not hear about it. But there is a distinct possibility that you won't hear from me after today, so I wanted to express my feelings.

You were always a better Jew than I. Even Dad thought so, although of course he was too much of a mensch to say it. You were a better rabbi, too. But there are reasons for that, some of which may become apparent to you. But among the unsaid reasons is this: you are a righteous man. In the end, I find that I am not. If I were righteous, I would not be doing what I'm going to do today.

I hope you'll forgive me.

With all my love, from your brother,
Dan

He reread the short message several times, wishing he could write more. His finger hovered over the send button for a moment. Then he clicked it, and the deed was done.

"I hope you'll forgive the cautions," said the Pope to Amy Weiss. "There was a disturbance here last night."

"No problem," Amy said, although in fact the whole affair had disturbed her. Her interview had been scheduled for two weeks; she'd passed through the background check the Vatican had required. One would have thought the metal detector and the bag search would have been enough. But the thin, soft-spoken man had come along with a nun in tow and had insisted on a complete search of her clothing and person. If all Amy had been after was the puff piece, she would have walked out. But she was now on the trail of a legitimate page one story. "In fact, I'd like to ask about that."

The Pope's eyes twinkled charmingly as he replied in his softly accented English, "I find the Unity Conference to be a much more pleasant topic, don't you?"

Amy felt the force of his charm and his authority, and tried to resist it. "Well, the two are related, aren't they? Do you consider the attacks here last night to be a threat? Are they related?"

"That is a question for a policeman, not a priest," John Paul said dismissively. "In any case, the conference will not be stopped. It is, I believe, the most important thing in the world."

"This conference?" she asked.

"Its purpose," John Paul said, putting a hand on her arm gently, almost pleadingly. "East and West; Christian, Muslim, and Jew. They are at war, or they soon will be. It is a war that may cover the world in flame. It must be averted."

Amy wanted to talk about the murders; she had been told to talk about the murders. But this old man, so small and yet so infused with power, charmed her with his sincere and plaintive voice. "But the Catholic Church has been the cause of strife, hasn't it? Are you the appropriate party to end it?"

John Paul smiled. "Who better?"

8:14 A.M. PST
CTU Headquarters, Los Angeles

Jamey Farrell spent several minutes updating Christopher Henderson on her recent findings. Henderson looked terrible, but then she probably didn't look fresh as a daisy herself. She'd seen Henderson dozing on the couch in his office, but she knew from experience that that sort of sleep had little lasting effect.

"This is the case that won't die," Henderson grumbled as she finished. "Why couldn't it have just ended when we arrested the Sweetzer Three?"

Jamey shrugged. "I'm not a field operator, but if you ask me, I think someone's been expecting us to come along. I think we're chasing lots of decoys."

Henderson shook his head. "Those bikers weren't

a red herring. They were really going to blow up the city's water reserves."

"I didn't say red herrings. I said decoys. We chased that threat because it was real, but it's got nothing to do with some other plot. Something we haven't found yet."

"Your missing C–4."

"Jesus, I hope you're wrong," said Jack Bauer, walking into the room. "I've been shot at enough for one day."

"You got here fast," Henderson noted.

Jack shrugged. "It's easy if you ignore all the traffic laws." He sat down on the couch where Henderson had earlier slept. "Look, how sure are we about this? Aren't you guys the ones who said the Ramin and Muslim connection was a different plot that had already been stopped?"

"Director Chappelle, not me," Jamey said. "And all I'm really saying is that there is still C–4 missing. And that there was a Muslim connection at the start."

"But no suspects left," Jack said. "And no target."

Nina Myers walked into the middle of the conversation. "I have a new suspect for you." She described her surveillance of Diana Christie.

When she was done, Jack tried to rub away his headache. "None of it makes sense. What the hell would an NTSB investigator be doing with a small-time arms dealer? And what does it mean for us? The lead she gave us from that conversation was real! It put us in Dean's way."

"Jamey thinks decoys," Henderson said.

Jack considered this. "Yasin. He knows we know

he's in the country. That's why Ramin's dead. Maybe he expected it, and planned this. But it's pretty elaborate."

"Not so much," Nina said. "All it really took was giving away some of the C–4 to someone who wanted to do something with it. And maybe asking them to plan their event for today. Yasin's attack may be on a different day entirely."

Jack shook his head. "Ramin thought today, and he was on that side of the equation. Okay." He gathered himself with a breath. "Are we back at square one again?"

His answer came in the form of his ringing cell phone. He gestured an apology when he saw the number, then answered. "Hey, Harry."

"Jack, you heard what happened to me?" Driscoll said quickly. When Jack replied in the negative, Harry filled him in, and Jack felt the aching pulse in his forehead increase. Biehn. Jack hadn't thought of Biehn in a couple of hours. There was a connection between Biehn and Yasin that he hadn't resolved yet. Biehn claimed he'd been kidnapped when he got close to Collins. Now Driscoll had been ambushed when he arrested Collins, and the priest had been killed. "You searched the body, right?"

"Of course. Nothing there. I did get one thing, though. I have a partial plate on the Chrysler that attacked me. I want to run it down, and I want your help."

"Okay, but why do you want help from me? You can do that on your own."

"Hmm-mmm," Driscoll refused. "I gotta tell you, Jack. The minute that guy yelled, 'Get the body,' I freaked. There's something going on here that's a lot bigger than some guy in Robbery-Homicide. There's spook stuff happening, and you're a spook."

"Okay, give me the partial."

Jack wrote it down, and handed it to Jamey. "Can you run this right away?"

Jamey blinked. "This Chrysler. You know how popular it is? There are going to be a lot of them."

"So far, you've been brilliant. You'll do it."

Jamey Farrell's glare indicated that the flattery hadn't worked. But she took the scrap of paper and left the office.

"I don't get paid enough for this," Henderson said.

"But think of all the nice people you get to spend time with." Jack laughed. He left Henderson moping at his desk and followed behind Jamey. She'd gone to one of CTU's working computers. He stood behind her as her fingers flew over the keyboard.

She knew he was there without looking. "We're authorized to tap into all kinds of databases. If it's a California plate—oh, damn."

She'd just finished, and a long list of license plates appeared. There were more than two hundred black Chrysler 300Cs. "Maybe we could get LAPD to help us track them down."

"Yeah," Jack said. "But let's play a hunch. How many of those are rental cars?"

Jamey's finger clicked again. "Five."

"Okay, let's get on the phone and find out if any of them are leased in Los Angeles right now."

They worked together, and it was done in a few minutes. There were two. One had been rented to a Sharon Mishler. They ran her information and found her to be a resident of New York, having recently arrived on a flight from JFK to LAX. They recorded her information and funneled it to LAPD to investigate. The other had been rented by a Bas Holcomb, resident of Los Angeles. Before Jack could say a word, Jamey was running down his information.

"No nothing, really," she said as she assembled information from the DMV, IRS, and several credit bureaus. "No criminal record. Certainly no connection to anything like a terrorist organization."

"He's still our best lead," Jack said. "I'll run this down with my LAPD contact."

8:39 A.M. PST
Coffee Bean & Tea Leaf, Encino, California

Yasin sat in the coffeehouse and read the news on a laptop computer while he sipped tea. He would have preferred the food and drink at Aroma Café, which was a few miles down the road, but he could not risk it. That café was frequented by dozens of Israeli immigrants, and unlike the ignorant Americans, the Israelis were perceptive enough to recognize him as an Arab, and a suspicious one at that.

Yasin himself was an American, having been born in Bloomington, Indiana—a fact that he believed he could correct only by striking a blow against his despised homeland. 1993 had been a start, but it had not satisfied him. He wasn't sure that today would scratch his itch, either, but it would do for the moment. Those he worked with in al-Qaeda desired this blow, and that was enough for him.

The method, though, had been entirely his idea. Not just the method for delivering the explosives—

although he admitted smugly that the method was brilliant—but also for the associates he had shanghaied into helping him. That had been a unique twist.

Yasin thought back to the day he had first met Abdul Mohammed, who'd been born Casey Stanwell, a Catholic until he'd been driven away from the infidel faith. It was his story that had given Yasin the idea.

Yasin sipped his tea again. He might have felt less satisfaction if he'd known that Father Collins had been killed. And that his body lay in the coroner's office ready to be autopsied. And that a Federal agent named Jack Bauer was tracking down the associates Yasin had so carefully coerced.

8:44 A.M. PST
Los Angeles

Jack pulled into a mini-mall parking lot, and the fireplug of a detective got into the car.

"You have any idea what kind of night I've had?" Driscoll said by way of hello.

"A pretty good idea, yeah," Jack replied.

"What is this we're doing now?"

Jack explained. "We traced the partial plate you gave us. There were a lot of possibilities, but we narrowed it down to a couple possibles. You and I are going after the most likely one. Rented to a Bas Holcomb, business address a mile from here."

Driscoll nodded. "If Mr. Holcomb shot up my car, I would definitely like to have a word with him."

Holcomb's address was a landscaping business

on Crescent Heights a few miles away, much more difficult to travel now that the morning traffic was in full swing. It was an old adobe-style garage converted to office space and equipment storage. There were three narrow parking spaces, one of which was occupied by a newish-looking half-ton pickup. Jack pulled into one of the others, and the two men got out. Driscoll unbuttoned the safety strap on his gun holster as they passed under a sign that read ST. FRANCIS LANDSCAPING.

The front door led to a tiny office with a desk covered in stacks of manila folders and invoices like ramparts of a castle. An old lady sat behind the desk, punching numbers into an old beige calculator that rattled off sums and spewed out tape. She looked startled to see someone walk through the door.

"Hi," Jack said in his friendliest manner. "Is Bas around?"

She didn't stand up, but she stopped banging on the calculator. "The owner hasn't been around much, lately. Not since we got that big client."

"You know where we can find him?"

The lady shrugged and started losing interest. "Probably there. Mr. Holcomb takes the work seriously."

"Where would that be?"

"The mosque down in Inglewood."

8:52 A.M. PST
Los Angeles

As the two men walked out of the office, the old woman reached for the telephone and dialed.

"Clarissa?" Mr. Pembrook said by way of answer.

She replied in a whisper, even though she knew the visitors were gone. She wasn't used to espionage. "Yes, sir. You asked me to tell you if anyone came around the office looking for Mr. Holcomb. Two men just did."

Pause. "Did they say who they were?"

"No. No, and I didn't think to ask. Is everything all right? Do we owe money?"

"No trouble, darling. Probably old friends. What did they look like?"

Clarissa described them. "A blond man, nice-looking I guess, about as tall as you. The other man was short, a black man. Looked like a weight lifter. I told them Mr. Holcomb was over at the Inglewood mosque. Do you know if he's there?"

"I can't say I know for sure," Pembrook replied.

"I hope I didn't lead them astray. Are they old friends of your partner's?"

"Oh, yeah," Pembrook said. "They're old friends, all right. Thanks, Clarissa."

8:53 A.M. PST
Renaissance Hotel, West Hollywood

Pembrook hung up his cell phone and leaned back in his chair, trying to breathe away the tightness in his chest. He wasn't as good at this as Michael. And, somehow, he hadn't expected it to go this far. The master plan had been beyond him: all Michael had ever asked of him was to act as backup muscle, which he'd been doing since their days in Special Forces.

They'd bonded back then, not just over a shared

love of violence, but over religion. They were both Catholics, and both shared similar views of certain church activities. They'd been friends ever since, and although he had a small landscaping business he shared with Bas Holcomb, his real job flowed from Michael's security work for the church.

Now Pembrook called Michael with a trembling hand. "You know what's going on?" He detailed his conversation with the assistant at his company. "We've got to disappear."

"That was true no matter what happened today," Michael said. His voice was steady. "Have we sent them on their way?"

"Yes, they're on their way to the mosque. They have Holcomb's name, too. I have to say, I'm scared shitless, but that was a good idea. It's a deflection and an early warning system all built into one."

"You can thank my Arab friend for that. He seems very good at twists and turns."

"As long as none of the twists turn back on us," Pembrook prayed.

"Amen," Michael said. "Anyway, pack. Tonight we're both getting out of here."

. . . .

THE FOLLOWING TAKES PLACE
BETWEEN THE HOURS OF
9 A.M. AND 10 A.M.
PACIFIC STANDARD TIME

. . . .

9:00 a.m.
CTU Headquarters, Los Angeles

Nina Myers decided that she had a love-hate relationship with Jack Bauer already. She liked his no-nonsense, name-taking, ass-kicking style, except when he turned it on her. She had a strong lead with this Diana Christie anomaly, and she knew it. He'd made a mistake in brushing it aside, in brushing her aside, and that pissed her off. Like a schoolgirl, she'd gone from admiring him to despising him after a single moment of neglect. She was aware of that, and it made her even angrier.

She left CTU and got into her car, laying the address to the NTSB agent's apartment on the passenger seat. She was going to confront Diana Christie on her own . . . but somewhere in the no-BS zone in her brain, she knew that she was doing it not because it was her job, but because Jack Bauer had spurned her. That made her angriest of all, and she planned on taking it out on Diana Christie.

9:03 A.M. PST
CTU Headquarters, Los Angeles

"What I'm looking for is a reason not to pull your funding and scrap the Counter Terrorist Unit right here and now," said Senator Armand from Mississippi.

It was not the best way to start a video conference, and Ryan Chappelle could feel sweat dripping down his sides beneath his dress shirt.

"That wasn't a rhetorical question, Director," Armand added into the silence that followed.

"I'm sorry, Senator," Chappelle said. "I was gathering my thoughts. May I speak freely?"

Several of the senators and congressmen on the Joint Subcommittee on National Security chuckled. Armand himself grimaced. "I prefer it to ankle licking, Director. Let's cut the bullshit and speak truth to power."

Chappelle nodded. "Because bad things are happening right now, and more bad things are on the way."

"Bad things?" Armand leaned forward, as though trying to push right through the monitor from three thousand miles away. "You sound like my four-year-old."

"If you want more details than just 'bad things,'

Senator, then give us the funding we need," Chappelle retorted. "Right now I've got three analysts, which is currently okay because I have only two working computer terminals. Only four or five field agents. You have more aides on your staff than I have agents to protect the western United States. So until you give me funding, all you get is 'bad things.'"
Take that, you pompous son of a bitch.

Another committee member, Malpartida from Texas, responded. "That's the safe reply, Director. You aren't fully funded yet, so we shouldn't expect results. I get it. But what you have done, so far, is drag your agency into the murder of a priest and several other killings. This is all very public for an agency that is supposed to be covert."

Chappelle had been ready for this, and he'd been practicing the reply for an hour, wanting it to sound crisp but not rehearsed. "We are not operating in Somalia, Congressman. We're not operating in Angola or Sarajevo. We're in downtown Los Angeles. We are not going to be able to hide everything we do."

"But what you do seems to involve murders and shootings, not stopping terrorists!" Armand broke in. "I'm getting off-the-record reports about shootings in the hills, people getting blown up on motorcycles. Is this how you're running things?"

"No, sir," Chappelle said, ready for this as well. "That wasn't one of my people. That's an operative on loan from the CIA. His case crossed ours. CTU can't be held responsible for his actions."

"What the hell was he doing blowing people up?" Armand drawled.

Chappelle explained the Castaic Dam incident to the best of his knowledge, doing his best to highlight

Bauer's maverick personality and independence from CTU. When he was done, Representative Malpartida spoke up. "I hear you. He's a loose cannon. But are you saying he single-handedly stopped these terrorists or bikers or whatever from blowing up a dam?"

The CTU Director hadn't seen the trap until too late. "Uh, well, nothing is that simple, but—"

"But?" Malpartida persisted.

"—yes, sir," Chappelle said reluctantly.

The Congressman snorted and half-spun in his chair, glancing left and right at the other assembled politicians. "Forgive me, gentlemen, but it sounds to me like we don't just need more funding, we need men like this agent!" He looked at Chappelle through the monitor. "Can't be held responsible for him? Damn, sir, it sounds like you should be begging to get some of the credit for putting him on the case!"

Chappelle's neck turned red. "Yes . . . yes, sir," he found himself stammering unhappily. "We're . . . we're trying to recruit him to the team." Even as he said it, Chappelle suspected that he would regret that statement for the rest of his life.

9:08 A.M. PST
Inglewood, California

This time, they took Harry Driscoll's car, lit up in red and blue and wailing like a banshee. Without the lights and sirens, they never would have reached Inglewood, a suburb south of downtown and near the airport, in under twenty minutes.

The mosque was an unobtrusive structure, built with discretion in mind. Harry and Jack pulled into the parking lot and looked up, seeing a short tower with the faintest resemblance to a minaret. The lawn was well-tended but nondescript, and instantly Jack wondered why they needed a landscaper. His question was answered, though, when they passed the outer wall into a courtyard that was all fountains, flower beds, and pathways, like something out of *1001 Arabian Nights*. Beyond the garden lay the mosque proper.

There was a short, thin, brown-skinned man in gray work trousers and a gray work shirt, down on one knee, pulling weeds from one of the flower beds. He didn't look up until they were standing almost on his ankles.

"Bas Holcomb?" Driscoll demanded.

"*Que?*" the man replied.

"Are you Bas Holcomb?"

"Oh. No!" the man said, smiling and standing, clapping dirt off his hands. He spoke in quiet, clipped English, as though uncomfortable with his command of the language. "My name is Javier. Espinoza. I work for St. Francis Landscaping. That's—"

"His company, we know," Driscoll interrupted. "Is he here somewhere?"

Jack's cell phone rang, and Harry continued the interrogation while Jack stepped aside.

The gardener shook his head. "I no see him. He supposed to be here?"

"You tell me," Driscoll retorted.

The gardener shrugged. "'S not my usual job. I covering for the regular guy. He sick. I usually work at another place for them."

Jack closed his phone and looked at Driscoll irritably. "My people just got ahold of the car rental agency. The Chrysler was supposed to have been returned yesterday. Holcomb's house is vacant, and he hasn't made a call from there in forty-eight hours."

"He skipped town," the detective deduced.

"It gets worse. The Chrysler was found this morning abandoned on a side street. No prints. No one's heard from him in days."

Driscoll knew what Jack was thinking, but they couldn't discuss it in front of a civilian. "Okay," he said to the gardener. "If we need to talk to you, can we reach you through the landscaper?"

"Sure," Javier Espinoza said, "or most days at the other place. That's where I work for them."

"What's the other place?"

"Sante Monica."

9:18 A.M. PST
Santa Monica, California

Nina didn't hesitate. She pulled her car up to the little postwar bungalow on Twenty-sixth Street below Pico, walked up the little path, and kicked in the door. She didn't throw around that much weight, but what she lacked in size, she made up for in technique. Her foot connected right where the bolt should be, and the door flew inward, banging against the wall, and Nina was already inside, scanning the room over the top of her muzzle.

Diana Christie ran halfway into the room, startled by the noise. Her left arm was in a sling and she held a small semi-automatic in her right hand, but she didn't raise it. When she saw Nina, her eyes filled with fear.

"Drop the weapon!" Nina ordered.

Diana did so immediately. She held up her good arm and backed away from Nina. "Oh god," she said in sheer terror. "Get out of here. They'll know! They'll know!" She sounded on the verge of hysterics.

"Down on the ground!" Nina demanded, advancing steadily.

"No, please, you don't understand—"

"Get on the ground, now!" Nina was almost within arm's reach. Suddenly, Diana Christie bolted. She ran out of the living room and down a hallway, then through another door. Nina followed a few steps behind, and they ended up in a small, cramped garage, with Diana on the far end pressed against the door, and Nina at the interior door, her sights level on Christie's chest.

"Get out of here!" Christie pleaded, tears streaming down her face. "Get out of here!"

Nina was about to respond, but a bomb went off, and a gruesome image of bright lights and blood splashed across her retina.

9:25 A.M. PST
St. Monica's Cathedral, Downtown Los Angeles

Mulrooney heard Michael enter his office. He could always tell it was Michael by the sound, or rather, the near-lack of it. Michael's footsteps reminded him of the padding of cat's paws from his childhood.

"Big day, Michael," Mulrooney said.

"Very big, Your Eminence," the security man agreed.

Mulrooney noticed that Michael had lost some

of his gleam. There had always been a sort of sheen around the man, a halo, for lack of a better word. Now it was tarnished. "Is everything all right with our . . . problem?"

Michael shrugged uncertainly, a gesture as uncommon as the fatigue that showed on his face. "I believe so, Your Eminence, but I can't be sure. Dortmund is no longer a problem, and of course Giggs is gone. Collins is also dead."

The Cardinal felt no remorse. "Monsters all. If it weren't to protect the church, I'd have thrown them out myself. Is there any . . . are there any witnesses?"

The security man said, "No one firsthand, Your Eminence. I don't know what Father Collins might have told the police officer, but at least Collins himself cannot testify to anything." Michael could not bring himself to mention the other man who knew so much about the abhorrent acts of the clergy, and the church's attempts to cover them up: that bastard Yasin, whom Michael would deal with someday.

Mulrooney nodded with satisfaction. "Then you've done as much as you can, Michael. Thank you. You are a soldier for the true church."

Mulrooney said, and Michael received, the phrase *the true church* with a profound respect. When Michael didn't reply, Mulrooney continued. "I can't wait until this damned conference is over. I want that false Pope out of my diocese!"

"It will be over soon, Your Eminence," Michael promised. "But on that count, I have a favor to ask of you. You must excuse yourself from the Unity Conference. Make an appearance at the reception, but then beg off."

Mulrooney almost passed over the request, disregarded it, but it stung him after the fact, like the butterscotch taste of whiskey that burns the throat a moment later. He stopped—his every muscle locked into place where he sat, as he might have done if a wild dog had suddenly appeared in his office, growling at him.

"Michael, what is going on?" he asked.

Michael had been preparing for this conversation, but in no version had it seemed satisfactory. "Your Eminence, there is nothing for you to know. Or, rather, there are two things. First, that you must be out of the reception hall a few minutes after it begins. Second, that everything I do, I do to protect the true church."

Mulrooney studied Michael, and felt in that moment that although the man had worked for him for several years, and that (though the Cardinal would barely admit it to himself) Michael had done many unscrupulous deeds at his request, he didn't really know the man at all. "Have you . . . are you going to do something?"

"Not me, Your Eminence," he said matter-of-factly. "But a thing will be done. The less you know, the better."

With that, Michael turned and walked out, leaving the Cardinal of Los Angeles to wrestle with a conscience he had ignored for many, many years.

9:33 A.M. PST
Santa Monica

Nina Myers picked herself up off the floor. She could hear nothing but a loud ringing in her ears.

The garage was on fire. She saw the smoke and the flames, but she couldn't hear the noise. If fire trucks were on their way, she had no idea. The garage—what she could see of it through clouds of dust and smoke—had been blasted by the bomb. Chunks of wall had been blown away, and the big garage door was twisted on its hinges.

She knew she'd been unconscious, but she didn't know for how long. Her mind had constructed a fantasy of sleep and vacation. Was she on vacation? Had she been sleeping? No, she didn't sleep in a garage. A bomb. A bomb had exploded. She'd been concussed. She might be seriously injured. Nina's eyes swam in and out of focus, so from a kneeling position she patted her hands up and down her body. She felt skin, and clothes, and wetness that was probably her blood. She was cut! No, not her blood. Diana Christie's blood, splattered all over her. Diana had been blown up.

Weirdly, it occurred to Nina that Jack Bauer had first come to CTU the night before after being nearly blown up. Shit, she was coming in second to him already. She felt professional jealousy rear its ugly head.

You are delirious, lady. Unrattle your brain!

Nina grabbed hold of something sturdy—a tabletop?—and pulled herself to her feet. She shook her head but still couldn't see, so she felt her way to a wall, and then to the interior door. She had to get out. She had to stop the ringing in her head. And she was sure there was something important about the bomb that had just gone off. Something she couldn't quite draw into the clear part of her brain . . .

Jon Boorstein liked his brand-new BMW 730i. He liked ordering Armani (in the same waist size for the last seven years, thanks to his trainer Gunnar). He liked Cannes and he liked the after-parties at the Oscars.

He did not, however, like his job. His job was the price he paid for the good things in life.

"But what a fuckin' price," he muttered as he glided his Beemer through the self-opening gate of Mark Gelson's Malibu home.

He hopped out and walked through the door, which was opened by Lucia, without breaking stride. He didn't look at the elaborately carved crucifix hanging on the wall—the thing always gave him the creeps. Walking by that thing was about the only time Boorstein ever appreciated his Judaism, which forbade graven images.

Mark was sitting on the deck overlooking the sand and the Pacific, reading the *Times*. Though he was good-looking by any other standard, in Hollywood he was over the hill. Some actors, especially men, aged into new roles and remained sex symbols—hell, Bruce Willis was heading toward fifty, wasn't he? Others couldn't let go of the man they'd been in their twenties, so they got grouchier as they aged, and the resentment showed.

Boorstein had tried, a year or two ago, to encourage Gelson to move past his *Future Fighter* persona. If he'd managed the aging process well, he'd have a whole new set of doors opening for him. But Gelson couldn't, so he didn't, and now he was slowly dropping down on Boorstein's must-call-back list.

"Hey, Jon," Gelson said, as though surprised to see him. "What's up?"

"Headlines," Boorstein said, sitting down. "They're up all over the place, and they're talking about you. But not the way we want."

"Don't PR guys say there's no such thing as bad publicity?"

"They do say that," Boorstein agreed irritably. "But they don't have clients who talk about blowing people up."

"Don't worry about it," Gelson said. "It'll all blow over soon enough."

Boorstein heaved a dramatic sigh. "Maybe, maybe not. Here's the problem, my friend. You are moving out of the where-are-they-now file and into the what-have-they-done-with-their-life file. That means that people aren't doing bios on you, but when you fall on your face, they want to tell that story."

"Thanks for reminding me," Gelson said. "You pitch that to *Entertainment Weekly*?"

Boorstein snorted. "Them I tell about your next this, your upcoming that. But you I level with. The mug shot was already in the paper. But I know two reporters who are doing a follow-up, digging up dirt." Boorstein's voice grew suddenly grave, and his cavalier movements settled into focused attentiveness. "So tell me, is anyone going to find out about this whole Catholic Church thing?"

Gelson looked calm, almost serene. "I don't think I care anymore, Jonny. I don't scream and shout about it. Why should they care?"

"Because Catholics go see movies. And if they hear that you are a schizophrenic—"

"Schismatic," Gelson corrected.

"Yeah, that. Then they might stop going to see your movies, and then people would stop paying you, and I wouldn't get paid, and that would be bad."

Gelson looked out at the ocean. "You know, the Catholic Church is the oldest continuously existing entity in the Western world. That's a powerful thing all by itself. Then of course you add the grace of God and—well, never mind. But it's been around. And it's worked. It brought education and enlightenment. It was Catholic priests in Ireland that preserved Western civilization during the Dark Ages. One church, unbroken, unchanged. That's why it lasted. It remained true. Until the sixties."

Boorstein wished he didn't need the history lesson, but he did. If anyone had ever told him about Vatican II, and the massive changes the Pope had ordered, he didn't remember. But Gelson told him in detail about the changes in the catechisms, in the Mass, and so many other vital parts of the service.

"Hundreds of years, Jonny. Hundreds. And then, wham! It all gets changed by one man."

"By . . . the Pope," Boorstein reminded him.

"Not my Pope," Gelson said.

Boorstein shrugged. "Look, none of your fans are going to care about a theological debate. Just don't say or do anything crazy. Okay?"

Gelson shrugged. "No promises."

• •

THE FOLLOWING TAKES PLACE
BETWEEN THE HOURS OF
10 A.M. AND 11 A.M.
PACIFIC STANDARD TIME

• •

10:00 A.M. PST
Mid-Wilshire Area, Los Angeles

"You know, I came across an honest-to-god coincidence once," Harry Driscoll said as he and Jack Bauer drove back to Jack's car. "When I got out of the academy, I moved into apartment 432 at 1812 Delaware Avenue, and I got a new phone number. Swear to god the phone number was 432–1812."

"No kidding," Jack said.

"No kidding," Harry repeated. "But in twenty years of detective work, that's the only goddamned coincidence I ever came across. There are no coincidences. Ever."

"St. Monica's," Jack said, cutting to the chase.

"Saint friggin' Monica's," the fireplug of a detective replied. "Why is it you go there twice in one night. The priest that I arrest, who works there, gets shot. And now the guy who rented the car that shot me up, who seems to have disappeared, runs a business that takes care of the place." Harry shook his head in disbelief. "You keep chasing this C–4 all over the city, and we keep ending up back at St. Monica's every time."

"I'm with you," Jack said, "but where's the next step? At least, where is it as far as the terrorists are concerned? You've absolutely got a criminal investigation to chase down, with child molestation and priests who should probably be castrated. But what about the plastic explosives? There's no connection for me, as far as I can tell."

Driscoll said, "You know the connection. Biehn said that whoever kidnapped him also knew about the terrorist, Yasin's his name, right?" Jack nodded. "So the kidnapper takes Biehn, who was shadowing Collins. Same kidnapper has knowledge of some terrorist thing connected with Yasin. You got to figure that the same terrorist tried to kill me when I went after Collins."

"We need that autopsy," Jack said.

10:05 A.M. PST
Santa Monica

We need our own forensics team, Nina thought. *Add it to the list.*

Not that Santa Monica PD's team was bad. But even if they did everything by the book, there would be bureaucracy. Information would have to flow up the chain at the local PD, then back down through the Federal agencies. And by that time it might be too late.

These guys hadn't even treated her like a colleague. The fire truck and black-and-white that arrived together on the scene had first treated her like an accident victim, then the cops had briefly put handcuffs on her when they realized a bomb had gone off, and then they had ignored her when someone checked her credentials through the State Department.

Now one of the forensics techs, a tall, ugly man with lanky black hair and pockmarks, approached her with a quizzical look on his face. "Ma'am, a question?"

"Fire away," she said. "What have you guys got?"

"Well," he said, then stopped. He furrowed his brow, creating deep lines above his pockmarked cheeks. Finally, he asked, "Was the victim . . . was she holding anything when the bomb went off?"

Nina tried to think back. At first her memory was fuzzy, but then she recalled Christie dropping her handgun. Her right hand had been empty. Her left arm had been in a sling. "No. Not unless she was hiding something in the sling on her arm. Why?"

The tech's quizzical look deepened. "Well, only because the explosion . . . well, the explosion looks like it happened right where she was standing. Was she wearing a bomb?"

Nina shook her head. "I guess she might have been. I didn't see anything big on her. But my brain is pretty banged up."

"Okay, thanks," the tech said, but he left looking even more perplexed.

Nina took out her cell phone, thankful that it still worked, and dialed the number for Jack Bauer. He answered quickly. "It's Nina Myers," she said.

"Hey," he said. "I'm headed back to CTU. Are you there?"

"Santa Monica. I've got news for you. I went to see Diana Christie to talk to her about her and Farrigian."

"What did she say."

"She blew up." Nina described her brief, explosive encounter with the NTSB investigator. She was gratified when Bauer said, "It sounds like Ramin. You may have been right. Are we running a background check on her?"

"I'll do it. But you know this thing is getting crazier, right? Yesterday she was the one pushing for an investigation. Then last night she sends us on a wild-goose chase. Today she blows up."

Jack agreed. "This whole thing is convoluted. Someone set it up that way."

"Yasin?"

"Has to be. But there's someone else. Someone on the front line who can move around without arousing suspicion. And they planned so that we've spent the last twelve hours running after everything but their target."

"What do you want to do?"

"I'm done playing. I'm going to go ask some people some hard questions. Starting with that weasel of an arms dealer."

10:12 A.M. PST
Melrose Avenue, Los Angeles

Gary Khalid lifted his demitasse with a trembling hand. He couldn't get it to stop shaking. Anyone watching would have laid the blame on the four triple espressos he had drunk. But it wasn't so. Khalid was excited and terrified and ready to get out of the country. He dared not return home. Considering the fact that the priest's body was in the hands of the authorities, it was only a matter of time before the police uncovered their carefully laid plan. And eventually, Yasin had assured him, they would reexamine the history of Ghulam Meraj Khalid.

10:13 A.M. PST
CTU Headquarters, Los Angeles

"I already gave you the best example I can, sir," Chappelle said. He was disciplined enough to keep the fatigue and annoyance out of his voice. If they thought redundancy and tedium could wear him down, they had seriously underestimated Ryan Chappelle. "But let me do so again. Right now I have agents spread thin all over Los Angeles, running from place to place because I don't have manpower to chase down several leads at once . . ."

10:14 A.M. PST
Mid-Wilshire Area, Los Angeles

Jack sped back to Farrigian's warehouse with a grim look on his face. He was sick of being bounced around. He was going to ask questions and keep asking until he got answers.

10:15 A.M. PST
CTU Headquarters, Los Angeles

". . . drafted other agencies into our pursuit of terrorists," Chappelle said into the video monitors.

"Isn't that positive?" a Congresswoman asked. "Multiagency involvement means greater pooling of knowledge, doesn't it?"

"And a greater chance of leaks, or worse, ma'am," Chappelle said. "And different agencies have different agendas, and different command structures. Even if the people themselves are good, we won't know what kinds of bureaucracies they'll have to deal with."

10:16 A.M. PST
Los Angeles Department of Coroner
Forensic Sciences Lab

Harry Driscoll felt his bones start to ache. He was getting too old for this sort of work. Pulling all-nighters and getting shot at, that was a young man's work. But this next job, at least, was specially designed for an old veteran like him.

He walked into the coroner's office to find Patricia Siegman waiting for him. "I know I promised you noon, Detective, but we're doing the best we—"

"Step into my office, please," he said, and half dragged her into the men's room before she could resist.

"Look and listen," he said. He was short enough for them to see eye to eye, but he was twice as broad. "I'm with LAPD but I'm doing work with a government unit. They believe terrorists are going to make some kind of attack today. Now. But they don't know what. I think this guy was involved somehow, I don't know exactly. I think this autopsy could give us an answer, so I need you to move some other stiff off the table and put my guy on it or people may die and it'll be your fault."

10:18 A.M. PST
CTU Headquarters, Los Angeles

". . . terrorists are out there," Chappelle concluded with just the right hint of righteous indignation. "You all believe that, or this meeting would never have been called. We don't know where they are exactly, but I do know we have the resources to root them out, if we commit those resources to action. If not, they will hide in convenient places, waiting for convenient moments, and then they will strike."

10:19 A.M. PST
Playa del Rey

Yasin had moved, as was his habit these days. He'd spent a short time in the San Fernando Valley, and now he was headed toward the suburbs near the airport. He doubted the authorities had any idea of his location, but even with the simple changes he'd made to his appearance, someone might recognize him. It was better to be unpredictable.

He was impressed with how well this more elaborate plan was working. '93 had been simple, but ineffective. Yes, there had been headlines, but they had succeeded only in angering the Americans, not terrorizing them. This plan had required much more subtlety, much more planning, but so far it had worked. Yasin was not blind to the fact that Federal agents were scouring the city, but he had foreseen that possibility, and, through Michael, he had set up intricate avenues and mazes to lead them here and there. So far, so good. Allah was willing.

10:20 A.M. PST
Farrigian's Warehouse, West Los Angeles

Jack drove into the parking lot of Farrigian's Warehouse and walked in the front door, SigSauer in hand. He'd been here only ten hours earlier, but it seemed like a lifetime. He walked over to the little office and opened the door without knocking.

Farrigian was inside. He squealed when he saw Jack Bauer, but there was nowhere to run. Jack grabbed the front of his shirt, gathering up cloth and chest hairs into a tight fist, and dragged the petty criminal across the desk, scattering papers. He slammed Farrigian down onto the floor as invoices fluttered around them. Jack put his knee into Farrigian's chest and his gun against his cheek.

"What the f—?" Farrigian gagged.

A guy dressed in jeans, work boots, and a T-shirt came around the corner, attracted by the noise. "Hey Andre, everything okay?" He pulled up short when Jack, kneeling, brought the Sig around to the height of his groin.

"Everything is okay," Jack stated. "Got that?"

"Sure thing, boss. Holy shit!" the worker said, melting away.

"All right," Jack said, pressing his knee harder into Farrigian's sternum. "I'm sick of all this crap. You sold a package of C–4 to a bunch of Arab terrorists, right?"

Farrigian shook his head no as vigorously as he could with the gun jammed back into his cheek.

Jack had had enough. He had never been a huge advocate of torture, mostly because he himself had been an operator with Delta, and the possibility of capture and torture were very real and very unclean to him. But he'd been run around like a dog in heat all night, and he was done.

He used the Sig's sights to cut a red streak along Farrigian's forehead.

10:26 A.M. PST
CTU Headquarters, Los Angeles

Senator Armand moved on to the next topic. "You must be aware, Director, that your methods are being called into question this morning. What can justify the fact that an operative escorted a suspect in a murder investigation around Los Angeles and apparently let him attack and nearly murder someone?"

Nothing can justify it, Chappelle wanted to shout. *He's a thug and I don't want him on my team!*

But he'd already painted himself into that corner once. If Bauer wasn't going to be a pain in his neck, Chappelle would at least put him to good use. "This was the same operative this committee praised earlier for stopping Castaic Dam. I have spoken with him"—that was true—"and he's assured me that his actions were based on urgent needs and time constraints."

Chappelle couldn't believe he was sitting here defending that moron Jack Bauer. But if Bauer's actions could ensure his funding, he'd take it. "Bauer is out there now, working loose ends of this case. But I can assure you he is doing everything possible to stay within the letter of the law."

10:29 A.M. PST
Farrigian's Warehouse, West Los Angeles

"Oh, ahhh!" Farrigian howled. "Oh god, it's the truth! I didn't sell the stuff to Arabs."

"They had it," Jack spat. "How'd they get it?"

"How the fuck should—ow! I don't know. Not from me. I bought from Arabs. I *bought* from them!"

Bought from Arabs, Jack thought. *From Yasin? Had Yasin arranged this from the other end?*

"Names," Jack demanded.

"I don't know. I'll give you all the shipping information, but I can tell you it was nothing. Some joke of a gangster in Cairo named Farouk. Middleman like me."

Jack held back a curse. Farouk was where he'd started. Farouk had led him to Ramin. He already knew that Farouk knew almost nothing. He couldn't go in circles.

"You sold to someone. Give me those names. And don't say the bikers," he warned, gouging another hole in Farrigian's forehead.

"Aah! I did sell to them. I was told to. But some I sold to this other guy who was in charge. I don't know his name, I swear I don't!" he added in a panic as Jack aimed the sights at a fresh spot. "He was American. He never let me see him, but he talked like an American. He only wanted a little for himself. The rest he said to sell to Dog and Dean."

"How did he know them?" Jack asked.

"Don't know. They weren't the same type, that's for sure. And they didn't know my guy at all. They kept talking about Mark or Mike or something, but that definitely wasn't the guy who arranged the whole thing."

"What was he going to do with it?"

"Are you kidding me?"

Jack wasn't kidding. He cut another red line across the arms dealer's forehead. But he doubted Farrigian could answer his question. The mastermind behind the C–4 had gone to great lengths to keep the authorities busy with other problems. There was no way he would tell his master plan to the likes of this.

"What did you to do Diana Christie?" Jack asked.

"I didn't do anything. I didn't even meet her. I made you guys when you came last time. I didn't trust you, but you weren't my problem, you were Dean's, so I sent you to him. Guys want to pay me to keep my mouth shut, they pay me, right? Otherwise it's the law of the jungle. When she came back, the boss man was here to meet her, not me. Did they kill her?"

"Eventually," Jack said.

"Oh, man, look, none of this is my thing. I just buy and sell, you know?"

Jack asked how much C–4 the mysterious leader

had kept for himself. Jamey Farrell would have been pleased when Farrigian said, "About ten pounds."

10:40 A.M. PST
Culver City

Marwan al-Hassan had one more act to perform before leaving for the Unity Conference, a sort of purification ritual. Slowly, carefully, he slid his left arm out of its sling. Then he began to unwrap the bandage that covered his arm. It took several minutes, and every movement was painful, but he forced himself to continue until the bandage was gone. His forearm looked sickly and pale, but under long sleeves it would not be noticeable. There would be pain, but the pain was a small price to pay for the glory that was to come.

10:59 A.M.
West Los Angeles

Jack's phone rang. "Harry, what's happening? Are you at the coroner's office?"

"Yeah, and you need to get down here. Now."

"They did the autopsy?"

"Yeah, but you need to see this to believe it."

. . . .

THE FOLLOWING TAKES PLACE
BETWEEN THE HOURS OF
11 A.M. AND 12 P.M.
PACIFIC STANDARD TIME

. . . .

11:00 A.M. PST
Four Seasons Hotel, Los Angeles

Security for the Unity Conference was subtle but efficient. Guests passed through two sets of metal detectors in the lobby and took a specially designated elevator to the top floor, where Swiss Guards dressed in elegant black suits politely relieved all guests of their unnecessary bags and coats. As they did, a hidden camera snapped a high-resolution photo of their faces and a computer matched it against a predetermined guest list. Guards surreptitiously passed swatches of chemically treated cloth over some part of each guest, and the swatches were casually passed back to a coatroom that had been turned into a laboratory. The swatches were examined—one that turned black indicated the presence of explosive agents.

The man who called himself Abdul al-Hassan passed casually through all this security, even patiently allowing the Swiss Guards to probe his arm sling. The only moment of trouble he had was walking through the second metal detector, which, unbeknownst to him, was set at a higher sensitivity. The detector made no sound, but a single light went off on the far side of the metal frame, and a young man in Armani smoothly gestured for al-Hassan to step to the side.

"Do you have any metal on you, sir?" he asked in lightly accented English.

"Metal?" al-Hassan said. "No. The other detector didn't—"

The young man smiled. "They are temperamental sometimes." He held up a metal wand. "May I?" Before al-Hassan could respond, he began to wave the handheld detector over the attendee. The wand hummed steadily until the guard passed it over al-Hassan's arm.

"Ah," he said. "I broke my arm. There is a metal plate in there."

The guard nodded. He gently fingered the cloth sling again, and then waved al-Hassan through.

"Can you believe the security here?" said a woman who appeared suddenly beside him.

Marwan al-Hassan knew immediately that this was a Jew. Only his training kept the look of disdain off his face. "Necessary, I suppose." He turned away from her.

"Well, no need to be rude, Mr. al-Hassan," the woman said. "Are you saying you don't remember me?"

Marwan looked at her calmly, but he felt his heart

pound against the side of his neck. Could he be undone so quickly? "I'm sorry?"

"Amy Weiss." The woman laughed. "I interviewed you on Thursday about the conference."

"Ah, of course," he said apologetically. "I'm so sorry. The last few days have been very hectic."

"I'm sure," Amy Weiss said. "That's just twice now, after I did that story on your peace efforts after the '93 bombing."

Marwan fought the urge to squeeze her neck until her head popped off. "We all have our failings," he said sweetly. "Now, if you'll excuse me."

11:11 A.M. PST
I–10 Freeway

Boo McElroy had never picked up his room as a kid, so now he was stuck picking up trash on Interstate 5. Boo (his real name was Bradley, but no one called him that) didn't have the vocabulary to use the word *irony*, but that's what he felt. He'd always told his mom she could go stuff herself every time she tried to get him to clean up. He was a tough kid, independent, doing his own thing.

Until he got caught robbing a 7-Eleven, his third robbery since turning eighteen. Now he was serving a year in county, and working off some of that time wearing an orange vest and raking up trash along the freeway with a crew of cons.

He couldn't believe how much shit people tossed out of their cars. Come on, he tossed a bottle or can now and then, but his own personal shit couldn't amount to much. It was all these other bastards who treated the city like it was a toilet.

He used his poker to jab a can and then lift it up into his trash bag. He moved on and saw a large canvas bag. It was his size and half covered in dust and leaves. It looked full. Well, hell, he thought, no way was he picking up that big thing. They couldn't make him—

He stopped mid-gripe and blinked. He used his poker to push aside some leaves.

There was a cold, gray hand sticking out of the bag.

11:14 A.M. PST
Los Angeles Department of Coroner
Forensic Sciences Lab

Jack saw Harry Driscoll waiting outside the door of the forensics lab.

"What couldn't you tell me over the phone?" Jack asked, slightly annoyed.

"Inside," Harry said. "You wouldn't believe it if I told you. You have to see it."

Jack followed Harry inside, where they were both greeted by a woman in a lab coat who introduced herself as Dr. Siegman. She looked astounded and fascinated and was clearly eager to get back to the autopsy room. Outside, they donned surgical masks, then entered.

The naked corpse of the priest lay on the examination table. Its left arm had been cut open and splayed out.

"This is why we wanted you to come down," the coroner said. "Look at the arm."

Jack approached the table and looked at the sickeningly butchered arm. The bone was exposed, but along the bone there was a steel plate, around which had been packed strips of what looked like very wet putty.

"C–4?" Jack asked.

Siegman shrugged. "That's not my field, but from what the detective tells me, that may be the case."

Siegman picked up a probe and used it to push aside some of the dead tissue. "Look how it's designed. A plate like this is normally used to brace a badly broken bone. But this one is a lot weaker. And look how the explosives are packed in there. I think if this were to explode, all this metal would go flying outward."

"Show him the receiver," Harry said.

Siegman used a pair of tongs to lift a small circuit. "Again, not my field, but if this is an explosive, I'm guessing this is a receiver."

The ramifications of what he was seeing were instantly clear to Jack. Father Collins had turned himself into a human bomb. Jack's knowledge of ordnance wasn't strong enough to estimate the power of the blast, but he'd just seen what a brick of C–4 could do to a packed earth wall.

The small room seemed eerily silent with the three of them staring at the mutilated corpse. Finally, Harry Driscoll said something to break the dead quiet. "This is the most twisted thing I've ever seen. I mean, I've heard of suicide bombers, of course—"

"It's not that far off," Jack cut in. "Either way, the bomber is going to die. This delivery system—"

"Delivery system!" Dr. Siegman gasped, horrified. "This is a human being!"

But Jack was beyond her sense of morality, assessing the threat. "It's not as efficient as a suicide vest. You can pack that with more C–4, and use nails, bolts, other stuff to make yourself a claymore mine. But this would be undetectable."

"There's that metal plate, though," Harry pointed out.

Siegman was finding the same page Jack was on. "It wouldn't matter. Most metal detectors aren't set to go off when they find that density of metal. The plates are made that way. And even when they are, what would the security guard do, ask you to open your arm?"

"Was the transmitter on him?" Jack asked.

They searched through the few possessions that had arrived with the corpse, but found nothing of interest. "It might be anything," Jack said. "A cell phone. The keyless entry on a car. Anything."

"He wasn't going after anything when I arrested him," Harry said. "Man, he played that cool. But I guess if you're willing to have a bomb planted in your arm, you can handle a few questions from a cop."

Jack stepped back from the corpse, as though the physical distance might lend him mental perspective. The discovery lent him a small sense of relief— whatever Collins had been planning to do, it clearly wasn't going to happen now. And at least now they knew why Driscoll's attackers had wanted to reclaim that body. But it also raised a hundred questions, and at least a dozen of them were urgent. What had been the intended target? Who had helped him with the horrific surgery? Was there a connection between Father Collins, the human bomb, and Father Collins, the child molester? Other questions swirled around in Jack's brain. He needed to organize them.

"Background check on Collins," he said out loud, reciting the first thing he needed. "We need to know who this guy was. This has got to be the C–4 missing from the—oh, damn." A depressing thought struck him. He looked at Siegman. "I don't suppose there's ten pounds of the stuff in there."

Siegman looked at the arm. "I can give you an exact weight in a little while," she said, "but no way. Whoever did this did it well, but there's no ten pounds. They did this well. Look, there's a sterilized wrap around the explosive, so it doesn't break off and start moving around in the body and get reactions from the immune system. But I guarantee you, this guy was feeling even this amount. He must have been in some serious pain. The human body doesn't like a lot of foreign objects invading it."

Jack felt some of the energy drain out him, and he tried to put a mental stopper in the leak. It had been a long night, and he still couldn't catch up to the plastic explosives, or the actual plot. Every time he caught up with some of it, more seemed to be missing.

11:33 A.M. PST
CTU Headquarters, Los Angeles

Jamey had long ago given up any thought of going home, so it didn't bother her when Jack Bauer called.

"I need everything you can get me on Sam Collins, a priest at St. Monica's in Los Angeles, and I mean everything, including his medical records. He had surgery on his arm recently and I want all that information as well."

"Give me ten minutes and I'll tell you how much money he got from the tooth fairy," Jamey said. She started typing.

11:35 A.M. PST
Los Angeles Department of Coroner
Forensic Sciences Lab

Jack hung up and turned back to Dr. Siegman. "Doctor, I'm assuming that this was done with the man's cooperation, yes? There's no way this was done without his knowledge?"

Siegman looked startled, as though she hadn't even considered the possibility. "Well, I guess it's possible, once someone's under, but what doctor would do that? Besides, you'd have to be a complete idiot. There'd be a lot of discomfort."

Jack nodded his understanding and moved on. "Harry, we've got to figure out what the motive is, and the target. You know the Pope is in town, right?"

"Yeah, half our unit is assigned to it this week. He would be the obvious target. But a priest kill the Pope?"

"Maybe he's a renegade," Jack said. "Someone was telling me just recently about a group of people called schismatics who—"

"Yeah, they don't think there's been a real Pope since Vatican II," Dr. Siegman said. "Usually very orthodox Catholics."

"Are you Catholic?" Jack asked.

"Me? I'm Jewish. But my sister married a Catholic, and he's a schismatic. Family dinners are murder."

Jack felt all the pieces fall into place. If Jamey came back with information connecting Collins to the schismatics, then he had his target and his motive. It was possible—although he felt the stretch here—that this Catholic renegade had contacted Yasin to learn how to plan the attack. Mercenary work wasn't Yasin's style, but he might be unable to resist a chance to help strike a major symbol of Western civilization like the Pope. If that was the case, then they might have nipped this whole incident in the bud.

Jamey Farrell called back a moment later and gave him a preamble. "I don't think this is what you wanted to hear."

Harry eavesdropped on the conversation, but Dr. Siegman returned to her examination of the bullet-damaged receiver.

"What I want to hear is that the priest was part of a renegade sect that hated and opposed the Pope and wanted him replaced. It'd also be like whip cream on top if, say, Yasin's phone number appeared a few dozen times in Collins's phone logs."

"How about a guy so squeaky clean you could eat off his stomach. This guy, Collins, was a friggin' saint."

"He was a child-molesting monster," Jack replied.

"Well, not according to any record of him anywhere that we can dig up. Grew up in Orange County, went to a Catholic high school where his grade point average was exactly that—average. Served as Vice President on the student council, played on the baseball team. College at Pepperdine. Seminary school after that. His name is listed on the boards of about fifty charitable organizations. I can't even find a friggin' parking ticket on this guy."

"He can be all that and still hate the Pope," Jack said.

"He could," Jamey retorted, "or he could be co-chair of something called the Eternal City Project, which raises money for underprivileged Catholic kids to go to Rome and see the Pope. Not to mention having received a meritorious service award from the Council of Bishops, which was presented to him by, um, yeah, the Pope himself two years ago."

"Jesus," Jack muttered, no pun intended. "All this is so much easier if he just hates the Pope. That would explain my target. Without that, I have no idea why a priest turned himself into a human bomb."

"All that motive could still be hidden under this stuff," Jamey pointed out. "It wouldn't be the first time."

"By the way," Jack asked, "is there any way at all, any possible way, that you were off in your calculations, and that the box of C–4 was missing only a pound or so?"

"No way. If that thing was packed full, then ten pounds is missing." She paused. "You saying there aren't ten pounds where you are?"

"Yeah."

"This case just won't die, will it?" she asked.

"Medical records?"

"He checked into Cedars-Sinai a month ago after a car wreck. I have all the records from that surgery online."

Jack thanked her and hung up. He was aware that Harry Driscoll and Dr. Siegman were staring at him, but he ignored them. He had to think, and his insights were coming few and far between. He wished he'd had at least a few minutes of sleep when he'd been home—not for his own comfort, but so that his brain would have had time to reset. Maybe it'd be working better now.

"Okay," he said at last. "This is what we have to go on. There is roughly ten pounds of plastic explosives out in the open. Some fraction of that is here, in Father Collins's arm. The rest isn't enough to do any huge damage to any buildings or important structures, so we can rule out that sort of terrorist attack.

"Father Collins apparently had no motive to murder anyone, and was working toward becoming the next Mother Teresa. But we know that's not true because he stuck a bomb in his arm. I'm going back to the office to start working on this."

"Mr. Bauer?" Dr. Siegman said, holding up the tiny electronic device. "This might interest you. You should take it and have it double-checked, because I might be wrong about this thing."

"It's not a receiver?"

"Oh, it's definitely a receiver. But unless I'm mistake, there's also a little timer built into it. A kind of fail-safe, maybe."

"A timer."

"Set to go off at five-thirty today."

. . . .

THE FOLLOWING TAKES PLACE
BETWEEN THE HOURS OF
12 P.M. AND 1 P.M.
PACIFIC STANDARD TIME

. . . .

12:00 P.M. PST
Four Seasons Hotel, Los Angeles

Rabbi Dan Bender had to admit that he was enjoying himself. It had been years since he'd attended a truly splendid party, and the reception that preceded the official start of the Unity Conference was nothing if not splendid. Clerics and holy men from a number of religions were in attendance—not just rabbis, imams, and Christian clergy, but also a few Sikhs, Hindus, and Buddhists. The Dalai Lama had been invited, but was unable to attend due to illness.

Although he tried not to appear obvious about it, he searched the crowd for Father Collins. He didn't like the man, but for reasons obvious to himself, Bender felt it very important to know the man's whereabouts.

He could not find Collins, which concerned him very much. But he did spot Abdul al-Hassan who, quite out of character, was standing by himself near a tall indoor plant in a large pot. Bender sidled over to him. "I've never known you to avoid a crowd, Abdul, at least not when you thought you could turn it into an audience."

Abdul turned on him sharply, and for the briefest of moments, Bender thought he saw real hatred in the Muslim's eyes. But the emotion, whatever it was, vanished in a flicker. "Well, I suppose I am just trying to hold back," he said quietly. "This is the Christians' affair, after all. It would not be good to step on toes."

Bender laughed. "What, haven't you read the brochure? This event is for all of us."

"It is a political stunt for the leader of the Crusaders to appear to be the leader of us all," al-Hassan said simply.

Bender hesitated. "Are you in an especially bad mood, Abdul?"

Marwan hesitated. He knew his brother shared that view—he'd heard him speak against the paternalistic approach taken by the Christian Pope. Had he said something wrong? "No, why?"

Bender shrugged. "There's an edge in your voice. I hope everything is all right."

"Fine," Marwan said, thinking of what was to come. "I am absolutely fine."

Go back to the beginning.

Jack remembered hearing that somewhere, though he couldn't recall where. The truth is that he had been picking up his investigative skills in a sort of on-the-job training program. His training with LAPD SWAT, and in Delta, and with the CIA, had much more to do with field operations than mystery solving. But someone somewhere had once told him that when the clues start slipping out of your mental grip, go back to the beginning.

"What's the earliest event?" he said aloud, alone in his car. Driscoll was trailing him. "If we count it, there's the airline bombing that Diana Christie was working on. No," he corrected, "there's the timeline Farouk gave me. The purchase of C–4 out of Cairo and its shipment to the U.S. When was that?

"Six weeks ago, he said," Jack answered himself. "Then the airline accident or bombing, whichever it is. Four weeks ago. Yasin arrives in Los Angeles four days ago. I question Ramin yesterday, and the house blows up."

Jack was still reciting the timeline of events as he pulled his car up to CTU's nondescript building and walked inside. He caught the attention of Nina Myers, Jamey Farrell, and Christopher Henderson and motioned them toward the conference room. They followed, and he began to repeat his timeline so far, this time writing it on a whiteboard in the almost-bare room.

Jamey Farrell shook her head. "You missed something. Nina arrested the Sweetzer Three. That was two days ago. One day before you went to Ramin's house."

Jack nodded and crammed that onto the whiteboard above Ramin.

"Well, that's a thing to think about," Christopher Henderson mused. "Yasin—assuming it's Yasin we're talking about here—didn't care at all about the three Muslims we captured with a load of plastic explosives. But the minute you questioned Ramin, he blew the place up."

"Maybe he couldn't get to them when they were arrested," Nina suggested.

Jack saw where he was headed. "Could be. But he was ready and waiting for Ramin. That bomb was planted long before we got there. Not these three, though. Why not?"

"They're too important to kill?" Henderson proposed.

But Nina was headed in the other direction. "No. They weren't important enough." Her eyes met Jack's, and both realized the other was thinking the same thing.

"They don't know anything," Jack said first. "They were meant to live, so we would waste time on them. They were the first decoy, just in case we were on the trail of the C–4."

"So the airplane, then," Nina wondered. "Where does that fit in? If Christie was right, then they blew it up. Why?"

"Something about Ali, the guy in the seat," Jack said. "You did a thorough background on him?"

Nina crossed her heart. "Trust me. Nothing in his past. Squeaky clean."

"Like Collins," Jack said. He paused, then said,

"Forget his past. What was his future? Where was he going?"

Jamey Farrell blushed. "I never looked for that. Give me a minute." She hurried out of the room.

12:15 P.M. PST
En Route from St. Monica's Cathedral,
Downtown Los Angeles

Michael rode shotgun in the Cardinal's car, but his mind had leaped five miles and more than an hour ahead.

Almost, he thought. *Almost there.*

After so much work, only a short time to wait, and then the heresy of Vatican II would be eradicated.

12:16 P.M. PST
CTU Headquarters, Los Angeles

Jamey Farrell reentered the conference room with a look of pure embarrassment on her face. "It was there all the time," she said meekly. "If only I'd thought to look."

"What is it?" Jack said, although he thought he already knew.

"Abdul Ali was arriving in Los Angeles to attend several meetings. The most important one was the Unity Conference. He was scheduled to meet with the Pope."

12:18 P.M. PST
Four Seasons Hotel, Los Angeles

Giancarlo swept the reception hall as he planned to do several times in the next hour or more prior to the arrival of the Holy Father. Every precaution had been taken, of course, but he did not feel right unless he had personally walked every inch of the area. In order to better mingle with the crowd of eighty or ninety clerics in the hall, he was dressed in the black robes of a priest, and, if necessary, he could speak eloquently on various theological topics. But at this moment he avoided all conversation, simply smiling and tipping his head to anyone who made eye contact with him.

Another "priest"—actually one of his Swiss Guards in a similar disguise—approached him and said quietly in Italian, "There is a telephone call for you. It may be urgent."

Giancarlo bowed and turned, gliding out of the room. In the hallway outside, he opened a nondescript door that led to a separate room filled with video monitors. In this room, there was no attempt to hide security. Four men in body armor and wearing automatic weapons slung over their shoulders waited with professional patience, while three others watched the video screens intently.

One of them handed a headset to Giancarlo. He slipped it over his head and said in English, "This is the Chief of Security, may I help you?"

"This is Federal agent Jack Bauer," said the voice on the other end of the line. "I'm concerned that there may be an attempt on the life of the Pope."

Jack admired calm, and the man on the other end of the line sounded almost serene. "I see," he said. "I am aware that my people have already vetted this call, but can you tell me what agency you're with?"

"Well," Jack said, almost smiling at the complex answer to such a simple question, "I am in a special capacity with the State Department."

"You are CIA," the man, Giancarlo, interpreted.

"I'm currently working with a special counterterrorism unit on a domestic case. It's led us to believe that there may be a plot for suicide bombers to assassinate the Pope."

Giancarlo allowed himself the faintest flicker of a smile. "Be assured, sir, there is no way for a suicide bomber to get anywhere near His Holiness."

In the most straightforward way that he could, Jack described the hunt for the C–4, the horrific discovery of the bomb planted inside Father Collins.

As Jack ended his story, the security man seemed nonplussed. "That is startling," he said without inflection, "but I don't understand. You say that you have found the C–4, and that you have stopped this suicidal priest. Do you think the Holy Father's life is still in danger?"

Jack explained their theory about Abdul Ali. "We're not sure if we're right about Ali. And if we're right, we're not even sure if the priest was a replacement for Ali, or if they were both supposed to be there. But I thought you should know."

Giancarlo said, "Thank you. I will inform His Holiness, but I fear that without solid proof, he will not cancel this conference. He has committed himself to see it to the end."

Jack sighed. "Let's just hope the end doesn't come too soon."

12:30 P.M. PST
Santa Monica Boulevard

Gary Khalid's hands still shook, but he was starting to feel better. He had one more hurdle to clear—an enormous hurdle, to be sure, but only one. He had to stop by his hiding place. He had decided to leave Los Angeles for good, but first he had to pick up his secret travel bag with cash and identification that would carry him through this crisis. He was smart enough not to hide the bag in his own home (but, he thought wryly, not smart enough to keep the travel bag with him at all times). The bag was, in fact, in the last place anyone would look for him.

Maybe they aren't looking for me yet, he thought. But even so, that was the best time to run. He would go to Venezuela, where he would be out of reach of the U.S. authorities. From Venezuela, he could make his way back to Pakistan, and from there to the Northern Provinces, or maybe to Afghanistan, where the Taliban were building a truly Muslim community.

But first he had to get that bag.

12:33 P.M. PST
Beverly Hills, California

Nina had volunteered to track down the doctor
who'd done surgery on Father Collins. She felt the
need to pursue this most morbid aspect of the case,
having watched Diana Christie blow up. Nina was
not a big fan of emotion, and she would have slapped
anyone who suggested she needed a good cry, but she
suspected there would be some sort of catharsis in
confronting the actual procedure.

David Silver was the surgeon of record who had
repaired Collins's broken arm. A few phone calls had
located him at his Beverly Hills office, on Camden
Drive just north of Wilshire. Inside the office, she
leaned over the counter where the receptionist sat,
and surreptitiously showed her identification. "It's
urgent, I'm afraid," she said softly but firmly.

"We're already backed up by forty-five minutes,"
the receptionist pleaded.

"Let's round it out to an hour," Nina replied,
and pushed through the door to the back offices.
The receptionist, flustered, guided her to Dr. Silver's
office, where she sat. The doctor himself appeared a
moment later. He was young, with dark brown hair.
He was also about five foot two, and he was already
forming a helicopter pad on the top. He had a habit
of making a wet, sucking sound at the corners of his
mouth every few breaths. A catch on paper, Nina
thought, but in real life, he was catch and release.

"Can I help you?" he asked, looking more than a
little concerned.

Nina introduced herself and then dove right in. "I
am interested in a patient of yours from several weeks

ago. Samuel Collins, a priest, who had a broken arm that you set." Nina's voice was casual and her posture relaxed, but her right hand never strayed far from the Glock 17 at her hip under her jacket.

Dr. Silver chewed his lip. "A priest? Collins . . . that doesn't ring a bell." He pressed the intercom. Nina tensed. If there was going to be trouble, it would happen now. "Marianna, can you look up records for a Samuel Collins? Broken arm."

He looked up. "I usually remember all my patients. Certainly recent ones, and I think I'd remember a priest, but . . ."

The buzzer sounded. "Dr. Silver, did you say Collins? I don't have a Sam Collins anywhere. We don't have a patient with that name."

"Thank you." He looked at Nina. "I'm sorry. I'm not sure what to say."

Nina's bullshit meter wasn't going off. This guy didn't feel like a con man, and there was nothing about his operation that raised red flags. But she wasn't giving up yet. "Cedars-Sinai's records indicate that Collins had surgery at that hospital almost four weeks ago, on Tuesday the twelfth. You are listed as the surgeon. Can you tell me where you were that day?"

Silver looked shocked. "Am I in trouble?"

"That depends on where you were."

Silver's eyes went up and to the left, which told Nina he was accessing some visually remembered memory. "The twelfth? I could check my calendar and—oh! The twelfth. That's easy. I was at my place in Jackson Hole. We were there all week."

Now it was Nina's turn to look perplexed. "You can prove this? Are there witnesses?"

Silver said, "Yeah. My wife, my twin daughters, the caretaker who watches the place when we're not around, Hank the fly fishing instructor . . ."

"I get it," Nina said, standing up. "Thanks for your time."

12:40 P.M. PST
CTU Headquarters, Los Angeles

Jack was still pacing back and forth, deciding that he had to go over to that Unity Conference himself, when Nina called back.

"You can forget Dr. Silver. He wasn't even in town when this operation is said to have happened. He has a ton of witnesses."

"We have to run them down, though," Jack said into the phone.

"Trust me," she answered. "This is a nerdy Jewish doctor in Beverly Hills. He's not blowing up anyone."

Jack put her on speakerphone and addressed Jamey and Christopher Henderson. "So now we're saying someone doctored his records and basically faked an operation. A conspiracy can only go so wide before leaks start happening, and the only leak we've ever found here is back in Cairo, and then Ramin. Everyone else has stayed pretty quiet. Are we now saying there's a doctor out there who has something against the Pope, did these operations, faked records, and has flown under our radar?"

"This case is getting weirder," Henderson said.

No one spoke for a minute, until Harry Driscoll cleared his throat. He'd been there the whole time, but he'd faded into the background, whether out of fatigue or frustration, Jack didn't know. "Who says it has to be a doctor? I mean, a real doctor? Collins wasn't planning on staying alive, right? So if the operation wasn't perfect, who cares?"

"That doesn't help much, though," Nina said over the phone. "It widens our pool, it doesn't narrow—"

"Start with the suspects we have," Driscoll suggested. "Could one of them have done it?"

Jack shrugged. "It's worth a try. Jamey, can you—"

"Already doing it." She had dragged a laptop into the conference room.

Henderson frowned. "No wireless networks are allowed in here."

Jamey shrugged. "With all respect, I will absolutely follow that rule when you get more than two working computers in here. In the meantime . . . hmm."

"Something?" Jack asked.

"Well. Yeah." She looked up. "I just ran Nina's original list of suspects against any information on medical school, medicine, etcetera. You know who graduated from medical school before moving here?"

"Who?"

"Gary Khalid."

12:48 P.M. PST
Sweetzer Avenue, Los Angeles

Gary Khalid drove up the street in a borrowed car, but he didn't see anything unusual. If someone was watching the house, their countersurveillance skills were much better than his meager talents. It couldn't be helped. He had to get inside his house. He cruised his neighborhood several more times, searching for he knew not what.

Though he gave the appearance of an affable, simple man, Khalid was highly intelligent. At a certain point, he realized that he was being foolish. The way the Americans worked, if they had figured out his involvement in the affair, they would have ransacked his house by now. And if they were lying in ambush, they would have pounced on him long before now.

Still, he pulled his car to the end of the block and waited. He had waited many long years to strike a blow against the Zionists and Crusaders. He could wait another hour.

12:57 P.M. PST
CTU Headquarters, Los Angeles

Jack finished reviewing the records on Khalid's education in Pakistan. Like so many clues, they had been right in front of him, but they'd meant nothing until he knew what to look for.

Khalid had not only finished medical school in Islamabad, he had practiced as a surgeon and served as a doctor in the army.

"Last night this was in his favor," Jack said to no one in particular. "Educated, capable. Didn't fit the profile of a terrorist. Now it puts him right back in our sights."

He looked at Christopher Henderson. "Do you know what all this tells me?"

Henderson shook his head.

"It tells me we're not ready for this," Jack admitted. "It tells me these guys can come here and make us chase our own tails and do whatever they want. We'd better catch up."

Henderson noted with a slight smile that Jack now said *we*, but he said nothing.

Jamey Farrell hung up a telephone. "LAPD sent a car to Khalid's residence for us. No one's home. They searched, didn't find anything unusual. He may have already run out on us."

"I would if I were him," Jack said. "He must have cut Diana Christie up pretty quickly and horribly to turn her into a bomb. He probably panicked."

"Yeah, but he's not out of the country yet."

"Mexico's only a couple hours away."

"But he wasn't ready for it," she pointed out. "I mean, how could he be? This thing with Diana Christie had to be last-minute, because you didn't even know she'd come along until last night. So she went to that meeting and they ambushed her, did . . . whatever"—Jamey shuddered—"and then sent her off. So maybe after that, Khalid decides it's time to get out of town."

"If I were him, I'd just get in the car and go," Jack said.

"But he's not you. He's a guy who's been interviewed at bunch of times and passed with flying colors. He probably feels like he's safe."

Jack was impressed. "You should do fieldwork," he said.

"Nah, I'm not a big fan of getting shot at," she said.

Jack phoned Nina Myers, who was en route, and filled her in. "But he's not home," Jack said finally. "So if you have any ideas . . ."

"I do," Nina said. "Unless you need me at the conference, I'll go get Khalid."

"Who said I'm going to the conference?" Jack replied.

Nina just laughed, and hung up.

1 2 3 4 5 6 7 8 9
10 11 12 13 14 15 16 17
18 19 **20** 21 22 23 24

....

THE FOLLOWING TAKES PLACE
BETWEEN THE HOURS OF
1 P.M. AND 2 P.M.
PACIFIC STANDARD TIME

....

1:00 P.M. PST
CTU Headquarters, Los Angeles

"You really think there's still a threat?" Driscoll asked. "I mean, didn't we stop the guy?"

"The missing C–4," Jack said by way of explanation. "And the fact this whole damned thing is never-ending, and I can't seem to get my hands around it. It's like these guys make a religion out of being devious."

"Yeah, instead of the Father, the Son, and the Holy Spirit, we got the bomber, the stooge, and the plastic explosives."

It was a bad pun, and Driscoll would have forgotten he'd even said it except that Jack suddenly stopped, his eyes growing distant. "Threes," Jack said. His eyes focused again, and he looked at Driscoll in astonishment. "Ramin said that. That Yasin would do things in threes. There are going to be three attackers and we've only got one."

"How can you be sure?" the detective asked.

"I'm not," Jack said, suddenly animated. "But I bet if you check with Dr. Siegman, she'll say that there was just about enough missing C–4 to create two more bombs like the one in Collins's arm. Three bombers. And there've been three areas to investigate: the bikers, the Sweetzer Three"—saying the word itself was almost like the click of a puzzle piece—"and the Unity Conference."

"Don't forget the child molestation thing."

Jack shivered—it was not forgettable. "But that wasn't one of Yasin's plans. In fact, that's where it all started to go wrong for them," he pointed out. "Think about it, Harry. Where would we be if Don Biehn hadn't come along? I'd have stopped a two-bit biker thug, and maybe I'd have followed that lead to Castaic Dam. CTU would have kept the Sweetzer Three on ice, and figured they'd bagged all the C–4. We'd be sitting on our butts right now while Collins was getting ready to blow himself up. We need to get over there."

1:05 P.M. PST
Four Seasons Hotel, Los Angeles

Michael said the Ave Maria to himself in Latin, the only way that it should be said, as he followed Cardinal Mulrooney through the reception at a polite distance. He glanced at his watch. The Cardinal had to leave soon of his own accord. If not, Michael would make him leave.

In Michael's mind, Mulrooney ought to be in line for the papacy. Not because he was an especially moral man, but because he, like Michael, could see the false path down which the church had traveled these past forty years. They were few and far between in the church. Michael had to admit that. But Jesus had only a few followers when he started to spread the word. The true word of God could not be contained. By the will of the Lord, Michael would strike a blow against the heretics. There were several among the cardinals who were secret leaders of the schismatic movement. Several of them stood a decent chance of becoming Pope after John Paul was blown to hell.

It hadn't been easy, that first meeting with Yasin. In another time and place, Michael would have killed the man and rejoiced at it. But Yasin had come to him with evidence of the church's secret sin—the unwholesome appetites of some of its priests, who preyed on the children in their care. Michael knew of it, of course. He was in charge of security, and more than once he had acted as the intimidating presence in the background while a kindly priest convinced a child or a parent to keep quiet and allow the incident to drift into the past. The priests, meanwhile, were always moved to a new diocese to avoid any further unpleasantness.

Somehow, Yasin had known of this. Maybe a guilty priest had confessed, or an abused child had found his way to him. Michael didn't know, and never would. But Yasin had shown him several letters, and video footage that a priest had taken of one of the . . . incidents. The evidence was damning.

Even so, Michael would never have let himself or the church be blackmailed, until he realized what Yasin was proposing: the assassination of Pope John Paul II. And, better yet, an assassination that Michael could blame on the Muslims, who were more than willing to take credit for it. For Michael, it was a wondrous triptych: the death of the heretical Pope; the awakening of Christians to the threat of Islam; and the ability to escape unsuspected. All he had to do was agree to work with Yasin.

It had seemed easy, all those months ago. And, in fact, it had all gone smoothly until just a few days ago. Yasin had warned them that the Federal government might track the crate of C-4, so they had created a red herring with three fundamentalist Islamists who, while totally innocent, fit the profile the Americans feared. Then, for good measure, Michael had used a very strong contact within the schismatic movement to create another false trail with the Hell's Angels. And, finally, there was the real plot. These three channels had worked to confuse and befuddle the Federals. Yasin had called it, jokingly, his unholy Trinity. Michael had not appreciated the humor.

There was a buzz throughout the room, and Michael heard a voice whisper into his earpiece: "His Holiness is arriving."

The crowd parted, as though unseen hands were separating them. Reluctantly, Michael felt that will and moved with Mulrooney to one side. A set of tall doors opened inward, and the Pope entered, followed by four or five cardinals who had traveled from Rome. There was no music, no pomp of any kind, in fact. John Paul eschewed it. But the wizened old man entered with such understated authority that one could not help but feel a sort of tremble in the air, as though music was playing somewhere. "The song of an invisible choir," some writer had described it. Michael grimaced.

The Pope stopped a few feet into the room, raised his hands, and spoke a short blessing. "May God in all his graciousness bless the attendees, and the purpose of this conference. Amen." By long-standing agreement, he had kept his prayer neutral and, therefore, to Michael's way of thinking, vacuous.

As soon as the Pope had finished, a line formed to greet him. As Cardinal of the host city, Mulrooney was among the first, and soon he had knelt before John Paul and kissed his ring. As he stood, he canted forward and whispered, "Your Holiness, please forgive me. Something urgent is calling me back to St. Monica's."

John Paul looked up at him with those piercing eyes. "Very well, Your Eminence." As Mulrooney tried to disengage himself, the Pope held his hand in a viselike grip. "God alone decides our destinies, Your Eminence. May you see the true path he has set for you."

Then he let go.

1:19 P.M. PST
En Route to the Four Seasons Hotel

"There's got to be someone!' Jack said, feeling frustrated.

"You've got the whole list in front of you, Jack," Jamey Farrell said through his cell phone. "I'm running everyone through every database I can find, but it's not like the Vatican's people haven't done this. This list has been vetted by everyone all the way up to God!"

Jack tried not to let his frustration spill over onto Jamey Farrell. She wasn't the cause of it. He was pissed that he'd interviewed Gary Khalid—sat in the man's house, in fact—and never realized he was a prime suspect. The other side was kicking his ass on his case, and he was tired of it.

There has to be someone, he wanted to say again, but repeating himself would just cause tempers to flare. They were all working on no sleep. He had to gather himself before they got to the hotel. He needed to be sharp.

"Keep checking," he said. He gave her the contact information for Carlos at the National Security Agency. "Call him. He'll give you a hard time, but ignore it. Ask him to run everyone through every source he's got."

"You want me to ask a guy I've never met to run a hundred people through everything everywhere?"

"Unless you have a better idea," Jack said. "I'm getting desperate." He thought of the fail-safe implanted into Collins, set for five-thirty. He was guessing he didn't have that much time.

1:21 P.M. PST
Four Seasons Hotel, Los Angeles

Pope John Paul spent a moment with each person who had come to the conference. The truth was, as far as he was concerned, this *was* the conference. There would be a roundtable discussion tomorrow, and several symposia on various topics, led by clergymen with impressive credentials from around the world. But this was the real victory—to get these people of various faiths, fundamental and progressive, into one room together, to discuss the need for religious tolerance . . . that was an act of God all by itself.

John Paul glanced over the shoulder of the American televangelist who was speaking to him, and saw a bearded imam partway down the line. He thought he recognized the man and dragged his name out of memory: al-Hassan. He'd read the man's book. It had been an unforgiving but insightful critique of the West's view of Islam. Exactly the sort of man John Paul needed at his side. He was eager for al-Hassan to make his way forward.

1:23 P.M. PST
Four Seasons Hotel, Los Angeles

Jack pulled up to the valet stand at the Four Seasons. He and Driscoll flashed their badges and hurried into the elegant lobby. There was a trim, well-dressed man standing by the elevators, and Jack approached him. "Federal agent Jack Bauer," he said in a low voice. "I need to get up to the conference."

The man studied Jack's credentials carefully, and did the same with Driscoll's. He also looked into Jack's eyes, as though trying to read something else there. Then he muttered into the mic in his sleeve. Finally, he stepped aside, and Jack entered the private elevator that rose to the hotel's penthouse.

When the elevator door opened, he was greeted

by a thin, unimposing man, but Jack's instincts told him this was a man to be reckoned with.

"Your credentials, please," he said. Jack and Harry both complied. When Giancarlo had examined them to his satisfaction, he escorted them down the hallway—not the reception room, but the adjacent security office.

"Giancarlo," Jack said as soon as they were inside, "I don't know how to impress on you the urgency—"

"You have already impressed this on me," the other man said in finely accented English. "My job is the security of His Holiness, and I have told him already my opinion."

"Then let's get him out of here," Jack said. "Drag him kicking and screaming if you have to—"

Giancarlo's look was reproachful. "Clearly, that cannot be done. The Holy Father has committed his life to this peace effort."

"And we're all in the business of making sure his life is long enough to see it through. Look, let's make it simple. Just pull the fire alarm or something. Have someone get sick. It doesn't matter how, just get the Pope out of that room."

Giancarlo looked at Jack with sympathetic eyes. "I admire your desire, but I cannot do it. His Holiness has expressly forbidden anything that will damage the peace effort."

"Goddamned martyrs." That was Harry Driscoll, muttering under his breath. He realized he'd spoken aloud only when everyone looked at him. He shrank back as much as a two-hundred-pound man could. "Just thinking out loud," he apologized, but Jack knew he was right.

The serenity of Giancarlo was starting to annoy

Jack. The Vatican man said, "It is odd, isn't it, that in our line of work we give our lives freely, but we call the sacrifices of others selfish."

Jack replied, "Because when we die, it doesn't turn the politics of the world upside down."

1:30 P.M. PST
West Los Angeles Police Station

Detective Mercy Bennett looked at the note attached to the file on her desk. She buzzed her captain. "Hey, Cap, what is CTU? I have a note here to call them."

The captain made a low, quizzical noise, trying to remember it himself. "Oh, yeah. Counter Terrorism Unit, or something like that. New protocol. Anything we get that might involve religious fundamentalists, we send them a Post-it note."

"Religious fundamentalists?" she asked.

"Really, we're talking about Islamic nutcases who want to blow themselves up," the captain said in his own inimitable style. "But we can't say that on the record. Anyway, just buzz them with the info."

Mercy shrugged and redialed. It took several rings for someone to answer. "Jamey Farrell."

"Mercy Bennett, LAPD," she said. "Listen, I got word to call you guys. We picked up a body earlier. We haven't done forensics on it, but we ran prints. The deceased is Abdul al-Hassan."

There was a pause. "Um, okay. Anything else?"

"That's it. I was just told to call."

1:32 P.M. PST
CTU Headquarters, Los Angeles

Jamey Farrell put down the phone and went back to her database. She was so focused on her searches that she nearly forgot the message as soon as she'd hung up. Just in time, she grabbed a pen and scribbled the name on the back of some other notes. Someday they'd need receptionists and lower-level staff for that sort of thing.

1:33 P.M. PST
Sweetzer Avenue, Los Angeles

Khalid decided he'd waited long enough. There had been no activity on the street. For all he knew, the police might be combing the city for him, but they weren't looking here. This was Khalid's old mail route, and he knew every car that parked here regularly. Nothing was out of order.

Khalid got out of his car and walked down the street toward the house where Mousa and the others had lived. The three men were more complicit than they let on, of course, but much less than the authorities had suspected. In the end, they were dupes, enjoying the thrill of living on the edge of danger but really knowing nothing of what went on. If they'd known the crate had contained explosives, they probably would have run screaming like girls.

Gerry walked up to the Sweetzer house and opened it with a key hidden under a rock in the garden. He ducked under the police tape still strung across the porch and opened the door. He was sure the authorities would not have taken his bag. It was well-hidden, and the documents and cash inside were in a secret compartment.

Khalid walked through the living room and toward the bedroom when he heard the female voice behind him. "Hello, Gary."

1:40 P.M. PST
Four Seasons Hotel, Los Angeles

Jack moved through the reception hall, every sense heightened, as though he might be able to hear or smell a bomb. There was still a substantial reception line waiting to greet the Pope, and he walked along it casually. It was a surreal moment, imagining that one of them was a human bomb.

"Jack Bauer," said someone in line.

Bauer, who had been looking at hands and bodies, focused on a face and recognized Amy Weiss, the *L.A. Times* reporter. He remembered her as fairly new back when he was on SWAT, the kind of journeyman who did all the legwork but got only a "contributed" line at the bottom of the articles.

She was canny enough not to mention his profession when he was in plainclothes. "Amy," he said. "You've become enlightened, I guess." He pointed to the religious leaders all around her.

She laughed. "Well, I do write the truth for a living," she said. "But I still do it for the papers. I just got to interview the Pope, so I was given an invitation to the reception."

Amy's voice was light, but her eyes were staring into Jack, and he was instantly on his guard. He could practically read her thoughts: murder at St. Monica's, Pope's reception, LAPD undercover. She'd have flipped if she'd known he was now with the CIA.

"Are you enjoying it so far?" he asked.

"I love standing in line!" she joked. "But yeah, I have to tell you, I talked to him this morning, and he's committed to this. He believes it will save the world."

"He's definitely committed," Jack agreed, still glancing around.

"Is there something I should know about?" she asked casually.

"No," he said. "But if you wanted to go powder your nose for a couple of hours, that wouldn't be a bad idea."

Amy's face went pale.

1:43 P.M. PST
Sweetzer Avenue, Los Angeles

Nina had proned Khalid out, putting his face in the carpet, and did a cursory search. As she reached to cuff one of his wrists, he spun quickly. He was much stronger than his lanky frame indicated. She tried to jam her knee into his neck, but she lost her balance and fell back. He tried to jump her, but she kicked his shin and he staggered back. She leveled her weapon, but didn't try to shoot him.

He ran.

1:45 P.M. PST
CTU Headquarters, Los Angeles

Jamey was coming up with nothing. It was a stupid assignment anyway. There was no way the Vatican's security people had missed anything in the backgrounds of these guests.

She sat back in her chair and rubbed her eyes. As she brought her knuckles away from her face, her eyes focused on the note on the back of the papers. Abdul al-Hassan.

"Oh shit," she said.

1:46 P.M. PST
Sweetzer Avenue, Los Angeles

Nina vaulted over a backyard fence three houses down. Khalid was taller and maybe faster, but he wasn't nearly as stubborn as she was, so she caught up to him by the fourth backyard and dragged him off the fence. Before he could use his size and strength against her, she kicked him in the groin while he was down. He curled up into a ball and she stomped on his ankle. He screamed, and she stomped on his elbow, too.

1:48 P.M. PST
Four Seasons Hotel, Los Angeles

Only two people left, Marwan thought. It would have been unbearable, to stand in this line to greet the spiritual leader of the Crusaders; unbearable, if not for the fact that the Pope would soon be dead, and he himself would be in Paradise.

The room's length away, Michael reached into his pocket for the keyless entry remote control that he had not surrendered to the valet.

1:49 P.M. PST
Four Seasons Hotel, Los Angeles

Jack's cell phone vibrated in his pocket. "Bauer," he said formally, although he knew it was Jamey Farrell.

"Abdul al-Hassan!" she blurted out. "He's an impostor."

"What do you—?"

"They found his dead body dumped off the freeway this morning. You're looking for Abdul al-Hassan."

Jack snapped the phone shut. He scanned the crowded room for Giancarlo and hurried over to the Swiss Guard. "The bomber is Abdul al-Hassan. Which one is he? We need to know now!"

To his credit, Giancarlo did not waste words or motions. He spoke quickly in Italian to his security office. Unseen cameras whirred around the crowded room. Giancarlo touched a hand to his ear as he listened. His eyes went wide. "The bearded man. With the Pope!"

They bolted forward together.

1:51 P.M. PST
Four Seasons Hotel, Los Angeles

Michael watched Marwan al-Hassan, smiling pleasantly, take the hand of the Pope. Gingerly, according to plan, al-Hassan put his left hand atop their clasped grip. It was only in that moment that anyone might have noticed his shriveled left arm.

Michael pointed the keyless remote toward them and . . .

. . . a body came flying across his field of vision, tackling Marwan away from the heretical Pope. People screamed and scattered away from the sudden violence. Black-suited Swiss Guards materialized out of nowhere to surround John Paul.

Michael hesitated to trigger the bomb. If Marwan could get close enough . . .

1:52 P.M. PST
Four Seasons Hotel, Los Angeles

Jack tried to take al-Hassan all the way to the floor, but the man was as hard to hold as a cat. He shook free of Jack and tried to claw at him, screaming something in Arabic and surging toward the wall of black suits surrounding the Pope.

Jack grabbed him from behind. *He's a bomb,* Jack thought. *He's a grenade. Get him out of here.*

Jack lunged toward a set of French doors to his left and crashed through them, al-Hassan in tow. The human bomb spun toward him and scratched at his face. He was not a human being, he was an animal. But Jack was not so different from him. He dug a thumb into al-Hassan's eye and raked his fingernails across the terrorist's face, scooping out flesh. Al-Hassan screamed.

Jack didn't know how powerful the bomb would be, so he had to get rid of al-Hassan now. He pushed the man up against the balcony wall and hefted him over. Al-Hassan, suddenly terrified, grabbed hold of Jack's arm and pulled him off balance.

1:55 P.M. PST
Four Seasons Hotel, Los Angeles

It's lost, Michael thought. *Time to get rid of the evidence*. He pressed the button, but nothing happened. Marwan had fallen out of range. Michael ran forward with the rest of the astonished crowd.

In that same moment, Jack had the briefest sensation of falling, then he hit water. Striking the swimming pool after a two-hundred-foot fall at thirty-two feet per second was better than hitting a concrete floor, but not by all that much. The breath went out of him. He and al-Hassan were both under water. The terrorist kicked at Jack, getting a foot in his face and using it to push off.

Jack was about to swim after him when al-Hassan disappeared behind light and turbulence. Jack felt himself lifted up and out of the water as the sound of the explosion enveloped him like a bubble.

There was chaos in the hall. A wedge of Swiss Guards had surrounded the Pope and were driving their way through the crowd, out into the hallway, toward the safe room.

Less professional people might have called it a panic room but Giancarlo did not prefer that term. It was a room with reinforced doors and windows, stocked with supplies, where they could hold out for hours if necessary. They moved toward the room in a herd, radios blaring in their ears, Giancarlo shouting instructions. It was all well-planned and well-executed, but even for men of their expertise, this sort of thing did not happen every day.

None of them, not even Giancarlo, noticed in that moment the inclusion of an additional member. Rabbi Dan Bender had slipped into the panic room with them.

· ·

THE FOLLOWING TAKES PLACE
BETWEEN THE HOURS OF
2 P.M. AND 3 P.M.
PACIFIC STANDARD TIME

· ·

2:00 P.M. PST
Four Seasons Hotel, Los Angeles

Somewhere in the last few seconds Jack's world had turned from water to concrete. He was lying on his side on a hard surface, but he was soaking wet, and he felt like someone had jammed their thumbs into his ears.

He sat up. Al-Hassan had exploded. That much made sense. He'd killed himself and no one else. That much was right with the world.

But Jack felt no sense of relief. Three bombers. He was right about that. Collins had been one. Al-Hassan had been number two. Where was the third?

Jack staggered to his feet just as shocked bystanders from the hotel lobby came out to help him. He pushed them aside and, soaking wet, lumbered toward the doors. The Swiss Guards would be evacuating the Pope. He had to make sure they knew what to watch for.

Jack reached the elevators, but the Swiss Guard stationed there was gone. He pulled out his cell phone, but it was dead. Either the water or the explosion or both had killed it. He needed to find Giancarlo, but he didn't know their escape protocol. Would they barricade in, or exfil immediately?

As Jack stood there for a moment, dripping pinkish water onto the lobby tiles and trying to collect himself, Harry Driscoll appeared out of an opening elevator.

"Jack!" he yelled. "Are you—Jesus, I can't believe it!"

"Where'd they go?" he asked.

"They're evacuating everyone," Harry said, guessing at Jack's line of thought. "If there's a third bomber, they won't find him. They're driving everyone away from the Pope. How did you live through that?"

It was only then that the reality of the last two minutes occurred to Jack. He'd just fallen two hundred feet into a pool and then been concussed by a man who exploded not ten feet away from him.

Jack's knees weakened. His hands shook momentarily. He would have been excused, he thought, if he'd just passed out. But he didn't. His knees firmed up. He willed his hands to stop shaking. There was work to be done.

"I need your phone." He called CTU and got Christopher Henderson because Jamey was on the phone with someone from the NSA. "Christopher, get me in touch with Giancarlo, the head of the security team."

"You're kidding, right?" Christopher said. "Every line we have just lit up like a Christmas tree. No one over there is answering anything, I've got—"

Jack hung up on him. A car. They would move the Pope out of the hotel the moment they thought the ambush was over. Jack hurried to the parking lot with Driscoll dragging along in his wake.

2:07 P.M. PST
Safe Room, Four Seasons Hotel, Los Angeles

"You are uninjured, Holy Father?" Giancarlo said.

John Paul felt dizzy, not from injury, but from the rush and chaos of the last few minutes. Sharp though he was in mind, he was an old man in body, and his frail heart was racing under his brittle chest. "I . . . I'm not injured. Was there . . . I heard an explosion."

Giancarlo nodded. "There was an attempt on your life. We are secure for the moment, but we need to move you. Are you able to travel?"

"By the grace of God," the Pope said. "And you, Giancarlo."

And Jack Bauer, the Swiss Guard thought. He was a good man, to have sacrificed himself like that.

"Prepare to move," Giancarlo said into his microphone. "Bring the cars around."

2:10 P.M. PST
CTU Headquarters, Los Angeles

Nina Myers half dragged Gary Khalid into CTU, ignoring the shocked looks of the skeleton crew of analysts and computer techs, ignoring even Christopher Henderson's astonished face.

She led Khalid, who limped and whimpered behind her, into an empty room down the hall and pushed him onto the bare floor.

"Now you and I are going to talk," she said. "And believe me, the only way you're leaving this room, ever, is if you tell me everything you know."

2:11 P.M. PST
Safe Room, Four Seasons Hotel, Los Angeles

Advance men told Giancarlo that the hallway was quiet, and the delivery doors were clear. He gave the signal, and the Pope's retinue moved out of the safe room and straight to the service elevator.

2:13 P.M. PST
Four Seasons Delivery Dock

Jack waited by the delivery dock, not knowing but guessing it to be the most logical point of exfiltration.

"You're a friggin' mess," Harry Driscoll said.

"You want a prettier partner, take up ballroom dancing."

Harry's cell phone rang. Jack handed it to Harry, who handed it right back. "Your people."

"Jack," Jamey said. "We got Khalid. Nina is questioning him now."

"Good."

"Also, I've got news for you. Your guy at the NSA works miracles. He's got a possible for you."

"Go," Jack said. He thought he heard a car approaching.

"Daniel Bender, a rabbi. The records that exist for him are all on the up-and-up, nothing to indicate any sort of questionable activity. But you'd expect that or he wouldn't have been invited."

"So?" Tires squealed. To his right, the service elevator bell chimed.

"So, he doesn't seem to exist prior to 1996. There is plenty of information on him after that, but nothing beforehand. Your guy Carlos noticed that." There was a hint of professional jealousy in her voice.

"Well, it's something," Jack said, a little enthusiastically.

"There's more. Your NSA guy tracked his communications. He sent an e-mail to his brother, a rabbi in Jerusalem. The e-mail was some kind of apology. I'm sending you a picture of Bender."

The elevator doors opened. The phone bleeped, and Jack pressed the text message button. A picture of a jovial, round-faced man appeared.

"Okay, thanks." Jack stood up and made himself as obvious as possible as he walked toward the crowd of black suits that emerged. Instantly, guns were pointed in his direction, and he was ordered to freeze in four or five languages.

"Giancarlo," he said, searching the compact group.

"*Dio mio*," Giancarlo said, stepping forward. "Bauer? That was very impressive." He said something in Italian, waving the phalanx of security men, with the Pope somewhere in the middle, toward the three Ford Broncos that were pulling into the dock. "I want to thank you for—"

But he never finished. Jack looked over his shoulder at one of the men in the phalanx. He shoved past Giancarlo and dove at the man's knees, taking him down heavily. "Go, go, go!" he shouted.

Giancarlo reacted instantly. The quick-moving phalanx doubled its pace. Some of them shoved the Pope into the middle car. They had all vanished in an instant, and the cars were peeling away.

Jack felt the man struggle; he was big, looking fat but feeling solid. Jack rolled, and came up on top of him. He straddled the man and punched him once in the face, but before he could strike him a second time, the man bucked his hips and grabbed at Jack's hands, rolling him over and reversing their positions.

"Wait, wait!" the big man yelled.

Driscoll came up behind and clipped him with the butt of his handgun. The big man winced and glared at Driscoll, yelling, "Stop! I'm with you!"

Jack back-rolled away. His gun was gone, but he readied himself to lunge. It was Dan Bender; Jack recognized his face from the photo he'd just seen.

"I'm on your side!" Bender claimed.

"Talk," Jack demanded. "Keep your finger on the trigger, Harry."

Bender wisely did not move, but he waited a moment to catch his breath. "You're Jack Bauer, with the CIA. My name is Dan Bender. I am Mossad."

"Bullshit," Jack said.

"The truth," Bender replied. "I am Mossad stationed here in the United States. I was assigned to observe the conference. We got wind that there might be some trouble. We weren't sure that your services were prepared to handle it."

"Well, we were," Jack said. "At least, so far. How can I believe you?"

"Who do you think it was who put you on the trail of the C–4 in the first place?"

That was good enough for Jack. He still called in Bender's name, and they waited while Henderson routed it through various channels, but Jack was already sure. His original tip on the C–4 had come from the Israelis. Having worked with them before, Jack knew they were talented enough and arrogant enough to want to follow the trail on their own.

After a few minutes and a return call, they let Bender rise to his feet. "To be honest, we weren't sure you guys were aware enough to believe there'd be an attack on U.S. soil," Bender said. "We figured the lead on the explosives would get lost in the bureaucracy."

"1993 was a wake-up call for us," Jack said. "We know they're out there. I followed the trail from Cairo back to Los Angeles. We had separate agencies working it. Did you know about the suicide bombers?"

"No idea," Bender admitted. "I'm about all the resources we have here at the moment. There's a lot going on back home, from Gaza all the way to Baghdad."

"This is so far over my pay grade," Driscoll muttered.

"That was nice work," Bender said. "I saw you go over the wall; that had to be the end of you. You ought to be Israeli."

"Or a cat," Driscoll added. "Can we find somewhere else to stand?"

"I don't think they're done," Jack said to Bender. "I think there's one more bomber." He explained his theory of the three attackers.

"We should get over to St. Monica's," Bender said. "Those Swiss Guards are good, but they don't get enough practice. They should have carved me out of their group much earlier than they did. If something else is going down, they might not be ready for it. Hey," he added. "How did you ID me?"

"You sent an e-mail," Jack said. "Some kind of apology to your brother. We thought it was a good-bye note before your suicide."

Bender laughed. "Funny how the little things trip you up. My brother's a real rabbi. One of the most righteous men I know. I was apologizing for giving the rabbis a bad name."

2:26 P.M. PST
CTU Headquarters, Los Angeles

Maybe, if the cameras had been installed, Nina would have gone a little lighter. As it happened, there were no security cameras in the room that would eventually become a holding cell, so she was free to do her worst on Gary Khalid. She had handcuffed his wrists and ankles, and she spent her time walking around his prone body. Every time she circled around to his feet, she walked on the ankle she'd broken a short time earlier.

Gary himself suffered two kinds of torment. One was the physical pain, which was growing worse by the moment. The other was psychological: to be under the control of a woman, of all things. It was ludicrous. Humiliating.

He had held out for several minutes already, but in the end, Khalid was no hero. He felt the bones grind in his ankles, and he knew that he was done.

"You performed the operation on Father Collins?"

"Yes."

"And the guy who pretended to be Abdul al-Hassan."

"Yes, I did."

"How did you kill Diana Christie?"

Khalid explained quickly. He didn't know Farrigian well. From what he understood, Farrigian had told the people Khalid worked for about her, and they'd set a trap. Khalid had been brought in to work on her. It had been brutal and quick. They'd captured her and anesthetized her, then planted the bomb in her arm.

"Was she told to give that false lead on purpose?"

Yes, Khalid sobbed, ashamed but unwilling to bear any more pain. His employers had set up a separate attack, hoping that if the authorities were following the C–4, they would travel in that direction. The NTSB agent had been used to validate that plot.

"How many people did you operate on aside from Christie?"

Khalid hesitated, but only until Nina rested her toe on his broken ankle. "Four. But there were only supposed to be three. One of them blew up accidentally."

Abdul Ali. None of them understood how it happened. He was the first recipient, and he had been done early on so that his arm would have plenty of time to heal. He had come into Los Angeles for work and to prepare for the conference, but something had caused the receiver in his arm to trigger the detonator. The whole plane had gone down, and they had needed to find a replacement.

"Who was the replacement?"

"I don't know. Really!" he pleaded when she raised her foot. "I didn't know any of them. All I know is that one of them had no idea he was involved. They created credentials for me at Cedars and I went in to do the operation. He had no idea what had happened to him. The other two were part of the plan."

"Tell me about them."

"One of them was a Muslim. The other was American. He looked kind of familiar to me, but I don't know where from."

Nina crouched down beside him. "I need more than that, Khalid," she said sweetly.

He looked up at her in fear and hatred. "I don't know any more. I didn't know them. I never knew their names."

"Tell me who you worked for. Who hired you to do this?"

"It began with Yasin," Khalid admitted. "But years ago. He got the idea to deliver a bomb this way, and he told me he wanted me to do it. I moved here, to the U.S., to be ready. And then one day I got the message to start the work."

"Did Yasin come here to coordinate it?"

"I didn't work with Yasin after that," Khalid answered. "There was someone else. A non-Muslim."

"What non-Muslim?" Nina asked.

"I don't know. Yasin approved him. I didn't ask any more than that."

Nina tried to think of who was left. There were no non-Muslims on her original suspect sheet. She decided to call Bauer.

2:31 P.M. PST
Four Seasons Hotel, Los Angeles

After flashing his badge, and with some additional help from Harry Driscoll, Jack had managed to scrounge a change of clothes from the hotel management. He was dry, but that was the best that could be said for him. Every muscle in his body was sore; every bone felt bruised. It occurred to him with great irony that he had recently told Christopher Henderson that he enjoyed overseas work with the CIA because that's where the action was.

Driscoll's phone rang again as he was dressing, and he listened to Nina debrief him on the Khalid interrogation. Somewhere in the back of his mind, Jack had hoped that Khalid himself was the mastermind behind the whole plot, but that was not the case.

"We know there's a third bomber out there, based on clues and the leftover C–4," Jack said. "You can't get any more information out of him?"

"I've already leaned on him," she replied blandly. "He'll go into shock soon."

"Keep at it. We need to know who the final bomb is."

"Agreed, but the Pope is safe, isn't he? If he's at St. Monica's, surrounded by his people, he's as safe as he can be."

2:43 P.M. PST
St. Monica's Cathedral, Downtown Los Angeles

Michael admired and hated Yasin with a passion that rivaled his love for the true church. Yasin had built backup after backup into his plan, and it was working now to perfection. Of course, it had been Michael himself who executed that plan, but the brainchild had been Yasin's. Michael had always assumed that, once the Pope had been killed, he himself would find Yasin and kill him, to eliminate the threat of any future blackmail. Now he wondered quite honestly if he was up to the task.

A few moments later, the Pope's retinue arrived at St. Monica's. Michael had arrived seconds before, and he was already posting his own security people all around the cathedral. As the three black Broncos appeared, and the Pope, shielded by his men, was hustled into the great chapel, Michael shook hands with Giancarlo.

"That was quite a scare," he said.

"More than a scare," Giancarlo said. He turned to speak to several of his Swiss Guards, then he turned back. "We will be here for only an hour. I have radioed to the Vatican's private airplane. It is being prepared now. We will head to the airport and get back to Rome."

Michael made himself look perplexed. "Do you think there is more danger?"

"I don't know," Giancarlo admitted, "but as the Arabs say, 'Trust God, but tether your camel.' After what has happened here in the last twenty hours, the safest place for us is St. Peter's. In the meantime, is the entire facility secured?"

"Yes," Michael said.

2:50 P.M. PST
St. Monica's Cathedral, Downtown Los Angeles

A new arrival entered through a small door in the north wall of the cathedral grounds, a door that should have been locked and guarded by Michael's men, but it was not. He closed the door quietly and stepped behind a small bird-of-paradise. As planned, a plastic bag lay there. He quickly slipped on a black suit similar to the kind worn by the plainclothes Swiss Guards. In just a few minutes he was ready.

This would be a good end, a final part to play.

. . . .

THE FOLLOWING TAKES PLACE
BETWEEN THE HOURS OF
3 P.M. AND 4 P.M.
PACIFIC STANDARD TIME

. . . .

3:00 P.M. PST
St. Monica's Cathedral, Downtown Los Angeles

"I would like to be alone for a moment, Giancarlo," John Paul said. "Except for Cardinal Mulrooney. Please ask him to come."

Giancarlo could not fully honor that request. He refused to leave the Pontiff unguarded. But he ordered his men to guard all the doors to the cathedral, and they had left him alone at the altar. Despite the pain in his knees, John Paul knelt at the altar and put his head in his hands.

What, what, O Lord, was he to do with such hatred? That someone would blow himself up to stop him from holding a peace conference was, to him, practically inconceivable. He had gone out of his way to invite diverse opinions and represent all possible sides of the argument. And still it was not enough.

"Your Holiness?"

John Paul looked up to see Mulrooney, tall and lean and hawkish, standing over him. "Your Eminence. Please, sit with me."

Mulrooney sat, and for a moment, John Paul knelt beside him in silence. Finally: "Giancarlo spoke with an American agent. Do you know the man actually carried the explosives inside his body?"

"Horrible," Mulrooney whispered.

"It may surprise you to hear me say this, Allen, but I believe our differences to be petty. In the face of this sort of unspeakable hatred, the schism in the church is meaningless."

Mulrooney shifted ever so slightly.

"It's true," John Paul said. "We must get past them if we are to survive. What unites us is greater than what divides us. A war is coming, and we must prevent it."

"I support you, Your Holiness. But why are you telling this to me?"

"Because I know you are a leader of the schismatics."

The statement hung there in that sanctified air. "Your Holin—"

"Please do not waste my time or yours by denying it," John Paul said. "You believe I am a heretic. A traitor to the church."

Mulrooney felt the blood rise into his cheeks. This damned old man had done it to him again, looking so frail but then challenging him so directly. "This really can't be the best time to discuss this . . ."

"What better time?" the old man said. "The world is entering a religious war, my friend. How will we help if we are at war within ourselves?"

Mulrooney realized where the Pope's thoughts were leading him. "I was not there, Your Holiness, but I was told the bomber was a Muslim, not a Catholic."

"He was neither," John Paul said. "Whatever he was, whoever he worked for, he was not a man of God. Men of God reject violence. That will be all, Your Eminence."

3:10 P.M. PST
Outside St. Monica's Cathedral,
Downtown Los Angeles

Jack, Harry Driscoll, and Dan Bender pulled up to the cathedral and got out.

"Are you really expecting trouble here?" Driscoll asked.

Jack laughed. "There's been nothing but trouble here."

At the front of the cathedral, they were met by one of the Swiss Guards. He detained them briefly until a radio call to Giancarlo cleared them.

The chief of the Swiss Guards met them in the courtyard. He shook Jack's hand with both of his and said, "I did not have time to thank you properly before. You saved his life. Millions will thank you for it."

"I think there's one more bomber. And we still haven't found out who is transmitting the signal." He explained the design of the bomb found in Father

Collins. "Someone set that bomb off, probably someone at the reception itself, since they would have waited until the bomber was next to the target."

"No one from the reception is here," Giancarlo said. "We've evacuated the entire cathedral except for our people."

"You have a plan for evacuating him from here?"

"Yes," Giancarlo said simply. "In approximately an hour. Come with me to the library. Tell me what you know."

3:15 P.M. PST
Chapel at St. Monica's Cathedral,
Downtown Los Angeles

Michael walked around the outside of the chapel. There was a guard there, one of the Swiss Guards from the Pope's retinue. Michael smiled and nodded to him. "I am making my rounds," he said simply. "To check security."

"Giancarlo does the same," the man replied.

Michael smiled again and whipped his hand across the man's neck. The small blade sliced his throat like butter. The man gurgled once, his eyes staring wildly, then he fell on his face.

Michael moved on to the next one.

3:19 P.M. PST
Library at St. Monica's Cathedral,
Downtown Los Angeles

"The problem is not knowing the source of the threat," Giancarlo said as Jack finished his debrief.

"Well, ultimately it's Yasin, but he's got someone here working for him," Jack said with both determination and weariness in his voice. "I've been chasing them down all night. Whoever set this up has run me around in circles. But I'll come across them eventually."

3:21 P.M. PST
Chapel at St. Monica's Cathedral,
Downtown Los Angeles

John Paul sat in silent meditation for quite some time, searching his soul for some answer. He was aware of his own arrogance, to think that he could solve problems that had plagued the world for hundreds of years. But if not he, then who?

He heard footsteps approaching. At first he ignored them, assuming they were a guard checking on him. But the footsteps stopped, and after a few minutes the Pope was drawn out of his meditation. He looked up. There was a man sitting in one of the pews, smiling. He was dressed like a Swiss Guard, but John Paul knew that he was not.

"Who are you?" the Pope asked.

"My name is Mark Gelson."

3:28 P.M. PST
Library at St. Monica's Cathedral,
Downtown Los Angeles

"I talked with my headquarters on the way over," Jack continued. "All we know of the third bomber is that he is probably Caucasian. The problem is, we don't have any Caucasian suspects at all on our suspect list. Not unless you can think of anyone, Harry."

"This bomber poses a danger," Giancarlo agreed. "I'm just not sure—"

"I can't think of anyone," Harry mused.

"Me neither."

"Unless it's Mark Gelson," Harry finished.

That brought Jack up short. "Gelson? He's no one."

Giancarlo looked at them both. "Do you mean Mark Gelson, the American actor?"

"Yeah, but it—"

"He is a schismatic," Giancarlo said. "He belongs to a sect of Catholicism that rejects everything and everyone that came out of Vatican II. His father actually founded the sect. They're about twenty thousand strong in the United States. We've had Gelson on our watch list for several years."

3:31 P.M. PST
Chapel at St. Monica's Cathedral,
Downtown Los Angeles

"He was a good man, my father," Gelson was saying. "What you did broke him. He never wanted to cause a schism and form the Tridentine Society, and hated himself for it. But you gave him no choice."

John Paul had the urge to run, but it had been years since he had run anywhere. Besides, he abhorred the idea of an inelegant death. "My son," he said, "there are many who disagree with parts of Vatican II. The Society of St. Pius X, for instance. But they do not resort to violence. There are cardinals in the Vatican itself who share the schismatic view, but they try to voice their opinions within the church."

"How much good does it do them?"

"To kill over matters of religion, this is the problem with the world. Our enemies twist their religion and use it as an excuse to kill. We must not do the same."

Gelson laughed. "The history of the church is the history of killing those who stray and refuse to rejoin the fold. I don't see why you should be any different."

"And you would take your own life along with mine?"

"I was ready to," Gelson said. "But now I don't have to."

"What of your reputation?" John Paul asked.

Gelson laughed again, this time bitterly. "My reputation. Yes, I am putting at risk my reputation as a broken-down former action hero who talks about blowing people up when he's drunk. I'll risk it."

"Still, you will be known as a murderer."

"Among those I love, I'll be a hero. The man who killed the heretical Pope."

3:40 P.M. PST
Courtyard at St. Monica's Cathedral,
Downtown Los Angeles

Jack and the others followed Giancarlo across the courtyard. "I'm sure the Holy Father would like to thank you in person. First let me enter the chapel to see if he has finished his medi . . ." His voice trailed off.

"Something?" Jack asked.

"My men."

Giancarlo bolted forward, with Jack and the others racing behind.

They burst into the chapel to see two men standing over the Pope. Jack recognized Gelson immediately. The other man looked familiar to Jack, but he had no time to dwell on it as the man raised his gun to the Pope's head.

"No!" Giancarlo shouted. His own weapon was out immediately and he fired, knocking Michael off his feet. Gelson jumped back, terrified by the loud noise. Jack and the others surged forward. Michael was not dead. He sat up and steadied his semi-automatic again. By the time he squeezed the trigger, Giancarlo had thrown his body over the Pope.

Jack stopped and put Michael in his sights, but gunfire erupted all around him. He fired as he dove for the cover of the church benches. More security men, the same ones who had attacked him last night. He hoped Driscoll and Bender had found cover.

Why would Mulrooney's security team try to kill the Pope?

Schismatics. The single word came to him, then

disappeared as he sat up and fired toward a man at a side door. The man fell away and did not reappear.

Jack glimpsed Bender, still standing in the open, pouring rounds at Michael. He knew what the Mossad agent was trying to do. If he kept Michael's head down, the man might not be able to shoot at his target.

It worked, but Bender paid a price for his bravery. Bulky and exposed, he was an easy target. A few seconds after he fired, red flowers blossomed on his chest and he fell to his knees.

By that time Jack was up and vaulting over the pews. He saw the security chief fire point-blank toward the Pope, and he assumed the Pontiff was dead, but he kept moving and firing. The assassin went down again, and then crawled for cover. He was wearing some kind of body armor. Gelson squealed and ran toward the altar, with Michael close behind him. Bullets still burned through the air all around.

"Driscoll! Left side!" he yelled, and turned to the right, firing at any angle from which bullets seemed to come. The return fire ceased as the security men retreated.

Jack grabbed Giancarlo. The Swiss Guard was heavy and lifeless as Jack dragged him off the Pope, who cowered beneath, covered in blood. "Are you hit!" he yelled.

"It's his blood," John Paul said. "His blood!"

"Driscoll?" Jack called out.

"Here," Harry called from behind him. "But I caught one."

Jack turned. Harry was holding his gun in his left hand. His right arm hung limp and loose at his side.

It was swelling hugely from the biceps down, where a bullet had torn away most of the muscle and shattered the bone.

"Jack," Driscoll said, "I think they're coming back."

· ·

THE FOLLOWING TAKES PLACE
BETWEEN THE HOURS OF
4 P.M. AND 5 P.M.
PACIFIC STANDARD TIME

· ·

4:00 P.M. PST
Courtyard at St. Monica's Cathedral,
Downtown Los Angeles

Pembrook and Wittenberg were still alive. Gelson, too, but Gelson wasn't much of a fighter.

"What are we doing?" Gelson whined. "Let's get the hell out of here."

"He's not dead," Michael snarled. "That damned bodyguard shielded him. He's not dead!"

"It's too late," Gelson said. "It's all gone to hell."

"Wittenberg, far side. Go in when you hear the gunfire. Pembrook, with me." Wittenberg nodded and hurried around the corner of the building.

"He got Aimes and Duvaine on the move," Pembrook said. "He's better than us."

"We'll see. Go."

4:01 P.M. PST
Chapel at St. Monica's Cathedral,
Downtown Los Angeles

They came in behind their gunfire, keeping Jack's head low. The cathedral echoed with loud, angry cracks of firearms. Driscoll tried to return fire, but Jack guessed what they were up to. He whirled around to the far side just in time to see the other man burst through the door. Jack squeezed three times, and the attacker stumbled as though he'd tripped over something. He did not get up again.

John Paul, terrified out of all sense, started to stand up. Jack tackled him, fearful that he might crush the old man but short on choices. Driscoll tried to cover them. Out of the corner of his eye, Jack saw the detective fire and then fall like a rag doll. The two security men fell back again.

Jack felt John Paul tremble beneath him and heard the man whispering something in Latin.

"Stay still," Jack whispered. "They're not gone. With this much gunfire, I promise you someone is on the way."

4:03 P.M. PST
Cardinal's Residence at St. Monica's
Cathedral, Downtown Los Angeles

Cardinal Mulrooney sat on his bed with his hands over his ears, rocking back and forth slightly. He was terrified. He'd had no idea of this. None. It wasn't his fault.

Those phrases kept repeating themselves in his mind.

4:04 P.M. PST
CTU Headquarters, Los Angeles

Nina Myers slammed down the phone, then clipped her pancake holster to her belt as she ran for the door, with Henderson right behind her.

4:05 P.M. PST
Courtyard at St. Monica's Cathedral,
Downtown Los Angeles

Michael was out of time and he knew it. He could already hear sirens wailing. Bauer didn't have to defeat them, just hold them off until help arrived. The elaborate plan had failed. All three of their suicide bombers had failed. Michael thought now only of escape.

"You're right, Gelson," he said. "Time to go."

4:06 P.M. PST
Chapel at St. Monica's Cathedral,
Downtown Los Angeles

Jack knew they were retreating and he wanted to give chase. He knew instinctively that Michael was the man he'd been looking for: the man behind the plot, and the man who could lead him to Yasin.

He scrambled over to Driscoll. "Harry, you with me?"

The detective answered weakly, "Unfortunately, yeah." His eyes lost focus, then returned to Jack.

"All in all, can't say I'm happy I called you, Jack."

"Can't blame you." Jack examined Driscoll's wounds. They were not good. His right arm might never work again, and the second wound had punched a hole through his lower left abdomen. "You hear those sirens?" They were loud now.

"Like music."

"Help is on the way. But the bad guys are leaving. I'm not letting them go."

Driscoll managed a thin smile. "That's Jack Bauer, all right." He lifted his gun. "Go."

Jack launched himself toward the door and burst into the courtyard just in time to see three figures slipping over the wall. Jack fired, the rounds tearing holes in the adobe, but he was certain none of them found their mark.

Jack sprinted after them and was over the wall in a second, carried by pure adrenaline. By the time he got to the street, they had disappeared.

4:08 P.M. PST
Main Street, Los Angeles

Michael and Pembrook guided Gelson into the car Michael had waiting on the street. It was a blind, totally legal and registered to one of the two false IDs that Michael had worked so hard to create for himself.

As soon as they were inside, Michael eased into traffic. Sirens wailed around them, but they were just one of many cars trying to get through the congested downtown area.

None of them spoke. Michael was astounded at how suddenly and completely his carefully laid plan had turned into a failure. Not just a failure. An utter disaster. He had to get to a safe place and reassess, figure out how to recover from this debacle. And he thought he knew just the person to help him.

4:11 P.M. PST
Chapel at St. Monica's Cathedral,
Downtown Los Angeles

Jack returned to the chapel as the adrenaline dump wore off, making him feel suddenly old and heavy. Uniformed officers were swarming the area, along with the LAPD SWAT unit he'd once belonged to. The Pope was gone, whisked away by whatever remained of his Swiss Guards.

Jack showed the cops his ID and gave them what description he could. Gelson was easy, but in the middle of the gunfire he'd never gotten a great look at Michael or the other man; their faces were accompanied by flashes of light and gunfire. He had a feeling that he should recognize one of them. Paramedics rushed in, and he directed them toward Harry Driscoll and Dan Bender. Three of them started working on Harry Driscoll immediately. Their urgent voices told Jack that the situation was dire.

He had just sat down, nearly collapsing under the weight of his day, when Christopher Henderson and Nina Myers rushed in. Henderson went immediately to the officer in charge while Nina checked on Jack.

"You're not hit?" she confirmed.

"Nah," he said, sitting in one of the church pews. "I figured the five-story fall and the concussion were enough."

"Glad you didn't overdo it." She paused, looking for something to say, and settled on, "Is this what working with you is going to be like? Because if it is, I'm going to have to bring my A game every day."

Jack shook his head. "Not funny. People are dead, and an old friend just got shot up."

"And you saved the Pope," she replied sharply. "More people would have died if you hadn't pushed this case, and you know it."

"We didn't get them," Jack said.

"We know who they are. Gelson at least won't get very far, not with a face that recognizable."

"We didn't get the planner, and we didn't get Yasin."

"Jack, you saved the *Pope*. Not everyone gets to do that."

Ryan Chappelle walked onto the scene. Jack saw him before he saw Jack, because Chappelle's eyes were drawn first to the carnage. He shook his head and talked with Christopher Henderson. With each passing word from Henderson, Chappelle looked more and more unhappy. Finally, Henderson pointed Jack's way, and Chappelle walked over to him.

He stared reproachfully at Bauer. Clearly there was a lot he wanted to say, but for once he seemed to have the presence of mind not to speak. In fact, he was reviewing the teleconference he'd had with the joint subcommittee and wondered what they would say about the unknown agent who got things done, if only they were standing in the middle of all this bloodshed. At last, he said simply, "I'll need a full report on this."

Nina's phone rang. She answered, listened, and said, "No shit. I've got Bauer here," and handed him the phone.

"Agent Bauer? This is Dr. Siegman over at the coroner's office. I hear that a whole lot went down and you're going to keep us busy down here." Jack had no response to that, so Siegman continued. "Listen, I guess it may be too late for this, but some of our techs down here were playing with this receiver embedded in the deceased."

"Okay," he said.

"Well, you know it's not a purely passive receiver. It's more like a cell phone receiver. It sends out a locator signal every fifteen seconds or so. I guess so that you can detonate it from far away."

Jack thought of the one Barny had strapped to his back. "I'm familiar with them."

"Well, if it's like a cell phone, my guys figure that it can be traced."

Jack thought of Mark Gelson riding in a car somewhere with Michael. "Dr. Siegman, that is the very best thing I've heard all day."

"Courtesy of your friendly neighborhood morgue."

4:38 P.M. PST
405 Freeway

It had always been the ace up Michael's sleeve, that he knew where Yasin was staying. The information had come to him by accident, and he had only intended to use it as a bartering chip if he was caught by the authorities. But he knew that he would only have been able to strike a bargain if he was caught before the attempt on the Pope. Now that so many had died, and with not one but two attempts against the Pontiff, he knew the Vatican would scuttle any deal he tried to make.

It had not been as hard to track Yasin as the Arab liked to think. Yasin had visited the United States several times to strike the bargain with Michael and Gelson, and each time he had met them at a different location, but always within an hour's time of the phone call. Michael had simply triangulated the area, which was somewhere near the airport. On subsequent occasions, and with some trial and error, he had staked out various arteries into the area and was able to follow Yasin to Playa del Rey.

Michael drove there now in the silent car, with Pembrook lost in thought and Gelson rubbing his left arm, which had suddenly become an alien object attached to his body. He wanted it off.

"We need to get to your doctor," Gelson said for the tenth time. "He needs to get this thing out of me."

"Khalid is either dead or in prison," Michael said. "But we can ask Yasin. He is the contact."

They exited the 405 and drove on surface streets down into the suburb of Playa del Rey, between the airport and the ocean.

4:43 P.M. PST
Cardinal's Residence
   at St. Monica's Cathedral,
Downtown Los Angeles

"Yeah, I got 'em," Jamey Farrell said to Jack Bauer on the phone. "At least I think I do. We're making some assumptions here. Specifically, what I have here is a cellular signature very similar to the one emitted by the one the coroner dug out of the body. If that's them, then they are headed down by the airport."

"Trying to get on a plane," Jack said from St. Monica's.

"No, more like going to ground. They're in Playa del Rey, it looks like."

"Got it. Let me know when you have a definite location."

Jack hung up and turned his attention back to the questioning of Cardinal Mulrooney. He'd been too exhausted to handle it himself, so he'd turned it over to Nina.

". . . as I've said, I had no idea, none, that this was going to happen. It's horrific," the Cardinal was saying, now indignant after being asked for the fourth time.

"But it looks like the guy in charge was your security chief, Mr. Mulrooney—"

"Cardinal Mulrooney. Or Your Eminence."

"Okay, Mr. Mulrooney. You hired him. He worked directly for you."

"Many people work directly for me. I can't be held responsible for all their actions, too."

Nina added, "And he was a schismatic. You also are a schismatic, is that true."

"No!" Mulrooney said. "Not when you ask like that. I have expressed my unhappiness over some of Rome's changes. But that doesn't mean I joined a cult."

"Mr. Mulrooney," Nina said confidentially, "frankly, it's not going to look good for you. The leader of your church, a man with whom you have had strong political disagreements, is attacked while in your care, by your security guards. That's a lot of circumstantial evidence."

Mulrooney stiffened. "I am in God's hands. And I want my lawyer."

4:47 P.M. PST
St. Monica's Cathedral, Downtown Los Angeles

Harry Driscoll could hear the paramedics working around him. He had the vaguest sensation of some kind of mask over his face, and he could hear watery breathing that must have been his own.

But he didn't feel pain, and something told him he would never feel pain again. He thought back to the beginning of his troubles, standing at the door of Don Biehn's home. He hadn't wanted to open that door. Part of him still wished he hadn't, but that was water under the bridge, now. Doors open; we move through them. That was how life worked.

Though his eyes were closed, Driscoll saw a new door appear before him. When it first appeared, Harry was filled with dread. He did not want to approach it. But the door came inexorably closer, and the nearer it came, the less Harry feared it. It was, after all, only a door; and Harry was a detective. Opening doors was his job.

The door opened, and Harry Driscoll stepped through.

4:55 P.M. PST
St. Monica's Cathedral, Downtown Los Angeles

Jack was watching Mulrooney walk away of his own free will. If Jack had had his way, the Cardinal would have been wearing handcuffs. Not for the assassination attempt—Jack thought he was lying, but who knew?—but for the children who had been molested. He was sure Mulrooney had been complicit there. If it were true, Jack thought he ought to be destroyed.

One of the paramedics stepped into his field of vision. "Sir, I'm sorry. Your partner, Detective Driscoll. He just died. I'm sorry. We tried."

Jack grimaced. Losing Driscoll was a blow, not just to him, but to decency in general. There was no way that Harry Driscoll should die and Mulrooney should walk away. Then he suddenly thought of something he could do to point justice in the Cardinal's direction. As he did it, Nina's cell phone, which he was holding, rang.

"Playa del Rey," Jamey said. "1622 Reina Avenue."

"Good." All the fatigue fell away as Jack jumped to his feet. He was going to end this once and for all.

1 2 3 4 5 6 7 8 9
10 11 12 13 14 15 16 17
18 19 20 21 22 23 **24**

• •

THE FOLLOWING TAKES PLACE
BETWEEN THE HOURS OF
5 P.M. AND 6 P.M.
PACIFIC STANDARD TIME

• •

5:00 P.M. PST
Playa del Rey

Yasin heard the knock on the door and reached for
his gun. He was in the upstairs room of the house,
in the back; the room that made for the quickest get-
away. He was inclined to simply bolt—no one in the
entire world had reason to knock on this door—but
something about the gentility of the knock kept him
from fleeing. He figured it was a salesman of some
sort, and he would ignore it. But to make sure, he
walked as quiet as a cat to the front part of the house
and peeked through the curtained window at the top
of the stairs, which gave him a view of the porch
below.

"Oh, shit," he growled. He always liked swearing

in English better than Arabic. This knock he could not ignore.

Yasin hurried downstairs and opened the door. They stood at his threshold like the three wise men of the Christian tale, or maybe like the three parts of the Catholic god that Yasin found so blasphemous. How could Allah be divided into three parts?

"Get inside," he said, and closed the door behind them. When they were inside, he pointed his gun at them. "What are you doing here? I won't even ask how you found this place. What are you doing here?"

Michael ignored the gun and sat down on the couch. The house was sparsely furnished, but there were a few pieces of furniture and some pictures to avoid curious questions. "It all went sideways," he said. "The Pope is still alive. Your man, al-Hassan, got blown up but no one else did. We tried to kill the Pope back at St. Monica's but some government agent stopped us."

Yasin closed his eyes deliberately, then opened them after a moment. "I told you not to underestimate the Federal agents. They are not always brilliant, but some are tenacious."

Michael didn't need to be reminded of that. "We need a way out, and you are our best chance."

Yasin scoffed. "I can't help you. If you've ruined things this badly, I may have trouble myself getting out." There were ways. The border with Mexico was porous. That was how he had reentered the United States several times after 1993. But he did not relish these alternate routes. "You must have set up your own exit plan."

"I did," Michael said. "But it involved confusion

and misdirection because of al-Hassan and Collins and Gelson."

"And I want this out now," Gelson demanded, holding up his left arm and revealing, for the first time, the wicked scar from his operation. "I was willing to trade my life for the heretic's, but that chance is gone. I want this out."

Yasin ignored Gelson. Gelson, though he was in his fifties, reminded him of the young suicide bombers from Gaza, so eager to prove their religious faith, so willing to give their lives. They were useful fools.

Superficially, Yasin was calm and collected. He offered them water and some leftover Chinese food. He suggested they sit down. But the wheels in his head were spinning. How could he get rid of them? How could he escape? He was sure his window of opportunity was growing narrower by the second.

"Tell me what they know," Yasin said.

5:13 P.M. PST
St. Monica's Cathedral, Downtown Los Angeles

Amy Weiss was not allowed inside the cathedral, though she'd tried several times to sneak around, over, and under the crime scene tape. Finally she'd given up, and stood outside the tape at the entrance to the cathedral, making note of who came in and out.

To her surprise, she saw a uniformed officer walk out the front door carrying a plastic bag. He scanned the crowd until his eyes fell on her, and he hurried forward.

"Ms. Weiss, this is for you. Jack Bauer left it."

Amy took the parcel, plastic bag and all. It appeared to be a journal of some kind. She just barely made out the name scribbled childishly along the spine. It read "Aaron Biehn."

5:18 P.M. PST
Playa del Rey

Jack should have waited for a backup team. That was just common sense. But he had been chasing this killer for twenty-three hours without stopping, and he felt that if he stopped now he would simply fall apart.

So he jumped out of the car before Nina had a chance to stop completely and charged the house on Reina Avenue. He just had time to glimpse Nina run around to the back before he kicked open the door with a violent crash.

Yasin moved faster than Jack expected. Before the door hit the wall, Yasin was rolling over the back of his couch while Jack fired rounds that vanished into the pillows and couch frame. Gelson practically screamed. Michael, too, rolled out of Jack's line of fire. The last man rose to a squat and aimed, but by that time Jack had pumped three rounds into his chest and face, and he crumpled.

Jack dove to his right, into a hallway, as both Michael and Yasin fired back, shattering the door's small plate-glass window. No more shots came, and Jack knew that both men were on the move. He heard footsteps thump upward. Yasin, or Michael? Jack decided he didn't care, and gave chase.

Fourteen steps went up to the second floor. Jack leaned around a corner and then pulled back as rounds discharged and four holes popped into the wall at his back. Jack stuck his hand around the corner and fired without looking. Then he rolled into the hallway and sprinted forward as a door slammed shut at the end of the hall.

Nothing for it now but to finish, he thought, kicking that door inward. Suddenly, there was Michael, his semi-automatic in Jack's face. Michael pulled the trigger as Jack grabbed the gun and moved it. The round discharged and Jack felt heat blossom under his hand, but he held on, and the sting was already fading as Jack jammed his own gun into Michael's neck.

Michael's eyes went suddenly wide, and strangely sad. He whispered in disbelief, "I thought God was on my side."

Jack said, "Everybody thinks that." Michael tried to grab for the gun, and Jack pulled the trigger.

5:21 P.M. PST
Playa del Rey

Nina jammed her knee into Yasin's crotch and felt his grip on her gun loosen. He'd surprised her as she came in through the back. She had grabbed his gun and he had grabbed hers, and for a moment they had been locked in a silent struggle, until her knee struck him and she was able to tear her gun free.

She backed up a step, tapped, racked, and cleared as she'd been taught . . . but the jammed round wouldn't clear. Yasin stood straight up, so Nina kicked him again. Instead of trying to clear her weapon, she punched it, muzzle first, into Yasin's face. She grabbed his gun from his hand just as he lunged forward to put her in a bear hug. She braced herself with one foot back to stop him from going down on her, then calmly put the muzzle of her confiscated gun in his side and fired twice. The gun clicked dry on the third trigger pull.

She was just pushing Yasin's now lifeless body away from her when she saw Gelson stick a gun in her face.

5:23 P.M. PST
Playa del Rey

Jack swept down the stairs, his muzzle leading the way, then pulled up short. Mark Gelson was there, standing behind Nina Myers, who looked much more pissed than terrified. Gelson was behind her, holding a gun to her head with his right hand, with his left arm wrapped around her neck.

"I'll kill her," Gelson said. He was panicked, out of his league, and he knew it. "I put a fucking bomb in my arm, you think I won't shoot her?"

"I think you'd probably miss," Jack said. "You're a screwup, Gelson. You got talked into paying for this debacle. You even got talked into blowing yourself up."

"I didn't get talked into it. I volunteered. I'm willing to die if I have to."

"Then you won't mind blowing up in a minute. We took the receiver out of Collins. It had a failsafe. It was going to blow up at five-thirty whether it received a signal or not. It's probably the same with you."

This caught Gelson by surprise. At the same moment, Nina snatched at the gun, pulling the muzzle away from her head. Her other hand came up and caught it as well, and she snapped it out of his grip. Before he could react, she elbowed him in the stomach, then in the face, and the former Future Fighter dropped like a rock.

"He's not really going to explode, is he?"

"I don't think so," Jack said. "I don't even know if he has one. And I think Jamey can jam it now that she has the signal. But let's stand over here just in case."

Other cars were arriving, and Christopher Henderson walked in behind a flood of uniformed officers.

"Yasin is dead," Jack said.

"Nice work," Henderson replied.

"You can thank Nina for that. She got him."

Jack felt the heaviness return to his limbs. He hadn't slept in forever. Had he been going nonstop for twenty-four hours? He walked outside to the sidewalk and sat down on the curb. He put his head in his hands and heaved a huge sigh.

He was, in fact, sitting in the same position he'd been the night before, when Christopher Henderson met him at Ramin's devastated house. Henderson sat down next to him, not talking for a while. Finally, he said, "After a day like this, Jack, I get it if you don't want to sign on."

"I'm signing on."

"What?"

Jack lifted his head and rubbed his eyes. He didn't look at Henderson, though; he looked down the street at the row of suburban houses. "We weren't ready for this, Christopher. Any of it. Not your organization, not the CIA. They had it all planned out and we were nearly blind."

Henderson nodded his head yes and then no. "We did all right in the end. You did."

Jack disagreed. "No offense, but CTU would have quit a day ago. I probably would have figured we were done after Castaic. You know the only reason we kept going? Don Biehn. His vendetta made the connection between Yasin and the church. We would have been blind without it. We need to do better."

"You ready to help us?" Christopher said.

Jack stood up and stretched. "Yeah. Just promise me I'm not going to have any more days like this."